W9-BKY-118

WEDDING RING

EMILIE RICHARDS

WEDDING RING

MIRA®

ISBN 0-7783-2063-4

WEDDING RING

www.MIRABooks.com

Printed in U.S.A.

First Printing: July 2004
10 9 8 7 6 5 4 3 2 1

For the women of Herpel Community in Stone County, Arkansas,
who first taught me the joys of quilting.

AUTHOR'S NOTE

My fascination with quilting began just after college, when my husband and I were sent to Stone County, Arkansas, as VISTA volunteers. In our time there we developed a love for roots music, a passionate appreciation of mountains and mountain people, and a deep admiration for quilts and the women who create them.

Years have passed, and now I'm a quilt maker, too. But since I'm also an author, the stories that quilts and quilters tell are as interesting to me as the quilts I create.

Wedding Ring is the first of three books in my new series, Shenandoah Album, about the Shenandoah Valley of Virginia, traditional quilts and the women whose lives they enrich and change. It began as the wisp of an idea and transformed into three novels centering around three different quilts. I hope you'll also enjoy *Endless Chain* and *Lover's Knot* in the years to come.

My thanks to those women of Stone County and to quilters everywhere who continually inspire me with their creativity, dedication and warmth.

CHAPTER
1

After she surrendered to the inevitable and gave up trying to make her grandmother open the front door, Tessa MacRae resigned herself to spending the rest of the sweltering morning in what passed for shade on the front porch. The time wasn't completely wasted. From the vantage point of a creaking old swing, she could observe almost everything she needed to know about her grandmother's world.

First, in an area renowned for its natural splendor, this little corner of the Shenandoah Valley was not holding up its end.

The evaluation was interrupted by the screech of a window being wrenched open just above her.

"You still down there, missy? I didn't ask you to come, you know, and I sure didn't ask for these!"

At thirty-seven, Tessa, a high-school English teacher, hadn't been a "missy" for a number of years, but this was not the moment to object. A rattling followed Helen Henry's words, and suddenly the air was filled not with much-needed rain, but with balls of paper sliding off the tin roof to the ground below. Tessa tried to count them as they fell. A dozen, at least. Then, after a pithy pause, half a dozen more.

The window above the porch slammed shut again.

Tessa waited, but the paper hailstorm had ended. She got to her feet, picked up and smoothed a wad that had landed on the front steps. Two women and a man, with broad smiles and glowing silver hair, stared back at her from a golf course fairway.

"'Green Springs Retirement Community,'" she read out loud. "'Because today is the first day of the rest of your life.'" Crumpling the page in her fist, she wondered how many similar brochures her mother, Nancy Whitlock, had sent Helen during the past weeks. When nothing else fell from above, she returned to the swing, drew her knees up to her chin and got on with her assessment.

On her drive to the small town of Toms Brook, Tessa had been charmed, as always, by the magnificent blue-green sweep of mountains, the Queen Anne's lace and wild chicory blooming by the roadside, the placid, heat-hypnotized cattle and horses dotting Virginia's hillsides and meadows. But that was a panorama, a rural still life, and unfortunately, her grandmother's farm, which was baking under an unrelenting sun, was something else altogether.

The drought that had affected the entire area had been particularly bad here. Corn was *not* going to be knee-high by the Fourth of July, which was only three days away. Several acres of field corn across the road from her grandmother's house looked like bonsai gardens gone awry, twisted and shriveling under the sun. Only the dandelions seemed to be holding their own. Unless the area got rain, and plenty of it, the corn wouldn't even be knee-high by Labor Day.

Then there was the heat. Virginia was no one's idea of a summertime oasis, but Tessa, a native, couldn't remember a hotter July. While waiting for her grandmother to reconsider her options, Tessa had probably sweated away an entire quart of bottled springwater. No air stirred. No bees hummed. The mud daubers that had built a castle under the eaves had pulled up their drawbridge and escaped into the keep. Even the blue jays had declared a truce with the crows and were probably napping side by side under the leafy branches of Helen's twin maples.

The window screeched again. "And take these, while you're at it!" Helen shouted. "You think I need your fancy presents?"

The nightgown, then the robe, that Tessa had bought her grandmother on her last birthday floated to the rambling rose that sprawled uncontrolled along the trellis and porch railing. They bloomed there in soft shades of violet and pink, as close to real blossoms as the rose had produced in years.

"Or your mother's!" Helen added.

Tessa hoped that Nancy hadn't given Helen a piano or a safe. She was glad when the only thing to flutter past was a garnet-red sweater on its way to the holly bush beside the rose.

The window slammed again.

The sweltering Tessa stared stoically out at the Massanutten Mountains in the far distance. Neither the Alleghenies nor the Massanuttens, which flanked this upper part of the Shenandoah Valley, were simple postcard views. They were touchable, habitable mountains, populated for centuries by stalwart homesteaders who had seen the slopes as challenges and the peaceful, flourishing valley in between as their reward. The entire valley was a testament that rural life, idealized and cherished by millions of city dwellers, existed still.

But today, life in general seemed to have mysteriously vanished here on Fitch Crossing Road. In all the time Tessa had sat there, sweated there and silently willed her grandmother to throw up her hands and invite her inside, not one car had passed. Once she had turned off Route 11 and headed toward the Shenandoah River, Tessa's small green Toyota had been King of the Road. No tractors, no hay wagons, no horse-crazy teenagers passing a lazy summer afternoon.

For all practical purposes, Helen seemed to have Fitch Crossing to herself. If her grandmother died in this house—as she fully intended—she might well be a desiccated, mummified corpse before anyone realized she was gone.

The window screeched again. Tessa visualized medieval knights pouring boiling oil from towers on the heads of invaders below. She rested her feet on the ground, her hands on her lap, and made a conscious effort to loosen the kinks in her neck.

"And don't forget this!" Helen said.

If the first paper blitz had resembled hailstones, this one resembled snow. Pastel-colored snow. One of the tiny shredded pieces drifted to the porch floor. Tessa could see it was the corner of a check, most likely one of the many her mother had sent— one of the many Helen Henry had never cashed.

She waited for the window to slam once more. When it did, she propelled her head back and forth, side to side, and tied up her conclusions.

Helen was not taking care of the farm. The Old Stoneburner Place—as it would be called until Doomsday—had never been a showplace. It was a working farm, the product of German immigrants who had crosscut timber to build their first dogtrot cabin, cleared fields with the help of mules and multitudes of sons, shivered through mountain-shadowed nights and shuddered under summer skies.

Helen, a Stoneburner by birth, had worked the farm with very little help for almost sixty years. Somehow she had eked out a living and held on to the land despite rising property taxes, managing somehow. Clearly she was not managing anymore.

The farmyard looked neglected. On the way up to the house, Tessa had been forced to maneuver ruts in the driveway as deep as the drainage ditches lining it. The day lilies and peonies that had multiplied decades ago to border the ditches were being choked out by weeds and waist-high saplings; the fence around the vegetable garden was sagging and torn.

The house looked neglected, too. There were a thousand farm-houses like it in rural Virginia. Long, deep front porch, tin roof, white clapboard siding always in need of touching up. A screen door stood between a heavier door and the world outside, welcoming breezes and neighbors.

Today it was a typical farmhouse fast declining. Problems with the exterior were almost too extensive to catalog. And inside? The interior was a mystery, a black hole of gruesome possibilities. All Tessa knew, all *anybody* knew, was what one neighbor had told Tessa's mother.

When recounting that conversation Nancy Henry Whitlock had stampeded through the sentences as if she was afraid the end might be out of reach.

"I don't know how Ron Claiborne got my phone number, but he did somehow, and that's neither here nor there, I suppose. Then he said—" and Nancy's voice had changed to mimic his: "'Ma'am, I'm sorry to say it, but your ma's in a bad way. She don't come outside anymore, and she don't let nobody in. But I seen what I seen through her front door. And it like to have stopped my heart. She being the neat…well, prissy old woman that she is. You understand what I mean?'"

Nancy had paused at that point before she added in her own incredulous voice, "Like he thought maybe I really didn't understand."

Tessa still wasn't sure if her mother had been more aghast at the message or the messenger who had delivered it. A Claiborne? A hard-drinking, fast-living Claiborne tattling on a Henry?

Tessa, of course, had been the first person Nancy called after she hung up on Mr. Claiborne. God forbid that Nancy would look into this or any problem on her own. No, there was a ritual Nancy followed at moments like these. The wringing and fluttering of hands, the public gnashing of teeth, the litanies of "I told you there was a problem," and "If somebody would listen to me once in a while…"

As for the problem itself, neither Nancy nor Tessa really knew the full extent. Helen had refused to allow Nancy or Tessa's father, Billy, inside the farmhouse to see what Mr. Claiborne had meant, meeting them at the soda fountain at the Walton and Smoot Pharmacy, instead, after Nancy threatened to alert the health department or the sheriff.

According to Nancy, Helen had looked unkempt at that meeting, but, of course, Nancy, whose self-grooming sacrament took a full hour of each morning, thought that anyone who hadn't just stepped out of a full-service salon was worse for wear.

Helen had been surly, too, Nancy claimed. That, also, was nothing new. On a good day, people said that Helen was feisty, strong-minded, no-nonsense. Good days were rare. More often she was said to be mean-spirited, difficult, the woman most likely to snatch poor Toto from Dorothy's arms and turn him over to the sheriff.

So the news, at that point, had only been expected. Then the story had taken a sharp turn. Helen—and this was still hard for Tessa to believe—Helen had admitted that she was slowing down. Under Billy's patient questioning, she had admitted that no, she couldn't keep up as well as before, that no, the house wasn't as clean as it should be, that yes, she wasn't quite sure what to do about it. Helen Stoneburner Henry, a senior Superwoman in a housedress, had admitted that yes, she might possibly, just *might,* need a little help.

Of course, even though she hadn't been there, Tessa understood exactly what must have triggered the next exchange. While Billy had gently teased the truth from Helen's lips, Nancy had surely quoted county ordinances, conversations with officials at the health department, the nuggets of information Nancy had gleaned with regard to declaring an aging relative incompetent. Then, as a finale, she had probably sung the praises of every retirement community within ten miles of the Richmond city limits.

According to Tessa's father, the conversation had ended with

Helen's furious denouncement: "You're not moving me to some fancy old folks home hundreds of miles from here, not while I'm still breathing. And you're not coming inside my house ever again. Not unless you bring that daughter of yours along. At least Tessa has some sense!"

So now Tessa waited, poised for the fun to begin. She was not amused by the irony. She was caught squarely between two women she really didn't want to know any better, forced to spend the remainder of her summer vacation watching them dance and feint like boxers in a ring. On top of that, if the inside of the house was anything like the outside, she would be painting and patching for all of July and August.

But what did it really matter? What was waiting for her at home in Fairfax? *Who* was waiting for her?

A cloud of dust announced that, indeed, there was life on Fitch Crossing Road after all. Tessa turned her head to watch the cloud move toward her. In the center was a black sedan, her mother's sleek Mercedes, now coated with Fitch Crossing's gritty charms. The car slowed, and the cloud drifted home. Nancy was still going too fast when she turned into the driveway. She narrowly avoided the northern ditch, overcompensated, and straightened just in time to avoid the southern.

Tessa didn't move. She felt the remainder of the summer closing in on her. *Life* was closing in on her. She was not strong enough for this, might never be strong enough again. Yet here she was, dutiful daughter, solicitous granddaughter, peacekeeper. Tessa MacRae, high-school English teacher, wife of a successful attorney, survivor. She had already been through the worst that life could throw at her. She reminded herself there was nothing that could happen here to rival it.

She tried to gain comfort from that and failed. She waited until Nancy's door slammed and her mother was halfway up the overgrown path before she rose to her feet.

* * *

Nancy Whitlock's heart always beat faster when she saw her daughter. The phenomenon had begun in the hospital delivery room at the instant of Tessa's birth. After a torturous, prolonged delivery, Nancy had been drugged almost to a point where her heart should have stopped completely. But she had taken one groggy look at the scrawny, vernix-slick baby she had expelled from her womb, and, with her heart pounding in her ears, she had realized that everything, *everything,* that had come before had been worth it.

Through the years she had waited for the humdrum of motherhood to set in. Friends took their children in stride. They talked of other things, looked forward to nights out, made routine dates for tennis and golf. Those other pleasures had never truly captured Nancy's speeding, rapturous heart.

Now, as she walked up the path toward her daughter, she noted Tessa's pallor, weight loss, the tension in her perfect posture. Tessa stood remarkably still, as if she had schooled every human instinct into submission. She never fidgeted. If she had ever scratched an itch, it had not been scratched in public. She was a marble Madonna, terrifyingly beautiful in her serenity. Or rather, once upon a time she had been beautiful—at least in Nancy's eyes— and serene. These days she just looked tired, older than her thirty- seven years, haunted.

Right now, she looked resigned.

"I meant to get here earlier." Nancy started talking before she reached the porch. The words started as a trickle and ended as a cascade. "The traffic in Richmond was horrible. Then I had to stop and get gas. By that time I was starving. I'd have bought you a sandwich, just in case, if I thought you'd eat it. You don't eat enough, and it shows. Why are you still on the porch? Did you just get here, too?"

"Gram's not answering the door. And no, I got here on time."

The last was not a reprimand. The words were matter-of-fact.

Tessa had been on time. Of course she had been on time. Nancy was the one who got distracted, who tried and failed to be punctual, confident, cool. Nancy, who knew that she failed everyone she loved with every word and gesture.

Nancy responded only to the first statement. "Not answering the door? Why are her clothes out here?" She gestured to the rose bush. "And all this paper?"

"She hasn't answered for the hour or more I've been here, but she's home. I've heard her at the bedroom window."

Nancy stopped before climbing the porch steps, shaded her eyes with a cupped hand and squinted at the window in question. "Heard her? The window's shut and the curtains are drawn."

"They're drawn *now*."

"She closed the windows and drew the curtains, knowing you were waiting down here? In this heat? She left you to bake out here?"

"It's probably cooler outside than in."

"Maybe she's sick." Nancy took the steps as fast as her legs would carry her. She threw open the screen door and tried the doorknob. When it didn't turn, she began to pound. "Mother! Mother!"

"I don't think that will help."

Nancy continued to pound. "Something could be wrong."

"Unless something's wrong with her hearing, that's not going to get us anywhere."

Nancy halted abruptly. "You have a better idea, Tessa? Seems to me you've just been sitting here not doing a blessed thing. Who knows? She could be dead in there."

"She was alive when I drove up, alive when she tossed things out the window, still alive when she closed the window and the drapes."

"You really think she's stonewalling us?"

"It's pretty clear."

Nancy stepped back, glaring at the door. Like everything else, it needed several coats of paint. The roof needed repairing; the porch needed shoring; the windows needed cleaning; the screen door needed patching.

The main door had survived generations of Stoneburners and looked it. Years ago Nancy had left the house through this door-way and never looked back. Now she banged on the door once more for good measure.

"I think she'll come down eventually," Tessa said. "When she's punished us long enough."

"Punished us?"

"For insisting she change the way she lives to suit us."

"I suppose you think I don't have that right." Nancy could feel her shoulders slump. She was sixty but looked younger, much younger, when she was rested and reasonably contented. She was neither now. Sweat steamed a path between breasts which were jammed together in a bra that was close kin to the Iron Maiden. She wanted to rip off her control-top panty hose, tie them to the unpainted porch rafters and hang herself. She had been up every night for a week worrying about the days to come. The bags under her eyes had bags of their own, and she could feel a new chin grow-ing and wobbling as she shook her head.

Tessa didn't sigh. She was a still, dark lake, and whatever churned beneath was hidden, as always. "We're here," Tessa said. "It's too late to reconsider. I've cleared my calendar for the rest of the summer, you've cleared yours. All we can do is move ahead."

"And how do we do that? She's locked herself in like a prisoner."

"I gather you don't have a key?"

"Why would I need a key? She never locks the door. I've told her and told her to lock it—"

"Well, it looks like this time she did what she was told."

Nancy glanced at her daughter and saw the shadow of a smile. The two women were nothing alike. Tessa was tall, with narrow hips, small breasts. Her eyes were tilted and green, her hair bone straight and a rich, silky brown. She wore it long, pulled back like a dancer's. She had, in fact, devoted herself to ballet until mid-adolescence, when the pleasures of a more normal life had called her away. She still had a dancer's posture, a dancer's grace, a dancer's simplicity. Today she wore cream-colored shorts that highlighted her long tanned legs and a matching raw silk blouse with a mandarin collar.

Nancy knew herself to be an aged cheerleader. Stocky, blond, as perky as any woman with arthritis and high blood pressure could be. Her hair curled at any provocation; her skin blistered in the sun. She exercised religiously and exorcized the ever-creeping pounds, subdued the hair with the help of Richmond's best hairdresser, wore expensive sunscreen under more expensive foundation that she shaded and contoured to soften her square face.

Today she wore a designer dress of baby pink and more undergarments than a flock of Victoria's Secret angels. And right now she was sorry about all of it.

"I think she just wants to show us who's boss," Tessa said. "When Gram is sure we've gotten her point, she'll let us in. We should make ourselves comfortable."

Nancy didn't have to think about that approach. "No."

"No?"

"Did you check the back door?"

"It will be locked."

"Then you didn't check."

"I didn't feel comfortable barging in, not when she so obviously wanted to keep me out."

"Well, *I* don't have that problem. Two can play this game. She's not the only stubborn Henry woman in the world. I've come a long way, and I'm not spending the night on this porch. The mosquitoes will eat—"

"We're a long way from the mosquito hour," Tessa interrupted. "Can't you just wait a bit, see if she lets us in now that we're both here?"

Nancy was cranking up. She had put her entire life on hold for this. She had given up a chance to chair a garden club luncheon next week. It was an honor she'd long coveted and might not be offered again. She had left her husband in Richmond, and without her constant presence at his side, she was afraid he would have too much time to reflect on all the things that were missing in their marriage. "And what for?" she spoke out loud, as if Tessa had been privy to her thoughts. "Not to stand out here and plead to be admitted to my mother's inner sanctum."

She pivoted and started down the steps, only glancing behind her once to see if her daughter had followed. Tessa was trailing behind, but she didn't look pleased.

"Good," Nancy said. "We'll find a way. There's a door into the basement from the fruit cellar."

Tessa didn't respond.

The back door was locked. The fruit cellar door was locked. Most of the first-floor windows were closed and probably locked. Except one. Nancy stood below the window that led to the room her mother called a parlor and gazed up at it. Since the ground sloped, the first floor was higher here and the window was out of reach. But the window was open. Wide open and large enough for Nancy to squirm through.

"Did you sneak in and out this way as a teenager?" Tessa asked.

"Where would I have sneaked to? Look around. This is the middle of nowhere. There's probably a sign to that effect somewhere. I'm sure I passed it at the beginning of Fitch."

"You must have had friends. With cars."

"I didn't have time for friends. By the time I finished all the chores your grandmother gave me, there was no time for fun."

"Even if I thought creeping through windows was a good idea, I wouldn't suggest starting here and now. The window's too high."

Nancy registered her daughter's reasonable tone. Tessa sounded like a mother trying to be patient with a recalcitrant preschooler, a diplomat asking for concessions from warring nations. Combined with the heat, it was a fatal mixture. Nancy pulled herself up to her full five foot four. "There's a ladder in the garage. Or there used to be."

Tessa put her hand on her mother's arm. "We should wait."

Nancy shook her off. "Look, we need to establish ground rules right away. Your grandmother cannot be in control of what happens here this summer. If she puts up roadblocks every time we try to help, nothing's going to get done." She started for the garage, a freestanding structure that was as dilapidated as the house.

"So you're going to show her who's boss?"

"I wouldn't put it that way."

"It doesn't matter how you put it."

Nancy stopped mid-bustle and turned. "I lived with her for twenty-two years. No matter what you *think* you know about your grandmother, I know more."

Tessa stood quietly, but her expression said it all. She disapproved. She did not understand—and never would—what drove her mother. No matter how hard Nancy tried to get through to her, to enlist her support, Tessa, just like her father, would never regard her mother as anything more than a lightweight, beautifully wrapped burden.

"It's going to be a long, hot summer," Nancy said. "And it's going to seem even longer if you spend the rest of it passing judgment on me, Tessa."

Without watching to see the effect of her words, she started for the garage again. Only when she heard a loud *thunk* did she stop and turn. Tessa shrugged, then stepped back and gazed up at the window above her head. What had just been an open window was now firmly closed. As Nancy watched, the woman inside drew the curtain across this window, too, and completely shut out the world.

* * *

Panic was an old enemy, one that Helen Henry could usually subdue the way she had subdued most of the enemies she had confronted in her eighty-two years. Now it clawed at her gut and wrapped its hands around her throat so that she could hardly breathe.

Of course there was always the chance she was having problems filling her lungs because there were no longer any window open in the house and the temperature inside was inching its way into the triple digits.

She stood with her back to the small portion of empty wall beside the parlor window and tried to catch her breath. While the window was open she had stood in this very place and listened to her only living relatives discuss the relative merits of storming her house. Only then had she succumbed to the panic that had hovered an arm's length away for a week.

They were here. Sooner or later they were going to come inside. They were going to *see*.

Her head fell forward in despair, and she noticed that her blue housedress was missing two buttons so that it gaped over her pendulous breasts. She had a thousand buttons to choose from, but no energy for the task of repairing it. She was pear-shaped, and she wore the dress and others of its ilk to hide her wide hips. Good hips for childbearing, her own mother had told her. Right now Helen was sorry her mother had been right.

"Mother!"

At Nancy's summons, Helen gritted her teeth, which were still mostly her own. It was common knowledge that Stoneburner teeth outlived many a Stoneburner. She considered praying that hers would outlast her, that she would die right here and now. But she doubted the Lord would take her quickly on such a flimsy pretext. She had to save that prayer, just in case things got really tough.

Right now, she had to either fish or cut bait. She was not a coward. Her life had not been easy, but she had marched through it, keeping panic at bay with one hand as she hacked a path through her personal wilderness with the other. The hand that had done the hacking was the only hand she'd allowed anyone to see since her husband's death, and it was the hand she needed to show right now.

If she didn't show that hand, if she allowed her daughter and granddaughter to see any other part of her, they would descend on her, prey on her weakness. She pictured wolves with Nancy and Tessa's faces, and was only vaguely ashamed.

"Mother!"

She thought she heard Tessa trying to shush Nancy. She could have told her granddaughter that the effort was useless, although she supposed Tessa knew that and just couldn't help herself. To the rest of the world Nancy might look flighty, even foolish at times, but Helen knew the granite those more superficial layers had been built upon. Nancy usually got what she wanted. Her pampered, made-to-order life was a testimony to that.

Helen lifted a corner of the parlor curtain and peeked out the window. The two women were still standing with the sun blazing down on them. Nancy was wilting like a carnation in the sunlight. Helen felt a twinge of sympathy. Sweat was pouring down her own back, and her dress was soaked under the arms. Unfortunately, she was the one who was inflicting this misery on everybody.

Helen dropped the curtain and straightened. The time had come. If she waited any longer, she wouldn't find the strength. Her choices were gone, and the only choice now was to act as if she was in charge, even if it wasn't true.

She wound her way toward the front door, trying not to look too closely at her surroundings. The dead bolt screeched when she turned it, as if it hadn't been used very often—which it hadn't. The air that rushed in was hot, but it was air. She breathed deeply; then she closed the door behind her, stepped gingerly out on the porch and made her way to the railing.

The robe and gown she had thrown from the window were just in reach, and again, she felt vaguely ashamed. She hadn't worn them yet. She had plenty of older things to wear out first. But she had taken them out sometimes to look at them, to feel the silky fabric against her callused fingertips. She gathered them over her arm now, then reached for the sweater that Nancy had given her for Christmas, pricking her finger on a holly leaf as she did.

They hadn't come back to the front yet. She was certain they were on their way; after all, what kind of ninnies stood outside in full sunshine when they didn't have to? She debated how best to greet them when they showed up.

She didn't have to debate long.

Tessa appeared first, which was not surprising, since Nancy was probably still scheming and steaming unnecessarily. Tessa paused when she saw her grandmother on the porch, but said nothing. Helen awarded her points for that. She could count on Tessa not to make a fuss. She was a regular Jackie Kennedy in times of crisis.

"Well, come on up." Helen stepped away from the railing. "Since it looks like you're not about to take my hint and go home."

"I was afraid you were going to start tossing all the furniture out that window." Tessa climbed the steps but stopped on the top one. "How are you, Gram?"

"Just like I was the last time you asked me. And now that you know, you can go on home again."

Nancy rounded the corner and glared at her mother. "I suppose you think this was cute, Mother? Doesn't the Bible say something about making guests welcome?"

"Some folks might think a rattlesnake winding his way up the front steps was a guest, but me, I've got some common sense to go with my Bible verses."

Nancy started forward. "Is that the way a Christian woman talks about the loved ones who want to help her?"

Helen stood her ground. "You're here because you invited yourself."

Nancy started to respond, but Tessa stepped in front of her and stood firmly between the two older women.

"Look," Tessa said. "If you two don't stop, this summer is going to be impossible. Gram, I wish you had let me in when I arrived, but I guess it's your right to keep me waiting. It *is* your house."

"Durned right it is."

"And, Mom, you had a right to be worried about Gram."

"We don't need a negotiator, Tessa, and of course I was worried."

Tessa stepped back so she could see them both. "Let's just go in now and forget the rest."

Helen knew it was time to make one last pathetic stand. "I don't want you here. I can take care of myself. I've been taking care of myself for years and years."

Nancy started to list all the obvious signs that Helen couldn't take care of anyone, but Tessa held up her hand. "Let us help," she said to her grandmother.

Helen released a long breath and fell silent. *Help.* It was a word that had only the vaguest meaning, a word that applied to other people but never to her. She noted her granddaughter's expression. Tessa was like Helen herself, seldom showing what she was feeling. But at this crucial moment, concern shone in her eyes. The concern was that of one human being for another, not the heartfelt worry of family members who had warm, shared memories. But Helen grabbed it and held on. She had nothing else.

"I don't want to hear a word, you understand? Not a word about how I've let the place go. You think I don't know?"

Tessa didn't reply. Nancy sighed. "Let's just go inside."

"It doesn't matter what you find," Helen said. "I'm not leaving this house. Not until the Lord calls me home." She didn't wait for confirmation; she turned and stiffly hobbled toward the house.

Behind her, she heard Tessa murmur to her mother, "You heard what she said, right?"

"I hear just fine."

Helen didn't point out that *she* heard just fine, too. She shoved the door open, then stepped to one side once she was in the hallway. She watched the other women.

At the threshold, Tessa stepped aside to let her mother enter first. Helen watched as Nancy's eyes took a moment to adjust to the darkness. Tessa came in behind her and gave a low whistle. And after her own warning, it was Tessa who spoke first.

"My God," she said softly.

Without looking, Helen knew exactly what her daughter and granddaughter saw. Piles and piles and more piles lining walls, making corridors in the middle of rooms, towering like fortresses that stretched and tipped just feet from the ceiling. Cereal boxes flattened into wafers, empty jars glinting in front of a window, rescued magazines and books that the careless citizens of Toms Brook, Mauertown and Woodstock had thrown away in their trash, blankets, towels folded neatly and placed in their proper stacks. Kitchen appliances she would fix someday once she found the right parts, plastic bags filled with more bags—and what was more wasteful than throwing those into some landfill while they were still in one piece? Seed catalogues with photographs too lovely not to be enjoyed again, plastic flowerpots waiting for a new plant to fill them.

And more, so much more.

"Well, don't look so stunned. It's just my stuff," Helen said. "I'll use every last bit of it. Some folks never learn how to make do, to save and take care of things, to use something old again instead of throwing away and buying more. Well, I'm proud I know how. Nothing I need that I don't have right here. Nothing at all, and how many people can say as much?"

Then, because she couldn't bear to see the shock and pity on the faces of the only two people in the world who loved her even a little, Helen turned, picked her way up the cluttered stairwell and along the upstairs hallway, and closed her bedroom door behind her.

CHAPTER
2

Tessa realized that Nancy needed a place to sit and recover. There wasn't one, of course. Every chair in sight was simply a base for more stacks of "stuff," as Helen had put it. Tessa helped her mother remove thick books of wallpaper and upholstery samples from an armchair in the corner, making several trips to the porch, because there was no place inside to put them without cutting off access to the rest of the house forever.

When she returned after hauling out the final bunch, she found Nancy sitting with her head in her hands.

"All right," Tessa conceded. "It's bad. Worse than we imagined."

"I'm waiting for a rat to run over my foot."

For once, Nancy wasn't exaggerating. The house had that feel. Disturb a pile and unleash an onslaught of vermin. Maybe Helen had been collecting rodents, too, hoping to discover a use for them sometime in the foreseeable future.

"What do you suppose she was doing with wallpaper and upholstery samples?" Nancy asked. "Maybe she intended to paper over all these piles, hoping we wouldn't notice?"

"They're labeled. They're from an interior decorator's shop in Strasburg. I'd guess she saw them on a trash pile when she was there one day and rescued them."

Nancy groaned.

"You were right." Tessa had to give credit where it was due, even though it felt unfamiliar. "I guess I thought..." She didn't know how to phrase the rest.

"You thought I invented a problem here because I don't have anything better to do." Nancy lifted her head. "You think I don't know?"

"This is not a good time to delve into the mysteries of our relationship. I was trying to let you know I'm sorry I doubted the seriousness of this."

"It *is* serious." Nancy swept the room with a hand. "One match, Tessa. A spark. That's all it would take."

"I'll lure her outside if you're willing to do the deed. It would save a lot of time."

Nancy smiled, and Tessa was unexpectedly warmed by it. Nancy smiled too often, and her smiles usually hung on too long, as if she was pleading to be noticed and appreciated. This smile was not trying to accomplish anything. It was released, and it ended quickly.

"Can we sleep in the house tonight?" Nancy asked. "Without putting our lives in danger?"

"As hot as it is, we should probably worry about spontaneous combustion." Tessa paused. "And what are the chances the beds have space for us?"

"I've pleaded with her for years to let me put in air-conditioning. I even brought in a man to rewire the house for it a few years ago, but that was as far as I could get. She was furious. And the heat strains her heart. I don't understand her. I have the money. It's a small thing to me."

"Not to her."

"Well, she's upstairs now. We'd better decide what we're going to do while we still can."

"Or before she goes collecting again." Tessa ran one finger over a pyramid of dusty florist-issue vases. "How long has it been since you've been in the house?"

"Too long, obviously." Nancy touched her thumb to her fingers as if she was counting. "Last summer? No, that's not right. I've seen her, certainly, but it's always somewhere else. We'd meet at church or at the drugstore, then afterwards she'd say, 'Don't bother coming home with me, I have things to do,' or 'I can see to myself just fine.'" Nancy wrinkled her forehead. "I remember we came back here after Kayley died. I——" She stopped abruptly.

Tessa was silent. After Kayley died. Nearly three years ago. She supposed they all marked their days that way. Before Kayley, after Kayley. *I was happy before Kayley died. I was despondent afterwards.* The day of Kayley's death was a clear, vital demarcation in time.

The day that Tessa's five-year-old daughter had been struck and killed by a drunk driver.

"That was the last time I'm absolutely sure I was inside." Nancy was talking too fast again. "I'm sorry, I wasn't thinking——"

"Kayley died. We can't pretend she didn't." Tessa put her hands against the small of her back and pressed, stretching tall and swaying. "I came here after the funeral, too. The house looked fine, didn't it?" Of course, the house could have been swallowed by the Shenandoah that day and she would not have noticed she was treading water.

"It didn't look like this," Nancy said. "Tessa, what kind of a daughter am I?"

Tessa frowned. "One who was never invited into the house. She didn't want you to know. If you hadn't pushed this, none of us would know."

"What are we going to do?" Nancy's hands twisted in her lap. She looked to be on the verge of tears.

Tessa had been asking herself the same question. The smallest things now loomed like giants on the horizon. Was it safe to sleep here tonight? Was there a *place* to sleep, to eat? Was the lone bathroom in working order? Even if the windows were opened again, could enough air circulate through the house to keep the women from smothering?

And how had Helen allowed her life to come to this?

"We can't burn it down," Tessa said. "She'd go up with it, just to spite us. And we can't spend the night somewhere else. If we do, she won't let us back inside tomorrow."

"I'm amazed she let us in today."

"She knows she needs help, Mom. But it took her so long to admit it because she was scared."

"She's never been scared of anything in her whole life. You should have seen her when I was a little girl. She could——"

Tessa only half listened as her mother recounted stories of her grandmother's courage against copperheads and rattlesnakes, and once a big black bear that had been determined to visit the chicken coop. She knew there was no point in arguing the point. She glanced at her watch, a slender gold band with gemstone chips where numbers should have been. Mack, her husband, had given it to her on her last birthday. She had found that odd. Didn't he realize that one moment was the same as the next now that Kayley was gone? This was just one more way he no longer understood her.

She looked up again at Nancy, who had run out of steam. "We have about seven hours until the sun goes down. In seven hours we can haul a lot outside."

Nancy looked defeated. "You're serious?"

"We have to start with the paper trash. At the very least, the worst of that has to go outside before nightfall."

"Where in the world are we going to put it?"

"Out in the front yard for now. We can hide it with a tarp until we can dispose of it. I'm sure she has one."

"She probably has at least a dozen, in a wide variety of sizes and colors. All neatly folded and stacked in the shower stall or the woodstove."

"Tomorrow we'll see about finding someone to help us haul it away."

"She won't let anybody else inside to help. You do realize that, don't you?"

Tessa was afraid that was true. More than an hour had passed before Helen had let them in. No one outside the family would be allowed any farther than the porch. As easy as it would be to pay a crew to come inside and haul away the contents of the house, it was not going to be possible without agitating Helen to the point of mania.

"Are you going to tell her we're clearing out the place, or do you want to leave that up to me?"

"I'll do it." Nancy didn't move.

"Let me. I'm just the granddaughter. She doesn't have as much to prove."

"She'll throw a fit."

Tessa wondered. On some level, Helen realized the piles had to come down. Perhaps she even wished they would disappear so that she could move easily around her house again. Tessa was still wrestling with the psychology of this. Why would anyone hoard so many useless items that she no longer had room to live a normal life? She had heard of pack rats, but this gave new meaning to the term.

"I'd better get it over with," she said.

"Maybe we should tie a rope to your waist in case you get lost. I'd tell you to drop bread crumbs, but why bring the mice out of hiding?" Nancy got to her feet. "I'll be hauling newspapers."

"Let's both be careful of our backs. Just one small stack at a time."

Nancy touched her daughter's arm. "You have to be firm, Tessa.

We can't feel sorry for her. The stuff has to go, or *she* has to go. It's that simple."

"She knows that. You've already threatened her with the health department."

"I would have sent them months ago if I'd had any idea it was this bad."

Involving the authorities might have been the more sensible approach, yet what would it have done to Helen? The farm, the house, were her life. Unlike her mother, Tessa did not believe that moving her grandmother to a spiffy retirement home in a strange city would do anything except hasten her death.

She abandoned the muttering Nancy to the stacks and picked her way upstairs. Helen had left just enough space on each step for one foot. One misstep could easily provoke a tumble to the bottom. Tessa made a note to tackle the stairs just as soon as the paper trash had been hauled outside. All Helen needed was a broken hip.

She couldn't remember when she had last been on the second floor. The house was spacious, added on to here and there through the decades when rooms were needed for an overflow of children or aging relatives who had come back home to be cared for. She paused on the landing, mapping a route to what she thought was her grandmother's bedroom.

The piles of choice in the upstairs hallway were clothes. To Helen's credit she *did* know how to organize. Overalls and jeans were in one pile, the organizing principle being denim, apparently. Another pile looked to be shirts. Yet another was dresses. Rolled socks swelled into mounds, a stack of shoeboxes contained not shoes but frayed underwear. These piles weren't as high as those downstairs, but there were many of them, most at least knee-deep.

Tessa picked her way through the maze. This was the repository of dish towels, too, she noticed, and sheets that were only good for Halloween costumes. She came upon a tower of threadbare towels, and it leaned precariously when her hip brushed against it.

"Gram?"

Helen didn't answer, of course. That would have been too easy. Tessa thought of a trip she, Mack and Kayley had taken to London four years ago. Mack had flown over for a conference, and Tessa and Kayley, then four, had joined him to sightsee. Together they had taken the scenic boat trip down the Thames to Hampton Court, where Kayley had been entranced with the maze, giggling and hiding there as children had since the eighteenth century. Perhaps, if Kayley were still alive, she would be entranced with this one, too.

All their friends had told Tessa and Mack that Kayley was too young to enjoy a trip of that distance, that the little girl wouldn't even remember the vacation when she was older. Tessa had a million regrets about the brief years of her daughter's life. The books she hadn't read her, the walks they hadn't taken, the games unplayed. But she was still so very glad that she had followed her own heart and taken Kayley to London that summer.

She made her way to the closest bedroom door, the one overlooking the front of the house, where Helen had lobbed her missiles. She knocked, then tried the knob when no one answered. The room was dark, curtains still drawn. She flipped the switch and saw that Helen wasn't there. Of course Helen *couldn't* be there, since there was no room for a human being to move. There was one narrow aisle that led to the front window. The rest of the room was waist-to-shoulder-deep in black plastic bags.

"Terrific." She sniffed the air and was relieved not to smell rotting garbage. If they were lucky, Helen had simply housed more of her "collections" here, in trash bags, perhaps yet unsorted.

Back in the hallway maze, she found her way to another bedroom, this one a library of outdated volumes. The room had the musty smell of a rare bookshop, although she doubted that these books were particularly rare or valuable. Only half the floor here was cluttered. The other half had been cleared to allow passage to a bed. Tessa suspected that either she or her mother was to sleep here tonight.

Another room had been half cleared, too, lending support to her theory. She found Helen in the next one.

Helen's door wasn't closed all the way, but she didn't answer when Tessa knocked. Tessa let herself in to find her grandmother sitting at the window, looking out over the farm pond.

Helen had always been a large woman, broad shoulders and hips, big bones and breasts. Now, despite her substantial physical size, she looked fragile, almost shrunken, as if some unseen force had sucked away everything that had once kept her moving confidently through life. Her hair was wispy and white, and she had worn it in an unattractive Dutch Boy bob as long as Tessa could remember. Helen trimmed it herself—a mistake—but today it looked as if she hadn't bothered in months.

Tessa had seen photographs of her grandmother as a young woman. There weren't many. That kind of vanity had been frowned on in her strict Lutheran family, and the Depression had curbed any such tendencies, anyway. But once upon a time Helen had been considered "a fine figure of a woman," a woman who turned heads and easily dominated a room.

Now her face showed a lifetime of hardship. The decades were carved there as if to keep any displays of emotion from overlapping their deeply grooved boundaries. She had developed a perpetual squint, because she refused to replace her glasses regularly, waiting to visit a doctor until even the addition of a magnifying glass couldn't bring print into focus.

"Gram?"

Helen didn't turn or speak.

"I need to talk to you." Tessa stepped inside. This bedroom was surprisingly spacious, with a row of windows at the back where her grandmother sat. The floor here would be cluttered by normal standards, but not by the standards of this house. Fabric was stacked neatly on shelves built of concrete blocks and boards; sewing tools hung from a pegboard. Of course, there were piles here, as well, but at least they were pushed to the side so that the middle of the room was clear.

"I don't want to talk," Helen said at last. "Talk is useless."

"Then I'm afraid you'll just to have to listen." Tessa walked to the windows and stood beside her grandmother's chair, staring out at the pond.

The pond, like the land, was parched and dry. She remembered it in better days, when its surface had lapped at the roots of weeping willows planted along its borders. She estimated that it had shrunk by a third, stranding or crowding fish and making mud flats of the rim.

"It's been a terrible, dry summer, hasn't it?" Tessa said.

Helen didn't answer.

Tessa wondered if her grandmother's life had been the same. Had she begun her collections for something to do? Had the piles of abandoned objects filled that aching, thirsty place within her brought on by loneliness and aging?

"We have to clear out the rooms," Tessa said softly. "You know that, I think. The place is a health hazard, a safety hazard. And you need space to live and move around without falling. If you tripped over something, you could break a hip or an arm."

Again Helen didn't answer.

"It would be easiest if you let us hire somebody to haul it all away," Tessa said. "That way it could be done quickly."

That got the expected rise out of her grandmother. "Nobody's coming inside! I don't want you here, either."

Tessa rested her fingertips on her grandmother's shoulder. "That's pretty clear. I thought I was going to have to camp on your doorstep."

Helen snorted. "You? You're too soft. What would you know about roughing it?"

"Staying inside this house for the rest of the summer will teach me everything I don't know already."

"You're staying?"

"What did you expect? That we'd see the situation here and leave you to deal with it by yourself?"

"I don't need your charity."

Tessa struggled with phrasing. "Maybe not, but you could use the company, couldn't you? And there's a lot of work here, Gram. More than one person should have to do alone."

Helen was silent for so long that Tessa was afraid she wasn't going to answer. Then the old woman sighed. "I don't know how this happened."

Tessa, who had struggled not to feel anything since she arrived, felt sympathy streak right past her defenses. She understood her grandmother's words too well. Tessa had watched her own life spin out of control, and she, like Helen, still seemed powerless to stop it.

By the time they had made a start on removing the newspapers, magazines and cardboard from the downstairs, the sun had slipped behind the horizon. It was a little easier to move around now, and with all the windows wide open and fans in the cleared areas, the temperature was almost bearable.

Nancy stretched, holding her hands over her head. "I need a shower. More than I need a drink and dinner, although it's close."

Tessa needed one, too, but she had a bad feeling about the water supply. If the pond was slowly drying up, what about the well?

A month, more likely two, without air-conditioning or an ample supply of water to bathe in. A summer shared by three women who had little in common except DNA.

"Why don't you go ahead, and I'll see what we can do about dinner," Tessa said. "I think I can get to the stove and at least one of the cupboards."

Nancy finished her stretch. "I brought some groceries with me and put them on the table. Nothing perishable, thank God, since I'm afraid to look in the refrigerator, but some boxes and cans. Some fruit, too, and a loaf of bread. I didn't know what we'd run into here."

Tessa knew her mother to be an interesting mixture of drill sergeant and powderpuff. In her own limited sphere, Nancy was masterful. No one could organize a tea or a banquet better than she could. No one knew how to schmooze Richmond's elite with more finesse. She was on a first-name basis with most of the state legislature and knew precise details about the Confederate heritage, financial dealings and political ties of every leading family. Practical matters, though, like skinned knees or the location of circuit breakers or how many ounces equaled a pound seemed beyond her. To Tessa's knowledge, Nancy did not cook. Sarah, their housekeeper, had prepared every meal except the occasional bowl of cereal or sandwich. So it surprised Tessa that her mother had considered this problem and tackled it head-on.

"Peanut butter?" Tessa asked.

"Sarah packed the bag, but I think so. I asked for tuna, too, and a jar of mayonnaise."

"Good, then I'll do sandwiches."

"You're sure? You could shower first while I tackle the kitchen. I'm still moving, aren't I? Still on my feet?"

"I'm fine. Go on." Tessa had already told Nancy about the bedrooms. "Choose a room while you're at it. You'll find sheets in the hall. Lots and lots of them."

"It's been a long time since I've slept here," Nancy said.

"Which room was yours?"

"The one facing the woods."

The book room. "Gram has thoughtfully provided you with extra reading material for the summer," Tessa said, trying not to smile.

Nancy's eyelids fluttered shut for a moment, as if she was picturing what awaited her. "I'll get my overnight case." She started toward the front door, then she turned. "Wine. There's a bottle of wine, too. I just remembered."

Helen had a moderate attitude toward alcohol. Tessa knew she would not object, would even, perhaps, join them if they could get her downstairs again.

"Tessa, I..." Nancy stopped. "Well, maybe you'd rather we didn't drink at all? I didn't think. I didn't mean to push it at you that way. I know how you feel—"

"It's fine."

Nancy stopped herself from continuing, a measure of how powerful the subject was. She disappeared out the door.

There was a wider path to the kitchen now. Tessa had already divided the mess into two categories, at least in her head. The division was, as far as she could tell, dead even. The first consisted of things that simply needed to be disposed of. The second was going to be harder. Stacks of old correspondence, bills that might or might not have been paid, boxes of photographs, items that might still be useful to someone, even if not to Helen. At first she had hoped it would be as simple as throwing out nearly everything. But after hours of hauling, she had seen that would not be true.

The kitchen was a prime example of the second category. It was no surprise that Helen stored food. In case of national disaster, Fitch Crossing Road and the town of Toms Brook would be well fed. Now Tessa understood Helen's collection of jars in the living room. She used them for everything. Herbs, grains, pasta, cereal. She made her own jellies and used miscellaneous jars for those, as well. The food she canned—and an eclectic variety was represented here—resided in standard issue canning jars. Since Tessa hadn't yet come across that particular mountain, she wondered where those extra jars were stored. She was afraid to think what awaited in the root cellar.

Nancy had left the grocery bags on the only available cleared space, Helen's lone placemat at the small round table by the kitchen window. Tessa's first job was to clear a counter so she could prepare the meal. The obvious one held ancient cookbooks stacked three feet high. She moved them to the floor beside the back door, leaving just enough room for an emergency escape route.

Once cleared, she scoured the counter with a clean sponge—one of many—then set out bread, tuna fish and mayonnaise. In an overhead cabinet she found a wide choice of bowls, each one nested inside its larger neighbor to save space.

She was reminded of a Russian matroyshka. She'd had a set of the nesting dolls as a little girl, cats of assorted colors that her father had brought home from a business trip. She had given them to Kayley as soon as her daughter was old enough to understand how to put one inside the other. Kayley had given them names and played with them for hours.

She was still staring out the window when she heard a noise behind her. Minutes had passed since she took out the tuna, and she hadn't even opened the can.

"You're making supper?"

Tessa was surprised to find Helen in the doorway. "Does tuna fish sound good?"

"I have food, you know. You think I don't eat?"

"Gram, we didn't know what you'd have, so Mom brought a few supplies with her." She paused. "Including a bottle of wine. Would you like a glass?"

Helen shuffled over to the counter. "Haven't had wine in years."

"Does that mean you don't want to try some?"

"I suppose a glass might not hurt."

"Where will I find glasses?"

Helen chortled. "Just about any place you look."

Tessa was surprised her grandmother could make something so close to a joke about the situation. She pulled a glass from the drainer, then set it aside. It had a visible crack. Tomorrow, out from under Helen's watchful eye, it would go into the trash. The second was in better shape, even if it did feature a Flintstones cartoon in fading yellow relief. Circa 1965.

"You threw out all my newspapers. Who told you you could?" Helen said.

"Why were they piled up in there in the first place?" Tessa lifted the wine bottle out of the bag. She was grateful to see that Nancy had brought a corkscrew with her. She had no stomach for rummaging through the drawers tonight.

"I haven't read them."

"They're a fire hazard, Gram. Let's face it, if you don't read them the day they come out, you're never going to read them. Besides, you could start reading tonight and read through next Christmas and you'd still only finish a fraction."

"I've been making headway."

Nancy spoke from the doorway. "Mother, according to those newspapers, the World Trade Center's still gracing the Manhattan skyline, President Clinton is busily claiming he never had sex with that woman, and wives in Afghanistan aren't allowed out of the house unless they're covered head to toe."

"People throw out too much. Wasteful, that's what it is. Nobody knows how to take care of things anymore. And what have you done with my magazines?"

Tessa waited for her mother to throw fuel on that particular fire, too. She wrestled with the corkscrew and pulled out the cork. She poured Helen's wine, put it in front of her and searched for a glass for herself.

"There were some really interesting magazines in those piles," Nancy admitted, surprising her daughter into deeper silence. "I can see why it would be hard to part with them."

"Haven't even looked at half of them."

"Tell me which ones interest you most and I'll find the most recent issues for you," Tessa said, only trusting her mother's judgment so far. "You have subscriptions?"

"Subscriptions? Why? Doctor's offices throw them out once they get too old."

And Helen saved them from the landfill. The theme at the Old Stoneburner Place was becoming obvious. The aged, the outdated, had to be protected and cared for. It was Helen's duty, because no one else was doing it.

"Mom, would you like a glass of wine?" Tessa asked Nancy.

"Tomorrow I'll just bring all those old things back inside, you know," Helen said. "You see if I don't. You don't have the right." She picked up her glass, squeezed past her daughter and was quickly swallowed up by piles of junk. They listened in silence as she slowly picked her way back upstairs.

"I'll take a sandwich up to her later," Tessa said.

"This isn't going to work, you know," Nancy said wearily. "I had a two-minute shower before the water dwindled to a drip, then I dried myself with a towel from the Eisenhower era. Mother's not eating, and I'm not sure she's bathing. She's not going to let us do what needs to be done here. We'll take stuff out, she'll bring it back in. It's ninety in here, at least. The screens need patching, and the mosquitoes are looking for a stiff drink and a good time." She swatted a forearm in emphasis. "She's gotten crazy as a loon, and reasoning with her is only going to make things worse."

Tessa handed her mother a glass of wine. "And your suggestion would be?"

They stared at each other. Nancy made a silent toast. Tessa acknowledged it. They drank without another word, slapping mosquitoes lethargically as they listened to the sound of crickets through the gaping holes in the screens.

CHAPTER
3

On Wednesday morning Tessa woke up when the first rays of sunshine filtered through her window. The previous morning she had removed the old dust-heavy curtains and cleared most of her bedroom floor of piles and boxes. She and Nancy had agreed over yesterday's breakfast that if they were going to sleep in the house, they had to start by making their bedrooms habitable.

"When I finally got to sleep," Nancy had said, "I dreamed I was walking down an unfamiliar street and things started falling out of the sky. I woke up, and there were these piles of books all around my bed. I lay there with my eyes open, waiting for them to fall on me, too."

Tessa's dreams hadn't been any better, except that her personal nightmare was the same every night, no matter where she slept.

Most of Tuesday had been taken up with sorting and carrying out the contents of their rooms. Helen had holed up in her bedroom, refusing to come down for meals. In a way, her absence had been a relief. At least while she stayed upstairs she could not make good on her threat to retrieve the trash they cleared away. She didn't speak when Tessa delivered food or drinks. She sat and sewed at her window in silence.

This morning Tessa could hear her grandmother moving around in the room beside her. Tessa knew the truce—and calling it a truce was a positive spin—wouldn't last forever. Eventually her grandmother was going to go outside, see everything that had been discarded and raise the proverbial roof.

She sat up and gripped her knees. The old Stoneburner place was, in some sense, her family home, but she felt like a stranger here. As a little girl she had not visited her grandmother for overnights or summer vacations. When it was required, she had come for brief visits with her parents, but Helen had always frightened her. Her grandmother had a booming voice and a towering presence. If she liked children, she never willingly demonstrated it. There were no overflowing cookie jars in Helen's house, no picture books to ponder together, no pampered pets to cuddle. Tessa had been encouraged to run and play outside, but the vast, lonely spaces had disconcerted the little girl. By the time she was a teenager, she had usually manufactured excuses not to go when her mother and father made their duty calls.

Now the house felt unfamiliar. Someday, she supposed, it would be hers. When Helen died, the farm might even be passed straight to Tessa instead of her mother, since Nancy was more vocal in her dislike of the land and the Virginia countryside in general. But there would be no emotional struggle for Tessa when the time came to sell it.

Next door, Helen was muttering. Tessa swung her feet to the floor and dressed in the clothes she'd laid out the night before. Unfortunately, she had few choices. She had accidentally left the suitcase containing most of her clothes at home and would need to retrieve it that afternoon unless she wanted to wash the same two outfits by hand every night. Although her house in Fairfax was only an hour and a half away in good traffic, she was sorry she had to make the trip. She and Nancy needed to do as much as they could quickly, before Helen changed her mind and threw them out.

Downstairs, she found her mother staring out the kitchen window as she shined the faucet. Nancy didn't even turn when Tessa entered the room.

"Do you know how many dishes I've done at this sink?" Nancy said.

"Same sink, I bet."

"It's probably the original, brought to the wilderness by mule teams."

"Was there *anything* you liked about living here?" Tessa could hear a lack of sleep in her own voice. A neater room had made very little difference.

"As a matter of fact, no." Nancy bent over to rinse a cup, fussing over it longer than she needed to. "There's coffee. It's still fresh."

"I'll take a cup up to Gram. She's awake."

"Don't, Tessa. We're not here to wait on her. She can come down and get it if she wants it."

"Look, she's old, confused, upset. I—"

"You won't make things any better by treating her like she's any of those things." Nancy faced her daughter, her hands twisting in front of her. She had already showered, and her hair and makeup were morning-fresh. Tessa wondered just how early her mother had risen to achieve this state of perfection.

"Look," Nancy said, "I know her better than you do. She doesn't want to be taken care of. Okay?"

"Then we ignore her?"

"I doubt we'll be accused of that. We're here because of her, aren't we? We're spending our whole summer trying to make her life better."

"My life is just fine." Helen hobbled into the kitchen. Tessa hadn't even heard her descend the stairs. For such a large woman, she was surprisingly light on her feet. "I didn't ask for your help."

"There's coffee," Nancy said. "To go with the approaching argument."

"No arguments!" Tessa's voice was sharp. It surprised even her. "Look, you two, I don't know why you treat each other the way that you do, but I'm not going to be a party to it. We have a job to do here, and it's going to take at least a month, maybe two—"

Helen interrupted. "I didn't—"

Tessa held up her hand. "I'm sorry, but it doesn't matter if you asked us to come or not, Gram. We're here. We're staying. When we leave, the house is not going to look the same. That's inevitable. We can get along or not. That part is optional, and as far as I'm concerned, it's up to the two of you. But if you have to pick at each other, do it when I'm not around, okay? Because I do *not* like to hear it."

She abandoned the house by the back door and started around it. Before she knew it, she was jogging, then running faster. Running had never been her tranquilizer of choice. Until Kayley's death, yoga had helped her deal with the normal stress of a happy life. Afterward, she had not been able to focus, and yoga, like everything else, had seemed worthless.

She was on Fitch Crossing Road, running down the dips and up the slopes, before she wondered what she was doing. But she didn't wonder long. Running made a great deal of sense to her. As a metaphor, nothing could beat it.

She wasn't sure how far she had run before the heat and the unaccustomed strain got the better of her. She slowed to a jog, then a fast walk. She was no longer bordering her grandmother's acres. The fields here were better tended, as if someone had been through recently with a plow, even though the acres of corn stretching back from the road as far as the river probably couldn't be saved. She realized she must have run as far as the Claiborne farm.

In the distance, on her right, she saw a brick ranch house with a fleet of vehicles parked in front of it. A small mobile home sat well behind the house, and behind that stood orchards.

A man driving a tractor was heading down the driveway in her direction. Tessa waved and waited to utter a few words of greeting. This was not the city. Neighbors here did not ignore each other, not unless they wanted to be ignored when they needed help. The man—Mr. Claiborne himself, she guessed—let the engine idle and got down to speak to her.

"Oh, I didn't mean for you to stop," Tessa said. "I was just going to say hello."

The man, late fifties and whipcord lean, wiped his hand on his denim-clad thigh and held it out. "Ron Claiborne."

She shook his hand. "Tessa MacRae. Helen's granddaughter."

"How's Helen doing?"

She shrugged. "We're grateful to you, Mr. Claiborne. She's hidden her problems from us for a long time, I'm afraid." She felt something else was expected, some explanation that a family could be so oblivious to the plight of an aging relative. But she didn't know what to add.

He took charge. "Helen don't say much to nobody. I can see how it happened."

"Well, thanks for that, but at least we know now. We're staying to clear out the house and put everything in order. Then we'll see where we go from there."

"You're going to need help."

"She won't let anyone else inside."

"No wonder." He removed his cap—an advertisement for a local storage company—and scratched his head. "What do you plan to do with, you know, the things you don't need."

For a moment Tessa wondered if hoarding was a way of life on Fitch Crossing; then she realized he was just offering to help. "Actually, I'm not sure. We're just taking things outside now and covering them with a tarp. But I guess we need to hire somebody to haul it all away."

"Don't need to hire nobody. Your grandma's been my neighbor

long as I been living here. I got me a small horse trailer that'll do
the job just fine. I'll bring it over today and park it in the yard.
Then every time it gets full, you just call, and I'll haul the stuff to
the landfill. And if you ever need my pickup for stuff you want to
give away, you can give me a holler and I'll have my boy Zeke bring
it right over. It's the least we can do." He paused. "I feel bad, you
know, that I didn't call sooner when she stopped going outside. I
made excuses to check on her a time or two, but I should have
called."

She had always heard from her mother that the Claibornes were
no-account white trash, hard drinkers and fighters. Odd how
wrong people could be. This man was obviously a gentleman. She
managed a smile. "You did more than most people would, and we
really would appreciate the trailer if you can spare it."

He nodded and jammed his cap back on his head. "I'll be by
later."

She lifted a hand in farewell and started back the way she'd come.
She was halfway back to her grandmother's when her cell phone
rang. She had dropped it in her shorts pocket when she'd dressed,
planning to leave a message for Mack after breakfast. She had wanted
him to know she would be coming back to pick up her suitcase. He
would be gone by then, and she wouldn't have to talk to him.

There never seemed to be anything to say to her husband anymore.

She dug for it and flipped it open to check caller ID. For a moment she considered not answering, but after the third ring she
gave in. Some things couldn't be avoided.

"Tessa?"

She cleared her throat. "Hello, Mack. On your way to work?"

"Not yet."

Silence. She wondered if he was searching to find something to say.

He skipped the small talk. "There's a suitcase beside the bed,
and it looks like it's full. I didn't notice it until this morning. It's
on your side."

"I know. I don't know how I left it there. I guess I was worrying about Gram."

"How is she?"

"You wouldn't believe it if you saw it. The house is a disaster."

"Is she letting you help?"

Mack had always liked Helen Henry, although he wasn't overly fond of Nancy. As an attorney, his job was to see through to the heart of matters—and people, too. Mack had always seen something in Helen that the rest of them missed. He had enjoyed their family trips here, using them to teach Kayley about farms and crops and animals. He could talk to Helen about the weather or the price of beef on the hoof like a farmer shooting the breeze with his cronies at the local Southern States co-op. Now Tessa heard real concern in his voice. She was vaguely ashamed that she hadn't called him to report.

"She's not happy," Tessa said, "but so far she's letting us clear out the rooms a little."

"Clear them out?"

"You wouldn't believe what she's collected. It's a mania, Mack. Nothing as simple as a little dust and a few windows to clean."

"Sounds like you're going to have your hands full for a while."

She wondered if that bothered or pleased him. "I doubt I'll be home to stay until I have to get ready for classes again in late August."

"Then you're going to need that suitcase."

She hadn't expected him to be saddened at her absence, but his utter lack of concern stung. She wasn't sure why it should.

He seemed to realize what he *hadn't* said. "I'll be over to visit you whenever I can get away. In fact, I'll come tonight and bring the suitcase. Anything else you need?"

"You don't have to do that. I was planning to skip out on Mom this afternoon and retrieve it myself."

"Are you needed there?"

She couldn't deny it. "It's a long trip to Toms Brook, Mack."

"I'll skip my meeting, but I may have to work late. I'll be there after dark."

His meeting. Compassionate Friends, the support group that had been his crutch since their daughter's death, but never hers. If he was willing to miss a meeting, he must feel that coming here and checking on Helen and the situation was important.

She gave in. "Well, that would really help. I appreciate it more than you know."

They were silent again. She spotted her grandmother's house in the distance. "Well, I'm almost home. I'm out jogging, I—"

"Jogging? In this heat?"

"I might just take it up permanently. It'll make me strong. I'm going to need help if I'm going to survive their bickering."

His laugh wasn't convincing. "Just take care of yourself."

"You too. I'll see you tonight."

She closed her phone and slowed her pace. She hadn't been looking forward to the day, and now she wasn't looking forward to the evening, either.

She wondered whether Mack felt this same sad reluctance to see her. If he did, it was one of the few things they shared.

CHAPTER
4

The Episcopal church where Mack's Compassionate Friends group met was cool and dark, designed as an oasis from the secular world. The meeting rooms continued the theme. The outside wall in this one was brick, with dark paneling on the inside walls. Twisted metal sculptures adorned them, not crosses, exactly, but something more abstract that still represented human suffering. Mack had always thought both the room and the sculptures were immensely appropriate for people who were trying to adjust to the loss of a child.

A casual friend had brought Mack to his first meeting here. Mack would not have come on his own. He was a man who had always handled his problems alone. He was a fixer, a solver, a windmill tilter who made a good living seeking justice for the aggrieved. When his father died unexpectedly between the seventeenth and eighteenth hole at Pebble Beach, Mack had flown to California, sobbed at the funeral, consoled his shattered mother, then set about making certain her finances were in order and her future secured.

When Kayley died, he couldn't remember to shave or brush his teeth.

The friend, whose grown son had died several years before in a skydiving accident, had come to Mack's house three weeks after Kayley's funeral, chosen clothes for him to wear, helped him into the car and driven him to the meeting. Mack had been attending ever since. The friend only showed up occasionally now, but Mack was not yet at the point where he could cope without the group.

Tessa had only attended once, at his insistence. He had no hope she would ever attend again.

This evening the room was empty. The meeting wouldn't start for another hour, and he had only come to drop off pamphlets he'd copied at his office before he headed for Helen's house with Tessa's suitcase. Erin Foster, another group member, had mentioned that they were running low. He did not want another grieving parent or sibling to be without information.

The room was already set up for the meeting. He opened his satchel and stacked the pamphlets on a table beside the door. Erin, who usually came early to be sure the room was set up correctly, would see them and take care of them afterwards.

He stood quietly for a moment, reluctant to leave for Toms Brook. Whatever peace he had found since his daughter's death, he had found here. Tessa considered his regular attendance a form of addiction, but he knew it for what it was. A lifeline for a drowning man.

The room was cool and quiet. He stared at the wall above the table, but he saw his wife's face instead. Once upon a time they would not have disagreed about anything so fundamental. From the start, their attitudes, their values, their hopes and dreams, had been the same. They were very different people, but they had seen the world through the same eyes, and breathed in and out in the same rhythm.

Now they were strangers.

"Mack?"

He looked up and saw Erin in the doorway. She was in her late twenties, a former Minnesota Butter Princess who had come south after college to work for the Department of Agriculture. Her round face was classically Midwestern, open, friendly, marred by nothing except a spattering of freckles. Her hair was pale rippling cornsilk, her smile as wholesome as a day at the State Fair. He had trusted her on first sight. But nowadays, he didn't trust himself when it came to Erin Foster.

She entered the room the way she did everything, bouncing with enthusiasm. "Mack, what are you doing here so early?"

"I just came to drop these off." He motioned to the pamphlets. "What are you doing here?"

"Oh, thanks for doing that. The board's going to meet for a few minutes before the meeting gets started. I wanted to get the coffee brewing." She favored him with a radiant smile. "Want to help me set out the cream and sugar?"

"I'm sorry, but I can't stay."

"You won't be here for the meeting?"

"Afraid not. My wife's out of town. She's staying over in Shenandoah County for the summer. I have to take her a suitcase she forgot."

"Oh, that's too bad. We'll miss you."

She sounded genuinely sad. He was an expert at deciphering unspoken messages—the skill served him well in his professional life. Now, though, he was as unsure of his own words as he was of her response.

He had just told Erin that for all practical purposes he would be a bachelor for the next two months. And he had neglected to make it clear that Tessa had left home because of family obligations. He might as well have lied and said that he and his wife were undergoing a trial separation.

And how much of a lie would it be?

"You look a little down about it. You're doing okay?" Erin said. "Need to talk?"

He was afraid that what he needed were Erin's strong arms around him, Erin in his life and in his bed. He needed her compassion, her warmth and, most of all, her desire for a future.

He needed to leave.

"I'm doing okay, thanks." He closed the satchel. "I'll be here next time, but I'd better not keep Tessa waiting. I'm getting a late start as it is."

"You need to be careful, Mack. It sounds like you're going to have a lot of free time to brood this summer. Make sure you spend some good time with friends."

Her gaze was unflinching. She had lost a younger brother to leukemia four years ago and suffered agonies over it. Erin understood how easy it was to fall into a chasm of despair.

There was nothing provocative in her expression or in her words, but Mack was fairly sure an invitation had been issued.

"Thanks." He bent and kissed her cheek. That was appropriate enough. They had been friends now for three years. But his reaction to that simple, quick kiss, to the cinnamon apple fragrance of her skin and hair, was anything but appropriate. "Have a good meeting."

In a moment he had left both temptation and solace behind.

After another day of backbreaking labor, Tessa had few choices on how to spend her evening. Faced with the prospect of socializing with her mother and grandmother in the newly cleared living room, sweltering alone in her bedroom as kamikaze moths and beetles threw themselves against her screens, or offering herself as a target for mosquitoes on the front porch, Tessa gladly chose the porch swing.

In the hottest part of the afternoon, she had made a quick run into Woodstock and come back with a cheap blue T-shirt, plastic barrettes to keep tendrils of hair off her neck, insect repellent and a trunk full of bottled springwater. Now she made use of all of them, showering quickly, donning the T-shirt, pulling her hair on top of her head and clasping it in place, and coating herself with the repellant. With a springwater in hand, she made herself comfortable on the porch swing and listened to the first swarm of mosquitoes chide her for a lack of cooperation.

The day had gone better than she'd feared, mostly because the three women had steered clear of each other. Nancy had spent significant portions of both morning and afternoon on her cell phone, no doubt shoring up her complicated social life. Nancy had worked so hard to reach her rung on the state capital's social ladder that nothing as insignificant as Helen's future was going to interfere with her continued ascent.

Tessa's life in Fairfax had intruded, as well. In between trips to the horse trailer that Ron Claiborne had parked in the front yard, she had fielded multiple phone calls from comrades in Mothers Against Drunk Driving. There was new legislation afoot, and they had sought Tessa's advice on how best to influence it.

Helen had stayed upstairs and quilted.

"Any breeze out here?"

Tessa didn't turn at her mother's voice. "Not so you'd notice."

"Mind if I join you?"

Tessa moved over to make room. "Where's Gram?"

Nancy plopped down beside her, and the swing screeched a mild protest. Tessa handed her the repellent, and Nancy began to rub it on her arms. "She's washing dishes."

On her trip to town Tessa had bought chicken salad from the Food Lion deli, and in a rare moment of agreement the three women had decided it was a good choice. "Maybe she's feeling a little better about everything."

"It was more along the lines of 'Get out of my kitchen, city scum, you don't belong here.'"

"See? She's sounding more like her old self."

Nancy laughed. "You have no idea how many hours I sat in this swing—or at least its predecessor—and waited for something to happen. There were hundreds of nights like this one. Just sitting."

Despite heat-induced lethargy, Tessa was curious. "You always make your years here sound so bleak."

Contrary to Tessa's expectation, Nancy didn't take the bit and run with it. "That was a long time ago. Maybe it wasn't as bleak as I remember. Sitting out here on summer nights, there were always a million stars, the smell of honeysuckle or wild roses. Sometimes your grandmother would come outside with me, at least until it got too dark for her to sew. She always had a quilt in progress, and she always worked late."

Honeysuckle scented the air tonight, and Tessa hadn't even noticed. She took a deep breath of it. "She's working on a quilt now. She put it in the frame this afternoon. I took iced tea up there about three, and she was struggling to get it tight enough."

"What does it look like?"

Tessa hadn't paid much attention. Helen's quilts were simply a fact of life. She and Mack had several that they swapped in and out for variety in their guest and master bedroom. In fact, Tessa had only realized that morning that the stacks in Helen's room weren't simply trash but projects she was working on, carefully separated into piles.

"Earth tones, I think," she said. "Lots of little squares."

"Probably Trip Around the World," Nancy said. "Or Irish Chain. She loves the traditional patterns."

Tessa was surprised her mother was so knowledgeable and started to say so, when she caught movement by the road. She leaned forward and squinted into the dusk. "Who's that?"

"Where?"

Tessa gestured with a twist of her head. "At the edge of the cornfield across the road."

Nancy shrugged. "Probably just somebody out for a walk."

"No, it looks like she's looking for something. I feel like stretching my legs. I'll go see."

"Don't mind me. I'll still be sitting right here waiting for something to happen."

Tessa ached everywhere. The unaccustomed run that morning, and hours of bending and lifting, had taken their toll. She moved slowly, but the woman across Fitch was oblivious to her, still standing in the same place.

Only when Tessa crossed the road did the woman—a girl, actually—notice her and speak. "Hi." She smiled shyly. "Nice evening, isn't it?"

The girl looked to be no older than seventeen. She was more ethereal than pretty, long wispy wheat-blond hair, pale lashes rimming blue eyes. Her skin was translucent, which made the multitude of freckles stand out in sharp relief.

She was also very, very pregnant.

"I'm Tessa MacRae." Tessa extended her hand. "Did you lose something out here?"

"Cissy Mowrey. I live over at the Claiborne place." She shook Tessa's hand, but dropped it immediately and clasped her own hands behind her back, as if to support the extra weight in front. "No ma'am, I was picking flowers."

Tessa's eyes flicked downward, where a neat bundle of dandelions lay at the girl's feet. They were scrawny and closing for the night, but there was a fair-sized cluster of them.

"Gram will thank you," Tessa said. "The more you pick, the fewer she'll have next year."

"Mrs. Henry's your grandma?"

"You know her?"

"No ma'am, not really. I seen her in church a time or two. I mean, I saw her."

The English teacher in Tessa applauded the correction. "Well, I don't want to keep you."

And she didn't. Tessa sensed something here, some need, some yearning that she had no desire and no resources to fulfill. The girl was walking alone a good distance from the Claiborne place, picking weeds for something to do on a summer evening. She looked to be somewhere in her second, even her final, trimester of pregnancy, and Tessa had already noticed there was no wedding band on her ring finger.

Tessa understood teenagers; she had developed a sixth sense for spotting trouble in their personal lives. Years ago, she had felt strong enough to involve herself when needed, to offer counsel, and if that wasn't warranted, a listening ear. Nowadays, no one came to Mrs. MacRae for anything except extra credit assignments.

"Oh, that's all right," Cissy said. "Zeke's off with his buddies. And there's nothing much good on television tonight."

"Zeke?" Tessa remembered that Ron had said his son Zeke would bring the pickup if they needed to borrow it.

"Zeke's my boyfriend. We live in the trailer up behind the house."

Tessa had seen the trailer that morning. She tried to imagine Cissy and the Claiborne son raising a baby there. Surely Cissy wasn't old enough to have finished high school. And how old or educated was Zeke? Tessa felt unwelcome concern for the baby they were going to bring into this world.

"What are you doing here?"

Tessa was startled by Helen's voice. She hadn't even heard her grandmother coming toward them.

She tried an introduction. "This is Cissy..." She couldn't remember the last name.

"Mowrey," Cissy said. "I'm Cissy Mowrey. You're Mrs. Henry. Mr. Claiborne's told me about you."

"Claiborne, huh?" Helen's glare was unmistakable, even as twilight was turning into night. "He send you over here to spy on me?"

Cissy's eyes widened. "No ma'am, he sure didn't."

"He's the one who called your mother, isn't he?" Helen demanded of Tessa. "I've never given those Claibornes a moment of trouble, and I've ignored their heathen ways all these years. And now look what I get for it."

Tessa winced. "Gram, he called Mom because you needed help. And besides, none of that's Cissy's fault, is it?"

"What *are* you doing here then?" Helen demanded. "If you didn't come to spy some more?"

"I seen—I saw these flowers by the roadside from Zeke's truck this morning. They reminded me of that quilt you had on the porch last week."

"What quilt?"

Tessa watched Cissy search hard for an appropriate answer. The girl certainly had common sense. Clearly she saw the minefield and was trying to avoid it.

"That gold quilt, you know, like a big, giant sunflower. Lots of different golds. Like these flowers here."

"Why were you looking at my front porch, anyway?"

"Gram!" Tessa had had enough. "Good grief, if you hang a quilt on the porch, especially a big, bright one, anybody who drives by is going to see it."

"I don't put my quilts outside to show them off. That's where I dry them. Nobody else's business."

Before Tessa could chide her grandmother again, Cissy broke in. "Oh, I know it's not really my business, but I just really couldn't help looking at it, you know? It was so bright, so, well, lively? It made me smile. Then I saw these flowers—" she gestured to the dandelions, which had just closed up shop for the night "—pretty sorry looking right now, I guess, but they made me think about the quilt, and I, well, I wanted some of that color for myself."

Even Helen could find no fault with the girl's explanation. She continued to glare, but she sealed her lips.

"See, my grandma made quilts," Cissy continued, when Helen

didn't answer. "I lived with her 'til she died. She promised to teach me how, but she, well, she didn't get very far before she passed on. Hers weren't as pretty as that one, but they were hers. You know?"

"Your grandma, she was from around here?" Helen asked grudgingly.

"Down in Augusta County."

"Then I wouldn't know her."

"No ma'am, I guess you wouldn't."

"You have her quilts?"

"They got sold. All her stuff was sold at auction after she died. I just have some bits and pieces nobody wanted."

Tessa could feel herself getting sucked into the girl's life story, and that was the last thing she wanted. She decided to end the conversation. "Do you need a ride home, Cissy?"

"Oh, no, the doctor says I should walk every day. I'll just take my time."

"Have a good one, then." Tessa took her grandmother's arm and firmly turned her back toward the house. Helen said a grudging goodbye, and they walked up the drive in silence.

"That girl's a baby herself," Helen said. "What is she doing having a baby? What kind of mother could she be?"

Tessa didn't even want to think about it.

CHAPTER
5

After she went back inside Helen tried to sew, but she couldn't manage it. She had always worked on more than one project at a time so that when she tired of one pattern she could pick up a different one. It was a luxury of sorts not to finish one quilt before starting another, one of the few things she did simply because it felt good. Pleasing herself that way felt almost sinful, but there it was. She was going to keep on doing it.

Tonight, switching to applique from hand-quilting hadn't helped. Her eyes were tired, and the tiny stitches anchoring each Christmas rose blurred, even when she hung her magnifier around her neck. Her hand ached, too, more than she could simply ignore. She was too old to sew for so many hours a day.

As she put the block she'd been working on in her sewing basket, the others came inside from the porch. Nancy went upstairs, but Tessa stayed down and fiddled with the screen door.

Now that the other women had come inside, Helen wanted to close herself off, but her bedroom felt more like a tomb than a refuge. Her screens still needed patching, and only one window could be opened without letting in every stinging insect in the county. She had planned to patch them, just never gotten around to it. There were a lot of things that fell into that category these days.

The living room was inviting, not that she was about to admit it out loud. She wasn't going to let Nancy and Tessa get away with dumping her stuff in the trailer. She aimed to go outside, climb in and sort through it before they hauled it away. She just hadn't gotten around to it quite yet.

She supposed it was the summer heat and that was all there was to it. It was hotter these days than she ever remembered. It was that greenhouse effect. If people just hadn't been so greedy, if they hadn't wanted every little thing that came down the road, if they'd learned to make do the way she had, then the world wouldn't be a greenhouse. The rain would fall the way it was supposed to, and she could keep busy.

She hadn't sat on her sofa for a while. It was old, but still comfortable enough if she avoided the place where the springs poked through. She could fix that, too, if the weather would just break.

"I can fix any damn thing you set in front of me, see if I can't!"

"I'm sorry, Gram, what did you say?"

Helen was brought up short. What exactly *had* she said? And didn't she know better than to talk to herself in front of other people? Just when had that started?

Tessa joined her, standing beside the sofa looking, for all the world, like finding her grandmother there was the normal state of things. "What can you fix?"

"I'm going upstairs." Helen struggled to her feet. She meant to sound firm. She sounded tired instead.

"Oh, don't. It's still hotter than the hinges of Hades up there." Tessa rested her fingertips on her grandmother's arm. "I bought lemonade at the store. Why don't you stay down here where it's cooler and let me get us some?"

"Where'd your mama go?"

"She's upstairs changing again."

"Oh, did she get a speck of dust on her skirt?"

Tessa laughed. Helen thought it was a fine sound and one she hadn't heard nearly often enough in the past few years. Tessa had lost weight and her sense of humor after Kayley's death. Both had just dropped away, until she was skin and bones physically and emotionally.

That was to be expected, of course. Helen understood far too well, although in her case, the weight had sure come back with a vengeance when the shock of Fate's death wore off. Of course, losing a husband, even losing one like she had, was something different than losing a child.

Today children grew up more often than they didn't. It hadn't always been so, of course, but even she, of a generation that had seen its share of tiny graves, had scarcely been able to believe that her great-granddaughter had been healthy and laughing one moment and gone from this world the next.

"You'll stay for lemonade?" Tessa said.

Helen felt the way Lee must have every time he had to give ground to Grant. "Then I'm going right off to bed."

"Can't blame you for that. Days start early around here."

Helen lowered herself to the sofa again. Maybe the living room wasn't much to look at, but it was hers. It was a small room that hadn't been painted in a long time, but the walls were still white enough to suit her. Landscapes in sagging frames left from her mama's day dotted them. The fireplace hadn't drawn well for a decade, and smoke had blackened the bricks. The mantel held several old clocks. She guessed she had just put a new one up when the old one stopped ticking and forgot to cart the old ones away.

Despite its many flaws, the room did look better when you could see more of it. She had to admit that much. There was no excuse for what Nancy and Tessa had done to her, that was certain, but even a blind hog found an acorn now and then. And the fact she could sit down in here now, well, that was her own personal acorn, she supposed.

Nancy bustled down the stairs, smoothing a fresh green skirt over her hips as she descended. She stopped at the bottom and stared at her mother. Helen waited, just waited, eyes narrowed, for her daughter to say something about her sitting on the sofa. That was all it would take and Helen would hightail it out of there.

"Tessa said something about lemonade earlier," Nancy said. "Want me to make sure she gets a glass for you, too?"

"She knows where I am."

Nancy's hair bobbed up and down as she nodded. Helen was reminded of the teenage Nancy and her silly hairdos. Teasing and curling and teasing some more until the bottom flipped up just so. The hours that girl had spent trying to make herself into something she wasn't. It was remarkable, in a way, that she had managed so well, at least on the surface.

"Tessa said you had a nice chat with the girl from down the road." Nancy looked for a place to sit, but nothing was as accommodating as the sofa. She took a few, tentative steps toward her mother.

"Just come on over," Helen growled. "I never bit you once, not once when you were growing up."

"Maybe not, but you sure tried a time or two." Nancy settled herself beside her mother. "Oh, good. Now there's a *spring* biting me."

"Keep you awake, more likely than not. Long enough to get that lemonade."

Nancy shifted left and sighed in relief. "Her name's Cissy?"

"That's what she says. Pregnant as a broodmare in March. And no ring in sight."

"Mother, you didn't mention that to her, did you?"

"You think I don't know how to bridle my tongue when it's called for?"

Nancy lifted an eyebrow. "Yes, that's what I think."

Helen couldn't help herself. She laughed. "Well, I did this time, so there."

"You know her story? What she's doing there?"

"I don't gossip with my neighbors. Don't hold with it and never did."

"Maybe not, but at least you used to see them now and then. You used to get out."

Helen sighed. It didn't sound like a criticism, although it might have. "I guess I did, didn't I?"

"I can see how it happens, you know. Sometimes I have to push myself out the door."

"You? You expect me to believe that?"

Tessa entered with a tray and three brimming glasses laden with ice. "Believe what?"

"That sometimes I'd just rather stay home and be by myself than go out in public," Nancy said.

"We're telling fairy tales for entertainment tonight?" Tessa said lightly. "I didn't know."

Nancy made a face. "Neither of you knows me, not the way you think you do."

"Who would know you better?" Helen took her glass and nodded grudgingly in thanks.

"Gram, what quilt was Cissy referring to?" Tessa said. "It sure made an impression on her."

"Don't carry on like you're interested. You never have showed the least bit of curiosity about my quilts."

Tessa settled herself in an armchair that Helen remembered her own grandmother sitting in. "Well, I haven't seen that many. Just the ones you gave me, and the ones you were working on whenever I visited. What have you done with all the quilts you made?"

"Packed away some of them. Others went here and there."

Nancy set down her lemonade and picked up a magazine from a stack of recent issues. She used it to fan herself. "Your grandmother used to make quilts for every baby at church, even if the family was brand new in town. And if somebody got burned out or their house got flooded, Mama was right there with quilts."

"What quilt was Cissy talking about?" Tessa asked. "Will you show it to us?"

"Don't see much point. For all I know you'll grab it and throw it in that horse trailer, along with everything else."

"Mama," Nancy said. "There's no chance of that and you know it."

Helen hadn't been called "Mama" in more years than she could count. Nancy had begun using the more formal "Mother" about the time she had decided to abandon Toms Brook and everything it represented. Helen was surprised how much she'd missed it.

Nancy got to her feet. "Tell me where it is and I'll go get it."

"Only if you promise not to touch another blessed thing in my room."

"Not a thing." Nancy crossed her heart. "Okay?"

"In the trunk at the end of my bed. It's the one on top."

Helen sipped her lemonade while she and Tessa waited for Nancy to return. When Nancy came back, she was carrying several quilts.

"Thought I'd show off a little," Nancy said. "Tessa should see these."

The night air was too hot for much complaining. Helen just grumbled incoherently to show she wasn't happy.

"First this." Nancy spread open Helen's most recent North Carolina Lily quilt. Helen had probably made half a dozen of that pattern over her lifetime, most in the traditional reds and greens on a white background. This time, though, she'd followed her own heart and made the lilies of bolder shades of pinks, purples and teal, and set them on black.

"Wow," Tessa said. "That's gorgeous."

Helen watched her granddaughter get up and move closer to hold an edge so she could see the quilting.

"It is, isn't it? Mama, when did you start experimenting with color like this?" Nancy asked.

"When I got good and tired of doing everything the same old way."

"Well, your same old way wasn't a bit shabby, but this is spectacular."

"These stitches are smaller than a flower seed," Tessa said. "How do you do it?"

"I practice. A lot."

"Help me hold up the next one," Nancy told Tessa. She unfolded the second quilt. It was a Log Cabin Star in red, white and blue. Helen had appliqued glaring American eagles in each corner of the wide navy border and quilted galaxies of stars in between.

"When did you make this?" Nancy paused; then she asked, "After September 11?"

"It kept me busy." Helen didn't add that she had quilted a star for each person lost at the Pentagon. It had been her way of saying goodbye to the people who had died in her home state. She knew, better than most, what their families would be going through.

"It's beautiful," Tessa said. "It's..." She shrugged. "Emotional."

"Don't get all big-eyed about it," Helen said. "It was just something to do when there wasn't nothing but the news on television."

She watched her daughter and granddaughter exchange looks.

"Get to that last one so I can go on up to bed." Helen was embarrassed.

The two younger women folded the second quilt and put it with the first. Nancy shook out the last one. "Incredible," she said. "Will you look at this, Tessa?"

Tessa whistled. "I need sunglasses."

The quilt was bright. Helen wasn't sure what had possessed her. It was a single flower with a multitude of petals that circled round and round. The background was minimal and the border merely a frame that set off the center. The flower took up most of the surface.

She had pieced it last winter, on the gloomiest days when she had yearned for sunshine. She had used nearly every yellow, gold and orange scrap she possessed. The result was, well... bright.

"I love this one," Nancy said. "Who wouldn't love it? It's a smile in quilt form. This would keep an Eskimo warm in an igloo."

"I don't know a single Eskimo," Helen scoffed.

Nancy bundled the quilt against her. "I had a quilt like this as a little girl, didn't I? What do you call it?"

"Giant Dahlia."

"Mine was pink. Do you remember?" she asked her mother.

Helen was surprised that Nancy did. "You were just a little thing. You like to have wore it out before you turned ten."

"I didn't want to part with it, even though the batting was all falling out."

"One day I washed it and there was nothing left but shreds when I was done."

"A sad day," Nancy said. "I cried."

"You cried more than any little girl in five counties."

Nancy hugged the quilt a little tighter.

"I can see why Cissy noticed it," Tessa said. "Gram, you're an artist. I've never seen anybody use color with more success."

"That's the thing about quilts," Nancy said. "They're art you can feel all around you. Not that many paintings you can hug this way."

"I had a quilt I loved," Tessa said. "Mom, *you* made it. Remember? Whatever happened to it?"

"Your mama? Your mama never made a quilt in her life," Helen said.

"I certainly did." Nancy folded the dahlia quilt with obvious reluctance and piled it on the others. "Am I right, or didn't you buy blueberry pie at the grocery store, Tessa?"

"I did. Would you like some?" At Nancy's nod, Tessa turned to her grandmother. "Gram?"

"I want to hear about this so-called quilt your mother made."

"I'll be right back," Tessa said. "No fair telling the story until I'm back."

Helen could hear her granddaughter rattling around the old kitchen. That room, too, had been nearly cleared out, although there were endless boxes and more boxes to sort through that had been carried to the back porch.

Tessa returned with the pie, and Helen took hers grudgingly. They were acting like a family when they weren't. They were related by blood, but surely that was different. Not knowing what all this meant made her uneasy.

Nancy took her first bite before she spoke. "It's good, but nothing like the blueberry pie your grandmother makes," she told Tessa. "Maybe, if we get a little cooler weather, she'll try one while we're here."

"I don't cook anymore," Helen said. "Nobody around here cares if I do or I don't."

"You are the orneriest old woman in the Valley," Nancy said. But she smiled as she did.

"You convince me you *ever* made a quilt, and I'll make a pie." Helen settled back to eat her slice.

"Well, I half made it. Does that count?"

"Half?" Tessa said. "It was a whole quilt. I remember it."

"Tessa's talking about the old wedding ring quilt," Nancy told her mother. "You pieced the top, remember? And after I was married, you took me upstairs where you had a pile of tops you hadn't quilted. You told me to pick out any one I wanted and finish it as a wedding quilt. Then you gave me some fabric you'd sewed together for the backing."

Helen was sorry this had come up. "Then I guess I only have to make half a pie, don't I? You only half made a quilt."

"Wedding ring," Tessa said to Nancy. "I remember now. You told me that's what it was called. It was made from dozens of fabrics—"

"Hundreds," Helen said. "It was mostly a feed-sack quilt. Do you know what that means?"

Tessa shook her head.

"When I was a girl, they sold chicken feed, flour, lots of things in sacks, only the people what made them figured out that if they made the feed sacks pretty, the women would push their men to buy certain ones so they could use them for clothes and quilts and stuff around the house. Bits of that one were made from little scraps my mama and others had saved."

"Only half a feed-sack quilt then," Nancy said.

"I think this story is only half told," Tessa said. "Mom, you don't sew. I don't remember a single thing you ever sewed for me as a little girl."

"Just one of the many ways I failed you?" Nancy said.

Tessa grimaced. "Don't make more of it than what I said. I'm just wondering whatever possessed you to make a quilt."

Nancy didn't reply.

Helen set down her plate. The others were still working on their pie, but she had downed hers like a starving waif. "I'll tell you why she did it. She was living with your daddy's folks in Richmond and didn't know a soul. She was going stir-crazy with nothing to do. In that way, she's more like me than she thinks. So the next time she and your daddy came back here to visit, I suggested she pick a top and do something besides sit and brood."

"That's not exactly what you said." Nancy set down her plate, too, but her pie had only been nibbled, because she worried about calories. "You said you'd give me a quilt top to finish, but there wasn't much point in it, since I didn't know how to do anything that useful."

"So you took it on a dare?" Tessa asked.

"I suppose." Nancy looked away, as if she was remembering. "It was a little late for a bridal quilt. Your daddy and I'd been married for months before I took the top. But I chose that one because it was a wedding ring pattern, and that seemed fitting. I didn't have a frame, but your grandmother gave me a lap hoop."

"I slept under it as a child. I loved it. I always slept better when you let me have it on my bed." Tessa paused. "Whatever happened to it? Did it fall apart in the wash the way your dahlia quilt did?"

"No, I learned my lesson about that. I always washed it carefully, but when it started to tear, I brought it back here to your grandmother." Nancy looked at her mother in question.

"It's up in the attic," Helen said. "Somewhere up there." She remembered exactly where the quilt was. She had packed it away herself, taking care to make sure it was out of sight. She had never really forgotten it, but over the years the memory had dimmed.

She lied now, because it was easier than telling the truth. "I planned to see if I could fix it someday, but I never got around to it."

"I never made another one," Nancy said. "I just got too busy, I guess."

"You just got too important," Helen picked up her plate and stood.

"That's really not fair," Nancy said. "The truth is, I could see right away I was never going to be any good at quilting, not the way you were. I love quilts, only I love looking at them, feeling them, examining the workmanship. I'll leave the making of them to the artists, like you."

For once, Helen really didn't know what to say.

CHAPTER
6

Helen went upstairs to bed, and Nancy retired to her room to make more phone calls in the long series she had begun that day. Tessa was tired, too, and her neck ached, a problem that had become chronic in the past few years. If Mack hadn't been coming, she would have gone upstairs with the others. As it was, she went back to the front porch, turning off the light, and settled back in the swing to watch the lightning bugs and wait for her husband.

She sat, hands folded quietly, breathing deeply in hopes it would help her relax. She tilted her head from side to side, then back and forth as her physical therapist had recommended, and after a few minutes the pain in her neck began to ease a little.

Mack would not forget to come or change his mind. In some ways her husband of ten years might be a stranger now, but she did know that he would honor his promise.

In the years since Kayley's death Mack had struggled, sometimes against incredible odds, not to let anybody down over the smallest things. His clients, who had been well served in the past, were better served now. He worked endless hours looking for any available loophole, any obscure statute, that might fulfill his promises to them. He had taken their cases, he would find them justice.

She understood why Mack acted that way, but she didn't know how to help him overcome it. Their daughter's death had changed them both so radically that now the pathways to each other's heart ended well before the destination. Mack's guilt was his to bear. She could not find her way there to help.

They hadn't always been so far apart. Love at first sight was too hackneyed and narrow to describe the instant attraction that had been as much about their souls as their hearts and bodies. Tessa Whitlock and Andrew MacRae had struck immediate sparks that had warmed their lives even as they torched their careers in conservative Richmond. Now, as she waited for him a decade later, she thought about that day.

Twenty-seven-year-old Tessa Whitlock had always believed she had boundless energy, but after almost five years of teaching English at one of Richmond's inner-city high schools, she was afraid she had nearly drained that well dry.

The first leak had sprung when her mother, distraught at her choice of employment, had approached the school principal before Tessa's contract had even been signed and begged him to reconsider hiring her daughter. The second had sprung on her first real day as a teacher. The students had taken one look at the privileged Windsor Farms neophyte and figured correctly that she had little to teach them and no way of enforcing the carefully-thought-out rules she had printed on the chalkboard.

She had never given up easily. Tessa strengthened her resolve, sought advice from everyone who would talk to her, and little by little gained control of her classroom while simultaneously gaining a reputation for being fair and nonjudgmental. By the end of the year she could measure success, but the required effort had drained away more of her energy.

Now, a month into her sixth year at the school, her personal resources were dangerously low again.

"Look, Tessa, you know you can't reach every student, don't you?" Samantha Johnson perched on the edge of Tessa's battered desk as she tried to make her point. Like Tessa, Samantha refused to sit at her desk during classes, and by the end of a day of walking in and out of rows as she lectured or quizzed students, her feet were swollen and sore.

Tessa rested her head in her hands. "But James? Not James. He's got so much promise. He's such a good kid, and he doesn't deserve this."

"Sure he does. You think because he says please and thank you, Miss Whitlock, he's got the right to bring a weapon into this school? If he blows you or me or one of your other students away with it, what difference are please and thank-you going to make?"

Tessa knew Sam had a point, as she usually did. Samantha Johnson had been teaching here for twelve years, a record for this particular high school. She had taken Tessa under her wing after a short probation period while Sam waited to see if the newly graduated white girl was going to flee to some nice private academy. Sam was middle-aged, comfortably padded and happily adjusted to both. She was not adjusted to bad manners, bad grades or bad study habits, and she made certain that the students who streamed through her classroom didn't become adjusted to them, either.

Tessa lifted her head. "But it wasn't James's gun. I don't think he even knew Malik had a gun in the backpack when he carried it in for him."

"You believe that?"

"I'm an incorrigible optimist."

"You lose that real fast in the neighborhoods these kids live in." Sam lifted her considerable bulk from the desk. "I'm sorry this happened, too, but don't beat yourself up over this one, Tessa. Just let go, because there's not a single thing you can do about it without losing your job. We got enough kids here you can make a real difference with. Just take your pick and have at it."

They said goodbye, and Tessa waited until her friend was gone before she began tidying the classroom so that the janitor could clean later that afternoon. She couldn't "let go," though. Not even a little.

A student named Malik Green had brought a loaded gun to school earlier in the week. Tessa had never been entirely certain why Malik was still enrolled at the high school. He was frequently absent, always in trouble, and the subject of frequent locker and backpack searches. His juvenile record looked like something a profiler might point to as an example of what to watch for when scouting out psychopaths.

The boy had a following, though. He was good-looking, bright and never without a stack of bills in his pocket, fastened casually with a chrome money clip adorned, ironically, by a gold DEA seal. He was always surrounded by a crowd, both male and female, some wannabes, some who rivaled him for making trouble, some who just wanted to bask in his radioactive glow.

Although Malik was not a student of Tessa's, one member of that latter group was, a young man named James Bates. James was a kid who rarely said much, but he always listened intently to her lectures. His papers held special promise, and several times she had asked him to help her after school as an excuse to find out about his plans for the future. She was sure he ought to be heading for college in two years, and she wanted to help him find the resources he needed to make that happen.

Unfortunately, the day Malik showed up with a 9 mm Glock in his backpack, James happened to be waiting outside for a friend. Malik, who saw two male teachers standing just inside the door and realized he might be searched, asked James to take his pack to their first class while he made a detour to the dean of students' office. James, flattered to be included in Malik's world, agreed.

Neither boy knew that the principal had instituted a policy of random backpack searches that week. James, who had never been in any trouble, was one of the students singled out for that honor. When the gun was found, James explained that the backpack belonged to Malik, which was easy enough to prove. But explaining why he had it was a different matter.

Tessa had no qualms about punishing students who disobeyed rules, and bringing a weapon to school was a rule that could never be bent. But the administration had refused to consider the circumstances or James's unblemished record. He had brought a weapon into the school, and so he was expelled until the following school year, and there were no alternative programs open to him.

Never mind that next year James would be a year older than the other students and less likely to finish high school because of it. Never mind that he would be out on the streets for a year with little to do except explore the scarier side of their fair city. Never mind that he was a United States citizen with all the rights that bestowed.

"Are you Tessa Whitlock?"

Tessa looked up to see a man standing in the doorway. For a moment she forgot to answer. Then she smiled, perhaps the first real smile of the day. "*You're* Andrew MacRae?"

"Call me Mack." He walked toward her, hand held out. "I was expecting someone older."

"So was I." She took his hand, a warm, solid hand that folded around hers with strength and energy. He had dark curly hair, an athletic body and the tan to go with it, and pale blue eyes that seemed almost silver against his skin.

He was, in one single package, everything she appreciated in a man.

She cocked her head. When she'd called the law firm where Mack was an associate, she had expected to be channeled to someone older and more buttoned-down. She had thought—and still did—that her father had given her the number of Mack's firm because it was the one most likely to dissuade her from trying to help James. Now she suspected that Billy had made an error.

"You know, you don't look like a lawyer," she said, assessing him further just because it was fun.

He examined her as she examined him. "And you don't look big enough to wrestle these kids to the ground when they need it."

She noticed that the skin around his eyes crinkled when he smiled, which made him look even younger. "You don't look like somebody who makes waves for a living."

"You don't look like somebody who would think seriously about jeopardizing her job."

She freed her hand, aware at last that she was still letting him hold it. "I know we're going to lose. Even after we explore all the legal channels, James will still be out on his ear until next fall. You'll have a loss on your record, your firm isn't going to be at all happy with you for taking this case in the first place, and I'll be looking for work."

He didn't reply right away. His eyes searched hers, but he didn't dispute her words. He spoke at last. "But here's what we *will* have. James will know that somebody cared enough to fight for him. I'll be on record for standing up for what's right. And you..."

She waited. "And me...?" she prompted.

He had a deep, gravelly voice with laughter built into it. "You, Tessa Whitlock, will have my undying devotion."

She smiled her second smile of the day and watched his face light slowly, too.

Then, and in all the months and years that followed, she had learned that the devotion of a man like Andrew MacRae was worth almost any price.

Tessa's memories were cut short by angry squawking coming from somewhere behind the back of the house. Years ago her grandmother had constructed an ingenious chicken coop on wheels, and now every time the chickens pecked their way through a portion of the field behind the house and rid it of pesky bugs and weeds, the coop was moved to a new location and the chicken wire fencing was re-erected.

Kayley had been enchanted by Helen's chickens. They were an odd enough flock. Practical to the bone marrow in most areas of her life, Helen's chickens were anything but. She was not a woman who had ever indulged in pets. Animals served a purpose, and affection was not one of them. She had a wheelbarrow load of unnamed barn cats who sometimes made their way to the front porch for a nap in the sunshine but never found their way inside. They were neutered and fed, and they killed mice and snakes in exchange. But it was purely a business deal.

Helen's chickens were as close to pets as anything in her life.

Helen collected unusual varieties, trading with other local farmers when she could. Tessa remembered the names of some of them because Helen had taught Kayley, and Kayley had recited them like a nursery rhyme. The sleek Araucanas, who laid green and blue eggs—Kayley's favorite. The stately, splendid Brahmas, with their black-and-white feathered shanks and hackles, the black Minorcas with their large red combs and wattles.

Kayley had never been afraid, not even when the chickens pecked at her sandal-clad feet on one memorable excursion into the coop. Blond pigtails flying, she had shooed them away like a veteran 4Her. Helen, not given to praise, had snorted and said that maybe at last somebody else in her sorry family had what it took to be a farmer.

The chicken alarm ended as suddenly as it had begun, and all was quiet again. Tessa stood and walked to the railing, leaning over it as she stared into the darkness. The night was still filled with sounds. Insects whirring and chirping, cows lowing in the distance. The first time Kayley had gone camping, Mack had encouraged her to listen to the night noises. She had renamed the nocturnal symphony "fright noises," demanding to know where each sound came from and what it was before she was reassured. She had always been more curious than afraid, a child who adjusted quickly and went on about the business of living.

Fitch Crossing brightened perceptibly as a car approached. In a moment Tess could see two distinct headlights; then, as she watched, the car slowed, nearly stopping before the turn into her grandmother's driveway. She heard the faint drift of music, most likely country, before Mack's blue Toyota—the fraternal twin to her car—pulled to a stop not far from the porch and the engine was silenced.

She didn't walk down the steps to greet him. She waited quietly, hands unclenched and still at her sides.

He appeared a moment later, rolling her suitcase behind him along the walkway. She waited until she could speak in a normal tone before she greeted him.

"Mack, I'm up here."

He lifted the suitcase and carried it up the steps, depositing it against the railing. "What are you doing out here in the dark?"

"The porch light would attract every moth in Shenandoah County. And Mom and Gram have already gone to bed."

"Country hours, huh?"

"There's not too much to do at night. Gram refuses to get a satellite dish, so TV reception depends on the wind and the will of the gods. She does have a pretty substantial library, though. Particularly if you like elementary textbooks."

"Textbooks?"

"I think she disagrees with the school board's decision to bring local classrooms into the twenty-first century. She's been visiting their Dumpsters."

Even in the faint light of moon and stars, Tessa thought Mack looked tired. He was still every bit as appealing as he had been at their first meeting. His hair hadn't thinned, and the new lines in his face added maturity. Most of the time he wore glasses now, wire-rimmed and unobtrusive, which only served to make his face a shade more scholarly.

"How many Dumpsters has she visited?" He hiked his thumb over his shoulder in the direction of the horse trailer, as if he had guessed what it was for.

"I'm thinking she knows the whereabouts of every promising pile of trash for at least twenty-five miles."

"That doesn't sound good, Tessa."

She resisted the urge to cross her arms. "She's doing better than I expected. So far she hasn't hauled anything back inside. She'd never say so, but I think she's grateful we're here."

"And your mother?"

She gave the slightest of shrugs. "She's running her social life in Richmond from the telephone, but I've got to hand it to her. In between phone calls, she works hard."

Mack crossed *his* arms and leaned against the porch post. "And the third member of the household?"

"Tired, hot, out of sorts a lot of the time. But glad to see we're getting things accomplished." She wondered if he would leave now that the duty questions were over, but he made no move to.

"The sun went down before I got to the prettiest part of the drive. How are things looking down the valley?"

Even though they were in the northern third of the Shenandoah Valley, they were "down the valley," because the Shenandoah River flowed north. The geography and history of the area had always fascinated Mack.

"The drought's done a lot of damage," Tessa said. "The river's down. You can hardly see it from the hill anymore. The pond's lost a third of its water, at least. If we don't start getting some rain, I'm afraid it's going to go dry."

He whistled softly. "I've never seen it that low." He hesitated. "Want to take a look at it with me?"

"Now?"

"Why not? I need to stretch my legs before I drive back."

"You could stay the night and go back in the morning if you'd rather," she offered belatedly. Mack's staying hadn't occurred to her before, a measure of how far apart they'd grown.

"No, I'm swamped with work, and I have an early breakfast meeting."

She realized she hadn't asked him one question about himself. "Is work going okay? I know you had a big trial coming up."

"Not for a while. But James had his first day in court this week."

James, the same James Bates who had cost them both their jobs in Richmond, was now a first-year associate at Mack's law firm in D.C. After Mack lost his lawsuit against the school administration, Tessa's father had found the young man a place in a small private school. James's record had been good enough that he'd gotten a scholarship to Virginia Commonwealth University right there in Richmond. By the time he graduated, his grades were good enough to get the needed financial aid to make it through law school at UVA.

Now James was proving to be a welcome addition to Mack's small firm.

"I was thinking about him earlier," Tessa confessed. "How did he do?"

"He lost his bid to have the charges against the client dismissed, but he scored a few points while he was at it. He did okay."

"I bet he did."

Mack pulled away from the post. "How about that walk?"

She remembered the last time they had been to the pond together and was about to make an excuse when he added, "I've got something I need to talk to you about, Tessa, and I don't want to do it here."

She couldn't very well refuse. He started down the steps, and she followed.

Out from under the shelter of the porch, she could just see the palest outline of a waning crescent moon in the clear dark sky overhead. Without clouds to hide them or city lights to outshine them, the stars were spectacular.

Mack waited until she was beside him before he set out on the well-worn path. A light breeze stirred, and the scent of something blooming—trumpet lilies along the driveway, perhaps—tinged the air. He didn't take her arm, but he stayed close, as if he was afraid she might stumble in the darkness.

"I remember the last time we were out at the pond together, too," he said, as if she had spoken her concerns out loud. "Kayley is everywhere here. The hill where we flew her kite the summer before she died, the old barn where she found that stray and her litter of kittens, the field where Biscuit scared up the covey of quail."

"Ruffled grouse." Biscuit, their old English sheepdog, had been nearly as surprised as everyone else when the grouse family had taken to the sky. Job completed, Biscuit had fallen to her rump and scratched behind her ear in celebration. Mack had said it was the equivalent of a gunfighter blowing the smoke from his six-gun.

"You're coping all right?" He kept his tone light, but she knew the question wasn't light at all.

"I see her everywhere at home, too," she said.

"But you're more used to that. And at home you've managed to remove a lot of the memories."

She heard censure, although she wasn't really sure it was there. They had quarreled in the past about the way she had systematically cleared Kayley's presence from their house. Now the decor in their home of six years was clean and spare, minimalist to the bone, and there were few traces of their only child.

Even Biscuit, who had grown from puppyhood as Kayley grew from toddlerhood, had gone to live elsewhere.

"I'm too busy to give it much thought," Tessa lied. "And Mom tiptoes around Kayley's death. Gram never mentions it at all."

"It's on their minds."

"Is that what you wanted to talk about? How to bring everything out in the open so we can all have a good cry together?" There were enough sharp edges in the question to shred them both. She blew out a long breath. "I'm sorry."

"Are you?" He didn't sound as if he thought so.

"I am. You didn't deserve that."

"The subject makes you uncomfortable."

"But not you?"

"I'm more used to talking about it."

She knew exactly what he was thinking. Because *he* had made use of a support group that she had rejected.

"It hasn't brought her back, has it?" she asked. "Talking about her hasn't brought her back."

"It's not supposed to."

"Thanks, but I'd rather spend my time making sure this never happens to another set of parents."

"And that hasn't brought her back, either, and won't."

"Maybe not, but at least I'll know there's a child graduating from high school or making his first home run or singing a solo in his church choir because the organization I work with got another drunk driver off the streets."

"MADD is a good organization, Tessa. You know I support everything you do for them."

"I don't know why we're arguing again," she said. But she did know. Neither of them had yet coped with their guilt and grief. Mack knocked himself out to live up to every promise he made, and she? Well, she put one foot in front of the other and hoped that someday, if she traveled far enough away from the past, she would find something approaching peace.

"Do you remember the day you told me you were pregnant?" he asked. "We were off on a walk, right about here."

That was just one of the memories she had hoped to avoid. That walk had been at Christmastime, a year after their wedding, and they had paid a duty visit to Toms Brook along with Tessa's parents. After the ritual exchange of presents, she and Mack had excused themselves, and on this path, on their way to view the frozen pond, she had told him she would deliver their first child the following summer.

The news had been welcome to both of them. From the moment they began to discuss marriage, Tessa and Mack had agreed they wanted children, and after a year of marital bliss, the decision to bring a child into their marriage had been an easy one. They were happy, healthy and stable. There had been no reason to wait, and Mack had been ecstatic at the announcement.

"It was probably the happiest moment of my life, up to that point," he said. "Except for the day I married you."

She wanted to ask him how happy he would have been if he had known the eventual outcome. But that was a conversation she would never be ready for, because her own answer was unclear. Had Kayley's life been worth the tragedy of Kayley's death? She really didn't know.

"I loved everything about the next nine months," he went on, when she didn't answer.

"That's because you weren't pregnant," she said. But in reality, the pregnancy had been easy. Tessa had gotten pregnant the first month she abandoned birth control, and as the months progressed, they had snuggled together at home, curtailing their social life to nest together. They made long lists of names, discussed how best to divide up the work, splurged on a plush rocker and mission oak nursery furniture.

He gave a short laugh, as if he was trying to keep the conversation casual, just warm happy memories shared between two normal people whose entire lives hadn't been torn apart and discarded.

"I was particularly glad I wasn't the one who had to go into labor," he said.

"You might as well have been. You were right there, letting me squeeze your hand. I nearly ripped it off."

"She was such a wonderful baby," he said. "So interested in the world that she hardly slept. Do you remember? Of course, we didn't care, because we loved having her awake."

Tessa's heart was breaking. She didn't know why she was letting him do this. "Mack..."

"The good memories still belong to us, Tessa. Nobody can destroy them, not unless we allow it. I can still see you nursing her. I would get up and get her from the crib, and you would be waiting for us, sitting propped up against the pillows, your hair loose over your shoulders. I don't want to forget the way you looked, the way I felt."

They had been so enthralled, they had known immediately that they wanted another child, but they had been jealous of their time with their daughter, and they had decided to wait, to enjoy both childhoods to their fullest.

She wondered now if that had been a mistake. How different would the aftermath of Kayley's death have been if they'd had another child to care for, too? Would they have been able to retreat so far from each other? To indulge their grief so separately? To spend so much time apart?

And yet, how could she have looked in the face of another child, Kayley's brother or sister, and not been destroyed anew each day? How would she have coped with the possibility of another loss? How could she have survived it?

"I go over and over our time with her," Mack said. "All the decisions we made. Do you do that, too?"

"Not if I can help it."

"I'm so glad you took that first year off with her, that you had that time together. But once you went back to work and Letty came to take care of her, she still did fine. She was so happy every day, so well adjusted."

Tessa had arranged her teaching schedule so that she had no late afternoon activities. They thought through every decision, every summer vacation, every holiday and holiday gift. All that had been part of the joy of being parents.

And then, when Kayley was five, the world had fallen apart.

With the story of Kayley's brief life hovering there, unconcluded, Tessa was forced to think about the rest of it as they made the remainder of the walk in silence.

Kayley, with two years of preschool behind her, had been more than excited about kindergarten. She was a bright, verbal child who made friends easily and could read most of her storybooks by herself. Her memory was extraordinary, and she seemed happiest when she was learning. Kindergarten in a "real" school was a dream about to come true for the little girl.

When the first day of kindergarten dawned, Kayley dressed herself in the clothes she and Tessa had carefully picked out the night before. Since it was Tessa's first day of the regular school year, as well, Mack was going to walk their daughter to the elementary school not far from their house. They had turned down a neighbor who had offered to pick up Kayley and bring her along with her own daughter. Mack had wanted to do the first-day honors himself.

But from the moment they came down to breakfast that morning, things began to go wrong. Tessa tore the skirt she'd donned, catching a pocket on the handle of a cupboard. She ran back upstairs to change, and when she came downstairs, Mack was pacing the floor.

There was an emergency with one of his cases, and he was needed in D.C. as quickly as possible at an arraignment. Could Tessa take Kayley to school instead?

Tessa realized she would be late getting to the high school if she did, yet what choice did she have? Mack's absence would cost his client far more than the minutes of planning time Tessa would miss. She agreed, grudgingly, and after a kiss and a hug for their daughter, Mack backed out of the house, apologizing as he went.

Kayley, who was sure this was the biggest day of her life, wanted to leave that very minute, but Tessa wasn't ready. She still had a few books and papers to gather and a follow-up phone call to Kayley's sitter, to be sure the afternoon plans were confirmed.

Kayley was beside herself with excitement. When she asked if she could walk to school alone, Tessa uttered a firm no, but Kayley wheedled. She would only walk to the corner and wait for Tessa there. She would not cross, but at least she would be closer, and she could watch the other children streaming toward the building.

Tessa knew there was a crossing guard who would watch out for her daughter until Tessa arrived. Kayley was a good child, and if she said she would wait, she would. This small concession, this evidence of her new maturity, would mean the world to her.

And so Tessa had agreed, going over the rules with her daughter as she flew around the kitchen trying to finish organizing herself to go to work. Kayley, blond hair soaring behind her as she ran out the door, was beside herself with joy.

Tessa followed no more than four minutes later. Four minutes that had changed all their lives forever. Four minutes when fate had looked down on them, decided, perhaps, that their lives were too perfect, and intervened.

Four minutes.

"I had no idea the drought was this bad," Mack said.

Tessa realized they had stopped. They were standing on the first planks of the old dock where Kayley had liked to fish. Now the dock extended across mud flats and ended before the shallowest reaches of the pond.

"Do you think any of the fish survived?" Mack said.

"I couldn't say."

"Do you remember the first time Kayley caught a fish here?"

"Why are you doing this?" She faced him. In the starlight, she could still make out his face. "I remember everything. A lot more than I want to. I remember that I let her walk to the corner by herself when I shouldn't have. I remember hearing the squeal of brakes when I hurried after her a few minutes later. I remember someone—an adult, I think—screaming. And when I got there, when I finally got there, I remember that animal Robert Owens staggering out of his car, looking down at our lifeless daughter and blaming her, blaming my beautiful little girl, for daring to wait there on the sidewalk when he was driving home so drunk he couldn't see an arm's length in front of him!"

Mack was silent while she regained her composure, as if he knew how much she would hate it if he touched her or tried to take her into his arms for comfort.

"You still blame yourself, don't you?" he said.

She took a deep breath before she trusted herself to speak again. "I have a long list of people I blame. I'm on it, yes."

"And so am I." It wasn't a question. "I should have been with her. The timing would have been different. When Owens swerved off the road, we wouldn't have been standing there, and if we were, I could have pushed her to safety."

"No." She turned away and looked over what was left of the pond. "I don't blame you anymore, Mack. I know I did at the beginning. But you didn't kill Kayley. You had every reason to think she would be safe with me. You would never have broken your promise to walk her to school if you could have avoided it."

"She *was* safe with you. And I would have let her walk to the corner alone, too, just the way you did. She'd done it before. She could be trusted. I don't blame you for what happened. Maybe I did at first, when I was trying to find someone or something to pin it on, but neither of us was responsible. You were a wonderful mother. Robert Owens and all the people who let him get behind the wheel of a car that morning killed her."

She wished his absolution helped, but it didn't. Like everything else, it couldn't bring Kayley back.

This time he did touch her. He reached over and cupped her nape with his hand, applying gentle pressure. His hand was large and warm, and he seemed to know exactly what he needed to do to make her feel better.

Making love had always been that way, too. From the beginning, they had been so attuned to each other's bodies that they only rarely had to ask each other for guidance. His touch reminded her how long it had been since that time.

"You've never really understood why it's so important to me to make sure that people like Owens get what they deserve," she said.

"Of course I understand."

"That was something we shared, right from the beginning of our relationship. We both wanted to fix the world."

"I'm still trying to fix it. You know what kind of cases I take on."

She did. Mack worked for justice wherever he was needed. In addition to representing clients who had no other place to turn, he served on the boards of several cutting edge social action agencies. His income was smaller than it could have been, because so many of his clients were poor, but she had always supported him. The money hadn't mattered.

"If you really understand," she said, "then why do you complain about the time I spend with MADD? Don't you see what Kayley's loss has done to us? We've gone from being a family with everything to two people who can barely carry on a conversation. I don't want anybody else to suffer this way."

He dropped his hand. She realized she had forced him to drop it by stepping away from him. She hadn't even realized it, and she didn't know if she regretted it.

"Are you so concerned about everybody else in the world that you've forgotten you still deserve a life and happiness, and so do I?" he asked.

She faced him, and this time, she gave in to the temptation to cross her arms and ward him off. "I have a life. Right now it revolves around making the world a safer place for children."

"Your life used to be *about* children. Now you even keep your students at arm's length."

She heard the unspoken corollary. *Now you keep me at arm's length, too.*

"I do what I have to so I can keep going," she said.

He nodded, as if she had confirmed what he already knew. "You don't see another way, do you?"

"What way would that be?"

"You were right when you said we can barely carry on a conversation, but I don't think you were right about why. It's not Kayley's death. It's because our lives are so separate now that we're not sure what to say to each other anymore." He held his hands out to her, but she didn't take them.

"Is that going to make what you have to say easier?" she asked. "Holding my hands?"

"What do you mean?"

"Why did you want me to take this walk? You said you had something to say. Have you said it? Or have you been saving it?"

He dropped his hands. "I've said part of it."

"You have a long drive back."

He was silent for a moment; then he shrugged. "All right. Here's the rest. I don't think we can continue this way."

The words hung between them long enough for her to think that as much as she had expected this, the reality still made her feel faint.

"I'm not asking for a divorce," he said. "I don't want a divorce—at least, I don't think I do. But I need to know we're doing something to repair this rift. We have to get into counseling."

"I've told you I don't—"

He held up his hand. "Yes, you have. You don't need or want

counseling. But I need you to be sure about that, Tessa. Because if our marriage isn't worth that much effort, then I think it's over."

"Your way or no way?"

"No, it's been your way for three years, and your way hasn't worked. We're dangerously close to a separation. This summer is a separation in more ways than one."

She considered carefully before she asked, "Is there someone else, Mack? Or do you just want the freedom to go looking?"

He didn't answer directly. "I want a real marriage, and if I can't have it with you, yes, I want it with someone else. I need a home and a wife and a family. I had that. I remember what it felt like. I'm young enough to have it again." He paused. "And so are you."

"You don't want a *real* marriage, whatever that means. We have a marriage. You want a wife who will do everything your way and be everything you want."

He shook his head, and his expression was sad. "No, Tessa, I only want a wife who wants to be one."

CHAPTER
7

Nancy wearily lifted her hair dryer, and the hot air blasting the side of her face wasn't that different from the air that had wafted through her window all night. She had been living in her childhood home for two weeks now, and she still wasn't used to the heat—or a lot of other things. But at least in that brief time she and Tessa had made noticeable progress on clearing the place out.

She juggled the hair dryer to her other hand, and the plug slipped out of the socket. Cursing under her breath, she plugged it in again.

"Mom, I'm back. But don't worry, take your time." Tessa's voice sounded just outside the door, then trailed off, as if she was passing by on her way to the kitchen. When Nancy had looked out her bedroom window a little earlier, Tessa had been a mere speck in the distance, running along Fitch Crossing.

Nancy turned on the dryer again, but she really couldn't do much with her hair in her mother's tiny bathroom. She'd had the same problem as a girl. In those days the major hurdle had been Helen pounding on the door, shouting about the curse of vanity.

Now the problem was lack of water, a paucity of electrical outlets and weary arms that really didn't want to hold a round brush or curling iron for the minutes required to lock every strand into place.

This morning the ritual was probably worth the effort. She was trying to prepare for Billy's arrival, and she was surprisingly flustered. She had not seen her husband since her arrival here. For the first week he had been in Atlanta at a conference. For the second he had simply been…busy. Or so he had said. She wondered and worried.

Satisfied her hair was dry enough, she unplugged the hair dryer and plugged in the curling iron. While she waited for it to heat, she leaned forward and gazed at herself in the mirror, not at all happy with what she saw.

She looked tired. That should have been a given. She had not done so much physical labor since adolescence.

She hadn't had a manicure since her arrival in Toms Brook, and this morning, before her two-minute shower, she had given up and clipped the ragged, discolored remnants nearly to the quick. Her nose was peeling from an unfortunate sojourn in the sun when she had helped Tessa repair the vegetable garden fence. The backs of her hands looked like the surface of the moon. Her knees and elbows felt like a cat's tongue.

Billy was coming to visit, and he was going to discover that his wife had aged a decade. Panic swept over her. She was fairly certain that Billy had stayed with her all these years for three reasons. First, their admirable sex life. Second, Tessa, whom he adored. And finally, Nancy's attention to presentation. In all the years of their marriage, she had never shamed her husband. She knew how to dress, what to say and to whom she should say it.

What was Billy going to think when he saw her here, in this house, looking the way she did now? All these years, all these difficult, panicky years, she had never forgotten that even though she might appear to be the epitome of the smart, sophisticated Southern matron, deep down inside she was still a barefoot farm girl with country manners, callused hands and dirt under her fingernails.

"Mom?"

Tessa sounded like she was right outside the door again. Nancy wrapped the ends of her hair around the curling iron and held on for dear life. "What?" she called.

"Daddy's here."

Early? Billy was early? For a moment Nancy allowed herself to hope that he hadn't been able to stay away, that he had missed her so much he had gotten up before dawn to make the trip.

"We're going bird-watching in a few minutes," Tessa said. "Do you want to say hello before we leave?"

Nancy's eyelids fluttered shut. "I'll be out in a moment."

"I'll get him some coffee."

Nancy unclamped her hair and did a halfhearted repeat on the other side. Then she yanked the cord from the wall and set the curling iron on the back of the toilet to cool. She'd hoped for another go-round with the mascara wand, but there was no time now. She fluffed her hair, tucked her crisply ironed white blouse into linen pants and went to find her husband.

Billy was sitting in the kitchen with Tessa, sipping steaming coffee from a pottery mug. Tessa was dressed in black running shorts and a tank top. A white hand towel hung over one shoulder, and as Nancy watched, she mopped her forehead.

Billy looked up and smiled, getting to his feet as a brief respectful salute. "Tessa tells me she's taken up jogging."

"She's going to have a heart attack in this heat," Nancy said, waving him back to his seat. "But she doesn't listen when I tell her. Why don't you try?"

"I think it's great," Billy said. A sip of coffee washed away most of his smile. "You look fresh and ready to greet the morning, Nancy."

"I stay as comfortable as I can." She tried to sound like a lady of leisure. She didn't tell him that just yesterday she and Tessa had hooked up her mother's tractor to the chicken coop, pulled up all the fence stakes, chased the chickens into the coop, and hauled the whole foolish enterprise to another part of the pasture, where they had reassembled it under Helen's watchful eye. Then, for a respite, they had climbed out on the roof and cleaned a decade's worth of leaves from rusting gutters.

"You're feeling well?" he asked.

She chided herself for feeling disappointed that he hadn't kissed her when he got to his feet. He wasn't shy, but Billy had never been demonstrative. He was charming, gallant and respectful of women. His Southern belle mother had done herself proud with her only child.

"I'm feeling hot, and I bet you are, too," she said. "I'm sorry my mother refuses to get central air or even a window unit. I'm sure you're wishing she weren't half as stubborn about now."

"There's a breeze coming through the window. I'm fine."

"We spent all day Wednesday making sure the air flows now," Tessa said. "I took some of the window frames into town for new screens. Gram and Mom patched the better ones. They look like little crazy quilts. Very artistic."

Nancy surreptitiously examined her husband, almost hoping that he had aged visibly, as well. But Billy looked just the same. He was a tall man, with wide shoulders that were always thrown back and a waist that had widened only marginally in the past decade. His once-dark hair was steel gray, but thick enough to be notable in a man nearing retirement age. His eyes were still the unusual silver-brown of mica-flecked stone.

Billy took care of himself, but not with the obsession of so many men at their country club. He spent most of his leisure time canoeing the James River or tramping through fields and swamps to add birds to his life list. He was a good man, still a handsome man, and Nancy loved him without reservation.

"Want another cup of coffee, Mom?" Tessa asked.

Startled, Nancy realized she had been staring. "I've had plenty, thanks. Did you make your dad a fresh pot?" Before Tessa could answer, Nancy addressed her husband. "If I'd realized you were coming this early, I would have put together some muffins."

"You don't have to fuss," Billy said. "It's fine."

Tessa excused herself and left the room to change, but Nancy hardly noticed. "It's just that I know you like your coffee stronger than we do."

"It's fine." He set down his cup. "The house looks a lot better than I expected."

Nancy had to admit that the farmhouse decor almost passed for bad housekeeping now, instead of making-do gone awry. Three trailers filled with junk had traveled their last miles to the landfill. "It does look better," she conceded, "but you should have seen it. Not that it was ever much to look at, but when we got here, it was unbelievable."

"A lot of life has been lived here."

She thought that was the kind of response he'd been trained to give from the moment he first babbled "Da-Da." Responses that were polite without any substance to speak of.

She was surprised at herself. That thought, that errant, arbitrary thought, felt disloyal. She brushed it aside. "The same could be said for our house in Richmond."

"That's an interesting comparison."

He hadn't smiled again, but the words could have been accompanied by one, because she detected a sliver of humor under them. Quite clearly, in Billy's mind, the two houses had nothing in common.

Maybe she was exhausted from the unaccustomed physical labor. Maybe she'd held the blow dryer to her head for seconds too long that morning. Maybe the fact that he hadn't kissed her when she'd appeared rankled more than she'd thought. But her next words surprised her.

"There's a very *strong* comparison," she said. "The people who built both houses were our ancestors. Yours and mine. For good and for bad. Frankly, this one appeals to me more and more because it's not pretentious."

He merely looked interested. "And ours is?" Billy and Nancy lived in a Georgian style mansion that had been built in the 1920s by Billy's extravagantly wealthy grandparents and lovingly cared for by the subsequent generation. Nancy had always been sinfully proud of it.

"What would you call it?" she asked.

"A showplace?"

"Architecturally, it's no slouch. I won't dispute that. But it was ostentatious when they built it, and it's a monster now."

"You've never seemed to mind."

Suddenly the whole conversation played back in her head. She wondered what exactly had gotten into her. The Whitlock house was a stop on every architectural tour of the Windsor Farms neighborhood. Living there had been a dream come true. Living *here* had been a nightmare.

She took a deep breath. "I'm sorry. I can't believe I'm criticizing the home your family has lived in for three generations."

"You've always seemed happy living there."

Had she been? Another astounding thought. But had she been happy there? And if not, if indeed she hadn't been, why hadn't she realized it before now? Was she really as shallow as everyone seemed to think?

"Of course I've been happy," she said, still wondering if it was true. "I guess I'm feeling a little sensitive about this house and my family. I haven't lived here for a long time."

He got up and took his cup to the sink. "You've *always* apologized for who you are and where you came from. And you've never said a good word about this place. I'm surprised you're defending it today."

"Billy, what are you talking about?"

He didn't answer. He looked as if he wanted to but had thought better of it.

"I'm not apologizing, and I'm not defending anything or anyone," she said when he didn't answer. "I just compared our childhood homes, that's all."

"But you didn't quite get to the heart of it, did you? You just skirted the edges."

"Meaning?"

"The differences in our backgrounds. Two dots on the Virginia map that are worlds apart. Lives so separate it's surprising we even glimpsed each other in passing."

She was stunned. It was as if Billy had launched himself straight to the heart of her inadequacies. Or at least what she had always perceived them to be. The fears that had nagged at her earlier bloomed fully now. Coming here, living here again, had highlighted the enormous gap between them.

Yet wasn't that absurd? Had all the years when she had struggled to deserve him mattered at all? Had all the love and attention she had showered on him and on their daughter meant nothing?

"I was talking about houses," she said. "You seem to be talking about something more important, like our entire life together."

"Never mind," he said at last. "I'm tired. I had to get up early to get here, and I guess it shows."

"You didn't have to come this early. I didn't expect—"

"I want to spend some time in the hills with Tessa before it gets too hot."

He had come to see their daughter. He had not come to see her. And now he clearly did not want to belabor this distasteful conversation. Pretenses were everything in the code Billy lived by, the code Nancy herself had adopted with such enthusiasm.

For a moment Nancy thought she was going to cry. But she

couldn't. Not in front of Billy. She didn't want him to see how vulnerable, how graceless, she really was.

"Well, run along," she said, turning away. "The birds are waking up, too."

"I'll see you when I get back." He stopped on his way out to put his hand on her shoulder. "Maybe we can go out for lunch."

She felt like an old hound dog who hadn't picked up a single scent during a long day's hunting. Maybe there would be a consolation bone waiting in the kennel, but there wouldn't be any new trips into the woods.

She was rarely angry at her husband, but suddenly, she was filled with it. The fiery weight of it, the enormity, blocked every other feeling. She could hardly catch her breath. She stepped out from under his hand before she could think twice about it.

"You know, I think I'm going to be busy at lunch," she said, pausing to inhale twice before the sentence was finished. "I told Mama I'd run some of her old magazines to a nursing home in Strasburg, and they're expecting me. But it was nice of you to ask."

Then she left the kitchen one step ahead of him and went up to her bedroom to cry alone.

By afternoon the sky had darkened and the temperature had dropped as if rain might be on its way. Tessa was pleasantly tired after trooping through the hills with her father. They had spotted a white-breasted nuthatch and the rarer brown creeper. The hooded warbler that Billy had seen last year just over the first ridge had eluded them or, more probably, set up residence in a wetter climate.

Billy had begun taking Tessa birding when she was still in diapers. At first she had traveled in a backpack, then she had graduated to hiking in on her own, carrying her own canteen and binoculars. Like Billy, she kept a life list of birds she had observed, although it was not annotated in detail the way her father's was, nor half as long.

Billy's list was so vast that he was inching toward membership in the 600 club. While Tessa was more than content just to look for birds wherever she happened to find them, Billy's dream was a trip to an isolated region of the Amazon with his binoculars, notebook and little else. Not surprisingly, that was not Nancy's idea of a vacation.

Billy was gone now, back to Richmond without saying goodbye to his wife. Midafternoon, an unrepentant Nancy had returned from doing her errands in town, her arms heaped with new curtains for the living room.

At the sight of them, Helen sniffed in disapproval. "The old ones were just fine," she said, before going upstairs to sulk at this new overstepping of boundaries. Earlier in the week, the old curtains had been added to the heap in the horse trailer.

"I'm going to get a start on the walls while I'm at it," Nancy told Tessa. "So be prepared for another eruption." She shooed Tessa out of the room, insisting that if Tessa didn't participate in the Great Makeover, Helen would only be angry at one of them.

With the temperature cooling perceptibly, Tessa decided to begin on the attic. She and Nancy needed a storage area for the items that couldn't be thrown away without Helen sacrificing herself on top of the trash pile—a Shenandoah twist on Hindu suttee. The attic seemed the most appropriate possibility, although that meant clearing it first. Luckily the room was large and well ventilated, with a high ceiling, windows that provided a cross draft and a surprisingly modern fan to draw out the hottest air. It would be bearable for a short time today, at least.

On the third floor she was greeted, as she knew she would be, by a scene similar to the one they had confronted on arrival. In places, the boxes and piles brushed the sloping ceiling. She wondered what else she would find among them. She might need to begin a life list of bugs, snakes and rodents.

She took stock to see if any form of order applied here. A closer look revealed that this mess was more or less organized along the lines of the downstairs version. At the very least, boxes contained similar items. Papers in one, broken pottery in another, gaily colored rectangles of fabric folded carefully in yet another toward the back.

She paused just as she was about to push that box back into line. This time she stooped so she could get a closer look when she folded the cardboard flaps back again. She picked up the first piece of fabric, large abstract strawberries in shades of bright pink and red, and examined it, standing at last to take it to the window where the light was better.

"Feed sacks." She smiled, delighted she'd been able to make the identification. Someone, perhaps her grandmother, perhaps a woman of an earlier generation, had taken out the stitching that made this rectangle a bag. Tessa could still see the holes. Then most likely the fabric had been washed and ironed and folded for future use.

For a moment, without even thinking about it, she held the scrap of cloth to her chest. She wasn't sure why this, of all the items she had handled over the past two weeks, moved her. Something about the care that had been taken with it, she supposed, the enthusiasm with which the sack had been readied. She imagined the woman who had folded this going to the store and choosing this particular flour or chicken feed sack because of color or pattern, knowing that she would use it someday to clothe her family or keep them warm. Women with very little not only making do, but making art as they did.

She replaced the sack, folding it carefully again, and pushed the box toward the steps. She thought it might be fun to go through the box with Helen at some later date. Some of the feed sacks had already been cut into strips and squares. She wondered if her grandmother could remember where pieces of those fabrics had ended up.

The box of fabric reminded her of something else she wanted

to find here. Her grandmother had said that the wedding ring quilt Tessa had so loved as a child was up here. She gazed around the room again, wondering where to look first. She supposed she had at most another half hour before she had to abandon the attic for a cooler space.

Surrounded by cardboard, there were three old trunks against one wall, like the flea-market finds that were often used for coffee tables. These weren't that nice. The leather was cracked and, in some places, missing. But the trunks looked sturdy enough. She made a trail to them by rearranging aisles of boxes. The first trunk held school papers. They were arranged in layers. The ones on the top belonged to her mother.

Tessa smiled, lifting a neatly written essay on Jonas Salk and the polio vaccine. She read a few sentences, impressed with the eleven-year-old Nancy's writing skills. She set it back inside, looking forward to going through the papers another day at her leisure.

The second trunk contained men's clothes. She realized who they belonged to after she scanned the paper on top and realized it was a condolence letter from the U.S. Navy on the death of Fayette Henry. She smoothed her hand over a sailor's Dixie Cup cap. All these years, her grandmother had kept her husband's effects. She'd had little enough time with him, but the grief had not abated. Not entirely, anyway.

Despite the heat, Tessa felt a chill. She closed the top and moved on quickly to the third trunk. This one seemed filled with yellowed newspaper clippings. Closer examination showed that these were quilt patterns with instructions, carefully cut out and saved. Some of the patterns had been glued to thin cardboard. She flipped a piece to look at the back and realized the cardboard was a cereal box. All-Bran, she guessed, although only part of the printing was still decipherable.

She sifted through the papers, enjoying the line drawings of women with pageboys and aprons. She could imagine that these patterns had been treasured at a time when there were few gifts or pleasures in the life of a farm wife.

The top layer gave way to another of cigar boxes filled with old spools of thread and buttons cut from garments—judging by the attached tufts of fabric. The third layer consisted of odd quilt blocks, rejects, she guessed, for projects Helen hadn't finished but hadn't wanted to throw away, either. She could see why some of them had been discarded, but several caught her eye, and she set them aside to see what Helen would say about them.

Three unfinished quilt tops made up the fourth layer, all made from scraps and not nearly as nice as the quilts Nancy had showed her.

The final layer, under a neatly folded white sheet, was the wedding ring quilt.

Tessa lifted it carefully, excitement mounting as she pulled it from the trunk. She had hoped that Helen had protected the quilt by placing it in a trunk where damage was less likely, but she was surprised she had guessed so well and so quickly. It was the same quilt, though. She would have recognized it anywhere.

The past seemed to be impregnated in the cloth. She was filled with memories of her childhood. Cuddling under the quilt when she was home from school with strep throat. Sitting on her father's lap as he read stories to her, both of them covered by the quilt. Waking for just a moment when Nancy came in late at night to tuck the quilt back around her after she had kicked it off unwittingly.

She wished Kayley were there in the attic with her, to see the quilt that Tessa had never thought to mention to her daughter, to hear the stories of Tessa's own childhood. She laid her cheek against the disintegrating cotton and wondered how many tears she had already cried against it.

Helen was getting used to being fed, and although she would never tell her daughter or granddaughter, she found herself looking forward each day to whatever they bought or cooked for her. Nancy wasn't worth much in the kitchen, but she could make a salad, not the way Helen had taught her, of course, but with fancy ingredients for which Helen was developing an alarming fondness. Canned artichoke hearts. Ears of corn as tiny as a baby's pinky. Avocados. Bean sprouts, although why anyone would take the time to sprout a bean, then eat it before it could produce more beans, well, that went beyond silly.

Tonight, though, Helen had ordered them out of the kitchen so that she could make a real meal. Country ham, crowder peas, sweet potatoes the way her mother had taught her when times were still good, and, to top it off, a home-baked blueberry pie. After all, she did owe Nancy half a pie for half completing a quilt, and since that was pretty hard to bake, she settled for the whole thing. She would eat half of the pie by herself, just so show them who was boss.

The kitchen hardly seemed like it belonged to her anymore. She couldn't find anything, although, in truth, she hadn't been able to find anything for months. At least now it was easier to search, and the way Nancy had organized utensils, pots and pans made a certain crazy kind of sense. She would redo it, of course, just as soon as they left. But for now, at least she could still cook.

By the time they filed in to eat, she was weary but proud. She might be old, but she could still turn out a decent meal. She waited for lectures about cholesterol and fat grams, but both women broke into delighted smiles at the sight of the supper table covered with dishes.

"I am absolutely, one hundred percent famished," Tessa said. "And this looks beyond good, Gram."

"Sometimes I wake up dreaming about food like this." Nancy hugged herself.

"Don't you dare say you can't eat it 'cause you'll gain weight," Helen said. "Don't you dare."

"I'm not going to," Nancy said. "What are a few pounds worth? Who's even going to notice?"

Helen thought there might be more to that last comment than met the ear, but she didn't ask. She wasn't good about asking questions like that. What a body felt, well, it was that body's business.

"Gram, you sit. I'll get the tea," Tessa said.

Helen made a long series of noises, like she didn't need the help, but she had seated herself long before the noises abated, and her feet were grateful. "It's in a pitcher in the refrigerator. Not much else in there. Your mother wants me to starve."

"You're on to me," Nancy said. "That was my sole reason for coming here this summer. I want you to starve so I can take over the farm and mass-produce ostriches and llamas."

"Don't forget arugula," Tessa said, returning with the pitcher, which she set on one of the few bare spots on the old oak table. "And all the other varieties of mesculun. Greenhouses filled with Chinese healing herbs. I can see it now."

Helen realized she was smiling. Worse, she realized the others had noticed. She watched them exchange smiles of their own.

"Did either of you do one sensible thing today?" Helen demanded. "Bird-watching and curtain hanging." She shook her head and started to pass the platters and bowls.

"Do you like the curtains?" Nancy asked, reaching for the sweet potatoes, which Helen had glazed with syrup and topped with crushed pineapple and pecans.

Helen sniffed. "I didn't even look. The others were just fine."

"The dust wasn't even holding those together anymore." Nancy didn't sound offended. "These let the light in. You'll enjoy them."

"You didn't even ask what color I wanted you to paint my walls."

"I thought you didn't look." Nancy passed the sweet potatoes and lifted a platter of corn bread. "And I didn't ask because I knew you'd say white. And peach suits the room, the new curtains and you. Any woman who can make a quilt like that gorgeous dahlia quilt deserves color on her walls."

Ever the peacemaker, Tessa changed the subject. "I spent some time in the attic this afternoon."

Helen knew she'd been bested on the paint-and-curtain issue. She was glad to move on. "Well, now, that wasn't very smart. Hotter'n the devil's own furnace up there, wasn't it?"

"It was just bearable. But I found some interesting things before I had to quit."

"If you'd asked, I'd have told you that's where I keep the old stuff." Helen buttered a slab of corn bread and slapped at her daughter's hand when Nancy tried to move the butter farther away. "Family stuff, mostly. Nobody's ideas of heirlooms, though. You don't have heirlooms 'less you have enough cash to buy them in the first place."

"I found a box of feed sacks," Tessa said. "I'm proud to say I recognized them. I'd like to go through them with you someday, just to see what you remember about them."

Helen was surprised. "Feed sacks? In the attic?"

"A whole box. They'd been taken apart, washed and folded."

"Used to be a woman I knew who used the string that bound those sacks together to crochet doilies. Took it out stitch by stitch and rolled it in a ball. Times were awful hard."

"They must have been."

"I guess I forgot they were there." Helen glared at the others. "Don't think it happens very often. It doesn't. Nothing wrong with my memory."

"Boy, that's the truth," Nancy said. "You remember everything I ever did that you didn't want me to."

"And then some," Helen said. "And don't forget it."

"And…" Tessa ladled crowder peas on her plate and passed them, although nobody else had much room left. "I found the wedding ring quilt. Not the first place I looked, but almost."

Helen was surprised. She hadn't hidden that quilt, exactly. After all, she was the only one who lived here. And a woman couldn't hide something like that from herself. But she had buried it deep and hoped, as she did, that it wouldn't resurface in her lifetime.

And now Tessa had found it.

"How's it look?" Nancy asked. "Did all my quilting fall out over the years?"

"I haven't had time to examine it, but I thought maybe we could do that after supper."

Nancy and Tessa chatted about other things, but Helen worked on her meal without another word, finishing before they did. She took her plate to the sink, then pulled the pie from the counter where it had been cooling. Without asking, she dished up three hearty slices and brought them to the table, followed by a quart of vanilla ice cream and a scoop. No one refused their share.

By the time they had finished their dessert, everyone, even Helen, had mellowed. She had to admit that sitting at the table with her daughter and granddaughter was not all bad. It was a pleasure to have her cooking so genuinely enjoyed. And it was nice to have someone to talk to—not that she had anything much to say.

"Let's look at the quilt now, then I'll do the dishes." Tessa rose and stretched. Helen admired how lithe and lean she was and just wished that the tension in her granddaughter's face would disappear, to be replaced by something that matched the overall impression of good health and inner strength.

They filed into the parlor, since the living room smelled of paint and the furniture was draped. The parlor was a small room, a useless ornament, really, for a farm family with nothing nice enough to save for company. Helen's own mother, Delilah, had realized this. When she was alive, the room had held a big quilting frame and little else but chairs to sit around it. During Delilah's reign there had been neighborhood quilting bees every Wednesday morning right here. The Fitch Crossing Ladies Homemakers' Society.

"This is a cozy room. It was my favorite as a little girl," Tessa said. "I used to curl up in here and read whenever we came to visit."

Helen switched on lamps that had shone during her mother's day. Delilah had always insisted on plenty of light in the parlor, because she claimed that quilting could ruin the eyes. "You were the reading-est child. Not like that daughter of yours. Kayley liked to run and play. She never even came to see me 'less she came with a kite or a ball."

There was a silence, the way there always was when Kayley's name was mentioned, then Nancy said, "Tessa would have been a tomboy, too, if I'd let her, but I was determined she had to be a young lady."

Helen shook her head. "In my day, nobody had time to think like that. Everybody got their hands dirty, and not by playing ball, I can tell you."

"That sounds bleak," Tessa said. "Did you ever have fun?"

"I never said we didn't have fun." Helen heard herself laughing, and the sound surprised her.

"I never found *any* of the chores I did here fun," Nancy said.

Helen was sorry that was true, although she understood the difference. "We had more fun than you can ever guess at. Nobody ever said you can't work and have fun at the same time."

She lowered her considerable bulk to an armchair and made herself comfortable. Nancy sat in the faded love seat where Tessa had always read as a child, and Tessa disappeared, returning in a moment with a bundle wrapped in a white sheet.

"This sheet was protecting it, so I thought I'd better bring it along." She placed the bundle on a table in the corner and began to carefully unfold it.

Tessa's movements were always fluid. Helen supposed that her granddaughter's natural poise and grace had come from Billy's side. No Stoneburner woman had found time to develop either, while Billy's mother and grandmother had honed both at fancy debutante cotillions. Helen watched Tessa unfold the sheet and smooth it over the sides of the table. Like a dance or an elaborate pantomime.

Next Tessa unfolded the quilt and smoothed it over the sheet. "This was like finding an old friend you were afraid had moved away for good." She finished and stepped back. "There are a lot of memories here."

Helen could have told her a thing or two about that, but she sat silently as Nancy got up to view the quilt. "Well, the stitches don't look like yours, Mama, but I have to say, they're not too shabby, either. I wasn't good, but I wasn't bad."

"There are so many colors and patterns." Tessa lightly stroked her hand across the top. "But it's really damaged. More than I re-member."

Helen got to her feet at last. She moved over to look at the quilt, too. It was about eighty by ninety inches. She wasn't sure why, exactly, except that she had probably thought that was a reasonably standard size. What had she known when she was only a poor teenaged girl with big dreams for her future? And how much time had there been at the end? She'd wanted to finish the top before her wedding day. For some reason that had seemed imperative.

"There are two wedding rings," Helen said. "The single wedding ring, which is a whole lot simpler. Then there's the double wed-ding ring, that's the one you see the most. This here's the double. I started piecing it when I was a girl. My mama thought it would be a good learning quilt because it teaches patience and accurate curved seams."

"Was it?" Nancy asked.

"I suppose." This wedding ring was a scrap quilt, plain and sim-ple. Only the corners of the intersecting ovals, a scalloped border and the backing were alike, a blue fabric that had meant so much to her as a young woman.

"There's damage here, here…" This time Tessa didn't touch the quilt, but she passed her finger over the worst areas. "Some of the fabric looks like it's disintegrating."

"It's a mess, all right," Helen said. "The way you and your mother throw away just about anything that doesn't have a sheen or a sparkle, seems to me you'd have this old heap in that horse trailer of Claiborne's before I could whistle 'Dixie.' I'm surprised you didn't get shed of it instead of bringing it down here."

"I didn't bring it back to you so we could just toss it in the trailer," Nancy said. "You know when I brought it I asked you to look it over and see if it could be fixed. I thought you'd do it a long time ago. But when I didn't hear anything about it, I guess I just forgot."

"It's an heirloom," Tessa said. "Not a stack of unread newspapers."

Helen was still fuming about their meddling and not about to give ground. "Fixing it would take a lot of work. Besides, I've got to say, I don't know how to go about it. I make tops, and I quilt. Sometimes I've put new binding on an old quilt that's wearing thin. But that's all I know how to do."

"I guess we could take it apart and start all over," Nancy said.

"No sense in that. You could make a brand-new quilt in the same time."

Tessa lifted an edge of the quilt, almost reverently. Despite herself, Helen was touched. She hadn't realized how many memories had been bound into it for her granddaughter.

"There are so many fabrics," Tessa said. "Where did they all come from?"

"It's a regular family bible, this quilt. I worked on it for a lot of years, a little here, a little there. Like I told you, some are feed sacks. Some of the pieces come from old dresses, mine and family's, friends'. Most likely those are the pieces with the most damage. I traded for some of the fabric, a piece of mine for a piece of theirs. I wanted each section to look different, which is why it took so long. We didn't have money in those days to just go buy something pretty we liked at the store. Nobody in these parts had any money."

"I'd like to hear about it. About the dresses and the feed sacks. About what it was like to make this quilt." Tessa looked up. "About your life, Gram."

"Why?" Helen frowned. "What do you care? It was a long time ago. Nobody left but me. I could tell you about the dresses and the people I traded with, about this." She pointed to a piece. "That belonged to my mama. It was cut from her favorite apron. That was the first section of this pattern I ever sewed." She pointed to another. "That piece right there, that was from my grandma's wedding dress. But why do you care? You'll never know them."

Tessa didn't fuss or try to make her feel better. "You don't have a TV that works well enough to see most of the time. It's early. I'm tired of reading."

Helen had been prepared to refuse. What did she have to tell her upstart daughter or her grieving granddaughter? She was just an old woman whose life was nothing in the world like theirs. But there was something about the offhanded way Tessa asked, something underneath it that tugged at Helen and made her think twice.

"I might tell you a little. But only if you scare up some of that wine we had the other night. I could do with a glass if I have to talk. Reminds me of the dandelion wine my papa always made in the spring, only his was sweet enough to make your teeth ache."

Tessa stretched and swayed a moment. "You get comfortable. I'll be right back." She left the room.

"What are you still doing here?" Helen demanded of her daughter. "I tried to tell you about your grandparents and such when you were living here. You didn't care then, and you probably don't care now."

Nancy leaned forward, and the smile that was always so hard for Helen to get behind disappeared. "You are one nasty, stubborn old woman, you know that? All my life, you've gone after me like that. I never said I wasn't interested in my own family. I just wasn't interested in being told how much better they were than I would ever be."

Helen stared at her. "I never said that. You're making that up."

"I was never good enough for you, Mama."

"You got that backwards. I was never good enough for *you*."

Nancy sat back in the love seat and crossed her arms. "These may be your memories to share or not to share, but when you're making up your mind, just remember this is my family, too. And I'm not going anywhere."

Helen flinched. There was no room for ambiguity in her life. She had lived so close to the edge that she'd had to make snap decisions and stick closely to them to keep from falling into the chasms of poverty and despair. But she had always known, deep in her heart, that there were problems with moving so quickly and decisively. Now one of them was sitting across the room from her.

"I never said I wouldn't tell you about your family," she said. "You show me when I said that, and I'll apologize."

Nancy didn't respond, which was so unlike her that Helen knew how important this was. She tried to find words that fit the turmoil inside her, and none occurred to her.

"I'm glad you want to hear," she said at last. She didn't sound glad. She knew that, but at least she'd managed something.

Nancy, arms still folded, nodded.

CHAPTER
8

1932

Helen knew better than to complain to her mama. Delilah Stoneburner moved faster than her husband Cuddy's best squirrel dog, and she got mad if she had to slow down. Like the other women who lived up and down Fitch, Delilah's workload had gotten heavier in the past years, but her step had only gotten quicker to make up for it. Now that Cuddy had a job unloading sacks of grain at the feed store, Delilah had her husband's chores, as well as the ones she had always done. Helen's brothers Tom and Obediah—Obed for short—did their share, and so did twelve-year-old Helen, but that still left too much work and not enough time.

Despite knowing her mama wouldn't take kindly to an interruption, Helen followed her out to the chicken yard. "Those two in the corner." Delilah pointed out two chickens pecking for insects at the far west edge of the coop. Tom, fourteen and already nearly as tall as Cuddy, looked like he wanted to protest, but he knew better. He might not like wrenching the necks of chickens the way Delilah had taught him, but it was his job. Besides, that meant there would be chicken on the supper table, a rare enough event these days.

Helen didn't want to watch. She fed the chickens every day, and even though she knew better, she secretly gave them names. She was pretty sure Daffodil and Lilac would be sitting next to the potatoes and gravy that night.

"Mama." Helen turned from the sight of Tom trying to corner the hens. "Mama, I want to quilt like everybody else. I don't want to watch the babies. I can quilt just as fast and straight——"

"You still here?" Delilah looked down at her daughter and frowned, as if everything about Helen from her glossy dark hair to the length of her toenails displeased her. "You still talking back to me?"

"Mama, I won't ask for another thing. I'll help with supper after the bee's all done, and I'll clean up the dishes all by myself. I'll put Aunt Sarah's baby to bed and stay in the room with the other children all night if you want. But, Mama——"

Delilah actually slowed her pace. "You still talking back to me? You still using those big brown eyes to show me how sad you are?"

Helen fell silent.

Delilah's voice softened. "Lenny, I told you before. We gotta have somebody watching the babies. Pretty soon one of the other girls'll be old enough to watch 'em. They'll help you today. But today you gotta be the one in charge. You understand?"

Helen did. "Maybe just a little? Just a little while?"

Delilah laughed. "Maybe. But you go on now. You got things to do before everybody gets here."

Trying to ignore the squawks coming from the vicinity of the chicken yard, a heartened Helen scampered down the path to the pond and raised the latch on the high wooden box her father had built just above the shoreline. She hoisted a scoop of corn and scattered it for the ducks and geese, then followed with another. Standing at the edge, she did a quick search for the ducklings that had hatched that week, but either something had gotten them or they were hiding in the tall grass at the pond's edge. Philosophically, she hoped for the latter.

An hour passed, and she filled it with chores. Delilah liked a clean house, and even if she had a hundred other chores to do, the house never suffered. Rugs got beaten. Floors got waxed whenever they needed it, and twice a month all the wood furniture got a coat of the beeswax and turpentine polish Delilah made herself.

These days Helen did most of the inside work. As the only daughter, the women's chores fell to her so that Delilah could do her husband's. Cuddy got home after dark and left before the sun rose, but nobody complained. For the first time in recent years there was a little money now to buy the things they couldn't provide for themselves like coffee, salt and sugar, things Delilah had tried to trade eggs and butter for when she could.

Helen emptied the slop jars first, a chore she despised and wanted to get out of the way. Then, after she washed her hands at the pump in the farmyard, she went back inside with her mother's feather duster and swept it across every surface in sight. Beds needed making; dishes needed doing. By the time the neighbor ladies and the Stoneburner and Lichliter women who lived near enough to walk or catch a ride in a wagon were supposed to arrive, the house was clean enough to suit Delilah. Helen knew her mother was pleased because she didn't point out a single thing Helen hadn't done.

Today was a special quilting bee. Each woman had made a friendship block and signed it for the teacher at their schoolhouse, who was moving away. Helen was sorry to see him go. He had loaned her books from his own bookshelf and helped her figure out the hardest words without making her feel foolish.

Helen's Aunt Mavis had gathered up all the blocks and sewn

them into a quilt top. Today, with everybody working on it, they could pretty nearly get it finished. Delilah would complete and bind it in time to present on the last day of school.

Aunt Mavis arrived first, with the top folded neatly under one arm. She was Helen's favorite aunt, Delilah's youngest sister, and Mavis always seemed to remember what it had felt like to be the youngest child in a family. Today she singled Helen out for a shoulder squeeze, the way she always did. Then she winked and presented her with a poke tied off at the top with a piece of string.

"Done brought these for you, Lenny," she said, exchanging the poke for the broom Helen was holding so that Helen could open it.

"What is it?" Helen picked at the knot in excitement. Her nimble fingers just couldn't seem to do the job right.

"Wait and see." Mavis swiped at a speck of dust on the threshold. "Anybody else here?"

"Not yet. I don't know who all's coming, but we got a room upstairs all ready for you. And there's chicken for supper."

"A good enough reason to stay."

Delilah's other three sisters lived closer to Front Royal than to Toms Brook, so any time they came, they stayed the night. Some of Cuddy's family lived well beyond Woodstock, and when they visited, they stayed, as well. Tonight the house would be full to bursting, because even some of the women who lived closer, like Mavis, were staying so they could work late into the night.

Helen finally loosened the knot, and in a moment the poke fell open to reveal fabric scraps in a rainbow of colors.

"Aunty Mavis!" She dug through it in excitement. "These are all for me?"

"Just a little of this and a little of that for your wedding ring quilt. Some dress goods from a neighbor, an old dress of mine that give way at the back 'til I couldn't fix it no more. And best of all, a little piece of the dress your own grandma was wearing when she got married." Mavis peered into the poke and dug around with one finger, lifting a square of fabric sprigged with tiny faded roses. "This here's the one. I know you wanted pretty pieces, and that's what I got for you."

"They *are* pretty. Now I can make some new blocks." Helen folded the top to seal it. "It's so much. Thank you."

Mavis pushed her niece's hair off her square face. "You'll think of me every time you see it. That's what I did it for. So you'd remember me." She rested the back of her hand against Helen's cheek for a moment before she went off to join the other women.

Spring had arrived early this year, but by ten the sun had gone behind clouds, and those women who hadn't dressed warmly enough were sorry. Helen took shawls and hats and hefted a baby on each hip when the mothers handed them over. She was surprised that nearly every one of them handed over a poke, just like the one Mavis had given her.

"For taking care of the babies today," one of the neighbor women said. "Your ma said you'd be real glad for the gift."

Helen was more than glad. Her mother had been thinking of her, and she had asked the other women to do the same. Rewards were unusual in the Stoneburner home and always treasured more for it.

She took control of the babies with a bit more enthusiasm, although she wanted nothing more than to steal upstairs and dump all her scraps on the floor of her bedroom to sort through them.

She didn't mind hard work, but she didn't like to mind children. Her older cousins couldn't find enough hours to talk about all the babies they would have and what they would do with them. Helen figured someday she might have to have a baby or two, just to keep her man happy, but she would sure rather be outdoors doing men's work or inside making quilt tops on her mother's sewing machine. And most of all, she would rather be sitting at a quilt frame, rocking her needle back and forth the way Delilah had taught her when she was only eight.

More children arrived, some who were walking or running, some who were still in arms. She greeted cousins and neighbors and the preacher's wife, who had brought a particularly ornery little boy for Helen to look after—along with half a brand-new flour sack patterned with tiny blue houses. Some older girls arrived, too, but they were only good for helping, not for talking to. At eight and nine, they knew very little.

The women drank coffee that Delilah had roasted and ground herself, and cut a large swath through a trio of coffee cakes she had risen at dawn to begin. The children were given bread and jam and fresh milk. Afterwards Helen took them outside and set the older girls to minding the toddlers while, baby on each hip, she took the children who could walk the distance down to the creek that was close kin to the Shenandoah river and fed into the pond.

The women were settled around the quilting frame when she returned with her charges. Helen's fingers ached to take their own place there, but she knew better than to ask so soon. With the help of the other two girls, she entertained the little ones, but by the time another hour had passed, the babies were fussing. She gave them to their mothers to feed, then put them down for naps in the front bedroom, where their cries could be heard when they awoke.

The older children were tired of the games Helen and the others had devised. Helen was tired, too. She wanted to be in the parlor where the women were laughing and telling stories. She could hear just enough to know what she was missing.

"I got an idea," she told the older girls.

There were four children to care for besides the napping babies. After a little preparation Helen led them all into the parlor. "They want to play groundhog under the quilt."

"Groundhog?" Delilah spoke first and looked suspicious.

"That'll be the groundhog's cozy old den. They'll be quiet underneath." She was fairly sure they would be, since all the children looked like they needed a good rest by now. This close to their mothers, they would probably curl up and go to sleep.

"You going under with them?" Delilah asked. "Or you leaving them here for us to mind?"

"I'm going under with them." Helen tried to look innocent. "I'll watch out they don't hurt nothing."

"You can try." Delilah sounded skeptical.

Helen was elated. Underneath wasn't as good as sitting beside the quilt with a needle in her hand, but at least she could hear what was going on. She herded the children between chairs and under the quilt; then she settled them in the middle, with old quilts she'd gathered, and dried apples and black walnuts from the autumn's harvest. At first their excited chatter drowned out whatever was being said above them. But just as she'd hoped, the children, snug and well fed, began to drift off to sleep. Only the preacher's devilish little boy continued to squirm, but even he stopped making so much of a fuss when one of the women thumped his head through the quilt with her thimble when he tried to stand up.

Helen curled up beside one of the sleeping children and listened to the talk above her.

A woman spoke, but Helen wasn't sure who. "Becky, Mavis here never did hear that story you tell 'bout the boy who didn't go to church of a Sunday."

Helen had never heard it, either, and she hoped Becky, a grandmotherly woman who lived about a mile down the road, would cooperate.

"You never did?" Becky's voice was easier to identify.

"I don't remember hearing it," Mavis said. "If you have a powerful need to tell it, I have a powerful need to listen."

The other women laughed. Becky followed up. "You won't never skip church again, once you hear it, I can tell you that."

"I never did hear it, either," another voice said. Helen recognized her cousin Lenore Lichliter, who was going to be married in June and made sure everybody in the whole wide world knew about it.

"Then I'll tell it," Becky said. "'Cause if I don't, you might find yourself in nearly the same situation one day."

One of the children turned over and kicked another. Helen held her breath, but the abused child didn't even stir. She breathed easier as Becky began the story.

"They tell this down to Page County, where my grandma went to spend her final days. They say it really happened, you know, and I believe them."

"Lots of these old stories really happened," someone said.

"You better believe they did. Well, this time it seemed there was a young boy name of Herman. Nobody ever said his last name, and I never did ask. You'll see why. Anyway, Herman woke up of a Sunday morning, and it was mighty hot that day. He decided he'd go a-swimming instead of sitting in church where it was bound to be hotter."

"I've felt that way a time or two," someone said, and the others laughed.

"Well, this Herman, he knew a good ol' swimming hole on the deacon's farm. And he figured the deacon would be at church like he was supposed to be. So he went over to the swimming hole, and he took off his clothes 'til he was stark naked. But just about the time he was planning to jump in, he heard a noise behind him."

Helen was holding her breath again, only this time it was because she could see the whole story like it was being acted out in front of her.

"What kinda noise?" Mavis asked.

"Well, not the kind you or me, we'd ever want to hear. It was the deacon's bull, a bad bull at that, who was usually kept in another pasture. Ol' Herman saw that bull coming right at him for a look-see, and he was scared to death, I can tell you."

"Scared and naked," Delilah said. Helen could almost hear her smile.

"Herman, he didn't have time to set and think about it. He did the only thing he could. He jumped to the left, just as the bull nearly got him with his horns, then, when the bull turned for another try, well, Herman, he just grabbed that bull's tail so he could stay behind him. The bull ran and ran with this naked boy hanging on to his tail, and finally he got tired and went to stand under a tree."

"That must have been a sight of running Herman did," a woman said. "A real sight."

"You better believe it was," Becky said. "But once that bull stood still to rest, well, Herman saw his chance. He climbed that tree, first a low branch, then a higher one. Before long he was high up in that tree, and he thought he was safe."

"But he wasn't?" Lenore said. "He wasn't safe?"

"Not a bit of it. You see, there was a hornets' nest in that tree, and the hornets took a good look at Herman and decided he needed stinging. And that's what they did. Sting, sting, sting."

Helen winced. She felt real sorry for the boy. Real sorry.

"Herman, well, he knew he had to do something. So he swung out on a branch, and he landed on that bull's back, and he hung on for dear life. That ol' bull wasn't used to being rode and such. So off he ran, faster and faster, 'til he broke through the fence and headed right off in the direction of the church."

"Oh no!" Lenore giggled. "Still all naked, too!"

"Herman, he thought he was gonna die, and wouldn't you? That bull bucked and that bull twisted, but Herman held on thinking those were his last moments on earth. And he was real sorry, I can tell you, chug full of sorry that he was heading right for that church, where he was going to meet his maker in front of all those folks, and naked, too. Altogether naked and no mistake about it."

"I guess he was wishing he'd just gone to church," Mavis said. "No sermon in the world as bad as all that."

"Not a one," Becky agreed. "Well, just about that time church was over. It had all taken so long to happen, you see. All the people were coming out of the church, and they saw the bull running toward them with something on his back. Women started scream- ing, and men started cursing, even though some of them still had one foot in God's house."

Everybody tsked.

"Anyway, the bull saw all those people coming out and decided he'd better turn around before he crashed into that old fence around the church building. So he twisted and started to run in the other direction. And when he did, Herman flew off like some kind of bird. And he landed in a patch of ivy just beside the church. A real soft patch, too, and he wasn't even hurt."

"But he was still naked!" Lenore said. "Naked in front of all those people."

"Do you think that boy ever skipped church again any Sunday of his life?" Becky said.

A wide-eyed Helen heard a chair scrape; then she saw her mother's face peeking under the quilt frame. "You think he did?" Delilah asked Helen.

Helen thought about it. Herman had had a good ride and some- thing he could sure tell his grandchildren about until the day he died. And he'd survived it all. She wasn't sure that being naked in front of the townspeople had really canceled all that out. She wasn't sure at all, but she knew what she was supposed to say. "No, Mama," she said.

Delilah winked before she disappeared.

CHAPTER
9

Tessa took the wedding ring quilt up to her room that night and draped it over the footboard, where it was the first thing she saw the next morning. She had been nightmare free that night, an unusual enough occurrence. She had not awakened to the terrifying screech of brakes, the wailing of strangers. She had awakened with the quilt folded neatly in front of her, the way it had been for so many mornings of her childhood.

One decision in her life was simple. She wasn't going to allow the quilt to disintegrate further, and she certainly wasn't going to discard it. That had become perfectly clear last night as her grandmother talked about her own mother and the other women who had given her fabric. Tessa's entire vision of Helen Stoneburner Henry had changed with that story, and so had her already high regard for the tattered remains on her footboard.

A knock sounded on her door; then her mother opened it just enough to peek inside. "You're awake?"

Tessa sat up and stretched. "You're up early."

"I had a hard time sleeping." Nancy came over and perched on the edge of Tessa's bed, the way she had when Tessa was a little girl. Then the purpose of the early morning visits had been to school Tessa in the social graces or organize every moment of her day— at least, Tessa had felt that was the purpose. This morning Nancy just looked troubled.

Since it was a Sunday, Tessa asked the obvious. "Were you planning to go to church?"

"Not unless your grandmother insists, and that's not likely. I don't think she goes very often these days."

"What's the problem?" Tessa asked. She reached for the bedside clock and squinted. "It's later than I thought. It's going to be too hot to jog if I don't get up and get going in a minute."

Nancy got to her feet. "I won't keep you."

Tessa reached out and grabbed her mother's arm before she could disappear. "Don't go. I'm just surprised I slept so long."

Nancy fell back to the bed. "I've been up for an hour."

"Why?"

If Nancy had been up for an hour, she hadn't used any of it for personal grooming. She might have combed her hair, although not carefully, but she was still in her bathrobe without a smidgen of makeup. Tessa only rarely saw her like this, and she was surprised how young her mother still looked, even with the expensive artificial layers stripped away. Young, and even more vulnerable than usual.

"I'm worried about your grandmother," Nancy said.

"Worried?"

"Aren't you?"

Tessa felt like a contestant in an early morning quiz show. She was not awake enough to name the myriad forms of sea life at the Great Barrier Reef or the past governors of Rhode Island, and she was not *nearly* awake enough to delve into her mother's psyche.

"Tessa?"

Tessa shrugged. "I think she's doing remarkably well. She hasn't thrown us out. She hasn't retrieved more than an item or two we've tossed in the trailer." She searched for something else to say, ending with another helpless shrug when she couldn't find it.

"Last night, Tessa. Remember?"

"Last night was lovely." She pulled the pillow from behind her and hugged it, leaning forward a little. "I used to wish I knew stories about the family, so I could share them with—" She looked away. "It bothered me that I knew so little. But whenever I tried to find out anything, I got the cold shoulder. I'd even forgotten Gram had brothers."

"Your grandmother didn't want to talk—"

"Not just Gram," Tessa said. "*You*. Mostly you, in fact. You just didn't want to talk about your family."

Nancy drew herself up straighter. "What did I know? She never told me that story, either. And besides, you knew hundreds of stories from your daddy's side of the family. That should have kept you happy."

"Truthfully? I got a little tired of the Civil War and stories about how great life was when the Whitlocks owned a tobacco plantation on the James River."

"Don't forget the part where the slaves never had to worry about being sold downriver, because the Whitlocks certainly weren't those kind of people."

Tessa smiled, and Nancy smiled back.

"You didn't buy that part, huh?" Tessa said.

"No, or the part where the field slaves carried on something terrible when the carpetbaggers forced them to leave the plantation after the war." Nancy sobered. "I'm sorry. Your Grandmother Whitlock was a good woman." She paused. "More or less," she added, considerably softer.

In all her years, Tessa had never heard anything resembling a critical word against her grandmother. "It was revisionist history, the South the way she and a lot of other people wished it had been, but I never believed it. What's funny, though, is that I thought you loved all that."

"It's possible you don't understand me as well as you think you do."

Tessa mulled that over. This was becoming a recurring theme.

Nancy straightened a little. "Anyway, since you can't figure out why you should be worrying about your grandmother, I'll tell you. She's undergone a personality change. Telling stories, baking pies and frying chicken for us? I've heard people soften up this way sometimes, right before they die." She paused. "I guess I'm not ready for her to go. And, Tessa, this is something we've purely skipped over. We haven't really given her health a thought. Maybe your grandmother let the house go to rack and ruin because she's sick. Maybe she was telling those stories last night because she knows the end is near."

This kind of thinking was more what Tessa was used to from her mother. She felt on firmer ground. "That's a huge leap in logic. Gram might just be glad to have us here."

Nancy waved that away. "When has she ever been glad? It's a good visit if she doesn't tell us she's tired of us before an hour is up."

Tessa laughed. "Let's make waffles this morning. You kept the waffle iron, didn't you?"

Nancy got to her feet. "You're not going to take me seriously, are you?"

"I'll watch for signs, but I've got to say, she eats as much as we do. She seems to sleep well. She's quilting up a storm. She's not going to live forever, but she'll get through the day." She threw back the sheet and swung her legs over the side of the bed. "There's a patch of blackberries beside the creek. I'll come back that way and pick some when I finish jogging. They'll be good on the waffles."

Nancy's eyes narrowed; then she relaxed. "No one ever listens to me."

Tessa was glad she didn't sound too worried about it.

* * *

Helen watched her daughter fussing over the waffle iron. "From the looks of it, I'd say the last time you made waffles was right there at that counter."

"I've made them since then."

"When?"

Nancy forked a half-formed waffle onto a plate and scowled at it. "Tessa was two, I think."

"Do you remember when I got that waffle iron?"

Nancy wiped the grill, sprayed it to keep it from sticking and closed it so it would heat again. "They hadn't invented Teflon, that's for sure."

"I won it at the church fair. You were eight."

Nancy leaned against the counter and folded her arms. "I wanted a pony, and we got a waffle iron. Now I remember."

"The pony wasn't fit for dog food. The waffle iron's lasted all these years. And you were so excited, I had to make waffles that very night for supper."

"And they were first rate." Nancy smiled. "Better than these are going to be. You tried to teach me to cook. I remember the lessons."

"There's nothing wrong with those salads you make."

Nancy looked surprised at the compliment. "Tessa's picking blackberries down by the creek on her way back. To put on top of the waffles."

"Is she, now? I wonder if she'll find the same thing I found down there one day."

The back door rattled, and Tessa walked in. "These were at their peak. But I'm guessing there were about half as many as you'd get in a good year." She placed a plastic bag with about two cups of berries in it on the counter. "Whew, it's hot out there already."

"You're going to melt away to nothing," Helen said. "And that's a right puny bunch of berries. We've had years when there weren't enough plastic bags like that in the whole world to hold all the berries we could pick."

Nancy went to the refrigerator and poured her daughter a glass of orange juice, holding it out to her. "You've got time to cool down before the waffles are done."

"I'm going to wash up. I'll be back in a minute."

Helen thought her granddaughter looked cooler when she returned. She'd washed her face and changed her shirt. She joined Helen at the table and sipped her juice.

Nancy approached with a colander filled with the freshly washed berries in one hand and a platter of reasonably edible waffles in the other. "At home I eat a small bowl of natural yogurt and a slice of whole wheat toast. I don't like it, but it fills me up. Then I come here, and I can't think of anything but food. If Tessa hadn't suggested waffles this morning, I was going to."

"We're using up a lot of calories. You're not going to gain a pound." Tessa took the waffles after Helen had dished up her own plate. She took hers and passed the platter to Nancy, who did the same.

"How's the swimming hole look?" Helen poured syrup on her waffles, then topped them with three big spoonfuls of berries.

"What swimming hole?"

"The one at the far side of the creek. Kayley could have showed you. She showed it to me once. She and Mack found it on a walk."

"I don't remember anything about a swimming hole," Tessa said.

Helen watched the way Tessa's face changed at the mention of her daughter. It didn't seem right to Helen that the subject was still forbidden. She ignored Nancy's warning glance.

"You've just forgotten," Helen said. "Because she told you all about it. I remember. You've shoved it away somewhere, filed it under the past in your head."

"Maybe." Tessa looked up. "Exactly where is it? Can you really swim there?"

Helen thought the exchange had gone well. Her granddaughter hadn't withdrawn completely, the way she usually did at the mention of Kayley's name. "More like a wading hole, unless it's been a real wet year. Then it's maybe shoulder deep. But it was deep enough so's all the young'uns what lived up and down Fitch Road liked to come and cool off there. A sight closer than going all the way down to the river."

"Why didn't they swim in the pond?"

"Snapping turtles. Bigger than a hubcap."

Tessa paused with her fork halfway to her mouth. "Still?"

Helen shrugged. "This drought could chase them away, although it's more likely that too much rain would do the trick. I wouldn't mind if they went. Then we could have ducklings again."

"I'd almost forgotten about the swimming hole," Nancy said. "You caught me out there once with a boy and nearly skinned me alive."

Helen scowled. "Because you hadn't told me where you were going and you liked to have scared me to death."

"Mom, were you skinny-dipping?" Tessa was smiling. "Is that why Gram was mad?"

"No, but I did skip my chores. And nothing made your grandmother madder than that. Not even if she'd found me stark naked."

"There wasn't another living soul to do them chores, 'cept me," Helen said bluntly. "And I had my hands full."

Nancy put her hand on her mother's for just a moment. "I know you did."

Helen was surprised. When had her daughter last touched her that way? When had anyone? For a moment she was mute.

"Well, I'm disappointed," Tessa said. "I thought there might be a good story there."

Helen recovered. "I'll tell you a good story, you want to hear it. In a way, it has to do with last night's, because it happened right after that, soon as the weather warmed up a little and the boys started swimming again."

She watched her daughter and granddaughter exchange glances, as if they were surprised or...

"Just what is that about?" she demanded. "You don't want to hear what I have to say, just tell me!"

Tessa leaned forward. "We'd love to hear it, only you don't usually talk about the past. And it's worrying Mom."

"Worrying you?" Helen couldn't believe it. "You're worried because I'm talking? Isn't it when people *stop* talking that you're supposed to get worried?"

Nancy glared at Tessa. "Did you have to tell her that?"

Tessa dove back into her waffles. "Uh-huh."

Helen tapped her daughter on the arm. "What exactly is worrying you, Nanny?"

"Are you...ill, Mama?"

Helen didn't understand. "Do I look ill to you?"

"I've just been wondering if maybe there's something you're not telling us."

This time Helen got it. "Like I'm dying?"

"Like that, yes."

Helen couldn't believe that one little story had produced such a reaction. She started to ridicule Nancy's concern, then thought better of it. "I just never had time for stories, that's all."

"You're feeling all right, then?"

"As all right as anyone my age can feel. And no, I haven't seen my doctor lately, and he hasn't given me bad news. Can't a woman just talk without getting herself in trouble?"

"You're sure?" Nancy said.

Helen nodded.

"I, for one, would like to hear that story," Tessa said. "Before the whole day gets away from us."

"I tell it, you're not going to accuse me of something else, are you?" Helen asked.

"No." Tessa held up the plate with the remaining waffles. "Fortify yourself, Gram. We're listening."

Helen took the plate. "Remember that old tale I heard when I was under the quilt frame that day? Well, in a way, it has to do with that."

"Did you ever get to quilt that day?" Nancy asked. "You didn't say."

"They let me at the frame late in the afternoon. Then the next day, when she thought I wasn't looking, my mama took out every stitch I'd put in. Not small or straight enough to suit her. But it was the last time. The very last time anybody ever took out even one of my stitches, I can tell you that."

The Claiborne family had owned their farm just about as long as the Stoneburners had owned theirs. In years past, the families had been friends, helping each other the way neighbors in the valley always did. They had raised barns for each other, made apple butter together, along with other nearby families, butchered hogs, even attended the same church. But then Sammy Claiborne—more than half drunk on bootleg whiskey—shot one of Cuddy Stoneburner's goats, dead certain he'd bagged a doe for the family supper table. When the truth was discovered, there was nothing offered as compensation except an apology, and even that was halfhearted.

Cuddy wasn't one to feud with anybody, but from that moment on, the Stoneburner family shunned the Claibornes.

All except Obed.

At fifteen, Obed Stoneburner was half a head taller than his brother Tom, and more than a year stronger. He was a good-looking boy, and a smart one, too, and Delilah and Cuddy struggled not to favor him over his quieter brother. They were strict with all their children, but more often than not Obed could find a way around the rules. And Obed, who understood he was nobility of a sort, took advantage of their affection.

Obed had been friends since early childhood with Sammy Claiborne's son, Gus. Even after their parents stopped talking to each other, the boys got together frequently to hunt squirrels or hike up into the mountains. Gus was as big as Obed, and even better looking, although not as clever in school or as popular with the other youth on Fitch Crossing.

Everybody knew that Gus had a hot temper and a mean streak. He would tease the younger children and play tricks on them until they were frantic to get away from him. Although no one had ever caught him at it, everyone knew it was Gus who left dead birds and animals impaled on the picket fence of a widow who caught him smoking and gambling in her barn.

None of this affected the boys' friendship. Gus was an only child, and Obed was the closest thing to a brother he had.

Until Fate Henry arrived.

Lafayette Henry—or Fate, as he was called by everyone—had lost both his parents to diphtheria when he was just a baby. His father's sister and her husband who lived in the Oklahoma panhandle stepped in to care for him, but when their tiny farm turned to dust and began to blow away, they sent Fate back east to Virginia to live with the Claibornes so they could travel farther west and look for work.

Since Fate's mother had been Samuel Claiborne's sister, the Claibornes had little recourse but to take the boy and finish raising him. In their own meager way, they tried to make him welcome. But Gus soon made sure Fate knew the real score.

On a particularly hot June afternoon, the twelve-year-old Helen sat on the front porch stringing beans. It seemed to her that Delilah had planted enough to feed all of Virginia, and Helen was the one required to pull every danged string and snap every danged end.

"You almost done, Lenny?" Delilah climbed the porch with a basket of freshly folded laundry on her hip. "I'm gonna pickle a bunch or two before I cook supper. They'll taste good come February, won't they?"

Helen was heat-dazed and ornery. The boys had finished their chores an hour ago and gone off on their own. She didn't know where they were, but she sure wished she was with them instead of sitting there snapping and stringing. "Why'd you grow so many?" She lifted handfuls and let them dribble through her fingers. "I won't be done with these 'fore it's time to bring in the cow and feed the chickens."

"It's a busy day."

"Not for Obed and Tom."

"Them boys've been up since way before you and worked the whole time. They want to go off a little while, I don't see no reason not to let them."

Helen saw lots of reasons, but she knew better than to list them. She understood that her mother was training her to be a farm wife, just like her. It was Cuddy's job to train their sons, but Cuddy was away most of the time now, and Delilah was just worn out by this late hour and couldn't make herself stay on top of them.

"You finish those beans, and I'll bring in the cow for you," Delilah said, relenting a little after a glance at her daughter's long face. "You can go on down to the creek when you're done, wade a little if you've a mind to, and come home with a pail of blackberries for tomorrow's pies."

Helen perked right up. "Really?"

"Uh-huh. But if you dawdle, won't be no time to get down there. No wading and no pie."

Helen's fingers flew after that. By three she was nearly finished. By three-thirty she had hauled all the beans into the kitchen, where Delilah had already set out vinegar and sugar to pickle them. Delilah shooed her daughter away and began scalding canning jars with water from the teakettle that was always set to heat on the wood cooking stove.

Helen felt like a canary set loose for the very first time. She took a bucket off the back porch peg, scrubbed clean and waiting for an afternoon of blackberry picking. She would harvest everything in sight, and, of course, she would eat a few, just to see if all that work was worthwhile.

Mostly she didn't wear shoes in the summertime, but Delilah was firm about wearing shoes near the creek. People weren't the only living things that enjoyed the shade and the water. Delilah had seen copperheads and rattlers on the creek bank, and she made sure her children were protected, even if last year's shoes pinched their toes. Helen donned her only pair of shoes, pushing hard to get her feet inside, then set off, limping, toward the creek.

The best patch of berries was upstream from the swimming hole. Even though it was nearly four o'clock, the sun was still beating down when she got there, and she was glad she'd worn an old straw hat to shade her eyes. Without even thinking about it, she checked for snakes and stepped farther into the brambles when she saw there were none. The warm, ripe berries slid off the canes and into her bucket as if they'd known all along she was coming for them. The bucket was a third full before she moved on. When she had half a bucket she decided to take a break and wade a little to cool down. Hiking her dress over her thighs, she tied knots in the hem as she moved down to the creek; then she removed her shoes and placed them carefully on a rock.

The water was cool, not cold, but she didn't care. The silky creek bottom oozed between her toes as she made her way downstream.

The summer had been a good one for the local farmers, making up a little for last summer's terrible drought, which had affected even the most prosperous. The creek was higher than Helen remembered in her lifetime, although here it was only knee-deep. Cuddy had made sure all his children knew how to swim, and even when she tripped over a rock and nearly went under, she only laughed.

She'd thought she might find her brothers at the swimming hole, but there was no noise coming from that direction. If she had been older and free for the whole afternoon, that was where she would have gone. Delilah had forbidden her to swim there alone, but she hoped that one day soon her mother would relent. Then she would really have a reason to hurry through her summer chores.

Humming, she stepped on stones and leaped over a log that blocked her passage. Just as she was about to turn back and finish picking, she heard a noise.

"Psst."

Helen stopped and listened. The woods along the creek were alive with birds and small animals rustled in the undergrowth. But this was different. The noise was more insistent.

"Psst. Over here..."

Startled she turned in the direction she thought the noise—now a voice—was coming from.

"Somebody there?" she called.

"Don't look."

That made no sense to her. Helen searched harder. "Who's there?"

"I said don't look!"

Since she'd yet to see anything anyway, she dropped her gaze to the creek. "Who's talking to me?"

"Listen, you gotta help me."

The voice was new to her, and the accent very unlike the accents of people in the valley. It was flatter, more nasal, and the way the boy pronounced vowels took some getting used to.

"I don't gotta do a single thing," she said. "Except listen to my mama and daddy and say my prayers. And who's that talking to me, anyway? Why're you hiding?"

"I gotta."

"No reason I can think of." She peeked from under her lashes. "Cept'in you done something wrong and don't want nobody to see."

"I ain't done nothing. Just, just got into some trouble, that's all."

She lifted her head and peered around. "What kinda trouble?"

"Don't look!"

"You tell me why, then maybe I won't!"

There was a long silence. She'd just about decided he was gone when he spoke at last.

"They took my clothes."

The voice was so soft that at first she wasn't sure she'd heard him right. "Clothes?"

"Ain't that what I just said?"

"Who? Who done it?"

This time the silence went uninterrupted. But Helen, the best at sums in her schoolroom, had put two and two together. "Who are you, anyway?"

"Fate."

For a moment she thought he was joking. Maybe he thought this was some sort of game where he pretended to be something no person could rightly be. Then she realized what he meant. "Fate? That boy what's living with the danged old Claibornes now? You that Fate?"

"Uh-huh." He sounded miserable, as if "danged old Claibornes" didn't even begin to describe his new family.

"Fate, huh?" She wondered what fate had brought him here to the creek and grinned at her own silent joke.

"You gonna help or not?"

Helen realized she was enjoying herself. Surely this was the most exciting thing that would happen to her for weeks and weeks. She knew better than to dismiss it lightly. "First you gotta tell me what happened," she said. "All of it. Purt near every bit of it, anyway."

"They made me come, told me I could swim."

"Who's they?" She thought she knew, but she asked anyway.

"Gus. He's my cousin. And a boy named Obed."

"How about Tom? He been here, too?"

"Nobody named Tom."

Helen thought that was probably good. When her father found out what Obed had done, only one Stoneburner boy would be begging for mercy tonight. This was just the kind of mischief Cuddy hated the most.

"So they brought you here," she said. "Then what?"

"They told me they always swum—" He didn't finish.

Considering the state he was in now, she knew what they'd told him. "Told you they always swum naked, didn't they?"

"Uh-huh."

"They was lying, you know. Got caught swimming like that one time and Mama near to took the skin off their bodies. She don't hold with it, there being girls on Fitch who might come along."

"Like you." He sounded absolutely miserable.

"You ain't see no bulls, have you?"

"Bulls?"

"You ain't swimming and avoiding something you were supposed to do, like going to church or helping a poor old widow woman?"

"What are you talking about?"

Clearly this was not going to be as exciting as the story that Becky had told at the quilt frame in the spring, but at least this one was happening to her. It was her job now to make sure that Fate didn't end up naked in front of half the world, like the boy in the story.

"You know what they did with your clothes?" she asked.

"You think they'd tell me?"

"Guess not." She pondered this. "Guess I'll have to get you some others, only it's not gonna be easy. My mama sees me, she won't let me go back outside. She'll make me stay inside and help with supper."

"Please, you gotta think of a way."

He sounded unhappy, but not afraid. And he wasn't whining. Nobody in the Stoneburner family was allowed to whine, and complaining was against the rules, as well—except maybe a little on important occasions. Fate just wanted his clothes so he could go about his business. And he didn't want to show the world every little piece of himself in the process.

"Since it's Monday, my mama did her washing today." She was putting together a plan now. She had seen her mother with a load of dry folded clothes. But she knew the routine. On a good day in the summer Delilah washed late in the morning because clothes dried quickly in the heat. The light clothes, their dresses, her father's shirts, dried first. Delilah folded them and took them inside to be ironed that evening when the weather cooled. But the heavier clothes, like overalls or the blue work pants her father wore at the feed store, stayed on the line until suppertime. If she was lucky, they would still be there.

"I'll be coming back," she said. "I won't leave you here. You best believe I'll help."

"I surely do appreciate it."

She couldn't think of anything else to say. Leaving the bucket behind she made her way toward the house, watching for her mother as she went. She stayed out of sight of the long kitchen window and hoped that Delilah was so busy pickling her string beans that she didn't have time to worry about her daughter.

She was nearly to the clothesline, palms sweating and breath coming swiftly, when she saw Obed and Gus. They were lying in the grass, gazing up at the clouds and laughing. Worse, there wasn't one piece of clothing left on the line. Delilah had been and gone with the whole load.

Anger shot through her. Obed had always been her hero, and even the crumbs of attention he tossed her way were treasured. Today, though, she saw him differently. Everybody knew that Gus had a mean streak, and now she was afraid her brother was taking after his friend. She thought it was about time Obed remembered he was just like everybody else.

She straightened her shoulders and started toward them. Neither boy saw her, and she was just about to tell them what she thought of them for playing this trick, when a better plan occurred to her. If she threatened them and insisted she would tell Cuddy if they didn't return Fate's clothes, she was afraid it might backfire. It was just like Gus to figure out some way to make this seem like it was her fault.

This newer plan was so different, so overwhelming, that for a moment she rejected it. Then she thought of poor Fate, alone behind a tree by the creek. Poor Fate, naked as a jaybird.

"Obed!" She forced herself to sound upset. "Obed, Gus. Oh, no, you gotta come quick."

Obed barely lifted his head. "What're you crowing about, Lenny Lou?"

"Crowing like some silly ole banty hen," Gus said. "Always thought you were an ole banty hen, Lenny."

She didn't react. "Obed, there's a boy down to the creek, and he's, he's. . ." She paused for effect and put her fist on her breastbone. "He's drowned. In the swimming hole, and I was just on my way to tell Mama."

Both boys sat up at the same moment and looked at each other. "Drowned?" Obed's deep voice squeaked back into adolescence. "Drowned?"

"Deader'n any doorknob."

"He can't be drowned. Said he swimmed."

Gus hissed at him. "Silent. Be silent!"

Obed was on his feet by now, and Gus was scrambling to his. "And he's got no clothes," Helen said tearfully. "Not so much as a stocking." She paused for effect. "What'll we do? I gotta go tell Mama."

"No!" Obed grabbed her arm. "No, you'll scare Mama all the way to Winchester and back. No, you come show me. There's something to tell her, that's what I'll do."

Helen let him drag her along. Gus was beside him, and the two were whispering, but she didn't care what they said. So far her plan was working just fine.

Minutes passed before they reached the creek and began to follow it toward the swimming hole. She sniffed periodically for effect, and wrung her hands a couple of times. From the corner of her eye she saw that Obed was white. Even Gus had lost his sneer, and honest fright shone from his eyes.

They reached the swimming hole. The water here was murky, and it was impossible to see to the bottom. Virginia's good red earth had made sure of that.

"Where?" Obed demanded. "Where is he?"

Helen wrung her hands again. She was becoming an expert. "He was right over there." She unclasped her hands long enough to point. "Hung up right there on that old log."

A felled tree hung over the side, grazing the surface. She knew that the boys jumped off of it when the water was high enough. Obed's eyes widened. "You're sure, Lenny? You're sure about this? He was really dead?"

She remembered how the hog they'd butchered in the fall had looked after her uncle shot him in the head. She gave an impassioned description. "His eyes were staring, like they was looking at something, but there weren't nothing to see. And he was stiff, you know, like nothing would bend no more." She cleared her throat, like she was trying not to cry.

"He's under there somewhere, that's for sure," Gus said. "We can just leave him there, can't we? Who's gonna know how he got there?"

"What do you mean?" Helen said. "How did he get there?"

Obed was already stripping off his overalls. "Lenny, you get outa here, only don't tell Mama. I'll tell her, I find anything. Promise me now? Promise you won't?"

"I oughta," she said. "She's gonna be so mad at me if I don't."

"Please?" His overalls were down to his waist and his undershirt was in a wad at his feet.

She nodded. He gave a sickly smile. "Now you go on."

She headed away, like she was in the worst of hurries to leave the scene.

About twenty yards away she stopped behind a big hickory tree that was flanked by tall undergrowth. She could hear the boys talking, but she couldn't hear a thing they were saying. Then she heard a splash.

"Hey..."

She whirled and saw a strange boy peeking at her from behind a sprawling nannyberry bush. She could only see his face and shoulders, but for a moment she stared. To her twelve-year-old eyes, Fate Henry was a fine figure indeed. Black curly hair, a strong, sloping nose and full lips. For a moment she couldn't say a thing.

"What're you doing?" he demanded.

"You'll see directly." Helen crept back the way she had come. Obed and Gus were so immersed in their search now that they didn't even think to look up to the bank. When they both dove under the water again she snatched their clothes, then went crashing through the brush back to where she'd left Fate.

"Here you go," she said, dropping the clothes just in front of the bush. "Put on whatever you want, then toss the rest way over there in the bushes. But you'd best hurry before they figure out what's going on."

He looked at the pile; then he looked at her. "What'll they do when they find their clothes are gone, do you suppose?"

She shrugged. "I don't aim to stay and find out. I just wish they'd end up in the churchyard naked as baby pigs, right there in front of everybody."

He cocked his head. She grinned; then, before he could ask for an explanation, she grabbed her berry bucket and her shoes and headed for home.

CHAPTER
10

Early Thursday afternoon, Helen plopped her housedress-and-sneaker-clad body on the porch swing and picked up a supermarket circular that had come in the morning's mail.

She fanned herself with it. "If there don't come a good rain soon, I'm going to stop moving, like an old clock that just run down and run down till there's no winding good enough."

Tessa knew it was just like her grandmother to find a practical use for the junk mail so that she wouldn't have to throw it away. Tessa and Nancy had taken to waiting until Helen's back was turned, scooping it off the rattan table beside the swing and spiriting it into the trash. They'd also secretly made a start on the huge mounds on Helen's desk in the dining room and in half a dozen laundry baskets beside it. The mail they'd uncovered there was just more of the same.

"I heard there was rain in the forecast." Tessa lowered herself to a chair beside the swing. Since the beginning of the week, she and her grandmother had taken breaks together every afternoon. Sometimes Nancy joined them, and sometimes she was too busy trying to run her Richmond life by cell phone or making quick trips back to the city. But the ritual was becoming important to Helen. Tessa could see that. She was someone who had spent her entire adult life pushing people away, but she was no longer keeping to the pattern.

"No rain can be enough." Helen sounded glum. "Corn's already gone. Even the trees are wilting. Those maples out there?" She nodded to the twin maples in front of the house. "Too many years of drought. They'll have to come down soon enough, unless things turn around."

"I can't imagine the house without those trees."

"Won't bother you none after I'm gone. You and your mama'll sell the old place without thinking twice anyway."

Tessa wondered if that was still true. She hadn't come to Toms Brook to forge new connections with her past. Most of the time she wished she could wipe the past clean and never be forced to confront it again. But in the two weeks she had been here, she had developed a reluctant attachment to her family's history. The Whitlocks had never interested her much, but the Stoneburners, despite poverty and sorrow, had struggled to make the best of what they'd been given. From Helen's brief descriptions, there had been love here, and strength.

"Just promise you won't sell off the family plot," Helen said, when Tessa didn't reassure her.

Tessa remembered that Helen had wanted Kayley to be buried on the hill behind the house with the Stoneburners. Tessa hadn't listened.

"There's room for me up there," Helen continued, her voice more strident. "Fate's there, and I want to be with him."

Tessa met her grandmother's eyes. "I'll make sure you're buried there. Don't worry."

Helen nodded once, as if the deal was set. Then she sat forward and peered out toward the road. "Who's that, do you suppose?"

Tessa followed her grandmother's gaze. A blue pickup had turned into the driveway. It bounced over ruts and sank into pot- holes before it stopped about twenty-five yards away.

The driver's door opened, and a girl came around the front, un- latching the hood and throwing it high. Steam poured from the en- gine, then began to dissipate.

"It's Cissy," Tessa said.

"Who?"

"Cissy." She couldn't remember the girl's last name. "The Cissy who lives at the Claiborne farm."

"She's getting big as a pumpkin."

In less than two weeks Cissy had gained weight, but Tessa thought it was only because the girl was slight and carrying the baby low. "I doubt she's in any danger of delivering it right here." She rose re- luctantly and walked to the steps to invite Cissy to join them.

Cissy waved, then, before Tessa could call to her, she went around the back of the truck, opened the back gate and lifted something out of the truck bed.

"Peaches." She held them out. "From Mr. and Mrs. Claiborne." She started toward them.

"What'd she say?" Helen demanded.

"It looks like the Claibornes have sent you peaches."

As Helen grumbled, Tessa went to meet the girl and lift the bas- ket from her arms. "You shouldn't be lifting anything this heavy, should you?"

"It's not so bad. Not a full bushel, on account of the drought." She smiled shyly at Tessa.

Tessa was struck by how appealing Cissy was. In a huge white maternity blouse and denim cutoffs that had probably belonged to a man with a potbelly, she looked tired and a bit too fragile for comfort. But her coloring was exquisite, and her complexion as fine grained and smooth as the peaches she carried. "How does all this hot weather agree with you?" Tessa asked.

"Oh, it seems worse than usual, I guess, 'cause the baby's heating things up to start with. But I just go about my business."

Tessa lowered her head and inhaled. "These smell wonderful. This is nice of Mr. and Mrs. Claiborne."

"The peaches are having a hard time of it this year. Not so many set fruit, and those what did, well, they're just shriveling up. But Mr. Claiborne says there's a good rain coming, and he knows those things."

"I hope he's right. Maybe it will help."

"Too late for the peaches, but it'll help the apples, for sure."

They had arrived at the porch. Cissy stepped back to let Tessa make the climb first, then she followed. Tessa set the basket on the porch. "Look at these, Gram. Aren't they pretty?"

Helen made a noise low in her throat that could mean almost anything. "Ron Claiborne's trying to butter me up for something. You just watch and see."

Cissy didn't appear to mind the insult. "No, ma'am, he told me, Cissy, you just take these peaches over to Mrs. Henry. And then he said—" She stopped. "I guess that's all he said."

"Ha! I just bet he said more. Gives me a bushel like this every year, just because I don't spray my own trees no more and get good peaches from them. I know he wants something."

Tessa understood this aversion to the Claibornes better now than she had before her grandmother had told the story of her first meeting with her future husband. "Gram, is Ron Claiborne Gus Claiborne's son by any chance? Is that why you're so rude to him?"

"Gus Claiborne never had a son. Ron's his cousin's son. Gus went off to California after the war and never came home again. Good riddance to bad rubbish. The cousins just moved on in once Sammy died."

"Then do you have something against Ron Claiborne's father?" Helen grumbled.

"Then you have no real reason to dislike him?" Tessa asked. "If I'm right, Mom and I are some kind of distant relative of his."

"Not a one of them Claibornes was as good to my Fate as they should have been."

"Mr. Claiborne picked these himself," Cissy said. "Wanted good ones for you, even if there ain't so many. I can't think what he'd want in return. He has everything he needs."

"Probably wants my land. Figures if he's nicey nice, then maybe Tessa here will sell it to him when I'm gone."

Cissy shook her head. "I don't want to argue, Miss Henry, but truth is, I heard him telling Zeke he's already leasing too much extra land these days and ain't got enough money to plant or graze it all. He's afraid he's gonna have to sell some of what he owns one of these days just to stay ahead. Lots of folks in the city want a piece of land out here to build a summer place."

"Well now, there's another good reason not to like that man," Helen said. "He'll have a fight on his hands, he tries selling bits and pieces of his land to developers. I can guarantee that. Don't need a bunch of senators out here playing gentleman farmer. No, we sure don't."

"He says just about the same thing."

Tessa tried to head off more discussion about the strengths and weaknesses of Ron Claiborne. "Everyone's taking a beating in this economy. We'll enjoy the peaches, Cissy. It was nice of you to bring them with you."

"I was glad to. Can't drive much farther than this in that old truck. It just about blows up after a mile or two." She stood quietly, arms wrapped around her huge belly. Tessa realized she was waiting for an invitation to sit.

Helen issued it. "Well, take a load off your feet, girl. Tessa will get us some tea."

"That would be awfully nice." Cissy looked around the porch, as if assessing what seat might be free. She chose the right one and lowered herself gingerly into an old metal chair with a raggedy cushion.

Tessa, who knew that fetching tea was a direct order, left for the kitchen. When she returned with a tray, Helen was lecturing the girl, complete with waving index finger.

"You got to plan, and you got to be accurate," Helen said, ignoring Tessa. "You can't just start cutting and sewing any old which way."

Cissy didn't seem upset. "I just don't know how to do it right. I decided I'd better just start somewhere or I'd never start at all."

Tessa set the tray down beside her grandmother and immediately saw the source of this discussion. Spread out on Cissy's lap was a square of fabric, at least it was supposed to be a square. It was longer on one side than the other, and made up of four uneven patches of different shades of gold.

Helen lifted it as Tessa watched and turned it to the wrong side. "You're sewing by hand?"

"I don't have a machine. Mrs. Claiborne's is busted, or I could use that. But she says it's older than the hills and not worth fixing." She smiled a little. "I think she's afraid she gets it fixed, she might have to use it. She hates to sew."

"At least she can cook," Helen said grudgingly. "Marian Claiborne makes the best sweet potato pie in the county, and she won't share her recipe with nobody. She's made an enemy or two over that, I can tell you."

"She's kind to me. She's never said a bad word, not even…" She didn't finish.

Tessa caught Helen's eye and gave a slight shake of her head. She did not want to encourage the young woman to bare her soul. They had enough to handle as it was.

"Anyway, I'm sewing with a plain old needle and thread. But I guess I'm not doing a very good job," Cissy said.

"What is it?" Tessa asked. She took a glass and handed it to Cissy. "Sweet tea okay?"

"Oh, yes. Thank you." Cissy took it and held the glass against her flushed cheek. "It's going to be a baby quilt. At least, I hope it is."

Tessa handed a glass to her grandmother and took her own. "I like the colors. Did they remind you of Gram's dahlia quilt?"

"That's why I picked gold."

Helen dropped the quilt block back in Cissy's lap. "Well, you're gonna have to do better than that, if you plan on being able to use it."

"I know. I guess I'll tear it out and try something different. I'll keep at it."

Helen was silent. Her mouth worked, like she was chewing the inside of her lip. "You want some advice?"

Cissy's expression changed, like the sun coming out on a gloomy day. "Would you have time for a little?"

"I don't give lessons. Never did, never will."

"Yes, ma'am, I understand. But maybe you could just tell me what I should do next?"

"Well, first, I wouldn't take out the stitches. I'd throw this away. You've stretched it and it's going to fray, besides."

Cissy looked uncomfortable, but she nodded.

"You got more fabric?"

"Zeke told me to go ahead and buy a yard of every piece I liked."

"Good. Did you wash it?"

"Well, no, I didn't know—"

"Then that's what you do next. Wash it good, and dry it, just the way you'll dry the baby's quilt."

"Oh. So it won't shrink later?"

"Then you iron it good, put a little starch on it if you can, then bring it here and I'll show you how to cut it nice and straight."

Cissy looked like someone had just given her a week in Tahiti. "You would do that?"

"Said I would, didn't I?"

Cissy got to her feet, clearly afraid she might wear out her welcome. "That's so nice of you. I'll do exactly what you said."

Cissy turned to Tessa, but before she spoke, her gaze fell to the book beside Tessa's chair. It was *Tess of the D'Urbervilles*, the novel

Tessa intended to use with her advanced placement English class in the fall. She hadn't taught the novel for a while, and she was rereading it so she could make lists of questions for discussion. She liked to switch books frequently to lessen the chance students would borrow notes and viewpoints from upperclassmen. That way she only had to worry about the Internet.

"Tess," Cissy read upside down. "That's your name. Is it a good story?"

"A classic. I teach it to my high-school classes."

Cissy lifted it and looked at the girl on the cover. "She's pretty, isn't she? And old-fashioned."

"It was written a long time ago."

Cissy didn't relinquish it. "That's what I miss most about school. Reading. You know? I always did love to read, only there weren't so many books around unless I was at school."

"What about the library?" Tessa asked the question without thinking. "You could check out as many as you wanted."

"I tried that, once I came here. But I couldn't get back into town often enough to turn them in without paying a fine. And I didn't want to bother Mr. and Mrs. Claiborne. Zeke, he'd go, but he's so tired time the day is done, I don't ask."

Cissy smiled, as if sharing a joke. "Lots of farm magazines at the Claibornes' house, though. Then there's the *World Book Encyclopedia*. I read all the way through C last month, till I figured out that Czechoslovakia isn't a country anymore, and the Iron Curtain came down a while ago. Figured I'd better find something newer to read or I'd have everything all wrong."

It was the longest speech the girl had made in Tessa's presence, and despite not wanting to be, she was touched. Perhaps if she'd suspected Cissy was hinting, she would feel differently. But the girl didn't seem a bit manipulative. And after years of teaching, Tessa could spot the difference.

"I could loan you the book," Tessa said reluctantly, "but I'll warn you, it's not for the faint of heart. Hardy's not easy to understand. As many times as I've read it, I always find something new to think about."

"Then it must be good." Cissy held it out to her. "But I didn't mean to sound like I wanted to take it home. I—"

Tessa pushed it back toward her. "Go ahead. Just bring it back when you're finished." Tessa suspected Cissy would be bringing it back unread soon enough.

"Well, that's so nice of you." Cissy clasped the book to her chest. "And, Miss Henry, I'll bring that cloth over, just like you said."

Helen harrumphed.

Cissy said goodbye, and both women watched her descend the stairs, slam the hood on the truck and drive away.

"I don't hold with that girl living in sin with the Claiborne boy," Helen said, as if to set Tessa straight. "But I'm a Christian woman, and she'll need something to cover that baby of hers. That's the only reason I offered to help her."

Tessa would have smiled, only she was too busy kicking herself for giving the book to Cissy. She didn't need a teenager so hungry for love and attention that she had chosen a house filled with feuding women to give it to her. She didn't know what had possessed her to help the girl that way, but whatever it was, it worried her.

Helen never would have guessed that chunks of fish belonged in a salad. Tomatoes, yes. Cucumbers, yes. But Nancy's supper salad had potatoes and chunks of tuna fish, even some salty kind of olive Helen had never tasted before. She was about to say something when she caught the expression on her daughter's face. Nancy looked worried. Helen hadn't seen her that way in too many years to count. These days, Nancy had all the answers. Only, maybe she didn't really.

"This dish got a name?" Helen asked.

"Salad Niçoise." Nancy passed a basket of rolls and tried to look nonchalant.

"Never had fish in a salad before, but I guess it's no different than having it sitting right beside one. Goes to the same place."

"It looks great, Mom," Tessa said. "I don't think I could have eaten anything hot. If this weather doesn't break tonight, I'm going to sleep outside in the nude."

"You'd be eaten alive," Helen said, taking two rolls and passing them to her granddaughter. "Just like Gus and Obed the day I stole their clothes. By the time they got up their courage to come back to the house, they was covered with welts, the likes of which I never did see again. And that was all that was covering them, too, except some vines they'd wrapped round and round their private parts."

Nancy laughed. "You were a rotten little girl."

"More power to you," Tessa said.

They ate in silence for a few minutes. Helen nearly cracked a tooth on an olive pit—just what was the point of leaving them inside?—but she was surprised at how good it all was. Even the rolls tasted fresh, although she knew for a fact Nancy had bought them frozen and warmed them up.

"So, just what did you all do today?" she asked, when the salad had made a substantial enough dent in her appetite to make conversation possible again. She watched her daughter and granddaughter exchange glances. She knew they didn't want to make a report, in case she got mad about whatever they'd thrown away.

"I got the new curtains up in the living room," Nancy said.

Helen had seen them. She couldn't believe it was the same room. Nancy had even rearranged the furniture so that when two people sat down together, they could see each other head on.

"What about you?" she asked Tessa.

"I worked in the attic this morning before it got hot, then I got a start on some paperwork."

Helen carefully sucked on an olive. "What kind of paperwork?"

"Little of this, little of that."

That was code, Helen knew, for "I threw away everything I touched."

"You just stay away from my desk in the dining room," Helen warned. "I don't want you touching a thing on it."

No one spoke.

Helen looked up, a frown deepening the wrinkles on her forehead. "I mean it," she said more forcefully. "There's stuff there nobody need concern herself with."

Tessa sighed and put down her fork. "Gram, that's where I was working. But I promise I didn't throw away a single thing except your old junk mail."

Despite the heat, Helen felt cold. "What junk mail?"

"You know. Advertisements, coupons that expired months ago, offers that are too good to be true. Junk."

Helen was on her feet before the final consonant sounded. She hurried out of the room, sorry she couldn't run anymore. As far as she could tell, growing old didn't have one thing in its favor.

In the dining room—where nobody'd had a meal in decades—the old secretary where she kept all her papers was now as neat as a pin. She didn't know when Tessa had cleared it out, but Helen suspected it had happened when she went upstairs to quilt after Cissy's visit.

She sorted frantically through the cubbyholes. Bills in one, up to date coupons in another, a form letter from her church pastor inviting everybody to an annual meeting and potluck supper in the third. She opened the top drawer, where neat piles of booklets and receipts and canceled checks sat side by side in organized glory. She opened the second drawer and found fresh paper, pens and other office supplies.

"Gram?"

Helen slammed the empty bottom drawer and faced her granddaughter. "What did you do with them?"

Tessa looked wary. "With what?"

Helen didn't answer. She pushed past and started for the front door. She knew what Tessa had done with the "junk" mail. She had tossed it in the horse trailer. All Helen had to do now was find it, bring it back inside, and store it under lock and key.

Tessa caught up with her and grabbed her arm. "What's the problem? What's missing?"

Helen was too upset to talk. She wrenched her arm free and started down the porch steps. She was halfway to the spot where the horse trailer had been sitting when she realized it wasn't there anymore.

"Where's the trailer? What have you done with it?"

"Zeke came and got it. He said he'd take it to the landfill and bring it back tomorrow morning."

Helen knew that must have happened while she was upstairs, too. "Then you just get in your car and take me over to the Claiborne house, you hear? Maybe he hasn't dumped it yet."

Tessa looked calm. Only a faint tightness around her mouth showed that she was not. "I'm sorry, but he was going to dump it on the way home. He had an old chest freezer in his pickup that had to go, as well."

Helen couldn't believe it. "Then we're going to the landfill."

"It closes at four. Zeke mentioned that."

Helen had known that, but she was too rattled now to think straight.

Nancy came to stand in the doorway. "Mama, get hold of yourself. Tell us what's wrong."

"My maps. My danged maps!"

Tessa looked perplexed. "I didn't throw away maps, Gram. I'm sure I didn't. But we can always buy you more, if you need them. I——"

"Hush!" Helen was trying hard to think. What would happen if she went to the landfill after hours?

"Whatever is bothering you, you don't have to handle it alone," Nancy said calmly. "That's why we're here."

"You're here to make a mess out of things! You think I need this kind of help? Everything. Gone!"

"We're just clearing out the clutter, Gram," Tessa said.

"That wasn't no clutter. That was my maps."

"What kind of maps?" Nancy crossed the room and rested a hand on her mother's shoulder. "Whatever it is, we'll fix it."

"Danged right you'll fix it!" Helen realized now there was only one choice left. "Change your clothes and get ready to dig. And I won't be taking no for an answer, so don't even give it a try."

"Nobody, Mama, absolutely nobody buries money anymore. What were you thinking?" Nancy slammed her heel against the old shovel and felt it sink another few inches in the ground.

Helen was digging, too, and not far away, Tessa was doing the same.

"I was thinking it was my money and I could do whatever I wanted with it." Helen slammed her foot against the shovel in rhythm to her words.

"It could have been making money for you in the bank or the market. Billy could have made sure you made the right investment decisions." Nancy hit a tree root and realized this couldn't be the right place. She abandoned the hole, shoveling the dirt she'd displaced back into it, and made a half-hearted attempt to tamp it down.

"You think I don't know what can happen? You think I wasn't born yet when the market crashed and the banks closed down and some people in these parts lost everything they had? Least my family didn't have nothing much to begin with. But Mama never kept what little butter and egg money she had anywhere but right here in the ground."

Nancy moved her shovel a yard away and began to dig again. "You always used a bank when I was growing up. You helped me start a savings account."

"Times were all right then. Times aren't so good now. I know the difference."

Nancy knew this was just another example of why her mother shouldn't be living alone or living in this house. She had lost the ability to make rational decisions. Now, it seemed, she'd lost all her savings, too.

Twilight had come and gone, and darkness was settling. Even the moon seemed to have left for parts unknown, and the stars were obscured by thick cloud cover. Helen had insisted they wait until darkness to begin to dig, and nothing Tessa or Nancy had said could dissuade her. She hadn't wanted anyone to see where the money was hidden.

Another example of irrational thinking.

"Try to visualize your map," Tessa said.

Helen slammed her shovel deeper. "If I could see it in my head, I wouldn't need it on paper, would I?"

"Do you know how much money we're looking for?"

"Enough, Missy. That's all you need to know."

"And you're sure you hid three different tins? Not more or less?" Nancy said.

"You think I don't know how many I buried?"

Nancy's temper was growing shorter. "Yes, as a matter of fact, that's exactly what I think. You don't know where they are, you admitted that. And you didn't think to put the location of the tins somewhere safe. No, you had to scrawl it on the back of some ad from Publishers Clearing House promising you'd won big money."

"You think I wanted it to be easy, so somebody could just waltz in and find it?"

"I think *this* would be easier if you two would stop fighting," Tessa said.

"Who said it ought to be easy?" Helen demanded. "You're the one that threw my papers away."

"I'm the one who didn't know my grandmother was drawing

treasure maps to her life savings on a four-year-old circular. You are right about that."

Nancy thought her daughter was beginning to sound irritated, too. They had worked all day, and Tessa had done a wonderful job of organizing her grandmother's papers. Now, instead of going to bed early, as she usually did, she was out in the sultry night, digging holes.

"You never asked," Helen said.

"Gram, that's not exactly the kind of question any reasonable person thinks of."

"You're saying I'm unreasonable?"

Tessa stopped and leaned on her shovel. "*This* is unreasonable. You knew we were cleaning and clearing. Why didn't you say something then? Why didn't you get the maps and store them up in your room?"

"How was I to know you would go through my private papers?"

"They were not private papers! It was junk mail. J...U...N...K!"

For a long moment, the only sound was the usual nighttime symphony of crickets and frogs.

"Well, you don't have to get so uppity," Helen said at last.

Nancy thought her mother sounded hurt. She could feel a tightness in her own throat, a need to say something, but nothing was there.

"I'm sorry." Tessa sighed. "It's this heat."

"Damn heat," Nancy said. "That's what it is."

"You'd think I did this on purpose, the way you two have carried on," Helen said. But she didn't sound angry. She sounded fragile and worried.

"We'll find the money." Tessa started to dig again. "We've got the rest of the summer."

"And then what?" Helen said. "You'll use this against me. You think I don't know? I can hear the lawyers gathering up their papers now. I can see the judge shaking her head, and the little men in white suits coming for me."

Nancy couldn't help herself. She began to giggle. "Little men in white suits?"

"You think this is funny, Nanny? You think I like knowing you're going to put me somewhere I don't want to be?"

"There *are* no little men in white suits, Mama. And hell, if there were, they could help us dig. I think we ought to call anybody who'll come and help."

"Don't cuss."

"Hell. Hell. Hell!"

There was a frog-filled pause again, then something rattled in Helen's throat. "I said, don't cuss." The noise rattled again.

"I am way too old for you to wash out my mouth with soap."

The rattle got louder, and suddenly it was a real belly laugh. "Don't you bet on it, girl! I'm still twice as big as you."

"You two!" Tessa sounded as though she was smiling. "How did you live together all those years? You must have driven each other nuts."

"Just the way you and I did," Nancy said. She was laughing now, too. "We were never meant to be together, the three of us."

"A celestial miscalculation," Tessa said. She was laughing, too.

"God doesn't make mistakes," Helen said. "But sometimes He mixes things up just to see what happens. Keeps things interesting."

"Well, it is interesting," Nancy agreed. "It's always been interesting. And I should know best, because I'm right in the middle of it. Mama, you're on one side pulling at me, Tessa, you've always been on the other. And I was never just right for either of you."

The skies chose that moment to open. There was no flash of lightning, no crack of thunder. One moment the only moisture in the air was the fierce humidity of a Shenandoah summer night. Then sheets of rain were gliding over them like a river tumbling toward the sea.

"Rain!" Helen shouted. "Rain at last!"

Nancy thought about her hair, fast plastering itself to her scalp.

She thought of the crisp linen blouse that was now dishrag limp, the sharply pleated dry-clean-only pants, the mascara that would run like claw marks down her cheeks.

She threw her hands toward the sky. "Rain!" Before she realized what she was doing, she dropped her shovel and launched herself forward to grab her mother's hand. "Rain." She began to dance.

"Quit that. Just quit that now!" Helen insisted. But she didn't pull away.

"Tessa?" Nancy held out her other hand. "Come here. We're going to do a rain dance."

Tessa stood rooted to the spot, staring at her mother and grand-mother.

"It's an order," Nancy said sharply. "Get that skinny butt of yours over here right now, and dance with your mother and grandmother."

Tessa moved slowly, as if she thought she might be nearing a lu-natic asylum. But she took Nancy's hand.

"You're the one needs the men in the white coats," Helen said.

"Rain, rain!" Nancy began to pull them back and forth, forward and backwards. "Kick those feet, ladies. Like this!" She did a grapevine step left over from an aerobics dancing class she had taken to keep herself fit and trim.

"Mom, this is odd behavior," Tessa said. But she was following closely, kicking her legs like a Rockette when it was time.

Helen tried to pull away, but Nancy wouldn't let her. "Come on, Mama, you can do it. When was the last time you danced?"

"None of your business."

"Dance with us now."

Helen harrumphed, but she began to move. Tentatively, grudg-ingly, but she was definitely moving.

The rain picked up. Tessa pulled them to the right, and they began to move around the fruitless holes they'd dug, weaving back and forth between holes and trees. Dancing, most likely, on some portion of Helen's life savings.

"Rain!" Nancy shouted again. "Thank you, God, for rain!"

"That's the first real prayer I've heard from you in a long time," Tessa said.

Exhausted, they stopped at last, in a small circle. Tessa grabbed her grandmother's other hand, and the three women, dripping now, sodden to the bone, stared at each other through rain-beaded lashes.

Finally, one by one, they dropped hands, but they didn't move apart.

"We'll find the money, Gram," Tessa said at last.

"I won't need it where you're going to send me."

Nancy did something she couldn't remember doing since she was a little girl. She put her arms around her mother and hugged her hard. Wet clothes sucked at wet clothes, and water drained down her legs. "Nobody's sending you anywhere," she said. "We'll make all our decisions together, Mama."

Helen frowned and nodded. But a frown in the middle of a cloudburst got washed away quickly.

For a moment, just the briefest moment, Helen's arms went around her daughter. For an even briefer moment, she squeezed.

CHAPTER
11

Tessa wasn't certain when her whole emotional life had begun to revolve around Mothers Against Drunk Driving. She stayed far away from the organization's victim support services, but in the years since Kayley's death, she had immersed herself at every other level.

She had begun her volunteer work with MADD by asking restaurants near her home if they would consider joining Northern Virginia's designated driver program. She persuaded several to offer free nonalcoholic drinks and a pep talk to one person at each table who agreed not to drink and drive that night. There were still restaurants where she wasn't particularly welcome because of the pressure she had applied.

After that, she had trained and worked as a court monitor, observing DUI cases and reporting back to the local and national offices. Now most of the county courthouse personnel knew her by name, even though she had graduated to training other monitors and didn't make as many personal appearances.

She organized victim impact panels, haunted shopping malls to present red ribbons to holiday shoppers who agreed not to drink and drive, solicited gifts of used cars to help fund MADD's programs. But everyone knew that Tessa's most important contribution was her unflagging devotion to administration. She was adept at finding grant money and writing proposals. She could organize phone trees, update websites, send bulk mailings over the Internet with the flip of her index finger.

The care she had once lavished on her family and students now went into phone calls and file folders, but she had still made a few friends along the way.

"Tessa! Did you tell anybody you were coming in this afternoon?" Sandy Stewart, the local chapter's dark-haired, fair-skinned program manager, gave Tessa a bear hug as soon as she walked into the MADD office. This was Tessa's first trip back to the city and the MADD office after the weeks in Toms Brook.

"I didn't plan to come. I wasn't even sure you'd still be here." Tessa gave the Amazonian Sandy an obligatory pat on the back before she pulled away. "But I had some bank business to take care of, and some shopping. I ended up nearby." She didn't add that she'd spent an hour at a local quilt shop getting tips and books on restoring old quilts. If she opened that door, Sandy would charge right through it, and Tessa knew she would have to tell the whole wedding ring quilt story.

"Can you stay?" Sandy looked at her watch. "At least until it's time to close up here? We can hit Starbucks for a latte."

"I thought I'd clear out my cubbyhole and see if there's anything I need to take care of. I'll be here a little while."

"The paper's been piling up. The Sisk Foundation turned down our grant proposal, but they'll be evaluating a new round next month and suggested some changes we could make to increase our chances."

Tessa was disappointed. The Sisk grant would have provided money to train high-school teachers on new classroom tactics to discourage drinking and driving. But the idea was good, and they would find a way to make sure it was funded.

"I'll take the changes with me and look them over," she promised.

"You just let me know when you're ready to go, and I'll close up shop for the day." The office was small, and six-foot-tall Sandy carefully made her way back to her desk, menacing anything that wasn't tied down. It was late enough in the afternoon that no one else was there.

Tessa cleared out her cubbyhole, not surprised by the amount of mail, annotated articles and memos that had stacked up in her absence. Most likely none of it was vital. The staff and most of the volunteers knew that she would be away for the summer, and they had her cell phone number in case her input or participation was crucial. Going through the clutter now would just make room for the next installment.

She took the stack of papers to a table in the back where she and the other volunteers usually worked, and made herself at home. In the background she could hear the rise and fall—mostly the rise—of Sandy's voice on the telephone as she made the final calls of the day.

Tessa sorted the papers into stacks, although her mind wasn't really on the task. She tried not to lie to herself, although sometimes it was the only way she made it through the day, but she knew that coming here had been a lie of sorts. She hadn't headed back to Toms Brook after her errands, and for once, MADD hadn't figured in the decision.

She missed Mack. She wanted to see him, and she hoped that she could catch him at home before she went back, perhaps even for a quick dinner.

She hadn't seen her husband for three weeks, not since he had dropped off her suitcase and told her that he had reached his limit with their relationship. Most of the time she had tried to put him out of her mind. He had called her occasionally. She had called him occasionally. They had talked about who should service their air conditioner, and whether they should renew their subscription to *Newsweek*. He had reported on his mother's latest boyfriend, and she had updated him on the treasure hunt for Helen's savings— one tin found, two to go.

Although she was realistic enough to know that his ultimatum must be resounding somewhere inside her, she had been careful to push it out of her thoughts. Sometimes she tried to imagine a life without Mack, what she would do and where she would go, just to prepare herself for a future that seemed inevitable. More often, she did nothing.

Tessa realized she was staring at a pink message slip, had been staring at it for some time. Maybe she was borrowing trouble to seek Mack out tonight, but was she really ready to give up a marriage that had once seemed nearly ideal? In the past three years she had taught herself a dozen ways to avoid the pain of Kayley's death. Was this just another? No husband equaled fewer reminders of her daughter?

She had to know. She was almost certain she wasn't ready to endure the marriage counseling Mack was insisting on, but she had to know if he was as adamant about that as he seemed. Perhaps there could be compromises as they continued to feel their way back into a world where Kayley no longer existed.

She set the message on top of the "to do" pile, then she realized the content still hadn't registered. She lifted it off the pile once more and forced herself to read it.

Someone who obviously didn't know or remember that she was out of town for the summer had scrawled a name and number across the surface, finishing with "important." Underlined. Frowning, she pulled the telephone a little closer, punched the button for a line that wouldn't conflict with Sandy's and lifted the receiver.

Mack wasn't sure why he had picked this particular restaurant for dinner with Erin. Siam Palace was one of Tessa's favorites, and it was close enough to their home that they ate here often. Kayley had never liked Thai food, so there were few memories of her here, but the place practically reeked of Tessa.

He wondered if he was lonely for his wife, that by coming here—even with another woman—he was trying to get closer to her. That seemed perverse and distinctly unattractive, but he wasn't certain it wasn't true. All he knew for sure was that Erin had mentioned a yen for Thai food, and Siam Palace had slipped past his tongue.

"So glad to see you, Mr. Mack." Frankie, the proprietor, honored him with a grin. He was a handsome man whose taste in clothing ran toward jewel-toned shirts open at the neck and dark pants. The restaurant was unpretentious, even plain, but the food was some of the best in Northern Virginia. The Friday night business alone could have kept the place afloat.

"Couldn't stay away," Mack assured him. "You have a table for two?"

"Mrs. Mack, she's coming, too?"

For a moment Mack didn't know what to say. Again he wondered what bad judgment had brought him here. "No, it's a business dinner."

Frankie led him to a window table. There was little to see except parking lot and traffic, but Mack took advantage of it so that he wouldn't have to answer any more questions.

When the server made her first stop, he ordered iced tea and some of the excellent *kanom jeeb* that were Tessa's favorite. She ate the same way she did most things, sparingly, gracefully, with concentrated appreciation. The bite-sized dumplings, with their delicately explosive flavor, were right up her alley.

Erin still hadn't arrived by the time his iced tea did, nor even by the time the *kanom jeeb* came out of the kitchen. He wondered if she had gotten lost, and just as he was about to look for a phone, she appeared in the doorway. She wore stretch jeans, and a bright blue tank top covered by an unbuttoned white shirt. She looked crisp and cool, and he wondered just how quickly Erin would melt if he kissed her.

He rose, not flustered, but disturbed by the thought. He wasn't surprised that sex was on his mind. He'd gone without for weeks, and before that he might as well have. Tessa, once so responsive that she could climax after the briefest foreplay, hadn't had an orgasm in months. She was stiff and unyielding when he touched her, and most of the time intimacy seemed more of an effort than a release.

He stepped around the table, took Erin's hands in his and kissed her cheek. Just over her shoulder he saw Frankie watching. Mack wondered if he imagined Frankie's disapproval.

"I'm so sorry I was late." Erin let him help her into her chair. "There was an accident on the beltway, and I was stuck in traffic. I was afraid you might not wait. I couldn't reach you on the cell phone."

"I left it at home this morning by mistake. Don't worry, I knew you'd be here." Erin, like Tessa, was completely reliable.

He realized that was the second time in a minute he had compared Erin to his wife.

"The two cars looked like they were totaled. There were a little boy and his mother standing by the police cars. They were both crying." She sighed. "I hope no one was killed."

Mack wondered if alcohol was lurking in that picture. One too many after-work drinks?

"Anyway, I'm starving," Erin said. "What's good here?"

"Everything. I ordered an appetizer. It just came. You'll have time to look over the menu before it gets cold."

She picked up the menu Frankie had left at her place and scanned it quickly before she put it down again. "So how are you?"

"Working too hard." And he was. He had spent the entire day driving from D.C. to Baltimore, then back again, trying to track down three character witnesses for a client who was about to go to trial. It was the kind of job he generally hired others to do, but he had needed a personal feel for the way these three witnesses lived and how reliable they might be. Not having the cell phone had made his day that much harder.

"You do look tired." Erin leaned forward. "It's hard without your wife at home, isn't it?"

"Not as hard as it sounds. When she's home she's not home."

"She's been through a lot."

Mack heard a dozen things behind the simple words. *Maybe it's not time to give up. I don't want you if you're bringing Tessa along with you. Are you sure, Mack, that you don't want to give your marriage more time? Because I'll wait.*

Or possibly he'd heard that last part wrong, and Erin was really saying that she wouldn't wait, so he'd better be sure of his options.

"The death of a child is one of the hardest things a marriage can undergo." Erin's tone was warm, compassionate, and he was sure he heard something more in it.

"It may well have brought this one to its end," Mack said, feeling for his words. "I'll know by the time summer's over."

Erin was feeling her way, too. It was obvious in her voice. "Mack, it's easy, when two people are sharing their feelings as closely as we've shared ours over the past years, to mistake the warmth we feel for each other for something it's not."

He looked up, and he knew Erin was trying to give him an out, to tell him that he still had that escape route if he wanted to take it.

"Are we laying our cards on the table?" He waited until Frankie took Erin's order before he continued. "Are you trying to keep me from making a mistake? Or trying to tell me there's nothing developing between us?"

Her fair skin colored a soft rose. "This is so hard."

"Take your time."

"I know better than to become emotionally involved with another member of the group, particularly a married one. It's dangerous for the organization."

"I see."

She looked up from her placemat. "You don't. I've asked Candace Grant to take over the jobs I volunteered for. She's warm and caring."

"And she's not involved with me."

She smiled a little. "I sure hope she isn't."

"I can't ask you to do that, Erin. I'll back off."

She reached across the table and touched the back of his hand. "Don't."

"I don't know where this is going. I don't know for sure that my marriage is over. I can't make any promises. I can't ask you for anything."

"I realize that, and I'm not rooting for your marriage to end. But in case it does, I'd like to be ready to test those waters."

He covered her hand with his. And that was when he looked up and saw Tessa standing five feet away, watching him.

His hand had already turned cold before he removed it. He stood and beckoned to Tessa. Her expression gave nothing away, but that had become increasingly true in the past three years. She had always been self-contained. These days she was hermetically sealed.

"What are you doing here?" He tried to sound welcoming. He wasn't sure he succeeded.

"That's the question I should be asking," she said pleasantly. He heard volumes behind it.

"You didn't tell me you were coming back to town. Is everything okay out in Toms Brook?"

"Fine. I had errands. I've been trying to call you all day, but your cell phone was turned off."

"I left it home this morning by mistake." He thought of all the mornings Tessa had trooped out to the car to hand him something he'd forgotten, just as he was pulling out of their driveway. His briefcase. His phone. Library books he had promised to return. She was the more organized of the two of them, the detail person. And he was the one who saw the bigger picture.

"I know," she said. "I went home to see if I could find you there. And I saw the phone on your desk."

Mack realized he had left Erin sitting at the table looking enormously uncomfortable. He introduced her, and Tessa looked down.

"Mack has mentioned you often," Tessa said. "In connection with Compassionate Friends. I know he thinks highly of you." She paused just a moment too long. "Very highly."

The words were measured, polite, and if he hadn't known better, he would have thought they were kind. But Erin understood the last two for what they were, and her cheeks colored again.

"Tessa, join us," Mack made an attempt to pull out a chair, but she waved him away.

"I already called in an order, and Frankie's got it ready for me up front. I was just here to pick it up."

"Don't be silly. Where are you going to eat it?" He wondered if Frankie had known it was Tessa's order. The Siam Palace owner had asked if Tessa was joining Mack. He must have wondered what was going on.

"I had something earlier at home. This is tomorrow's dinner. I'm going to introduce Gram to Thai."

He wasn't sure what to say next, but she saved him the trouble. "If you don't mind, I need a moment of your time." She glanced down at Erin. "May I borrow him for the time it takes to reach my car? He'll be right back."

Erin looked like she wanted to sink through the tile floor. "Please, I should go."

"Of course you shouldn't," Tessa said. "He'll be right back, and you can finish your conversation and your dinners." She nodded a goodbye and started toward the front without looking to see if Mack had followed.

"Don't leave," he told Erin. "Please."

"I'm going to ask the waiter to pack mine, too," she said firmly.

He didn't have time to argue. He followed in Tessa's footsteps. She was just paying for a large plastic bag loaded with takeout cartons when he reached her. She put her change back in her purse, smiled a taut goodbye at Frankie and started out the door.

Outside, cars whizzed by on the street as he followed her into the parking lot. The lamps jutting from cast-iron posts in the four corners were unlit. The sky was still light, and would probably remain so for part of her drive back to Shenandoah County. She stopped beside her Toyota, and he took the bag from her arms so she could unlock the door.

"We were having dinner to talk about the end-of-summer picnic that Compassionate Friends is hosting. I promised to be in charge of some of the arrangements. Erin's in charge of the rest."

Tessa opened the passenger door and set the bag on the seat. Then she shut the door and leaned against it. "You don't owe me an explanation. But I have to say, it didn't look like a discussion about who should bring the watermelon and who should bring the napkins."

He didn't deny it.

"Are you having an affair with her?" Tessa asked at last.

"No." He paused and decided to be honest. "Not yet."

Her expression didn't change. "Then that's what I interrupted? The whys and wherefores and whens?"

"No."

"She's very pretty. And young. She lost a child?"

"A brother. They were close."

"What's stopping you, exactly?"

Sometimes he wondered himself. How much rejection could any man suffer? How much pain was he required to bear alone?

How hopeless was a marriage supposed to be before a husband walked out on a wife?

"I love you," he said at last. "That's what's stopping me. At least, I think I love you, or the woman you used to be."

"Then you're not sure?"

"I need love. I need warmth. They're absent in my life now. They left when Kayley did. I miss them as much as I miss her."

He thought he saw a flicker in Tessa's eyes. A light that hadn't quite burned out, a response that hadn't yet been smothered.

"We can't go back in time." She looked away for a moment; then she met his eyes again. "You want to, but we can't."

"Then let me build something new with you. Don't shut me out. I've been shut out too long, Tessa, and I need something besides a black hole inside me."

As he watched, she seemed to give herself a mental shake. "Do you want to know why I was looking for you?"

"Yes."

"I got a message a couple of days ago, only I just found out about it today. From Robert Owens's attorney. From his assistant, actually."

He hadn't expected that. For a moment he struggled to adjust. "Owens's attorney?"

"It was a courtesy call. Apparently he tried to reach you at work and Grace wouldn't put him through fast enough, so the assistant called our home, but the answering machine wasn't on."

He heard himself explain. "I've been coming home to long taped calls from telephone solicitors. I figured anyone who needed to reach us knew how."

"Well, he did know how, as it turns out. He left a message for me at MADD. He knows about my involvement."

"What was the message?"

"They're releasing him next week. They're releasing Robert Owens."

The emotion that hadn't showed in her face before was there

now. Her eyes blazed. Her lips trembled. "Next week," she repeated in a strangled tone. "Three years for murdering our daughter. Three lousy years."

Mack drew a jagged breath. Robert Owens had been tried for involuntary manslaughter. He had been nineteen at the time of Kayley's death, and the sentence could have ranged from jail time served and community service to a more punitive one stretching for years and served at one of the state's adult facilities.

Since this wasn't Owens's first DUI, the lesser option hadn't been available to him. But Owens's mother had mortgaged her Manassas home and hired the best attorney she could find. The attorney's rendering of the young man's life story, replete with all the angst and dysfunctional underpinnings of a David Mamet play, had moved the judge, and the sentence had surprised them all. Owens had been sent to a special program for youthful offenders at the St. Bride's correctional center, where he was to undergo up to four years of intensive rehabilitation. When he finished, and if his time there had been productive, he was to be released into a year and a half of intensive probation.

But Mack and Tessa had been promised that Owens would serve the full four years, that the latitude in that particular sentence would not be utilized. He would serve the four years, then the additional intensively monitored probation. And if he slipped up even once, he would go back to prison and serve out the remainder of his suspended sentence, eight additional years.

"His attorney thought we should know," Tessa said. "The bastard thought we might need to prepare ourselves."

"What else did he say?" Mack realized he was flexing his hands into fists.

"That Robert was a model inmate, that he did everything he was required to do and more besides, that he's now a born-again Christian and the sponsor for several other boys in his AA group. That he's repentant, stable and deserves a better life."

"I'll talk to Judge Lutz."

For a moment Tessa looked vulnerable, even unsure of herself. The mask of indifference slipped. "Mack, will you...*can* you make a difference?"

He couldn't. He knew he couldn't. Owens's release was clearly a *fait accompli*, but he couldn't tell Tessa that. Not when that possibility was the only thing to give her hope. "I can try." He took her hands. They were ice cold despite a temperature hovering close to ninety. "I *will* try. But I don't want to mislead you."

"Just do what you can. Talk to him. Tell him... Tell him what that drunk bastard did to our lives!"

They stared at each other, as close physically as they had been in weeks. He could feel the soft knit of her jacket brushing his wrist, her thigh against his knee, her breath against the hollow of his throat. Then she wrenched her hands from his. He stepped back, and she rounded the car and opened the driver's door. He watched as she drove away.

Pain and confusion warred inside him. Things had been bad enough before, but this was a new and terrible blow. And just before discovering that Owens was going to be released, Mack had stood right here and admitted he was being pulled toward an affair with Erin.

Had he been that cruel out of a need for honesty, or simply because he was trying to shock Tessa into trying harder? Was he still, in some perverse way, trying to hold on to what they'd had?

Now he wondered if Tessa would ever be able to move on with her life unless he left her. He was a part of a happy past, and maybe she needed an absence of constant reminders of her pain before she could escape it. Maybe that past and their mutual agony were all that bound them together after all.

Ironically now, their mutual agony, in the form of one drunken murderer, had come forward to haunt them directly. Could he free her of Owens's presence for another year?

Could and should he free her of his own?

CHAPTER
12

The skies were dark, but a full moon hung over the valley as if a divine hand had set it there to light Tessa's way to her grandmother's house.

Tessa thought the whole world seemed to be operating that way tonight, as if everything in it was a sign or a signal, as if she were not a mere speck on this speck of existence, but somehow central to it all. The boy who had killed her daughter, then stood over the little girl's body and blamed her for standing on the sidewalk, was about to go free. Her husband was contemplating an affair. And her own heart was so constricted, so damaged, that she could no longer feel it beating.

She was a shell of the woman who had been Tessa MacRae. Had she not been so filled with fury, she would question whether she was still alive. But surely she had to be living and breathing to feel this much hatred for Robert Owens. She had felt little but hatred and anger since Kayley's death, and now it calmed her to know that at least she could still feel something.

It would calm her more if she could *do* something, as well. She knew that, and knew that tonight was not the night to decide exactly what. But she would not accept the young man's early release without a fight. She might not be able to change the inevitable, but she would find a way to make sure that Robert Owens never destroyed another life.

After Kayley's death, she had questioned why she still lived when her daughter did not. For months it had been the central question of her existence, fading a little as time went on and her faith that there was any plan to the universe faded with it. Now, though, she wondered if she understood at last why she had been left behind, why she had not been standing beside her daughter when Owens jumped the curb, why she had not been killed, as well.

Because it was her mission on earth to make sure he never killed again.

She was parked in her grandmother's driveway before she even realized she had made the turn onto Fitch Crossing. She tried to school her thoughts, but they tumbled unnaturally through her head. She held herself still, breathed deeply, tried to picture calm blue waters. But all she could see was Robert Owens's face as he stared drunkenly at her little girl, so drunk that he couldn't tell where a road ended and a sidewalk began.

She was sobbing before she could find a way to stop the tears. She rested her arms against the steering wheel and ducked her head. The tears were intruders, unwanted and uninvited, but the harder she tried not to cry, the harder she did.

She wasn't sure how much time passed until she finally had herself under control. She was glad it was late and that the other women had certainly gone to bed. She blew her nose, then gathered the takeout from Siam Palace and the bag from the quilt shop, and stepped out of the car.

The moon was surrounded by a canopy of stars, and the lightest of breezes rustled the twin maples' branches, and spread the scent of wild roses and parched earth. She stood quietly for a moment, forcing herself to notice, forcing herself to feel something besides pain and fury.

She wondered if Mack was right after all, and there was no reason to live with her now, no reason to continue their marriage. Why should another human being endure what she did every day? Shouldn't she just give up their life together? If she still felt anything for him, shouldn't she just set him free so he could try to move on?

Move on with Erin Foster. Move on to more children, a mortgage, sex whenever the mood struck—which it surely would often. Erin was pretty enough to be appealing to Mack and young enough to bear half a dozen children if he wanted them. They would always have a spare or two, if any of *their* children died.

The pettiness of that last thought shocked her, and she was horrified at herself. Mack had tried and tried hard to move through the bad times with her. Even now, poised on the brink of an affair, he was still trying to make their marriage work. And what encouragement had she given him? When had she gone to him, told him she still loved him, begged him to help her work things out? She knew, even now, even at this extraordinarily late date, that if she did those things, he would wait for her.

But what sign would he ask for? What change would signal that their marriage still had a chance? A genuine interest in exploring her pain with a marriage counselor? The promise of another pregnancy? Cutting her volunteer time with MADD in half so that they could rebuild their relationship?

She couldn't promise any of those things, not in good faith. Not now. Perhaps not ever.

She let herself inside by the front door, which Helen always left unlocked. Nancy lectured Helen about it repeatedly. Nancy would install a security system with motion detectors and flashing lights if Helen gave the nod. But Helen wasn't ready to abandon a world where doors remained unlocked at night and car keys perpetually hung from ignition switches. She'd made it clear that when she had to lock her doors against her neighbors, they might as well lay her in her casket whether she was dead or not.

Tessa closed the door behind her and stepped into the living room. Helen was sitting there in the dark, silently waiting.

Tessa drew in a sharp breath at the sight of her. "What are you doing there?"

"I think I live here, don't I?" Helen flicked on the lamp beside her chair. It glowed a warm gold—Nancy had replaced the old shade with a brand-new one. Helen was wearing the nightgown set that had floated off the roof the day of Tessa's arrival. "What are you doing sneaking inside like that? You like to give me a heart attack."

Tessa suspected that her grandmother had fallen asleep and only just now awakened. "Were you waiting for me?"

"Why would I bother? You're grown, aren't you? You can come in all hours of the day or night if it suits you. You don't have to call and let us know you're all right."

Tessa was ashamed. She'd been so filled with her own problems, she hadn't thought about her mother and grandmother, who had expected her back before this. Tonight the universe might be centered directly over Tessa's head, but Helen and Nancy hadn't gotten the word.

"I'm sorry." Tessa set her bags on the newly repaired and slip-covered sofa. "I didn't once think about calling you. That was an oversight."

"Your mama tried to get you, but your phone was turned off."

She had turned it off after her conversation with Mack at Siam Palace. She hadn't wanted him to call her for another installment.

More passive-aggressive behavior in a life now rich with it.

"Next time I'll be more thoughtful," Tessa promised. "But you never have to wait up. I'm a good driver. I'm careful."

"We both know that being careful doesn't keep you from dying, don't we?"

Tessa sank to the sofa beside her bags. "Do you ever think that dying isn't the worst thing that happens to us? That being left behind is the real blow?"

"It's not dying, and it's not being left behind. Maybe some day I'll tell you what it is."

"Tell me now."

"You're not ready to hear it."

Tessa knew she should go up to bed so that her grandmother could do the same. But even the thought of being alone in the tiny bedroom, thinking about Robert Owens, and Mack and Erin Foster, made her throat close and her stomach roll.

"I don't want to keep you up," Tessa said. "I'm sorry I kept you up this long."

"I'm up 'cause I want to be."

"Anything on television?"

"The answer to that's always no. Your mama keeps nagging me to let some foolish satellite cluttering the skies beam down television shows to me, like something in some sort of science fiction novel."

"And you, of course, being a purist at heart, say not a chance. So now you can't get most of what *is* available to watch."

"I'd snap it up in a minute if there was just something I wanted to see. I was a girl, we'd sit of an evening, all of us together, and listen to Grand Ole Opry music on WSM, all the way from Nashville. Mama'd make popcorn, and sometimes the neighbors would visit. Now that was entertainment."

Tessa smiled, and was surprised she still could. "I take after you. I don't like television that much, either. I'd rather read."

"And I'd rather quilt."

That reminded Tessa of the contents of the bag beside her. "Look what I found today." She opened the bag and pulled out a large book with a soft, shiny cover. "This is a handbook on repairing old quilts. And I got some good advice at the store, too and a few supplies they said I'd need. They've got an expert on staff, and she said I could bring the quilt in any time I have a question, and she'd look at it."

"You're going to let her do the work?"

Tessa had actually considered it, but in the end the thought of someone else making the repairs hadn't appealed to her. Helen had pieced the top. Nancy had quilted it. It only seemed right that Tessa should restore it.

"I'm going to do it." She thought she saw approval in Helen's eyes. "The first thing I have to do is figure out what can be left the way it is and what has to be replaced. Marilyn—she's the expert—said I should be on the lookout for fabrics that match the ones that are too rotten to save."

"New fabric?"

"Not unless that's all I can find. Old fabrics from the twenties and thirties, I guess. Like the ones you bought then. And if they look too new, I'm supposed to fade them."

"Bleach'll make them weak. Next generation will have to repair it all over again."

Tessa didn't point out that there was no next generation, that what was left of the Stoneburner genes had ended with her. "Marilyn suggested I put the scraps on a windowsill for a week or so and let the sun do the job."

Helen screwed up her face, as if she was thinking that over. "She sounds like she knows what she's talking about."

That was the ultimate expression of approval. Tessa was glad Helen was on board with the project. "Do you remember my telling you a couple of weeks ago that I found a box of feed sacks in the attic? Well, I'm hoping some of those will work as replacement pieces. What do you think?"

"They might do. But I've got boxes and boxes of old fabric. You won't have to go far to find what you need. I guess I don't need to tell you I don't throw much away."

Tessa smiled. "No, I guess you don't. I don't suppose..."

"What?"

"Well, I told Marilyn there's one particular fabric that shows up often, and that's the soft blue with the threads of white criss-crossing through it that's along the border. It almost looks like chambray or denim, but it's much finer. Some of it's intact, and some of it has to be replaced. She said since it's so prevalent throughout the quilt, we're going to have to find something that's a nearly perfect match, and that could be difficult."

Helen was silent for a moment; then she sighed. "I've got more. I didn't throw away a scrap of it. Not one. And I didn't use it in any other quilt. There might be enough."

Tessa was amazed that her grandmother could remember what she had done with scraps of fabric from nearly seventy years before. "You can't possibly remember that, can you? Do you remember every scrap of fabric in every quilt?"

"I sure remember that one." Helen got to her feet. "Come on. I'll show you."

"Where?"

"Up to the attic."

"We'll wake Mom."

"She wakes up, she was meant to."

Tessa supposed that now was as good a time as any. The attic would be cooler this time of night, and she needed the distraction. She lifted the bag from the restaurant. "There's food in here. I'll put it away and meet you upstairs."

On the second floor, Helen had just reached the attic door when Nancy came out of her bedroom, belting a white silk wrapper sprigged with tiny pink roses. "There's a parade, and I wasn't invited," she said flatly.

"I'm sorry, Mom, but Gram wants to show me something in the attic. It's a long story."

"Where have you been?"

"That sounds remarkably like something you used to ask back in the eighties."

"I was worried."

Tessa gave an almost verbatim repeat of her apology to her grandmother.

Nancy appeared to be appeased. "I'm just glad you're all right. Did you see Mack? How is he?"

Tessa could think of a dozen things not to say about her husband. "I did see him for a few minutes. He's okay. Busy."

"What's upstairs that you two just have to see?" Nancy asked her mother.

"Come take a look yourself, or, better yet, go make us some coffee and I'll bring it downstairs."

Nancy wrinkled her nose, as if considering. "Coffee," she said. She moved toward the stairwell.

Helen switched on the light and started up to the attic, and Tessa followed behind. She had done a lot of organizing here, but at night the remaining boxes hovered like monsters in the shadows. The floor creaked, and the smell of must and mothballs was worse after coming in from the fresh night air.

"Never did like this attic," Helen said. "I'll tell you true, I don't much come up here at night 'less I have to."

"Did you play here when it rained as a little girl?"

"We didn't play much, not the way you mean. We made fun out of the chores we did."

Tessa had already run out of small talk. "Let's get the fabric and get out of here."

"It's in that trunk over there." Helen pointed to the trunk that held what was left of her husband's personal effects. Tessa remembered it clearly.

"You're sure? I thought those were your husband's things."

"He was your grandpa. You never think of him that way, do you?"

Tessa was sorry, but she didn't. Not only hadn't she known

Fate Henry, her mother hadn't known him, either. For that matter, it seemed that Helen had hardly known him, at least as an adult.

"I guess I don't, but I should, shouldn't I? Why do you keep the fabric in there?"

"I'll tell you when we get downstairs. Your mama might want to hear."

A month ago, Tessa would have doubted that very much. Nancy had spent her adulthood pruning her Shenandoah Valley roots. But now Tessa thought she might well want to know more about her father. She seemed to know little enough.

"You'll find the fabric at the bottom of the trunk," Helen said. "You can bend over, and I can't. Not so well, anyway."

Tessa went to the trunk and opened it, lifting clothing and other effects until she was nearly at the bottom. She found the blue fabric, neatly folded along with some other large scraps. She guessed there might be as much as a yard of it left.

She closed the trunk and took the fabric back to her grandmother. "You were right. How long has it been there?"

"More years than your mama's been alive."

Tessa wanted to ask more questions. She needed to be asking questions tonight, to remember that other people had lives and sorrows, and she was not alone. But she knew she wouldn't get answers until they were downstairs again.

She followed her grandmother to the attic stairs and flipped off the light. Then she followed her down to the first floor, moving slowly as Helen took the steps with the care of someone who knew the dangers of a broken hip or ankle.

The coffee was brewing by the time they settled in the kitchen, and Nancy opened a tin of cookies that had been dropped off by a visitor from Helen's church that morning. "It's nice to know people are thinking of you, Mama," she said, as she set the tin on the table.

"Never did think I'd be one of those shut-ins gets a tin of cookies or a pot of chrysanthemums every couple of months from the ladies auxiliary. Never saw myself that way."

"I don't know about the chrysanthemums, but the cookies look great." Tessa reached for one and took a bite. "Chocolate chip." She remembered with the usual pang that they had been Kayley's favorite.

Nancy came back with mugs and a pint of half-and-half; then she brought the coffee and filled the mugs almost to the brim. "I'm glad you're both up. I couldn't sleep anyway."

"If you're going to complain about the heat, don't," Helen said.

Nancy sat down. "I don't mind the heat so much now that the screens are fixed. Besides, now if I have a hot flash, I've got something to blame it on besides growing old."

Tessa reached for another cookie. "You have hot flashes?"

"Why? You were hoping for a brother or sister?"

Tessa nearly choked on a cookie fragment. "I gave up hoping for that about thirty years ago. But now that we're on the subject, I always wondered why you didn't have more kids."

"I always thought there'd be plenty of time. Then, one day, there wasn't anymore."

Tessa thought there were a few things missing from that explanation, but she didn't want to probe. This was more than her mother had ever said.

"I always thought you just weren't sure your marriage was good enough," Helen said bluntly.

Nancy closed her eyes a moment and shook her head. "The things you say."

"I don't have enough time left to pussyfoot around, do I? Anything needs saying, needs saying right now."

Tessa the peacemaker emerged. "Why don't you say a few things about yourself then, Gram. Tell us about the blue fabric." She gave Nancy a short version of her trip to the quilt shop and Helen's promise of matching fabric. Then she sat back.

"You're sure you want to hear this?" Helen said. "It might take a while."

"We've got plenty of cookies," Nancy said. "Plenty of coffee."

"Since when did you start eating dessert?"

"I don't smoke. I hardly drink. I need a vice if I'm going to survive a summer with you." Nancy reached for a cookie and came away with several.

Helen settled in and looked almost eager to begin. "You probably guessed by now that the blue cloth has something to do with Fate, else why would it be in his trunk?"

"That makes sense," Tessa said.

"What you don't know yet is that he give it to me himself, when I was nearly twenty. That wasn't so young in those days, not so young as it is now. I wasn't a pretty girl, but there were still men who had their eye on me. There was only one man I wanted, though, and he didn't have a blame thing to give me. Or at least he didn't think so."

Tessa cradled her coffee mug and looked over the top at her grandmother. An hour ago she hadn't been sure she could face the next moment of her life. Now, in the coffee-scented kitchen, her grandmother on one side, her mother on the other, the world looked a little different.

She wondered if this was what Mack missed so deeply, this sense of caring and being cared for simply because one existed in the same time and place as people who shared life stories, a forgotten past, bloodlines. Was his need so very simple?

And no matter how hard she fought it, was hers?

CHAPTER
13

1940

Over the past two years, Delilah had slowed down considerably, unable some mornings to rise from her bed. In the winter of '38 scarlet fever had swept through the area and taken two children and an old man up closer to the river. Delilah had been sick for days, and Helen had nursed her faithfully. Once the fever broke, they had all expected her to recover quickly, but the malaise dragged on.

Determined to get better, Delilah had tried special herbal teas, even resorted to the local custom of "powwowing" with a practitioner who lived on lower Fitch. The old woman had stood at her shoulder and in a loud voice repeated words that sounded like they came straight from the Bible. Then she asked Delilah to plant and tend a garden of bleeding heart outside the kitchen door. But the mysterious incantation didn't help, and the flowers didn't thrive, because Delilah didn't have the strength to nurture them.

As a last resort, Cuddy borrowed money to take his wife to a doctor in Washington, D.C., but the doctor wasn't encouraging. He explained that the problem was Delilah's heart, probably as a result of the fever. The doctor told Cuddy that only a miracle would cure her now.

As the months of ill health had stretched into years, Helen and her brothers had taken over most of Delilah's chores. Weak and frighteningly pale, Delilah still cooked dinner and supper and did a bit of the cleaning. But Helen cooked breakfast, tended the vegetable garden and did most of the canning alone or with the help of her aunts. She slopped the hogs, milked the cow, fed the chickens and did all the washing and ironing.

She was a woman now, but there was precious little time to think about what that meant. Young men visited; she chatted with them at church, or when families and neighbors gathered to make apple butter or butcher hogs in the fall. But there was no time to worry about her future. For the time being her future was in Toms Brook, caring for her mother.

Helen had another reason for patience. Her world was a narrow one. Other girls mourned the absence of strangers in their isolated corner of the world. The boys they had grown up with interested them less than boys they would never know. But Helen didn't care if all the boys in the world were waiting just over the mountains. She knew who she wanted.

She just had to convince Fate Henry he had enough to offer her.

On the morning before Christmas, Delilah hobbled into the kitchen and made shooing motions with her hands. "I feel up to this now, Lenny. I told you I'd make the peanut brittle, and I will."

Helen reluctantly moved away from the stove and its welcome heat. Her mother looked even paler than usual, but Helen knew that no amount of coaxing would send Delilah back to bed. She had made peanut brittle every Christmas season that Helen could remember, even during the worst days of the Depression before Cuddy got his job at the feed store. The peanuts always came by mail from family down in southeastern Virginia; the sugar for holiday baking was put aside, a little at a time, throughout the year. There had never been money for fancy Christmas presents in the Stoneburner household or a belief they were necessary, but Delilah had always tried to make the holiday special.

"I was hoping you'd let me do it this time," Helen said. "I need to learn, don't I?"

"You could make it with your eyes closed. And I'm tired of doing nothing. Never did think I'd end up as useless as a scrawny old hen who can't lay an egg."

"You're not useless, Ma. You just need to rest and get better."

Delilah looked her daughter straight in the eye. "That's not gonna happen. We both know it, and it's time we all stopped pretending things are different from what they are. I'm having more bad spells, and the medicine the doctor give me isn't doing a thing for me anymore. Truth is—and I want you to hear this—I don't think I'll be with you next Christmas. So just one more time, I want to do this myself."

Delilah rarely minced words, but this was the first time she had addressed her impending death head on. Helen swallowed hard. "You can't get better if you say you're not going to."

Delilah managed a weak smile. "The Lord and I are up to date on this one, Lenny. And he's telling me to get my affairs in order. I've been given this one last Christmas, and I'm gonna make use of it."

Helen felt tears rising, but she knew that her mother would hate to see her cry. "Well, nobody makes peanut brittle nearly as good as yours. So I'm sure not going to stand in your way, even if I think you're wrong."

"You go on, now, and put the decorations on the tree. Your daddy's right proud of it. Cut down the best one he could find. You go on up to the attic and see what's there to make it pretty."

Helen made her way up to the attic with a heavy heart. Despite what she'd said, she knew her mother was right. Delilah was thin as a broom straw, and her hands shook so badly she had given up piecing quilts, although she still spent time each day at the quilt frame, where she could rest her hands as she worked. Helen pieced for her now, and Delilah quilted the results.

All except the wedding ring quilt. Helen planned to quilt that one herself, just as soon as it was finished. She had pieced more than two thirds of the oval sections since she first learned to quilt, but she had been choosy about fabrics, only using those she really liked or those with sentimental meaning. As the ovals had progressed and she had seen that nearly all of them contained different shades of blue, she had decided she needed one unifying fabric to bring the quilt together. She would use that fabric as connectors and a scalloped border.

She was in no hurry, though, because the man she wanted to marry hadn't yet asked her.

In the attic she found the box of Christmas ornaments. There weren't many. She and Tom had cut stars from colored paper and tin foil and hung them with bits of yarn. Last year Obed's girlfriend Dorothy had given them tissue paper bells to hang, and Obed had bought three glass ornaments made in Germany as a present for Delilah. Cuddy, who liked to whittle, had made a primitive village to put beneath the tree.

This Christmas Helen had a surprise for her mother, too. At night, while Delilah was sleeping, she had made tiny quilt squares from Delilah's favorite patterns, backed them and filled them with cotton batting, to hang on the tree. She knew Delilah would be pleased.

On this, her mother's last Christmas.

Helen sat on a pile of boxes and rested her face in her hands. She did not want to accept Delilah's prediction, but she knew it was the truth. What would she do once her mother was gone? Once he married Dorothy, Obed, who had a job with the Civilian Conservation Corps constructing overlooks and picnic areas on Skyline Drive, would move back home, and Dorothy would come to live at the Stoneburner farm. Helen liked her well enough and knew she was a hard worker. Dorothy would make sure that Cuddy was taken care of and the chores were done. Obed would run the farm with Tom's help. The farm would be shared by the two young men when Cuddy died, and since they had different skills and talents, the land would be in good hands.

But what would Helen do without her mother's love and guidance?

Eyes red, she descended the stairs at last with the box in her arms and took it into the living room.

Fate Henry was standing there, hat in his hands, looking as if he was afraid he might be shooed away.

"Fate." Helen put down the box, and her hands went to her brown hair, hoping it wasn't filmed with attic cobwebs. She was just glad she'd taken the time last night to put the short strands in pincurls.

"I just stopped by to borrow Tom's new ax. I want to show Uncle Sammy. He needs a new one."

Helen saw exactly how transparent the excuse was. Sammy Claiborne was so tightfisted, he would gnaw a tree like a beaver before he would invest in a new ax.

"I know Tom'll be proud to loan it to you," she said.

They stared at each other. Fate was easy to stare at. He had grown into his lanky long legs and wide shoulders. His curly black hair was short and slicked back over a high forehead, giving his eyes more prominence. They were green and heavily lashed, an adornment in a thoroughly masculine face. There wasn't a girl anywhere near Toms Brook who hadn't noticed him, but Fate seemed oblivious to every one of them.

Except, possibly, for Helen.

"You been doing all right?" she asked, reminding herself not to straighten her dress. It was an old one, but the green print suited her. She had made it herself and trimmed it with pique right off the bolt. It was worn now, but as pretty as anything in the Sears catalog when it was new.

"Sure. How about yourself?"

"Doing fine." She pointed to the box. "I'm going to put these on the Christmas tree. Do you have a tree this year?"

"Uncle Sammy don't believe in 'em. I think he's just too busy to cut one down, and Gus, well, he's not around much these days to do it. I tried one year myself, but there weren't nothing to put on it."

She knew by now that Fate's years with the Claiborne family hadn't been particularly good ones. He had not been treated as a son or a hired hand, but somewhere in the middle, with no rights at all. He would not inherit so much as a cup of dirt from the Claibornes, nor would he ever be paid as much as someone outside the family might earn. He was grateful to them for taking him in during hard times, but she also suspected he missed the real love and family he'd never had.

She wanted to give that to him, if only he would let her.

"Why don't you stay and help me decorate this one?" she said. "It won't take long. Just a few minutes."

"You wouldn't mind?"

Her breath caught. She had been fully prepared for him to say no. She wasn't sure what to do with yes.

She grabbed the box for something to do, but Fate took it right out of her arms. "Of course I wouldn't mind. I could use some help," she said.

"Here, let me."

She did, more flustered now that their wrists had brushed. "I got something else to put on it, something upstairs. Will you open the box and set stuff out while I run up there?"

"Sure."

She came back a few minutes later with the quilt squares she'd made. He had set everything in neat little piles, stars in one, the carefully wrapped glass ornaments in another. The tinsel they had saved strand by strand in an old Farmer's Almanac was laid neatly at the base of the tree. He was looking at the small cache as if he'd never seen such fine things.

"We had a Christmas tree every year in Oklahoma." He looked up and smiled, his teeth even and white. "Nothing much to put on it, but it was pretty anyway."

"Did you like Oklahoma better than Virginia?"

"I didn't belong there, either."

Her heart squeezed painfully. "You belong here, Fate. Just not with those Claibornes."

He smiled again. "What's that you got?"

Shyly, she opened her hands to show him the quilt blocks. "Nothing much, but I made them for Mama."

He took one of the squares, a tiny Jacob's ladder, and squinted at it. "You could put all these together and make a doll's quilt."

"I like making quilts better than just about everything."

"Have you made many?"

"I guess." She wasn't sure what came over her next, why she was suddenly so bold, but she added, "I've been making a bride's quilt for years and years. It's called wedding ring." She tried to look nonchalant.

"Why's it taking so long?"

"Oh, I only use material that means something to me. And right now I'm waiting 'til I can buy some of that blue cloth they have down at the store in Toms Brook. But I need yards and yards, so I have to wait a while." She shrugged.

"Blue cloth?"

The cloth she yearned for was particularly pretty, a robin's egg blue with white threads criss-crossing at intervals. She haunted the store on her rare trips to town, foolishly hoping the price might come down. So far, though, it was still more expensive than she could afford, even now that Delilah insisted she keep any money she made from selling eggs. If she used it to back the quilt—and that was what she hoped to do—she would need many yards. And at fourteen cents a yard, it was much more expensive than dress fabric usually sold for, nearly twice as much.

"Just something I'm waiting for," she said. "I'm just being foolish, that's all. And I guess there's no hurry, being as I'm not about to tie the knot."

She began to unwrap the glass ornaments and Fate stepped in to help her. They talked about where to put them, about what was happening in Europe now that England and Germany were at war, about whether they might get enough snow tomorrow so that Cuddy could hook up their old plow horse to the sleigh. But Helen was afraid her talk of the wedding ring quilt hung suspended in the air about them, waiting to swoop down and frighten Fate right out of the house forever. Her fear that she might have scared him away for good ruined the rest of their time together.

Christmas morning seemed like a present all its own. Helen didn't know if Delilah had told Tom and Obed what she'd told her, or if Cuddy himself knew how short his wife's time on earth was bound to be. But whatever had been said or not said, everyone in the family seemed to try harder to be kind and respectful to each other.

Tom and Obed had grown into good, strong men. Obed's wild streak had been tamed by hard work and a pretty woman. He announced at breakfast that he planned to ask Dorothy's father that evening if he could marry her.

Helen wondered if Obed wanted to hurry the wedding so that their mother could be there to see it.

They filled their stomachs with sausage from the hog they'd slaughtered in the fall and hominy they'd grown themselves. Helen had made a breakfast cake studded with black walnuts, and every crumb was gone by the time they rose to open presents beside the tree.

There were fresh oranges for everyone, as well as fudge and Delilah's peanut brittle. Tom had made Delilah a new cutting board for her kitchen and an identical one for Helen's hope chest. Obed had bought both women small bottles of toilet water, honeysuckle for Delilah and apple blossom for Helen. Cuddy had found a new sink for the kitchen that drained into the yard so that they no longer had to haul the dishwater outside. Better yet, he promised to install it before the new year.

The men got new shirts from Helen, sewn from fabric she'd bargained for at the store with eggs and fresh milk. Delilah and Mavis had made each family member a small fruitcake rich with nuts and dried fruit.

"It's a good Christmas," Delilah said when the last gift had been presented. "We are rich in the ways that matter."

Helen could feel that, too, that sense of having nearly everything she needed right here in this room and on this farm. But, for her, there was still one person missing. Fate Henry. And oddly enough, if she ever got to call Fate hers, he would take her away from her family.

They spent the rest of the morning doing only the most important chores; then Helen took to the kitchen again to help her mother finish preparing a feast centered around their very own country ham.

By the time she had cleaned up, family and neighbors began to arrive. They offered hot cider and roasted peanuts, and talked about the way the weather had warmed too much for a white Christmas. People came and went. Tom and Obed went off to visit friends, and Helen cleaned up after one group of guests just in time for a smaller group to arrive as twilight descended.

She had hoped that Fate might stop by, but he hadn't said anything when he helped decorate the tree. She wished she had asked him to come, but she had been afraid it might scare him after her talk of the wedding ring quilt. He was a quiet man, and shy to boot, and she was afraid she might never know what he felt for her unless she asked him outright. But if she did that, he would surely run away for good.

She was just serving more hot cider when there were shouts outside and the ringing of bells. She thought she heard a horn blowing, then another followed by a shout.

"Pelsnickles! Pelsnickles!"

Delilah faced her daughter. "Well, I haven't heard that for a year or two."

Helen's eyes were shining. "Somebody's pelsing us!"

"Well, don't just stand there talking about it. Go and let them in."

"But the cider—"

"I'll take care of everything. You just leave it to me, Lenny. Go on, now."

Helen charged into the living room just in time to see her father heading for the door. Cuddy was a tall, thin man, but years of throwing feed sacks into the backs of wagons had roped his lean arms with muscle. If he didn't want the pelsnicklers in his home, he could easily throw them out.

"Daddy, you're going to let them in, aren't you?" she demanded as he reached for the door.

Cuddy turned, and she saw he was grinning. "Why would I turn them away?"

"I thought maybe you was worried about Mama."

"It'll do her good. Never a Christmas passed without the pelsnicklers when she was a girl." He threw open the door, and there, standing on the porch, were eight monstrous strangers. "Come on in," he said, opening the door wider. "Just come on in this very minute."

The monsters grunted as they made their way inside. "You know who we are?" one questioned in a deep voice.

"I might or I might not," Cuddy said. "How about you, Helen?"

Helen stared. The men—although it was possible there were

women among them—were dressed in old ragged clothes padded everywhere so they looked to be twice as big as they were. Their hands were covered by old work gloves, and their faces were masked. Some wore decorated feed sacks over their heads with slits where their eyes and mouths were. Some masks were fancier, like they might have been bought at a store. All of them wore hats pulled low over their heads.

She recognized Tom immediately and was careful not to smile at him. She knew his gloves and the old shirt that was now stuffed until it was likely to split along the seams. "Don't know a one of them," she said. "Not a single one."

"Me either," Cuddy said, although clearly he did. "Let's have our guests figure this out. And your Mama, too."

Aunt Mavis had arrived with the last batch of guests, and she stood when the pelsnicklers strolled in. "Well, will you look at this, Delilah? Never saw a handsomer bunch, except maybe when your Cuddy came pelsnickeling the Christmas before you married him."

Delilah was seated, but her cheeks were flushed with excitement. "You're welcome here," she told the pelsnicklers. "We've got cider and candy, cake and nuts. You help yourself."

Mavis cornered her niece as the new arrivals loaded up plates. "Did you put the boys up to this, Lenny?"

"I didn't know a thing about it."

"They used to come every year, groups of them all through New Year's," Mavis said. "Your mama and me were the best at guessing who they were. It wouldn't have been Christmas without the pelsnicklers. Daddy always took them out back and gave them liquor. I suspect your daddy'll do the same."

Helen was sure he would. Making whiskey was a skill often employed in the hills above Fitch Crossing Road.

The pelsnickelers were getting rowdy, and although Delilah was laughing at their antics, she seemed to be gasping for air. Helen knew it was time to calm things down a little.

"I know who you are!" She pointed at one of the revelers who was smaller than the others. "Jacob Sommes, you take off your mask."

The mask came off and it *was* Jacob, a friend of Obed's, as she had predicted. There was laughter and much backslapping. Jacob shrugged and reached for another piece of peanut brittle.

The masks came off one by one as the boys were identified. Tom was one of the first to be caught, and Obed followed soon enough, until only three names hadn't been guessed.

Helen moved closer. "Mama, do you know who this is?" she asked, pointing at one of them.

Delilah nodded. "I do."

Helen was surprised, because she didn't. "Who is it?"

"It's the girl who's going to be my new daughter someday."

Helen felt a pang at the thought that anyone else could share that title. "Dorothy, you take off that mask," she said.

The mask—complete with yarn whiskers and floppy calico ears—came off, and Dorothy laughed as everyone broke into applause.

"I couldn't help it," Dorothy said. "Obed made me do it." She went to him, and he put his arm around her.

"Gus," Helen said, pointing at the shorter of the remaining two, "take off your mask."

"Aw heck, Lenny." Gus Claiborne stripped off his mask, a fearsome looking thing with dried leaves and acorns glued to it.

Helen's heart was beating too fast now. She was hoping she knew the identity of the last pelser. He was as round as a good potato, padded so thoroughly he could probably roll down a hill without injury. The mask was painted with black and white stripes, and the eyes were ringed with red. The mouth was painted blue and smiling.

"Go ahead, Lenny, guess," Tom said.

"I think you're Fate Henry," she said, pointing right at his chest. "I think Fate Henry's in that silly old costume somewhere."

There was a moment when she thought she might be wrong, because he didn't move. Then off came the mask, and she saw she'd been right.

Everybody laughed and applauded. In a moment everyone was in groups, talking, telling stories, eating and working on the cider she'd set out. But Fate was still facing her.

"You got time to go outside a minute?" he asked.

She looked at her mother and realized Delilah was watching them. Before she could ask, Delilah shooed her toward the door, then turned to say something to Cuddy. Cuddy began to corral the pelsers, and Helen knew what was coming next. Her father was going to take the boys outside and introduce them to the local moonshine. They would finish off the evening with firecrackers, the way they always finished Christmas Day.

"You're going to miss the fun," she told Fate. "Daddy's taking the boys out back."

"I'd rather be with you."

Helen's heart sped. "Let me get my coat. You got enough padding to keep you warm."

"I'll be out front."

She met him there a few minutes later. She wondered how any man dressed as he was could still make her breath catch in her chest.

"How many houses you been to?" she asked, trying to be casual even though her tongue suddenly seemed too large for her mouth.

"Just a few. Obed, he wanted your mama to see us, on account of..." He looked away.

"On account of her being sick," Helen said. She wasn't yet ready to admit out loud that her mother was dying.

"Uh-huh. She liked it, didn't she?"

"She liked it. She sure did." Helen didn't know what else to say. What did men and women say to each other? She could talk about chickens and cleaning house and how much starch to put in a Sunday shirt, but what else did she know about? What did Delilah say to Cuddy in their moments alone?

"You have a good Christmas?" he asked.

"I did. Was yours good, Fate? I wished, well, I wished you'd come over earlier. I was gonna ask you to, but I just didn't know…"

"Know what?"

"Well, if you'd think I was being forward."

He smiled, and just then the first firecracker went off out back. Helen hadn't expected it, and she jumped, brushing against him.

Fate put his hands on her arms to steady her. "Took you by surprise, didn't it?"

"It did. Now the chickens are going to be all mixed up for the rest of the evening, cackling and crowing and trying to get away." She looked up at him just in time to see his mouth descending to hers.

Nobody had to tell her what to do. She just leaned closer and turned her face up to his. The pressure of his lips against hers stole her breath. Her eyelids closed, and her lips parted.

He stepped away at last. "That's what I was hoping for to make my Christmas a good one," he said.

"Fate…" She smiled. She was dazed and ecstatically happy.

"I got you something," he said. "A present."

Unexpectedly, she wanted to cry. She swallowed hard. "You didn't have to. I didn't think—"

"I know you didn't, Helen. I never give you a reason to think much one way or the other, but it's not that I didn't want to. It's just…"

"You don't think you can afford a wife."

He nodded. "But that's gonna change. Open my present first, then I'll tell you how."

"Oh, you got to wait right there first. Can you wait?"

"I'm not going anywhere."

She turned on her heel and hurried back into the house and up to her room. She joined him again, holding something behind her back. "Who goes first?"

"You go."

She held out a pair of warm woolen socks she had knitted for him, hoping foolishly the entire time that she would be able to give them to him someday. "I made these from wool from Mrs. Mac-Namara's sheep. She spun it herself. They're real warm, and your boots never look warm enough to me."

"You been paying attention to my boots?" he asked with a smile.

"I been paying attention to everything," she admitted.

He held the socks against his cheek. "They sure are soft. I never had a pair this soft."

She was so happy she didn't know what to say.

"And now for you." Fate reached inside his shirt and felt around. She giggled, watching him, and the sound surprised her. When had there been time in her life to learn such a thing?

He pulled out a roll wrapped in brown paper and tied with string. "Here it is."

"Part of your costume?"

"Open and see."

He handed her the package, but no matter how hard she tried, she was too excited to untie the knots. He helped her at last, standing close, with his arms around her.

She folded back the paper, and there inside were yards and yards of the blue fabric she had wanted for her quilt. The wedding ring quilt.

"I want you to finish it," he said softly. "And I want you to think of me when you do."

She turned in his arms, and her eyes sparkled with tears. "Oh, Fate, it's so much money. It cost so much."

"I'd give you anything I can, Helen. I will—if you'll let me."

This time she kissed him. His arms came around her, and he pulled her against his silly padded chest with his silly padded arms. She thought nothing could have been more romantic.

"You'll marry me?" he asked at last.

"Oh, you know I will!"

"You gotta know what I've got planned, though, Helen. You know there's nothing for me here. And I don't want to be a farm-hand all my life."

She nodded, waiting.

"I'm joining the Navy. I already talked to them, and they said they'll have me. We won't have much time together at first, but after that, you can come and be with me, wherever I'm stationed. You'll see the world with me. It's the only way I can think of to make something of myself and make a home good enough for you."

"I can't leave my mama, not now, Fate. I can't go far away."

"You won't have to. You'll stay here until…she doesn't need you anymore. By that time, maybe I'll be settled somewhere, and you can come and be with me."

"But I want her to see me get married. I don't want to wait until…"

He touched her cheek. "Then marry me as soon as I'm done with my training. We'll be married, we just won't be together. Not for a while."

It was so perfect that no complications occurred to her. She would marry the man she loved. Fate would be a sailor, and she would stay home and take care of Delilah. Someday in the future she would join him. She would see new places, meet new people, have a life she'd never dared to dream about.

She knew Fate would be a success. He worked hard; he was in-telligent and strong. An endless happy progression of days stretched before them.

"When do you have to go?" she asked.

"Two days."

It was sooner than she'd thought, and not long enough to plan any kind of wedding. "And how long before you come home for a little while?"

"Three months, they tell me."

"Will you be here long enough then? Is there time to get married before you ship out?"

"It only takes a few minutes to say 'I do.'"

"I do," she repeated. "Oh yes, I do want to marry you!"

He flung his arms around her again, and as more firecrackers exploded and the wily guests streamed out to the front porch to congratulate them, Fate kissed her once more.

CHAPTER
14

At first Mack planned to see the judge who had sentenced Robert Owens by himself. The two men knew each other from political fund-raisers and had close mutual friends. Mack didn't practice law in Virginia, so there was no conflict in pressuring him on the subject of Robert's release. Avery Lutz suggested an early breakfast meeting and asked if Tessa would be coming.

Mack heard himself saying yes and wondered just what he thought might come of it.

He expected her to come into town the night before, but Tessa claimed her grandmother needed company at a Sunday night benefit supper for the local volunteer fire department. Instead she said she would drive in early to avoid the worst of rush hour. On Monday morning Mack was still in bed when she arrived. He heard her key turn in the lock, then her footsteps in the hallway. As he expected, they stopped well before the master bedroom.

He rose and shaved, showered and dressed. It wasn't even seven o'clock, but he had been wide awake for at least an hour. He wasn't sure how much sleep he'd gotten, and Tessa had probably gotten next to none, with the long drive and a pivotal breakfast meeting ahead of her.

Coffee scented the air by the time he entered the kitchen, adding a homey note that was otherwise lacking. The house's exterior was sleek and modern. The interior was the same. White walls, polished wood floors adorned by only a few muted Moroccan tribal rugs. At first glance their furniture looked uncomfortable, but, of course, it wasn't. It was simply pared down, as simple and functional as everything else in the house. Sometimes he longed for clutter, for too many pillows spilling off sofas, plants dropping leaves on the carpet, collections of Depression glass or Florida seashells.

The kitchen had frameless maple cabinets and black granite countertops. The appliances were stainless steel. Once he'd bought magnets, foolish plastic bananas and apples, to hang notes on the refrigerator, but at the last moment he had hidden them in his desk drawer, daunted by the perfect gray expanse unbroken by so much as a smudge.

The house had not been nearly so perfect when Kayley lived in it.

"Would you like a cup?" Tessa asked in greeting.

She wore white today, a dress that bared her arms and covered her knees. Turquoise earrings nestled in her earlobes, and her hair was pulled away from her face. She looked cool and casual, as if her entire world didn't hinge on Avery Lutz's decision.

"Maybe it will help me wake up." He watched as she poured. She swayed unconsciously, arched a wrist, cupped a hand around the porcelain mug. He had always loved the way his wife danced her way through the most common of chores. Now the sexual promise it implied only saddened him.

She added milk to his mug and passed it toward him. "You're nearly out of coffee."

"I'm nearly out of a lot of things. I've been eating most of my meals out."

"I guess it's a lot of trouble to cook for one person."

He didn't mind the cooking. He minded eating alone in this house. Tessa had systematically stripped it of their daughter's presence, but she hadn't been able to strip away the memories of their life together.

"How have you been, Mack?" She perched on a stool at the center island and propped her feet on the bottom rung.

"Busy."

"The work's pouring in?"

"More than we can handle. We're hiring another associate."

"That's good."

"For us, not for all the people in trouble."

She sipped her coffee. Clearly she had run out of small talk. He wondered what it felt like to have a conversation with his wife that wasn't laden with tension. He couldn't remember.

"How are things on Fitch Crossing?" he said to break the silence.

"We found another money tin. Gram was absolutely thrilled. It's almost like somebody else put it there and she just discovered it. Sometimes I think she's trying to forget it was her money in the first place because it's more fun that way."

He realized the calendar would be changing in three days. Nearly a month had passed since she'd moved to Toms Brook, and there still seemed to be so little to say to each other. "Are you planning to stay there for August?"

She gave the slightest of shrugs. "There's still so much to do. If she leaves and goes to Richmond with Mom, the house will have to be ready to sell. If she stays, we need to make sure the house is in good condition, and we need to find help for her. She just can't manage it alone."

"She won't like that."

"Oh, I know she won't. She's making sure there are no good alternatives."

He leaned against the island, an arm's length away. "Tessa, about this breakfast. Avery already told me not to get my hopes up. He's willing to talk to us, but he wasn't encouraging."

For the first time since her arrival, emotion flickered in her eyes. "How can they let that monster out to kill another child?"

He saw no point in answering that. What could he say? The state of Virginia was notoriously tough on crime, applying the death penalty with more exuberance than any state except Texas. MADD gave the state high ratings for the way it cracked down on drinking and driving, but there was probably no state that would refuse to give a young man like Robert Owens a second chance. By all accounts he had been a model inmate, participating in his own rehabilitation with enthusiasm and courage. Mack had spent a fair portion of his career struggling to find justice for men and women who hadn't performed half so well.

"Don't tell me you agree with this decision," Tessa demanded when he didn't answer.

"Tessa, if it were up to me, I'd sentence him to forever and a day. But that's a father talking, not an officer of the court."

"Will Judge Lutz listen? Will he hear anything we say? Should I bring Kayley's baby pictures?"

"Do we still *have* Kayley's baby pictures?"

She looked stricken, but she didn't answer. She stood and took her cup to the sink, pouring the contents down the drain, washing and rinsing it before she spoke. "I'm going to work hard to change his mind. I hope you'll help me."

He wanted to put his arms around her, to ask her forgiveness for what had been an ill-timed shot. But he knew better than to attempt such a thing.

"I'll say everything I can say, but please don't expect to change his mind," Mack said. "Avery Lutz heard every sentence of testimony at the trial. There's nothing new we can say to him. If the decision's been made to put Owens on probation, there's very little we can do."

* * *

After the breakfast with Judge Lutz, Tessa wanted to get in her car and drive back to her grandmother's house. But she had driven to the restaurant in Mack's car, and now she had to wait for him to take her back to Fairfax. And as upset as she was, she knew better than to leave him without a word. She and Mack had to talk. If they were going to preserve even a shred of their tattered marriage, they had to discuss what had just happened.

Mack pulled into their driveway and cut the engine. Neither of them had said anything since leaving the restaurant.

"I'm sorry," he said, and he sounded sincere. "I really am. I didn't think he would help us, I wasn't even sure he could, but I'm still disappointed."

She replayed the conversation they'd had over scrambled eggs from the breakfast buffet. At least they hadn't had to sit and engage in polite conversation while the waitress brought their meals. Instead, their food had been sitting right in front of them when the judge told them there was nothing he could do to help them.

"You know," she said at last, "when he told you it was out of his hands, you didn't sound disappointed. You were reasonable and thoughtful. If I hadn't known better, I would have believed you agreed with the decision."

"If Owens hadn't killed my daughter, I *would* have agreed with it."

"Maybe you should have mentioned that first part a little more, then. The part about him being a murderer."

Mack unhooked his seat belt, but he didn't get out. He turned so he could see her better. "Robert Owens is not a murderer, not in the strictest sense. He didn't set out to kill anybody."

"He drank himself into a stupor, then he got behind the wheel of a car. What else was he planning? To stop at every stop sign? To take nice neat corners and observe the speed limit?"

"He wasn't planning anything. He was *drunk*. Drunks don't plan.

Their judgment is impaired. Half the time they can't remember their own names and addresses."

"Anybody knows that, Mack. Surely Robert did, too. But he got in the car after a whole night of drinking God knows how much and drove away. That makes him a murderer."

"I'm not going to argue the fine points of the law with you. We don't have any control over it. And, unfortunately, we have to abide by decisions the same way Owens does. There's nothing we can do about this."

"Except put a big circle around his name in the newspaper next time he kills somebody."

"His license has been revoked," Mack said. "It will be a long time before he's able to drive again——"

"Do you think that will stop him?" Tessa heard her voice rising, but she was powerless to lower it. "Do you know how many people are driving Virginia's roads with suspended licenses? I'll be glad to send you the statistics next time I'm at the MADD office. The minute nobody's paying attention to him, Robert Owens will get back behind the wheel of a car and resume his normal life. And normal for him means drinking and driving. In that order."

"He's in AA, Tessa. You heard Avery. He plans to continue——in fact, continuing is part of his probation agreement."

"Wouldn't you say the same thing if you were in his shoes?"

"Yes, and I might mean it, too." Mack put his hand on her arm. "Do you think I miss her any less than you do? I don't. You know I don't. But do I have the right to insist this young man hasn't been rehabilitated? Do you? Do we have the right to assume he's the same person he was when he went to prison?"

"He's a drunk and a murderer!"

Mack shook his head. "It's the hardest thing we'll ever have to do, but now we have to give him the benefit of the doubt. So far he's done everything he was required to do and then some. He's going home to live with his mother, and from all accounts she's a good woman and a good influence."

"Then why didn't she stop him before he killed our daughter!"

But Tessa knew the story, and as Mack dropped his hand and waited for her to gain control of herself, the facts played through her head, the way they'd played out in the courtroom.

Robert Owens's parents divorced when he was thirteen. The boy suffered after the split, acting out and getting himself into minor scrapes. Although his mother had custody, he insisted she was too strict, so he ran away from her home in Manassas to live with his father in Fairfax. And despite his mother's pleas to the court, despite evidence that the father was a bad influence who made no attempts to control his son's behavior, the courts had not stepped in.

"She couldn't control him when he was a teenager," Tessa said. "What makes you think she can do it now?"

"Robert has to control himself," Mack said. "But she'll provide the kind of home he needs to get back on his feet. The father's not around any longer to corrupt the process."

Robert's father had died while he was in prison, and Tessa hadn't felt a pang of sympathy for the man or his son. She shifted in her seat, longing to get out. "Did you tell Judge Lutz this? When you were setting up the appointment? Did you tell him that *you* understood why they were setting Kayley's murderer free, but you thought I needed to hear it right from his lips?"

Anger flashed in his eyes. "No. I told him we were *both* upset, that we'd been assured that Owens would serve out the full four years before he was put on probation. I asked him to help us."

She felt a prick of shame. Mack was not manipulative. If anything, he was honest to a fault. She knew he would never have taken her to see the judge under false pretenses.

She looked away. She wanted to blame somebody for this travesty of justice, and Mack was sitting right there. She had blamed him after Kayley's death for the same reason. If only he had taken Kayley to school as he promised. If only he hadn't put his job first.

What she had learned in the sad aftermath was that there was really only one person to blame, and he had been sent to jail for only a few short years.

"I'm sorry." She stared out the window at the gray cedar siding, the careful groupings of evergreens, mulch and strategically placed rocks that were their front yard. "Of course you did."

"There is nothing we can do now," he said. "We have to let go of this, as hard as that's going to be. The law will follow through. Avery said he'll talk to Owens's probation officer himself and make sure he or she understands that any slip at all and he's back in prison serving out the full term. He'll monitor his progress himself. It's more than he has to do. Much more."

"What if there *was* something we could do?" She turned her head to look at him again. "What if we aren't helpless after all?"

He frowned. "Please tell me you're not talking about vigilante justice."

"I've thought of it." She watched his frown deepen. "And you haven't?"

"In the early days, yes. I wanted to kill him with my bare hands. That's normal enough. I've heard other parents who lost a child that way or worse say the same thing."

"But you're over that?"

"I'm over wanting to strangle him, yes. I haven't forgiven him."

"Are you trying to?"

"I'm just trying to find peace." He paused. "What did you mean about doing something?"

"I don't know yet. I'm not talking about anything illegal."

He seemed to relax a little. "It would be healthier not to do anything at all."

"How can you be so ready to leave this behind? Are you in such a hurry to move on to the rest of your life that you've forgotten the part you already lived?"

"We can't bring her back, Tessa, no matter what we do. Holding on to all the bad memories won't help. You've gotten rid of the good ones, but you're holding on to the bad ones so tightly they're destroying you. You have to let go and make room for the good ones again, and for a future. We deserve one. Do you think Kayley would want us to be unhappy?"

"I doubt that Kayley ever thought about it. She was five. Death was just a word to her until a drunk confused the accelerator with the brake, the road with the sidewalk."

Mack leaned forward. "She loved us the way only a child that age can. Making us happy was her joy. She's gone on to something else. I don't know what. I wish I did. I wish my faith was so simple and secure that I believed in a heaven where she's watching over us. But on the off chance it's true, is this what you want her to see? You'll break her heart, Tessa. You're breaking mine."

She couldn't look at him anymore. This was the kind of conversation he always needed to have, and the kind that made her stomach roll. He wanted to talk about feelings and moving forward. She wanted to talk about finding justice.

And if they couldn't communicate, what was the point of their marriage? Why hadn't they pulled the plug? After all, he had her replacement waiting in the wings. Why was he still trying?

Why was *she?*

"Don't do anything foolish," Mack said. "You're not rational about this, you know you're not."

"Are we talking about Robert Owens or our marriage?"

"Let's not mix the two."

She gave him one last glance. "But they *are* mixed. They're so twined around each other that I don't know where one ends and the other begins. Robert Owens killed our daughter, and now he's killing our marriage."

"No, we're doing *that* all by ourselves." He rested his hand on hers for the briefest of moments before she pulled away.

"Thanks for including me this morning," she said stiffly, reaching for the door handle.

"Don't go yet. Stay here with me today. I don't have a busy morning. I'll cancel my appointments."

She hesitated. What would they do? Make love? Talk more about things that should never be discussed? Could they go out together like two normal people, take a walk, perhaps, or browse through a museum? Watch a movie as if their own lives weren't drama enough?

"We can just be together," he said, as if answering her unspoken questions. "No strings. And no more talk of Owens. I miss you. I miss being with you."

For a moment she was tempted. Perhaps this was the only chance to find their way back together, one hour spent in each other's company, then another. One laugh, then another. One meal eaten without recrimination, followed by another, then another...

In the end, though, she couldn't bear it. Because no matter what they did together, there would always be an empty chair, a pause in conversation as they waited for a childish interjection, the desperate yearning for the high-pitched laughter of a little girl.

In the end, she was too much of a coward to search for Mack again.

"I have to get back." She opened her door. "A neighbor's coming this afternoon to see Gram, and I ought to be there. Gram has so little patience, I'm never sure what she's going to say."

"And your mother can't handle that?"

"You know my mother. The two of them will get into a fight, guest or no guest."

He didn't try to stop her. "All right. Give them both my love."

"I will." She was already standing on the driveway when he spoke again.

His words were soft, but she heard them anyway. "If you ever get tired of avoiding me, Tessa, you know where I live."

Cissy wore a striped top that looked like a beach umbrella over the bulge that was her baby-to-be. She had pinned her blond hair off her neck, but damp ringlets adorned her nape and forehead. Tessa thought she looked like the poster girl for corrupted innocence, Hester Prynne in her final months of confinement.

"Gram's upstairs getting some supplies together," Tessa said as Cissy lumbered up to the porch. "She'll be down in a bit." She lowered her voice. "She's really looking forward to this, no matter what she tells you. She's been sorting through threads and needles and patterns since lunch."

Cissy took the same chair she had last time, almost as if she had claimed it as her own. "I've been looking forward to it, too. I really want to make the baby a quilt. I don't know if it's a boy or girl. I told the doctor not to tell me, and Zeke says he don't care. But I think maybe he does."

Tessa was helpless not to respond. "He wants a boy?"

"No, ma'am, a girl. He says he'd like a girl that looked like me." Cissy's smooth skin turned a deeper peach. "He's a good man. I hope you don't think different about him."

"It's not my place to think anything." Tessa heard how rigid, how cold, she sounded, and that disconcerted her. She was still immersed in her conversation with Mack, even though it had occurred hours before. And she hadn't slept well last night. The nightmare had returned, and she had awakened at two in the morning to the terrifying squealing of brakes. She had never gotten back to sleep.

She tried to warm her voice. "What I mean is that this is your life, Cissy, and nobody else's."

"I know, but it worries me that people will think he's not good and decent, on account of my living with him and having his baby."

Tessa decided to avoid that minefield. She was too exhausted for confidences, too emotionally battered to get involved. She searched for a safer subject and hoped her grandmother would arrive soon. Nancy, busy sorting linens upstairs, wouldn't rescue her.

Cissy found a subject before she could. "I brought back that book you loaned me. *Tess*. It's a pretty name. Did your mother name you after the girl in the story?"

Tessa grimaced. "I hope not. No, Tessa's just a nickname." Nancy had chosen the more ostentatious Teresa Michelle, but Billy had shortened it to Tessa the first time he saw his baby daughter.

Cissy reached into the canvas bag she'd brought with her. She took out a square of neatly folded fabric and an old tomato pincushion studded with straight pins. Then she removed the book and held it out to Tessa.

Tessa hadn't expected to see Hardy's book again so soon, if ever. She was touched that Cissy had been so prompt and faithful. She wished she had searched Helen's motley book collection or the private stash she had brought with her for something that was more likely to have been read.

"If you'd like, I could look for another book you might like better," she said. "Gram has quite an assortment."

"Oh, I liked that one just fine. It wasn't the easiest book I ever read, but it made me think a lot, you know? And I like a book that does that."

Tessa was surprised. "So you finished it." She struggled not to make the words into a question.

"Last week. But I've been going through it some, looking for answers to some of the questions I had. So I held on to it a while. I hope that was okay? You didn't need it sooner?"

"No. No..." Tessa settled back in her chair. The teacher Tessa MacRae was powerless to resist continuing. "What kind of questions?"

"Well, you know, the times were different then. I understand that. And I guess in England, at least then, people got stuck a lot right where they were and couldn't really make changes.... I mean, a beggar couldn't really turn himself into a prince."

Except on the pages of Mark Twain. Tessa encouraged Cissy with a nod.

"But I think that being stuck was what Mr. Hardy, the writer, you know, that's what he thought the world was all about. It didn't seem to matter what Tess did or tried to do. Her fate was all decided. And who would believe that? I mean, if you can't fix anything in your life, why would you want to go on living?"

Tessa figured an explanation was in order. "Hardy lived at a difficult time. The world was going through enormous changes. He got caught between rural village life, which had a rhythm and security of sorts, and industrialization, which made so many abrupt changes in what people did and thought that everything was more or less thrown into chaos. That helped make his writing..." Tessa searched for the right word.

"Gloomy?"

Tessa realized she was enjoying this, even as she was taking herself to task for getting involved. She had assumed that Cissy, because of her accent and grammar, even her status in life, would not be able to glean anything from the novel. Like too many of the people in Hardy's work, Tessa's own prejudices about class and education had affected her judgment.

"Gloomy," Tessa admitted.

"You know, the world's like that now. Look at life out here in the country. I bet if you asked your grandmother, she'd tell you that everything's changing so fast there's not much point in making plans based on the way things used to be. Take Zeke. Not so many years ago, he would have just taken over his daddy's farm when Mr. Claiborne passed away. Well, him along with Gabe and Josh."

"Gabe and Josh?"

"His older brothers. Gabe lives up the road, but he works with Mr. Claiborne, and Josh drives a truck, but he comes home when they need him. Anyway, there's not enough work for the three of them all the time. Josh don't care, but Gabe wants to keep farming. So that leaves Zeke with nothing to do."

Tessa could hear the whooshing sound as she got sucked in further and further against her will. "That must be a problem for him."

"Oh, no. No, it's a good thing. See, Zeke don't—doesn't want to be a farmer. He wants to be a luthier."

"I'm sorry, what does that mean?"

"He's a musician himself, bluegrass and old-time mountain music. He can play anything. Guitar, fiddle, mandolin. But he wants to make instruments and repair them. He's been training for the repair part with an old man over in West Virginia."

"That must take a lot of skill."

"It does. So see, even though things change, you can adjust and find your place and happiness. I looked up Mr. Hardy in the encyclopedia, and it said he was the son of a man who built houses. But he became a writer, didn't he? He didn't have to be what his father was. So why does he believe people can't break away and be more than fate says they have to be?"

Tessa had simply loaned the girl a book. She had never expected this thoughtful analysis, or the way the story had brought out Cissy's own concerns about her life.

"And another thing," Cissy continued, before Tessa could answer. "I don't think God punishes girls for the things men do to them." She sat forward. "I don't believe in that kind of God, even if Hardy did. God is good, even if men aren't. God doesn't make bad things happen. Nobody will ever make me believe he does! I was glad I wasn't Tess. But I think I'm even gladder I'm not Thomas Hardy."

The girl hadn't had an easy life. The few things she'd said had confirmed that. Now she was pregnant out of wedlock, poor, unable to pursue the education she so obviously deserved. And still, she was God's very own champion. Put Thomas Hardy and Cissy Mowrey in the same room, and Tessa would be forced to bet on Cissy.

Tessa realized a schoolmarmish response wasn't what the girl needed, but she couldn't venture more. "I don't think he's quite as unfeeling as you make him sound. I think Hardy was trying to show that Tess was pure both before and after the birth of her baby. Her fate might have been predetermined, but she wasn't at fault. In that way his book was different from so many of the others written about that same time."

"Maybe so, but the baby still died, didn't she? And Tess dies, too." Cissy looked distressed. "They kill her."

Tessa couldn't help herself. She saw how personal the discussion had become. She leaned over and touched Cissy's hand. "You're going to be fine, Cissy. Your baby's going to be fine."

Cissy swallowed hard and nodded.

"I think you're a very intelligent young woman. Why don't you put some of your thoughts in writing? It would help you organize them a little. You have so many good things to say." Tessa sat back.

"Oh, no, ma'am, I can't write very well. I mean, I never really learned how. My family moved so much, and I wasn't in school as often as I should have been. So I didn't really..."

"Why don't you let me help you?" Tessa wasn't sure who was more surprised at the offer, Cissy or herself.

"Help me with my writing?"

It was too late to change her mind. Tessa managed a nod. "If you'd like."

"I wouldn't know where to start."

"Why don't you start by just saying what you thought about the book? Just list your thoughts about it and put them in some kind of order. Then we'll talk about what you did."

Cissy's mobile face wrinkled into a frown. "I'd be embarrassed."

"You don't need to be. I'm a teacher. You wouldn't believe the mistakes I've seen." She hesitated. "Or the progress. And, Cissy, if you ever need to get a job, you know, after the baby's born, then you'll need good writing skills. You're already a good reader. You can put your ideas into words. Writing them down won't be as hard as you think."

Cissy looked directly at Tessa. "You would do that for me?"

Even as she nodded, Tessa wondered if she understood all the reasons why she had offered. Who was she trying to help, Cissy or herself?

CHAPTER
15

Helen didn't know what good school was to a girl if she didn't learn to sew. Sure, she knew that most girls today bought their clothes, their bed linens and blankets. They ate out, too, or grabbed dinner through a window at some fast food place. But didn't any girl need to know how to sew on a button or hem a dress, never mind cook a meal for her children? Delilah had taught her daughter to be proud of her skills; she'd called them the womanly arts. But what was womanly or artistic about grabbing a skirt off a rack or eating a hamburger out of wrapping paper?

"I take it poor Cissy doesn't know how to sew?" Nancy joined her mother on the front porch before supper, easing herself down in the swing beside her.

Helen had been so engrossed in her thoughts, she hadn't heard the screen door open and close. It took her a while to make room for her daughter. "What makes you think that?"

"I heard you lecturing her earlier. I wonder if she'll come back? I had to sit through your lectures, you know, but that girl doesn't."

"I wasn't lecturing!" Helen thought about it. "Well, she needed a lecture or two, didn't she? Didn't even know how to tie the knot in her thread. And you? You needed a lot more than I ever gave you. Never did see a girl less inclined to work than you."

"I wasn't lazy." Nancy rested her head against the back of the swing. "You always thought I was. I was just different than you. I saw other possibilities for my life. Maybe I was more like my daddy."

Helen wondered if it was true. She wasn't sure anymore. Over the years, her memories of Fate had diminished.

"Do you think I'm like him?" Nancy prompted.

"It takes a lot of years to know a person, to find out what they're all about inside. I knew Fate as a boy, but just enough to know I wanted him as a man. I knew the man for too short a time to say much about him."

"Lord, that's sad."

"Don't get all weepy about it."

"I know. I know." Nancy waved her hand in front of her. "I cried more than any girl in Shenandoah County. You don't have to tell me again. At least you didn't send poor Cissy into tears today. Or did you?"

"She's got a spine, that girl. I can say that much for her."

"And I didn't." It wasn't a question.

Helen surprised herself. "You? You had the stiffest spine I ever did see. Maybe you cried buckets on the outside, but inside you had more determination and just plain guts than any girl I ever knew."

Nancy was silent. After a moment, Helen ventured a glance. Her daughter looked like someone had just thrown ice down her shirt. "Well, don't pretend you didn't know," Helen demanded.

"Now I might really cry. I think that's the nicest thing, maybe the *only* nice thing, you've ever said to me."

"Oh, go on."

"Well, it's true. I grew up thinking I was about the biggest disappointment in the state of Virginia."

"Never the biggest. You do love to exaggerate."

Nancy nudged her with an elbow. "And you do love to lecture."

"What's Gram lecturing about today?" Tessa came out on the porch with the wedding ring quilt folded under her arm. "Should I leave?"

"I thought you was making supper," Helen said. "I'm about to starve to death."

"I'll do a stir-fry as soon as the brown rice is cooked. Everything's all ready. Can you hold off another half hour or so?"

"If God wanted rice to be brown, that's how he would have made it."

"Exactly." Tessa settled herself in the chair catty-corner to the swing. "Did things go well with Cissy?"

"Well enough. She chose a pinwheel pattern, and I taught her how to cut and mark her fabric. Once she's all done with that, she's coming back."

"If your grandmother didn't scare her away," Nancy said.

"That girl don't scare." Helen paused, then she added, "I think she likes being here."

"She's lonely," Tessa agreed. "I don't think there's much for her to do over at the Claibornes' right now."

"There'll be plenty when that baby's born."

"Has she said anything about the baby?" Nancy asked. "Is she going to keep it?"

To Helen, the answer seemed perfectly obvious. "She's making a quilt, isn't she? Seems likely she's not planning to wrap that baby up tight and give it away."

Nancy gave an extravagant sigh. "It would be better for the baby if she did. How's she going to raise it? Between them, I'll just bet she and that boy don't have a plugged nickel."

Helen had worried some about that herself, so she couldn't fault her daughter for bringing it up. "You ever think about adopting?" She addressed her question to Tessa.

Tessa frowned. "No."

"You and Mack are the kind of people the county goes looking for. Can you say it hasn't crossed your mind you'd be better parents than Cissy and that Zeke could ever be?" Helen could feel her daughter's elbow in her ribs, poking and poking some more, but she didn't stop. "You know for sure you're good parents. You're experienced."

"I don't know anything for sure anymore." Tessa's lips were drawn in a tight line, and the words barely squeezed out. "Doesn't every woman look at a girl like Cissy, a girl who's still a child herself, and wonder if she could do a better job with her baby?"

Helen thought her granddaughter's answer was as good as a "yes." Tessa had imagined, even for just a moment, adopting the child. That struck Helen as progress.

"If Cissy wants to give up the baby, there will be five hundred well qualified couples standing on her doorstep the next day," Nancy said. "There aren't very many healthy babies out there for adoption, and fertility is declining. That means a lot of couples are childless who don't want to be."

"You read that in some women's magazine?" Helen said.

"No. I learned it firsthand. I volunteer on the children's ward of a hospital in Richmond. And I've talked to so many parents with sick children who tried and tried to give their child a brother or sister and never succeeded."

"What kind of volunteer work?" Tessa's frown had deepened. "I know you raise money for a lot of different groups, but this sounds personal."

"I work in the children's ward with an art therapist. I help the children express what they're feeling with crayons or chalk or paint. Then I take their pictures and frame them so they can put them right on the wall of their rooms, then take them home. If they go home..."

"You never told me that," Tessa said.

"You never asked. That's where I go when I go back to Richmond. There's a little gallery in Carytown that has its own framing studio in the back, and they sell me the supplies at cost. The owner taught me what to do. It's nothing fancy, but it makes the kids feel special."

"Carytown? When did you start?" Tessa asked.

Nancy hesitated. "A while ago."

"Three years?"

Nancy nodded. "Just about."

Tessa fell silent.

Helen felt the lapse in conversation like a weight dragging at them. She searched for a topic and found it right in front of her. Tessa was unfolding the quilt and refolding it. "What're you doing?"

"I'm going to take out part of this arc." Tessa tilted the folded quilt so Helen could see the section in question. "All these green fabrics have shredded, so there's hardly anything left. I thought I'd get a start. I'm supposed to just snip away any quilting that's holding it together." She looked up at her mother. "Maybe you can be the one to put the new stitches in."

"I'll leave that to you." Nancy leaned forward to look at the quilt, and the swing, which had been rocking gently, stopped. "Do you remember who gave you the green fabric or why?" she asked her mother.

Helen squinted. The green was so faded and torn that for a moment the memory evaded her. Then she remembered. "My Aunt Sally, bless her. It was left over from the first dress she made my cousin Minnie. Used to be a pretty soft green with tiny little polka dots." She shook her head.

"Sounds like something I can find a match for," Tessa said.

"Tessa, I think you should save scraps of each fabric you take out," Nancy said. "We can make a little journal to go with the quilt, and your grandmother can explain who gave each piece to her and why. An ongoing history."

Helen was amazed at the fuss. "All that for an old quilt?"

Nancy began to rock the swing again. "Not just any quilt. You know, I'm curious. You've told us a lot about the years when you were piecing it, but you haven't said why you never quilted it."

"I guess I didn't."

"Why didn't you?"

Helen tried on her responses and none of them fit.

"I just couldn't, that's all," she said at last.

"Wasn't it finished when you got married?"

"That was a long time ago," Helen said. "You're asking me to re-member a long ways."

Nancy twisted so she was looking at her mother. The swing stopped again. "You've never told me anything about the day you married my dad. Why don't you tell us now? The rice has to cook anyway."

"I'd like to hear, too, Gram," Tessa said, before Helen could re-fuse.

Helen wondered which was sadder, the fact that she had never told her own daughter and granddaughter about her wedding day, or the fact that she was so afraid to relive it that she didn't want to talk about it now.

She decided to tell the briefest version. "I told you Fate and I decided we'd wait to get married until after he joined the Navy and finished training. That way I could stay and take care of Mama until she didn't need taking care of no more. He joined up, just like he said he was going to. And while he was finishing off at boot camp at the Great Lakes Training Station over in Ohio, Mama took real sick."

She fell silent, remembering.

"Is that when she died?" Nancy asked.

"No, but we knew it was just a matter of weeks before we'd lose her. So I wrote Fate and told him we had to get married the very minute he got leave, so Mama could be there. I knew it would mean everything to her. Turned out though, that even though he was supposed to get twenty-one days off after his training, by the time he finished up, the government was saying there was a national emergency and he was going to have to ship right out."

"So your mother wasn't with you for the wedding?" Nancy asked.

Helen felt Nancy's hand patting hers, and the welcome weight of it made telling the story easier. "Let me tell it my way."

A morning finally came when Delilah just couldn't get out of bed. When Helen took her mother breakfast, Delilah could only pick at it, too weak to eat.

Downstairs again, Helen found Tom, who was lacing up his work boots to go and trim the apple trees in their substantial orchard. A winter of harsh winds and heavy snowstorms had brought down branches and left even more hanging. Tom would be out there for most of a week, sawing and hauling wood.

"Mama's feeling worse," she told him.

Cuddy had already been gone for an hour, and Obed and Dorothy, married the previous month, were staying with Dorothy's family during the week, because there was an old cabin on the property where they could be alone. Tom and Helen were in charge.

"Do you want me to get the doctor?" he asked.

The local doctor had already told them to prepare for the worst. He might come again, but Helen knew there was no real point in calling him. Not unless he could give Delilah a brand-new heart.

She shook her head even as she said, "But maybe you can come back for dinner? I was going to pack you something so you wouldn't have to bother, but it'd be nice knowing someone was coming back to check on things."

He smiled briefly. Too briefly. Tom had always been a serious boy. Now he was a serious young man, tall and thin like his father, with the same square face an ancestor had bequeathed Helen. If he'd ever had dreams or aspirations beyond their land and family, the Depression and Delilah's illness had extinguished them. He was even too busy for a serious sweetheart, although half a dozen local girls had their eyes on him.

"Course I'll come," he said. "You ring the bell about noon, and I'll come down. Or you ring it any time if you need me."

The bell, from an old schoolhouse, had seemed like a bit of foolishness on Cuddy's part when he'd lugged it home from town one day last fall and installed it near the house. But now Helen understood why it was there. Even then, her father had known that one day soon they would need a way to signal each other.

The house seemed too quiet after Tom left. She did the indoor chores, having risen before dawn to do the others while her father and brother were there to care for her mother. Since it was a Monday, she had planned to wash, hoping that Delilah would be well enough to sit at the quilting frame, where Helen could keep an eye on her through the window as she hung clothes on the line. It was a brisk March day, but the sun was shining, beckoning her to begin on the mound of laundry.

She decided to bake, instead. Delilah liked corn bread with milk poured over it, and Helen set out to make some for her mother's dinner. As she stirred the cornmeal and hot water, and heated the cast-iron skillet, she thought about the letter she had received the night before.

Fate liked to write her. She knew he took a long time composing the letters he sent. There was never a mistake, no words crossed out, no places where he ran off the page. She imagined him copying his words over and over until he got them just right. Ever since he had gone to Chillicothe for training, he had written once a week, telling her about his fellow recruits and the camp, how cold it was in Ohio and how much he missed seeing her. Cuddy picked up the letters in town and faithfully brought them back to her. She had kept every one.

Last night's letter had been a bitter disappointment. Fate's three-week leave, reward for three grueling months, had been canceled. He was to board a train for Long Beach, California, where the battleship *Oklahoma* was berthed, and he was to begin his naval career as an apprentice seaman.

Their marriage would be delayed indefinitely.

Helen had known they wouldn't be able to start their life together right away. Fate had to settle into the navy for a while before she could join him. She understood that, and besides, she had responsibilities here. But she had always counted on Delilah being with her when the pastor blessed her marriage to Fate, and she knew her mother had counted on it, too. Now, with Delilah's health rapidly worsening, she knew that simple wish would be denied them both.

Outside the kitchen window, crocuses bloomed along the path to the barn. She loved spring, particularly after a hard winter, but the next months seemed to stretch in front of her like a prison sentence.

At noon she rang the dinner bell for Tom; then she took a tray up to her mother again. She had checked on Delilah twice, and both times she had been sleeping. Now she took the tray to her bedside and gently shook her shoulder. "Mama?"

Delilah's eyes opened, and she stared for a moment; then she smiled. "I was having the nicest dream."

"I'm sorry I woke you up, then."

"I was with your granny, in a meadow filled with wildflowers."

"Next time take me along."

"I don't think you want to go there, Lenny. Not for a long time yet."

Helen didn't know what to say. More and more often, her mother talked about heaven and going home. Her religious convictions were strong, much stronger than Helen's own. Helen was glad the thought of heaven gave her mother comfort, but it gave her none at all. No matter where Delilah went, she wouldn't be here with her daughter.

Delilah struggled to sit, and Helen propped pillows behind her and smoothed the pile of quilts that covered her. These days Delilah was always cold, and the number of quilts mounted daily.

"I brought you corn bread and milk," Helen told her. "And some stewed apples, too. You can't keep up your strength if you don't eat."

"You best leave it and go down and feed Tom. It'll take me a while, but I'll eat every bite."

Helen felt encouraged. "I'll be back up just as soon as he's eaten."

"You eat, too, and take your time. You got to keep up your strength, too. Your granny told me to tell you that. She said you've got to stay strong, and you've got to stay calm and not worry. She said things have a habit of turning out right."

Helen stared at her mother. Delilah's cheeks actually had a little pink in them, a welcome change from the bluish tinge that had deepened ominously in the past weeks. "What things?"

Delilah smiled a little. "She said to get your hope chest all ready."

Helen hadn't yet told her mother that Fate couldn't get leave before he shipped out. Delilah had too many problems to burden her with more. Presented with this opportunity to set the record straight, Helen left the room instead. Let Delilah believe something good was about to happen. If it had brought a little color to her cheeks, so much the better.

She scrubbed floors in the afternoon and did a few more outside chores that didn't require long stretches of time away from the house. Cuddy would be home earlier tomorrow afternoon, and she could do a little washing then, and maybe get a start on planting potatoes in the vegetable garden while he sat with Delilah. A neighbor dropped by with an apple cake and left word that she'd seen Helen's Aunt Mavis in town yesterday, and Mavis had said she would be visiting in the morning.

She made ham pot pie, Delilah's favorite, for supper, simmering a ham bone from Sunday dinner with carrots and onions all afternoon as she went about her chores. When Cuddy arrived and Tom came in from the orchard, she removed the bone and shredded what meat hadn't already fallen into the broth, then she rolled pastry dough she'd mixed earlier into a thin layer and cut it into squares, adding them to the broth until they were cooked.

She was delighted when Delilah arrived at the table on Cuddy's arm. She looked pale but rested.

"I could smell it cooking all the way upstairs," Delilah said. "And didn't it smell good?"

"Nobody cooks as good as you, Ma," Tom said, "but Helen does all right, don't she?"

Helen beamed at the unexpected compliments.

Most of the time there wasn't much conversation over meals. Everyone worked hard and ate heartily, whether the table was spread with something special, like it was now, or simpler fare. But tonight Cuddy talked about people he'd seen at the feed store that day, and Tom told them how the sheriff had raided a still up on Massanutten Mountain and brought it back down to Woodstock strapped on the running board of his car. Two days later the lawyers who frequented that particular still had it hauled right back up again—or so the gossips said.

Cuddy waited until the end of the meal before he turned to Helen. "I got a telephone call at the store real early today, Lenny Lou."

There were no telephones yet on Fitch Crossing Road, and even if there had been, the Stoneburners would have done without. Everybody knew that old Mr. Fuchs, who owned and ran the store, frowned on using the telephone for personal business, so phone calls to Cuddy at the feed store usually meant bad news.

Helen had just started clearing the table. Now she sank back to her chair. "Somebody died?"

Her father grinned. "Not hardly."

She waited, but she realized he wanted her to guess. She tried to imagine who might have called him there. "Did Minnie have her baby?" Her cousin Minnie over near Front Royal was only seventeen and working on her second child, but that hardly seemed a reason for using the telephone.

"No, that weren't it."

She looked to Tom for help, but he shrugged. Delilah obviously knew, because she was smiling.

"Well, what was it, then?" she said. "I don't have any more guesses."

"It was about a wedding."

She tried to think who might be getting married, which cousin lived so far away he or she would have to call with the news. Only when she realized that both parents were beaming sunshine in her direction did she understand.

"Fate?" she asked, crossing her hands on her chest. "Did Fate call you?"

"He did. He'll be right here late this evening, and he wants to marry you tomorrow evening, right here in the parlor. They give him three days, on account of him doing so good on his training. One day to get here, one day to go back, and one day to stay and get married."

She thought about what a sacrifice this was, how Fate would get back to Ohio just in time to make the endless train trip out to California. He was doing this for her, and for her mother. Tears filled her eyes. "Right here. Will the pastor come?"

"I already asked, and he says yes. And Mr. Fuchs says Fate can drive his car to Woodstock tomorrow to get the license."

"Is there time to tell anybody?"

"Mr. Fuchs, he let me call your mama's sisters, and they'll get the word to everybody faster than any telephone could. Anybody who can come, will."

She knew they were having the wedding at home so that Delilah could be there. She had stopped going to church weeks ago because the trip took so much out of her.

"It won't be fancy," Cuddy warned, "but you'll be a married woman."

Helen thought of the dress she'd wanted to make and hadn't, of the way she had let her hair go after Fate's departure, of the ragged state of her nails and the garden soil embedded so deeply in her hands it was an indelible stain.

She thought of the man she loved, the only one she ever would.

"I don't want fancy, I just want Fate." She got to her feet. There were dishes to clear and a wedding to plan. And suddenly she had enough energy to conquer the world.

She was standing by the front gate late that evening when the Claibornes drove up in their old farm truck. They had agreed to pick up Fate at the station in Woodstock, a surprising act of generosity. He would bunk with Tom tonight, and tomorrow night, well, she wasn't sure she was ready to think about tomorrow at all.

She hadn't seen him in three months, but the moment he swept her into his arms, her shyness disappeared. He kissed her, and she kissed him right back for so long that she wasn't sure she remembered how to breathe once they'd finished. She stepped back and avidly examined him. He wore a white hat—he'd told her in one of his letters they called it a Dixie Cup—and a blue sailor's uniform covered by a thick wool peacoat. His hair was shorter than she'd ever seen it. As she watched, he scooped off the hat and stuffed it in the pocket of his jacket.

"You look wonderful, Fate." She grabbed his hands. "You never looked better."

"You look wonderful, too. Beautiful. Even more beautiful than I remembered."

The night was cool, and the wind ruffled Helen's hair, but she didn't want to go inside yet. She wanted him all to herself. "I couldn't believe it when Daddy told me you were coming after all."

"I had to do some fancy talking, but they let me do it because of your ma."

"She's livelier than we've seen her in weeks. The wedding means so much to her."

"And how about you? What's it mean to you?" he asked with a grin.

"Well, it just means the world, that's all."

"To me, too."

The shyness returned. She knew she wasn't beautiful, even if he'd said so. But this man loved her. He had traveled here to marry her, against the odds. Tomorrow they would be husband and wife. Tomorrow night. . .

"I kept thinking about you the whole time I was away," he said. The words were measured, as if he'd practiced them the way he practiced his letters to her. "I know I'm lucky to have you, Helen. But I promise I'll do everything I can to make our life good. I don't know where we'll have to go, but wherever it is, we'll be together. I'm sorry I'll be taking you away from your family, but we'll come and visit as much as we can."

She thought of her family and the farm, to which she was whole-heartedly devoted. Then she thought of the wide world beyond Fitch Crossing Road and the many sights and sounds she had never even hoped to experience. Fate Henry was giving her more than just himself. He was giving her a new life and new opportunities, and once she could, she would embrace them without reservation.

"I want to be with you, wherever you are." She squeezed his hands. He pulled her into his arms again and kissed her hungrily. The weight she had carried for so many months lifted. One life was ending, yes. But another was about to begin. This was what her mother had wanted for her. This was what seeing Helen safely married had really meant to Delilah.

CHAPTER
16

"The next day was busy, the way you'd imagine it to be considering that we had just that one day to make it all happen. Turned out my Aunt Mavis had made me a dress. I guess you'd think it was nothing special, but it was about the prettiest dress I'd ever seen, pale ivory with little teeny violets sprinkled all over it. Rayon, too, all the way from a store in Washington, D.C. And my Aunt Sally bought me a real pair of nylons. A whole dollar and a quarter they cost her, which in those days was a lot of money. I still remember. My first pair, and the only ones I ever had 'til well after the war, too."

Helen signaled Tessa to hand her the quilt. She turned it over, then over again, until she found what she was looking for. She had known, even then, that her wedding dress would not hold up to serious washing, but after Fate left for California and the *Oklahoma,* she had decided to use a scrap of the fabric provided by her aunt for one piece anyway.

"Here it is," she said. "Or what's left of it. Not much to see anymore." There was nothing much there except threads tacked to the batting by the lines of Nancy's quilting.

Nancy had listened to the story with rapt attention. She was sixty, well past the age when romance was supposed to thrill her, but clearly this was no ordinary story. Not to her. Helen was ashamed it had taken so long to tell it.

"You had the wedding right here?" Nancy asked.

"Inside, right there in the parlor. Mama had Tom move her quilt frame down to the fruit cellar, and we set up as many chairs as we could fit. The pastor stood in front of the windows, with me and Fate facing him. Fate wore his uniform. So many people came that they was standing all the way into the dining room and beyond."

Helen stared off into the distance, watching that night unfold again. "Everybody brought food. You never saw so much good food. Mama cried, and so did Aunt Mavis. After the pastor was finished with us, they cleared out the chairs, and the men brought out their instruments. We had a regular string band, and the music and singing and cutting-up went on until it got too late and people remembered they had to work the next morning."

"Did you and Fate—Dad—stay here that night?"

Helen glanced at her daughter. "Too much ruckus. No, Obed and Dorothy let us have their little cabin, over at Dorothy's parents' home place. The cabin's gone now. There's a big chicken house sitting right where it used to be. Back then it wasn't much, but it was quiet, and we could be alone."

"That was your only night alone together?" Tessa asked.

Helen was surprised, but her granddaughter seemed as interested as Nancy. Tessa had forgotten to keep her distance. Helen thought that was another good sign.

"Well, we weren't exactly alone," she said. She peeked at Nancy and Tessa, and saw their frowns. She wanted to laugh. It had taken this long, she guessed, to laugh about what had come next.

"You want me to tell you, don't you?" she demanded.

"May...be." Nancy didn't sound quite sure. "Unless it's too personal."

"The heck with that," Tessa said. "We've gotten this far. I want the rest."

"What about that rice?" Helen said. "Even brown rice gets soft after a while, don't it?"

"After supper, then," Tessa said. "I'll go make the stir-fry."

She disappeared into the house. Helen looked at her daughter. "Fate kept his thoughts to himself, just the way Tessa does. And when he loved somebody, he loved them with everything in his heart. She's like him in that way, too. In lots of ways. I knew it the moment she was born."

Nancy shook her head slowly. "You've never even hinted at that. Didn't you think I wanted to know?"

Helen reached out and touched her daughter's hand. Just the briefest touch. "Until now, I just didn't feel up to telling you."

Fate and Helen sneaked away from the music and the backslapping and the crying children. Obed had given Fate the keys to his old Model T, and for once it started without kicking and cursing. They were a mile down Fitch before either of them breathed easier. The only person they'd said goodbye to was Delilah.

"She looked so happy," Helen said. "Like she was all lit up inside. Does she look sicker to you? Since you been gone, I mean?"

He was quiet for a long time. "Helen, you got to love every moment you got left with her. But even if she's gone by morning, this night, well, it would have meant everything to her. She'll die happy now."

She knew that was his way of making her face the truth. But gently, with kindness. He had always been gentle.

She didn't say anything until they were nearly at the cabin. She knew they had to park at the bottom of the hill and walk up. The road into the farm was bad enough. They each had a bag with things they would need that night, and after he helped her out of the car, he took both bags and held out his hand. They started up the hill, following a well-worn, moonlit path.

The night was chilly, and Helen shivered. Dorothy had warned her the cabin was always cold, and that even though she and Obed had banked the hearth fire before they left for the wedding, it would probably have burned out by now. If they were lucky, there would be a few coals to start another.

Fate lifted her hand to his lips and kissed it, and she felt immediately warmer. The stars were a flickering, cloud-dusted canopy, and even though she was a little concerned about what awaited her inside, she was also anxious just to have Fate to herself. Since his arrival, they had been surrounded by activity and family, with very few private moments.

They stopped at the door, and Fate set the bags on the narrow porch floor and flipped a primitive latch. "Your pa told me I'd better not forget this." Before she could respond, he swept her off her feet and into his arms; then he nudged the door with his shoulder and stepped over the threshold.

"Put me down," she squealed. "I'm practically as big as you are!"

"Not nearly as strong, though," he teased. He set her on her feet, and before she could say another word, he kissed her. She clung to him, only stepping away reluctantly when she realized a frosty wind was sweeping through the open front door.

"If there was anything left of the fire, there won't be now." She shivered again and rubbed her hands up and down her arms. She had refused to wear her shabby old coat and cover her new dress.

"I'll get it burning again." He pulled her close once more, kissing her forehead; then he headed for the fireplace.

Helen got the bags inside and closed the door, latching it from the inside so it would stay that way. She had a moment to look around while Fate tended the fire. The cabin was one room, with stairs leading to an open loft where the bed must be. In the style of many old cabins in the valley, the fireplace and chimney were in the center.

The whole place was no bigger than a minute, but she was immediately envious of her brother and Dorothy, because the cabin was theirs, at least temporarily, and they could live in it together. Even though there were spaces in the chinking between logs, and the windows had gaps around the frames that had been stuffed with newspaper, Dorothy managed to keep it spotless. There were no cobwebs hanging from the rafters, no dust on the rag rug dotted floor.

"Come here and get warmed up," Fate said.

She joined him, holding out her hands as the fire began to flicker, nipping at the freshly split logs Obed had left for them.

"Your family's something special," Fate said. "I used to wish they were my family, too."

"Now they are," she said, slipping a slightly warmer hand into his.

"The Claibornes did all right by me. These are hard times. They took me in, even when they didn't have to."

They had taken him in, yes, but Helen knew how hard he'd had to work for his keep. She could not forgive the Claibornes for treating Fate so differently from the way they had treated their own son.

"You haven't told me hardly a word about Ohio and your training," Helen said.

"We'll have a whole life together for me to tell you things." He turned her to him, and she went willingly. "I'll tell you anything you want. Only later."

She had expected to feel shy. She didn't. She felt beautiful and desirable and lucky. As the cabin warmed—and so did they—and as he finally led her up the stairs to the loft and undressed her, she felt like she was just beginning to understand happiness.

Afterwards they lay in each other's arms, fitting together under a pile of old quilts as if they had always slept that way. Helen stirred and sat up after a time; then she swung her feet to the floor and stood.

"Where're you going?" Fate asked sleepily.

"Nowhere important. Go back to sleep."

She felt her way to her bag and dug through a few things to the very bottom, where she pulled out what she'd completed of the wedding ring top. She went back to the bed and spread it over Fate, crawling in beside him and pulling it over her shoulders, too. It was their wedding quilt. Maybe she hadn't finished it yet, but she wanted to remember they had used it this night.

She drifted to sleep. The darkness deepened.

Then the cowbells began to ring. The front door rattled, and men began to shout.

Fate muttered something but didn't wake up. Helen sat up and began to shake him.

"A belling," Helen said. "Tom and Obed promised they wouldn't!"

But by now Fate was awake. He stumbled to his feet and began pulling on his clothes. "You best put on something, too, Helen. They won't be satisfied 'less we come down."

"Can't you make them go away?"

"You know I can't."

She didn't have time for modesty. The latch was nothing more than a slender piece of wood on a leather thong. Enough jiggling and the door would fly wide open.

She was in her slip and robe when the latch gave way. Fate had his undershirt and pants on, and one sock.

"We're coming to get you!" Feet tramped on the steps, and Gus and Obed emerged.

"You promised!" she wailed.

"Sorry, Lenny, but better me than everybody without me." Obeddi didn't look sorry at all.

She heard women's voices calling her, and despite herself, she smiled. Fate didn't look upset, either, although goodness knows he needed some sleep, since he had to leave for the train station first thing the next morning.

Outside, someone was banging on pots and pans, and the cow-bells continued to chime. The men pretended to wrestle Fate, but it was all for show. They disappeared down the stairs, and, sighing and tightening the belt on her old flannel robe, Helen followed.

Outside, her brothers and their friends, her cousins and their friends, and every neighbor just a shade younger than her parents, were waiting. Everyone hooted and applauded when she arrived, and the clanging got louder.

"Now, Helen, you gonna cooperate or not?" Gus Claiborne asked.

She glared at him. As far as she was concerned, Gus Claiborne was one step below a rattlesnake. "I'm not getting in any old wheelbarrow, and there's nowhere to push one up here, anyway!"

"We got something else!" Gus pointed down the hillside, and Helen saw what awaited them. An old hay wagon hitched up to the Claibornes' team and filled to the top with hay.

"You don't come, we'll tie him up and throw him in," Gus shouted. "And he'll have to go without you." The clanging got louder.

Helen began to laugh. "We got but one night together before he ships off to California, and you want us to spend it in the hay?"

A series of ribald jokes flew through the air. She knew this was a sedate "shivaree" compared to some, where the groom was kid-napped and left tied up by the side of the road. She threw up her hands. "I'll go."

They were escorted by the crowd, pots banging and a washtub adding a deeper bass note to the clatter.

Fate helped her into the wagon, but she still fell face-first into the hay.

He laughed and fell in beside her, burrowing down and pulling her with him.

The hay wagon began to move, and as they circled the farm, then went for a slow ride down the road accompanied by shouts and bells and back again, Fate and Helen cuddled close.

* * *

Nancy tried to picture Helen's description of the wedding and the belling. The house she had grown up in—this very house, where Helen had been married—had always been silent and somber. She supposed that, when she'd been a girl, scattered relatives and neighbors had visited, but not often and not for long. Helen had never been a welcoming hostess. She had been too busy, too tired, too remote, for socializing. Nancy couldn't remember one festive moment, one holiday filled with the exuberant love of family and friends. She had always felt cheated.

Now she waited for the rest of the story, until she realized Helen was finished.

This was every moment of the time her mother and father had had together.

The three women had come back out to the front porch after the stir-fry supper to hear about the rest of Helen's wedding day. Twilight had deepened; the mosquito repellent had been passed around their small circle like a Shenandoah communion cup. Now the story had ended.

"You got your start that night in that old cabin," Helen said. "Your daddy left just after dawn to catch the train back to Ohio, then on to California. He wrote me as often as he could after that, even though they were out at sea a lot of the time. I couldn't reach him when Mama died a month later, but they wouldn't have let him come back, anyway, since he was doing more training. We had her funeral at the church, but she's buried up there on the hillside, where she wanted to be."

"I'm glad she lived to see you married," Tessa said.

"And didn't live to see everything that happened afterwards." Helen stared off into the distance. "Obed and Dorothy moved in after we buried Mama, and Dorothy helped me take care of things. I knew I was having a baby by then, and having Dorothy with me made things easier. Daddy was lost without Mama, but he tried to go on." Her voice grew softer. "I finished piecing the wedding ring top, then I put it away, to quilt when I was done grieving Mama."

"Then Pearl Harbor," Nancy said. The rest of the story was all too familiar.

Helen turned to Nancy. "Your daddy was so happy when he found out I was going to have a baby. He was happy in the Navy, too, happy seeing new places. He was a signalman by then, moving up fast. He didn't have much education, but he was smart as a whip, and they saw that right away. He wrote me all about Honolulu. He wished I could join him there, even for a week or two. We didn't have the money, of course, and you were very nearly here, Nanny, so of course I couldn't travel to Hawaii, but your daddy was fixing to come home the next time he got leave. He was going to come and see you...."

Helen fell silent.

Lafayette "Fate" Henry had died when the first bombs fell on December 7th, 1941. As a child, Nancy had been told that he was one of the luckiest victims, that he had been killed immediately, not left to struggle in the burning water or trapped aboard his sinking ship. Now she wondered if it was true and didn't want to know if it wasn't.

"I put the quilt top away for good after that," Helen said at last. "How could I quilt it? It was my wedding quilt, and my husband was dead."

"I was born just two weeks after he died." Nancy couldn't imagine what her mother had felt, giving birth to the daughter her husband would never see.

"Obed and Tom didn't wait to be drafted, even though they would have gotten deferments, at least for a while. Farmers got them back then. The country needed food, didn't it? But no, they had to go and fight. And I wanted them to, you know. I wanted them to kill the people who had killed my Fate. Only they died, too. Both of them. Tom in Guam in 1944, Obed in Italy the year before. Dorothy got a job working on F4U fighters over at Quantico, and we never saw much of her after that. At the end of the war she married a Marine she'd worked with and moved somewhere up north."

"And your dad?" Tessa asked.

"Worked himself to death. Grieved himself to death. There weren't no help to be had. The young men were all gone, and the women were off doing clerical jobs in Washington or working in defense plants. Daddy thought it was his duty to raise all the food he could. I helped as much as I knew how, but there weren't much I could do with a little baby and all the house chores, too. And the family was all scattered by then, off working in the cities or serving in the military, and there was no one else to lend a hand. Even Aunt Mavis and her family moved on down to Norfolk, then on to Jacksonville, and we never saw much of her after that. It cost too much to travel, and it was too hard. Daddy wore himself out, died of pneumonia. There weren't no antibiotics in those days, you know, not for people like us, and he just couldn't fight it."

Nancy had never realized the pace at which her mother's life had changed. Helen had grown up poor, yes, but there had been love and laughter in this house. Then, in the matter of a few short years, all the joy and comfort had disappeared. Suddenly everything that held meaning for her was gone. All except for one small child, the product of one night of love.

"How did you manage to hold on to the farm?" Tessa asked. "With nobody left to help you?"

"I had my widow's pension, though it weren't much, and the little bit Daddy had saved over the years for a rainy day. I paid the taxes before I paid anything else, so they couldn't take the farm away from me, the way they done during the Depression when people couldn't pay. Then I just made do. Once the war was over and men started coming back, I rented out what fields I could, hired help when it was cheap enough. A local boy took care of the orchards for me and picked all the fruit, and we split what profits there were. I took the smallest cornfield and turned it into a market garden, and trucked everything I grew into town to a little stand I set up by the roadside from May through October."

"And you raised me," Nancy said.

"I did my best. I just had to put the rest of it behind me and keep moving."

But for Nancy, that last part seemed to be the central question. Because the woman Helen had described, the young, optimistic woman Nancy had never known, seemed to have no connection to the careworn, bitter woman who had raised her.

"You put it behind you," Nancy said carefully. "Exactly what did you put behind you?" She glanced at her daughter and saw the slight shake of Tessa's head, the warning in her eyes, but stubbornly, she looked away. "The memories, Mama? Or the feelings, too? The love, the hope, the laughter?"

Helen appeared to ponder the question. She did not react with anger, as Nancy had expected. She seemed to struggle with her answer. "After your daddy died, I didn't want to look back. That's about all I can say."

"I feel like you've described a stranger. I never knew the woman you described. You never let me know her, or the people who loved her and would have loved me."

"They were gone."

Nancy leaned forward. "And so were you."

Helen didn't try to misunderstand. She didn't nod, but something in her eyes confirmed Nancy's words. She got to her feet and started toward the screen door, but she turned once her hand rested on the handle.

"I'd lost them all, you know, Nanny. Every single person I loved. You were a delicate child, always sick with something. Fate's little girl. There you were, just waiting to be lost, too."

* * *

Tessa waited to speak until the screen door's closing no longer echoed. The night wasn't silent. Not far away, a screech owl trilled its territorial call in one of the dogwoods. Coming from behind the house, she could hear the squawking of her grandmother's strange, exotic chickens, and in the far distance the rumbling of thunder from a storm system that would probably offer no rain.

"She'll check on the chickens, fuss over them a little, then she'll go out to the pond," Nancy said. "Whenever something upsets her, that's what she does. When I was a teenager, the chickens were in their element. They got extraordinary care."

Tessa had been prepared to bristle, to accuse her mother of insensitivity, but she heard the love in Nancy's voice. Had love and concern always been there, she wondered, and somehow she hadn't been able to hear them until now?

"It was a hard story to tell." Tessa still felt an unmistakable lump in her throat. She, like everyone else, had written off her grandmother as an odd old woman incapable of reaching out. She had never seen the young woman who had lost nearly everyone who mattered to her, the grieving widow who had been forced to go on anyway so she could support the baby who was her husband's parting gift.

"She was afraid to love me," Nancy said. "I never realized it. By keeping her distance, she thought she could protect me. If she didn't love me, maybe I would escape notice. I would survive."

Tessa was afraid her mother was right. "She does love you."

"I guess she does. But it was a terrible legacy. When you grow up without seeing love firsthand, you never learn how to give it. I've struggled with that all my life and never quite got it right."

Nancy was not above asking for reassurance. In fact, begging for it was as much a part of her character as her vanity and social climbing. But Tessa didn't think she was asking for reassurance now. She was simply stating what she believed.

Nancy had never seen into her own mother's heart. Tessa wondered if she had fallen into the same trap. Had she taken Nancy at face value and been blind to her strengths?

"There were men who were interested in your grandmother," Nancy said. "I remember two, in particular. Good, decent men. One was a widower with three boys. Another was an old bachelor who lived over in Woodstock and drove out of his way every Saturday to come to our vegetable stand. He'd get all slicked up, even wear a polka-dotted bow tie. You might not see it now, but she was a handsome woman. They noticed."

"But she didn't notice them?"

"She was cold as ice. She always said she didn't need a man to take care of, that she had enough to do."

Nancy stood and walked to the railing, looking toward the tree where the owl continued to trill. "Will you listen to that old owl? When I was growing up a screech owl this close to the house meant someone was about to die."

"There's been enough death here." Tessa wasn't thinking only of her grandmother's husband and family, but of Kayley, as well.

"I guess it's easy enough to lock yourself away from everything and everyone that matters to you, if you're afraid. When it comes right down to it, there's a screech owl in everybody's front yard, but only the people who've already lost too much ever hear it calling."

Tessa wondered if this desire for protection from pain was the very thing that made Mack want more children. Was he afraid that if he didn't reach out again, and soon, he would end up lonely and bitter? In its own way, was Mack's desire for another child an affirmation of life, a promise of sorts that he believed in a good universe, and he trusted enough to try again?

And if that were true, what did it say about her desire not to risk her heart?

Nancy turned to face her daughter. For once her hands were hanging loosely at her sides, as still as Tessa's own. "It took a lot for Mama to tell us everything tonight. Maybe we both need to ask ourselves why she did."

"I don't think it's so hard. She wanted you to know who you are, and what kind of people you came from."

"Everything she said was filled with regret. Didn't you hear it?"

"Of course she regrets it. Her world fell apart."

"No, you don't regret what you have no control over. You grieve, but you don't regret. Your grandmother regrets the way she shut herself off. And it says something good about her that she can reach out, at the end of her life, even if she couldn't reach out before."

Tessa didn't want more insights, and those she had, she didn't want to share. She stood. "I'm going to bed. This has been draining."

Surprisingly, Nancy didn't argue, and she didn't look hurt. "Sleep well, honey. The ghosts in this house are good ones, better than I ever knew. They'll keep you safe."

CHAPTER
17

Tessa and three other regular volunteers at the MADD office had a regular monthly dinner date at the Tyson's Corner Galleria. Tessa had planned to forgo it for the summer, but on the last day of July, in the early evening, she found herself at Maggiano's waiting for her three friends to join her. Jody, a tall, hollow vessel of nervous energy, arrived first, and Tessa suffered her hug. Then Diana, a petite, middle-aged redhead who played Jeff to Jody's Mutt, and Gayle, a silver-haired, sexy grandmother, joined them in line.

No one said much until they were sitting at their table in the noisy dining room; then everyone talked at once, catching up on summer activities.

They ordered family style, the way they always did, and only wrangled over the choice of pasta, settling on the chicken and spinach manicotti and the gnocchi with vodka sauce. They polished off the stuffed mushrooms and giant artichoke before there was a lull in the conversation.

"You haven't said much, Tessa," Gayle said. "Except that your grandmother's house is coming along."

Tessa considered what to tell them. These days, the three women and Sandy, the MADD program manager, were probably her closest friends. They had respected her right to work out her sorrow alone, but they had lingered nearby, encouraging and strengthening her as she did. They hadn't known her until after Kayley's death, so they never commented on changes in her personality or tearfully reminisced about her daughter. The level of intimacy was bearable.

"I had some bad news," she said at last.

The table fell silent, although the noise around them seemed to increase. A large group at the next table was clearly celebrating a birthday, and there were periodic catcalls and stomping of feet.

"Do you want to talk about it?" Gayle asked when Tessa didn't go on.

"Robert Owens is out on probation. A full year before he was supposed to be. He's living in Manassas with his mother."

No one asked who Robert Owens was. There was no need.

Diana was the first to respond. "How did that happen?"

Tessa told the story. "Mack says we have to give him a chance to prove he's rehabilitated himself," she finished.

Jody gave a humorless snort. "Unfortunately, Mack can find something good to say about anybody."

It was said without venom, and Tessa couldn't be angry. Mack was no pushover, but he believed in redemption and second chances, which Jody, who had nearly lost her own life to a drunk driver, did not. Mack's law practice was built on his faith in humanity, and sometimes it was too much for even their most liberal friends to swallow.

Diana put her hand on Tessa's and squeezed before she removed it. "At least he's out of the area. You won't see him at the grocery store or the dry cleaner."

"Out of sight, out of mind?" Tessa asked.

"No. But a couple of years after Jerry was killed, I saw the bastard who was behind the wheel, picking up his little girl from school. He'd been out of jail for months, and no one had warned me."

Diana's husband had died when his catering truck was struck head-on. Tessa tried to imagine happening on Robert Owens by mistake in her neighborhood. "What did you do?"

"He was with his wife. I was carrying a photograph of Jerry and me with our kids. I took it out of my purse, and I handed it to him. I told him to keep it as a souvenir."

Diana reached for her water glass. "He was arrested three months later for driving with a suspended license while intoxicated and went back to jail. That time he destroyed somebody's fence, not their life." She sighed. "It was years ago. Almost twenty years ago. He moved to Florida after he got out the second time. I hope he was eaten by a shark."

No one blinked. "Too quick," Jody said. "Much too easy."

"I wish I could have done something after my nephew was injured," Gayle said. "Everybody was so relieved Alex wasn't killed. They weren't with him during those months of rehabilitation, when he struggled to learn how to walk again, how to hold a fork, how to chew solid food."

"And the driver got off with a slap on the wrist," Diana said bitterly.

"Well, after all, Alex didn't die, and the driver was terribly sorry, so her sentence was light. Just a little jail time, lots of probation. The day her probation ended she celebrated with an old-fashioned bender and swiped a police car during the ensuing chase. Since it was a cop, the second sentence was stiffer. Alex had nearly recovered by the time she was released."

Tessa already knew their stories, and Jody's, too, but some things had to be said again and again. She supposed the other women were trying to make her feel better. They wanted her to understand that other people had suffered. They were still here to tell about it. They understood her anger and disillusionment and, most of all, her sense of futility. They weren't trying to one-up her. They were simply sharing their pain and their anger at a system that couldn't protect its law-abiding citizens from drunks on wheels. That was why they had made MADD such a large part of their lives.

"He'll kill somebody else," Tessa said. "I know he will. He knows what to say and when to say it, and I'm sure that's why they let him out of St. Bride's. I saw it at the trial. He played the jury like an angel plucking his harp. He'll be drinking and driving in a week or two, if he hasn't done both already. He'll figure out how busy his probation officer is, how limited her funds, how few and far between the phone calls and visits. He'll be working the system for all it's worth and having a ball on the side."

"And you want to do something about it." Jody waited until the appetizer platters had been removed and the salad course served before she continued. "Your frustration is obvious."

"I'm tired of waiting for the law to do the right thing. This kid is a time bomb. Can't they see it?" Tessa realized her voice had risen, but she didn't care. "If I knew what to do, I would. I don't want anybody else to go through what I did, and they will. He'll drink enough to lose any sense of reality, then he'll get behind the wheel of a car again, and somebody will be standing in his way. It's inevitable."

"Maybe not." Diana reached for more salad and spooned it on her plate. "What happens if somebody catches him driving? His license has been suspended, yes?"

"Of course it is, but who's going to turn him in? His mother? His friends? Unless he runs a red light or speeds, the cops won't catch him. And most of the time, they're not around to see those things anyway. They'll catch him when he kills somebody else."

"Would he go back to jail if he was caught behind the wheel? Never mind whether he'd been drinking or not. Just plain driving?"

Tessa grimaced. "The judge says that if he's caught stepping out of line even a little bit, he'll go back and serve the whole sentence. And it was a stiff one."

Jody and Diana were looking at each other and nodding. "I'm in, too," Gayle said. "You two can stop looking so pleased with yourselves."

"What are you talking about?" Tessa said.

Jody did the honors. "Look, if you weren't so upset right now, you'd see what has to be done. You're pretty sure that Owens is going to drive again. The cops can't sit around on his street to watch and see. His probation office can't either. His mom isn't going to turn him in if he does, and most of her neighbors probably have no idea what's going on. So somebody who *does* know what's up needs to watch him. And if he steps out of line, they have to call the police and report the behavior. Hopefully your judge friend will take care of the rest."

"Who's going to do it?"

"You are. We are."

Tessa sat very still, taking stock. "You're serious?"

"The most likely time for this Owens boy to get antsy and go off for a drive is in the evening after supper. We can take turns watching his mother's house and see what he's up to. There are four of us here. We can rotate. Once it's clear he's in for the night, we can head home. For obvious reasons we won't tell anybody else what we're doing. This isn't a MADD-sanctioned activity."

Tessa thought fast. Robert's license was suspended. If he was caught driving, he would surely go back to prison. But if one of the women caught him in a bar, and she called the probation officer and reported it, the officer could demand a blood test. If Owens's test was anything except normal, he might go back to prison for that, as well. The judge had promised to be vigilant.

But were the four women one step from becoming vigilantes?

"You can check with your husband," Diana said. "Ask him if

there are any legal problems with watching the house. We won't be stalking anybody. We'll just park and watch. And here's some really good news. I have a friend in the Manassas police department. He married my college roommate. If I explain what we're doing, he'll be on our side. We'll have a direct pipeline to the cops, and he'll make sure the kid's in police custody before his engine gets cold."

Tessa wondered what Mack would say. She was certain he wouldn't agree that this was the way to solve the problem of Robert Owens. But she didn't need Mack's permission. She needed justice.

"I can't ask you to take that much time out of your week," she said.

"You didn't ask," Jody said.

Tessa held up her hand. For a moment she couldn't speak. She had asked for nothing but listening ears, and they had given much more. They had given her a solution, a place to put her anger and concern. "I'll do it every other night. That way the three of you will only have to do it about once a week. Do you really have the time and patience?"

Jody reached for the bread basket and passed it around the table. "Honey, we have more than time and patience. We have a mission. Try to stop us."

"If Owens isn't doing anything wrong, we'll know that, too," Diana said. "And maybe knowing he really has changed will relieve your mind. And ours, too."

Tessa wondered if anything would ever be that simple again.

Nancy fluttered around the farmhouse living room, asking Mack yet again if he wanted something to drink. They had already indulged in three five-minute rounds of excruciatingly inane conversation, and he had already made multiple refusals of coffee and tea.

He wanted Nancy to leave, but he couldn't say so. He had never been fond of Tessa's mother. He thought of her as a bottomless pit into which the world could throw love and adoration for millennia to come, without ever, ever filling it. Her intentions were good, and he supposed that growing up with Helen Henry would turn even the most resolutely confident child into mush. But understanding and accepting were different. He understood why she was the woman she was, but he still didn't want her there.

Nancy plopped into the chair across from him at last, her duties as hostess shortcut by his final curt refusal. "You know, it's been clear to me from the first time we met that you don't like me."

Mack had sunk deeply into thought about Tessa's family dynamics, and it took mental strength to pull himself up and out of the mire. For a moment he was afraid he had put his thoughts about Nancy into words. "Excuse me?"

"Oh, Mack, give it up. You heard what I said." She sighed. "I guess it's to be expected. I don't like myself very well, either."

He felt as if he'd stepped through some invisible barrier to an alternate universe. Nancy never came right out and said anything. He didn't know how to respond.

She smiled a little, not unpleasantly, but with no intent to impress him. "Yes, I am a real person with real thoughts and feelings, and I have not quite forgotten how to express them."

He wondered how far his jaw had dropped, and if maxillofacial surgery was in his immediate future. "I never thought you weren't real," he said.

"That I doubt, though maybe you didn't phrase it that way in your head." Nancy reached for a magazine on a side table and began to fan herself. "Now tell me you've always liked me."

He didn't—couldn't—answer. He'd been set up, and there was no way out except a lie. And oddly, he didn't think she wanted that.

"This summer it's come to my attention that my head is screwed on sideways," Nancy said. "I've been so busy trying to do what I thought was right for everybody around me that I couldn't see what was directly in front of me."

"You've lost me," he said.

"I know you don't like the way I treat Tessa."

"I didn't come into this world to critique your performance as a mother, Nancy."

"When Tessa was born, I was so happy I thought I was going to die. I adored every little thing about her. You should have seen her. Those tiny little toes, that rosebud mouth. And hair? She had a full head of hair for weeks, and when that fell out, there were little curls that seemed to spring from nowhere. You'd never know that now, would you? Nobody's hair is straighter than Tessa's."

She pulled herself out of baby reminiscences. "And then the truth hit me. Here was this gorgeous little girl, and I was her mother. Me. I didn't know how to walk, how to talk. I had no education, no talents to trade on, I was passably pretty, but not in a sophisticated way. No, I was just little ol' Nancy Henry from Boondock, Virginia, with nothing but natural blond hair to offer. And my daughter, the grandchild of Harry and Caroline Whitlock, was going to suffer."

He was not sure why he rated the retelling of her life story, but despite his best inclinations, he was hooked. "And...?"

"And I decided that I couldn't allow her to suffer. My God, I loved her enough to throw myself in front of a train for her. I wanted to. I wanted to do something to prove myself. So I made it my mission to change everything, to become all the things I wasn't, and make sure Tessa came by all the social graces naturally." She paused. "Well, with a little instruction."

"With a lot of instruction, the way I heard it."

She didn't look hurt. "That's what happens when you put a hillbilly in Richmond society. Overcompensation."

"You were never a hillbilly. That word has no meaning, anyway."

She put her fist to her chest. "It means something if you feel it inside."

"Why are you telling me all this?"

"I don't know. I doubt it will change the way you feel about me. Maybe I'm just trying it on for size. There's not much else to do around here in the evenings."

Then she smiled. Not the tremulous, "love-me" smile he was used to, nor the manipulative "If-you-do-it-my-way-I'll-smile-bigger" smile that was a close second in her repertoire. This was simply a warm, embracing smile that sat well on her face and eased the lines of strain around her eyes.

He wondered what he should say or do next. She saved him the trouble. She stood and yawned. "I don't know why Tessa's this late, but I suspect she'll be here soon enough. Stay the night and I'll make waffles in the morning."

She nodded her good-night and disappeared into the hallway. He heard her climbing the stairs a moment later.

He had come to see Tessa, not her mother. He hadn't called, which was stupid, but he'd been in Front Royal speaking at the Virginia Bar Association's Capital Defense Workshop and found himself driving here afterwards with little thought and no consultation. He had expected to find his wife waiting, and it rankled that she could so easily drive back to Northern Virginia to have dinner with her friends, but found so few excuses to come back to be with him.

Nancy had persuaded him that Tessa would be back momentarily, but he wondered if she had decided to go to their home and stay the night. The only reason he didn't leave was because she hadn't called to announce her intentions, and he was sure she would have.

The living room looked much better since Nancy had worked her magic. His perception of Tessa's mother was going through a radical change, but one thing he knew for certain was her ability to create beauty. Tessa had inherited that ability, although his wife's taste was starker, more minimalist and dramatic. Nancy loved color and lavish displays. On the outside, the Whitlock family home in Richmond's Windsor Farms was a staid azalea-banked Georgian masterpiece, but inside it was a tasteful riot of contemporary art, antique furniture, lush Oriental carpets, aged bronze and polished brass.

She'd had nothing like that to work with here, but she had kept the farmhouse character while brightening and warming the rooms with paint and inexpensive fabrics. He doubted that even Helen could be unhappy with the outcome.

He got up and wandered fitfully, fingering a Depression glass vase filled with wildflowers, a green-and-white quilt draped over the sofa back, a hand-crocheted doily on an end table. He was at the side window gazing out over lilac bushes and overgrown forsythia when the front door opened.

"Mack?"

He turned and gazed at his wife. "I should have called."

"You came all the way out here and didn't let me know you were coming?"

He explained where he'd been and why. "I finished sooner than I expected. I wanted to talk to you, and I didn't want to waste this opportunity. But I should have called from Front Royal. I guess I just assumed you'd be here."

"I almost always am. And I bet you forgot your cell phone again."

He nodded a confirmation. She didn't look unhappy to see him. He supposed that was a good sign. She looked tired, but the drive back from the city was a long one.

"Did you have a good dinner?" he asked.

"Uh-huh. Did Mom or Gram feed you?"

"I ate at my meeting."

"Would you like some coffee or tea?"

He had already turned down pots, but he found himself nodding again. "I've got to get back on the road in a little while. Coffee's a good idea."

One heartbeat passed, then several. "You could stay here," she said.

He wasn't sure how to rate the hesitation between his sentence and hers. "I can't. I have to be in the office early for a staff meeting."

She didn't protest. She turned toward the kitchen, and he followed her.

Nancy, or someone, had worked magic in here, as well. The old cupboards had been given a coat of cream-colored paint. The walls, once spotted and stained, were now a becoming sky blue with framed collages of seed packets and prints of sassy crows in sunlit corn fields gracing them. Bright tomato-colored canisters lined the counters and a hand-painted sign over the sink claimed, "I taught Martha everything she knows."

He stood in the doorway. "Your mom's handiwork?"

"She's amazing." Tessa was at the sink filling the coffeepot. "She really works hard, and she does the fun stuff in the evening. Gram's loving the changes, even if she'd never admit it."

"Why is Nancy working this hard when she's planning to move your grandmother to Richmond?"

"You'd have to ask her."

"You haven't?"

"Time takes care of some things. It's better not to lock Mom into a position she has to defend. When the time comes to decide what Gram should do, she'll let Gram have the final say."

He was glad. He wouldn't have stood by if his mother-in-law tried to railroad the old woman. He doubted Tessa would have, either.

He waited to continue the conversation until she turned on the coffeemaker and joined him at the table. He drummed his fingertips on a flowered placemat while she settled across from him.

Tessa sat back in her chair. "You didn't come to socialize, did you?"

"I got a call from Harriet Jenkins at the library."

Tessa was silent a moment. Then her gaze drifted down to his drumming fingers. "How's the addition coming?"

The addition was a new room at their local library branch, a comfortable, carpeted space that very soon would be lined with low bookshelves crowded with picture books and toys for young children. Story hour would be held there every afternoon. Mothers could gather with their toddlers and preschoolers, and watch them explore and socialize with neighbors' children. There would be child-friendly computers in one corner and volunteers willing to help children learn to use them.

"It's going faster than they hoped," he said. "Not the usual story. Most of the time you hear the opposite, but there haven't been any delays or cost overruns. The new room is going to be ready to dedicate at the end of September." He paused. "They want one of us to speak at the ceremony. Harriet said that without Kayley's memorial fund, they never would have broken ground. They've decided to call it Kayley's Room."

He watched Tessa's breath catch. He waited for the barriers, for the impenetrable shield Tessa erected between them at the mention of their daughter's name. But her eyes misted instead. "How she would have loved it."

He could not have been more surprised. "You're all right with speaking, then? You'll be there for the dedication?"

A breath shuddered through her. "I don't want to speak, Mack. Will you? I wouldn't know what to say."

"Sure." He leaned forward a little. "It's the right memorial, isn't it? Kayley loved the library, and she always wanted to spend more time there, but it was always so crowded."

"It's the perfect thing." She looked down at her hands, folded neatly in front of her. "It's terrible, I guess, but I don't remember agreeing to it. I know I must have at some point. I did, didn't I? But I don't remember anything from those days except wanting to die."

"You gave your permission, but if I'd suggested we donate the money to a survivalist compound or a Doomsday cult, you would have agreed to that, too. Neither of us was capable of making decisions. Billy was the one who urged me on and finalized it."

"Dad?"

"I think your mom was involved, too." He thought about the Nancy who had spoken her mind to him that evening, the stranger he'd never gotten to know. He suspected that Nancy was the one who had helped bring about the perfect memorial.

"I wanted Kayley to love reading as much as I did," Tessa said. "I used to take her to the library and walk through the aisles with her when she was still teething on cloth picture books. I'd point out stories I'd read as a child and tell her about them." She looked up. "It was working."

Kayley had learned to read by the time she was four. No one had taught her. She had simply memorized her favorite books, then used the words she already knew to learn the words on the page. She had dictated her own stories to Tessa, who had carefully printed them so Kayley could read them back whenever she wanted. They had worried that school might bore her. They had never worried that she might die before she stepped inside the front door.

"What happened to the books she wrote?" Mack said. "The ones you worked on together?"

"They're packed away with all her things."

He felt such a surge of relief that for a moment he couldn't breathe. "You didn't..."

"Didn't what? Throw them away?"

He nodded.

"How could you think I'd do that?"

"I came home after a conference to find no sign we'd ever had a daughter. Even Biscuit was gone. You said you couldn't bear looking at her anymore, that you'd thrown things away——"

"I said I'd thrown *some* things away," she corrected him. "I told you then to go through the boxes in the basement if it made you feel better."

He hadn't, of course. He hadn't wanted to see what Tessa had left and what she had discarded. He hadn't wanted to think of his daughter's life reduced to the contents of a few cardboard boxes.

"I only threw away things that never mattered to her or us," Tessa said. "Everything that mattered is still there."

"The books? The photos?"

"Of course, Mack. And the photos aren't in the basement. I bought special photograph storage boxes. They're in the top of the coat closet."

She was hurt. He heard it in her voice. He didn't know what to say.

The coffee had finished dripping, and she got up and went for it, pouring it into spatterware mugs and adding milk before she came back to the table.

She put his in front of him. "And Biscuit was at such a loss without Kayley. She was languishing. She needed children. The Hitchcocks were happy to have her. They volunteered."

"You didn't ask me."

"That was more than two and a half years ago! You didn't say a word."

"I didn't want to hurt you."

"We've done nothing but hurt each other."

He rose. She was still standing beside the table, just a breath away. She looked defeated, sad, and more vulnerable than he could remember in years. He reached for her, and she went into his arms as if she had never left them.

She curved into his body as if it were a familiar destination. Her hip settled between his legs, the side of her breast against his chest, the silky length of her hair fell against his collarbone. Her arms crept around him; her hands locked at his waist. He laid his cheek against her forehead and felt her breath against his neck. His arms tightened around her.

His voice was hoarse. "I only want to make things better."

"I don't know how."

"Let's work on it together, then." He tilted her head, two fingers under her chin. Her eyes were the green of troubled waters, and there was nothing to be seen in them except sadness.

"Mack…" Her arms tightened a little. She didn't move closer so much as lean more heavily against him, as if she no longer wanted to carry her own weight.

"I could stay the night," he said softly. "I miss you so much, Tessa. You were so late tonight, and I was beginning to think I'd lost you, too, that you had disappeared from my life…." He lowered his lips to hers and felt resistance, then a slow soft blooming of desire.

He told himself to move slowly, not to push her into intimacy she wasn't ready for. He rubbed her back as he kissed her lips, her cheek, her chin, and felt her bending into him like a willow branch.

And then she moved away. Before he could show her his patience and concern. Before the fire inside him could ignite a matching blaze in her.

"You need to know where I was," she said. "Before this continues."

For a moment he wondered if *she* was having an affair, if all his struggles against his growing attraction to Erin had been ridiculous, that Tessa herself had found someone new. Then he saw that she felt no guilt, that whatever it was, it had not been that kind of betrayal.

"Does it matter?" he asked, refusing to relinquish his hold on her, even if she had taken a step backwards. "Can it wait?"

"I was sitting in a parked car across the street from the Owens house in Manassas, watching to see if he tried to drive, or went into town to a bar with his friends. I was spying on Robert Owens, and I'm going to continue until I catch him violating his probation agreement."

For a moment the words would not register. He tried to make sense of them and had no success. "You did what?"

She pulled away, and this time he let her go. "Some of the other volunteers are going to help me. We aren't breaking any laws. We aren't stalking him with intent to do harm. We're just watching to be sure he doesn't break the law."

"Tessa, have you lost your mind?"

"I've found a way to keep him from killing somebody else."

"That is not your job." His hand went to his hair, like a man waking from a bad dream. "You have to let go of this, of him. He's not your responsibility. You have a life. You have to move on."

"Making sure Robert Owens doesn't kill again *is* my life."

He started to speak; then he closed his lips and shook his head. "You need help."

The green eyes blazed with anger. "No, I just need to protect somebody else's daughter."

"You're looking for revenge. No matter what you tell yourself, that's what you want. Sure, you don't want him to kill someone else, but that's only part of it. You want him to suffer the way you did. And three years of his life wasn't good enough for you. You want him to suffer eternally."

"You're damned right I do! He killed my daughter!"

"And now you're letting him kill you one inch at a time. You've turned into a vigilante. You've shut out everyone who loves you. You've stopped letting yourself care about anything except avenging Kayley. And Kayley is dead! She's not asking anything from you. She wouldn't even recognize you if she were alive today. You've become somebody she wouldn't want to know."

"No, this is *me*. This is who I am. I'm her mother, and I love her enough to fight for her!"

"She...is...dead!" He looked away. He was breathing hard, because his chest felt like someone had slid a blade directly into his heart. "She is dead, and you are burying everything that's left of her under hatred and revenge."

She was quiet for so long he thought she might not answer. When she spoke at last, her voice was like a winter wind. "Not all of us can be as forgiving, as tolerant, as you are, Mack. I want him back in jail, I'll admit it. And I want him to suffer. I'll admit that, too. But I'm not going after him with a gun or an out-of-control Chevy. I'm going after him with the only weapon I would *ever* use. The law."

"It's not your job to enforce it."

"I'm a citizen of this great country of ours. Think of it as a neighborhood watch program on wheels." She threw her head back and turned away. "Go home. No one asked you for help. No one asked you to agree. Go home and live your life. I'm going to live mine the way it has to be lived."

He watched her walk away, watched until her footsteps faded and the house was silent.

He tried to remember that there had been a moment when she first arrived when he had felt they were coming together again. He tried to remember that she had been softer, warmer, opening to him and to her feelings the way he had so longed for, that even though he was appalled at what she was doing, she had talked to him. For once she had told him what was inside her.

But all he could really remember was the way her neck arched and her eyes blazed right before she turned away from him.

Again.

CHAPTER
18

Billy had come to visit exactly three times in the month Nancy had been in Toms Brook. After the first abortive encounter, she had arranged to be gone for the greater part of the last two visits. She wasn't sure Billy had noticed, since as far as she could tell, he was only there from duty or a desire to visit his daughter. She supposed her reasons for avoiding him ranged from payback for hurting her feelings to testing him to see if her absence mattered. At least part of it, though, was a very new, very tender need to define herself as Nancy, and not as Billy Whitlow's wife.

She might seem like an empty-headed, foolish woman to those she loved most, but Nancy was beginning to believe there was more to her than even she had known. Out from under the shadow of Richmond's dogwoods and magnolias, its Confederate monuments and grand old homes, she was finding herself again.

"I never have understood the way your mind works," Helen said. She was cozied up in her bedroom after a light lunch, with a glass of iced tea beside her and her misshapen, shoeless feet propped up on her sewing chair.

"You said it, I didn't." Nancy finished her last swallow of tea and wished she'd made a larger pitcher, but she knew better than to leave her mother alone. In the moments it would take to go downstairs and put the kettle on, Helen would vanish and her quilts would never be documented.

"You lived with me for all those years, visited me at least a million times, and you pick August, the hottest month of the summer, to look at my quilts. Makes me sweat just unfolding them to show you."

"I told you, Mama, I'm not asking you to do it so I can admire them. We're going to catalog them. See, I have my laptop computer up and running." She pointed to a space at the foot of the old four-poster bed. "And we don't have to do them all today. I know there are way too many."

"I don't see the point of this. They're just quilts. Who cares where they come from and why?"

"I do, for starters." Nancy wiped her hands on her dress. The dress was damp from a morning of perspiration and as wrinkled as an old dish towel. Today it didn't much matter to her how she looked. Who was going to see her anyway?

"Then let's get it over with so I can get busy and make some more." Shaking her head, Helen delved into the pile of quilts that were folded beside her chair.

"Why do you keep those quilts right there?" Nancy watched her mother unfold the first one.

"These are my giveaway quilts. Somebody gets burned out, or flooded, or a loved one dies, one of these goes to them. And don't get all soft-eyed about it, like I'm some kind of saint. I don't care much for these quilts. I'd rather give 'em away than keep 'em." She grimaced as she finished spreading one out. "See what I mean?"

The quilt in question was a symphony of soft peach and turquoise in diagonal drifts of color. "Jacob's Ladder, right?" Nancy asked.

"How'd you know?"

"I used to live here, remember?"

"Well, it's not Jacob's Ladder, Miss Smarty. At least, not exactly. It's a variation. Some call this one Road to the White House. Me, I wouldn't name a quilt in honor of any of those no-account Republicans you and that husband of yours are so fond of."

Nancy tried not to smile. "It's a Democrat's quilt, Mama. Look, if I turn it this way, the colors are leaning left."

Helen chortled. "So they are."

Nancy sat down on the trunk at the foot of the bed and positioned the laptop. She typed the name of the quilt and a brief description, including Helen's comments about the name. "How big is it?" She continued to type as Helen got out the tape measure and grudgingly answered her questions.

Once she had the basics, Nancy put the laptop down and went to examine the quilt closer. The quilting was as fine, as even, as it was in any of her mother's quilts.

"You're not really going to give this away to just anybody, are you?"

"Well, why not?"

"It's beautiful. I can't believe this is one of your rejects."

"Shows what you know." Helen pointed to several lines of quilting that veered perhaps a sixteenth of an inch from their companions. "The light must have been bad that day, or I wasn't paying close enough attention."

"No, you're just a perfectionist. Didn't you tell me once only God is allowed to be perfect, and in the old days, your grandmother and her friends would always make a mistake on purpose? Turned a flower upside down or used the wrong color in a block?"

"You remember that?"

Nancy plopped down to a chair beside her mother, where the window fan could ruffle her hair. "I'm sorry if it seemed like I didn't listen and I didn't care when you talked about your quilts. I was a teenager."

"I'm just surprised, that's all. But if you think this quilt is something else, I have others I like better."

"I want to see them all."

Helen carefully smoothed and folded the Road to the White House quilt and set it back on the pile. Nancy suspected that her mother liked it better than she had let on. And didn't that make the gift of it to a stranger in need that much sweeter?

Helen stood after a maximum amount of fuss and crossed the room, opening a wooden cupboard against the far wall. She returned with three quilts and set the bottom two on the bed, unfolding the top one and draping it over the footboard.

Nancy got up and moved closer. "My God, Mama, the work in that quilt. Is that a Baltimore Album?"

"What do *you* know about Baltimore Albums?"

"I saw one at a quilt exhibit at the Virginia Museum of Fine Arts a couple of years ago. Remember, I tried to bring you down to see it, and you told me you'd come to Richmond in a casket and not a moment before."

Helen was silent for a moment. Then she shook her head. "I didn't say that." She paused. "Did I?"

"You thought I was going to kidnap you."

"I didn't!" Helen paused again. "I guess I thought you'd be ashamed of me."

Nancy had brought that on herself. She knew it. She owned up to it silently before she exploded. "You're my mother. If I'm that shallow, then you should have just drowned me at birth."

"Wished a time or two I had."

The two women looked at each other, then burst out laughing. Nancy slipped her arm around Helen's waist. "I wouldn't have been ashamed. But I'd have bought you a new dress for the occasion."

"Could stand one, I guess. But there's nobody much to dress up for here."

Nancy hugged her harder. "Does it get lonely sometimes, Mama?"

"I'm used to it."

"I miss you when I'm down in Richmond. I think about you and wish you were closer."

"I'm not moving to that retirement village. Just count that out right now."

"I know."

They stood locked together, staring at the quilt, until Nancy finally concentrated on it again. "It *is* a Baltimore Album, isn't it?"

"This ain't Baltimore. It's a Shenandoah Album, and I made up all the designs on my own along with the name. I patterned it after the old *fraktur* from these parts, you know, like some of those pasted in that trunk up in the attic."

Fraktur was stylized, ornate printing and artwork brought from Germany by way of Pennsylvania by the early Shenandoah settlers. The designs had been used, among other things, to decorate birth announcements or baptisms.

The quilt was exquisite, twenty blocks, each one different. Nancy saw birds and trees, angels and flowers and a running stag. She stared at it and couldn't believe that such a thing had been created from scraps of fabric.

"Mama, this ought to be in a museum."

"Tsh..." Helen laughed. "It's just an old woman's fancy."

"It's unbelievable. How long did it take?"

"Too long. I could have made fifty quilts in the same time—and should have. My mama would say I'd purely lost my mind. Quilts are made to be used."

Nancy had seen the dozen or so quilts of Delilah's that Helen still owned, and she treasured them because they were made by the grandmother she'd never known. But Delilah's quilts had been simple and utilitarian. Helen's were something else entirely.

"Mama, you're an artist."

"I'm nothing of the sort, just a bored old woman with too much time on my hands now that I can't work outside much."

"Why haven't you entered this in the county fair? Or a quilt show?"

"I just quilt. That's all. Nothing much else to do here."

Nancy was surprised to hear shyness and uncertainty in her mother's voice, along with something more endearing. Just a hint of pride and pleasure that her daughter had found this quilt—so obviously a source of joy to its maker—to be worthy of praise.

"I couldn't change your mind, could I?" Nancy said. "There's got to be a quilt show in the area that will want to display this."

"I don't go to quilt shows, don't go to quilt meetings. I just quilt. Don't matter to me one bit if any of my quilts see the light of day."

Nancy heard the words but knew the truth beneath them. Helen was unsure of her own work, and she would never try on her own to have any of it displayed publicly.

But that was what daughters were for.

"Are there others as spectacular as this one?" Nancy asked, as nonchalantly as she could.

"Spectacular's a ten-dollar word, and it don't mean a thing."

"Mama..."

"I got a few more I'm not ashamed of. Nothing special in the scheme of things, but they please me enough."

"Then let's see them," Nancy said. "And tell me all about them."

She wondered, as Helen folded the Shenandoah Album so she could display the next quilt, what Billy would think if he saw her mother's best work. Would he, the educated collector of valuable abstract impressionists, think her mother's quilts were nothing more than primitive folk art from an old country woman? Or would he see them as part of a chain of artists that was centuries long, female artists who had used what was at hand to bring comfort and beauty to their modest homes?

And did she really care what Billy thought? In the long run, wasn't it what *she* loved that mattered? And wasn't it about time she understood the difference?

Tessa liked working in the attic best. The sorting downstairs was for the most part boring, going through and throwing out meaningless junk that Helen had rescued, and paperwork her grandmother had stacked and never adequately investigated.

Tessa had developed a schedule of sorts. House chores or repairs with Nancy in the coolest hours of the morning, sorting and hauling when the day was hottest, and trips to the attic in the late afternoon and evening when the temperatures dropped enough to make it comfortable.

She thought of the attic as dessert. In her hours here she had uncovered a wealth of Stoneburner memorabilia, in addition to the wedding ring quilt. Ladies' hats and men's suspenders and waistcoats. Shape-note hymnals and faded wildflowers preserved between panes of wavery glass. The tattered remnant of a Confederate flag that looked as if it had seen more than one battle. Nineteenth-century postcards from places like Natural Bridge and Virginia Beach. A painfully neat ledger listing farm expenses in bleached brown ink, along with notes about crops and cattle.

This afternoon she was glad to have an interesting way to pass the time. Last night's encounter with Mack had replayed through her mind all morning as she sorted through the black plastic bags in the spare bedroom. A lifetime supply of tattered tablecloths and dish towels hadn't offered much of a mental challenge, at least not enough to make her forget that, downstairs in her grandmother's kitchen, she'd shoved Mack away with both hands, probably far enough away that he would have trouble finding his way back.

And she would lose her way if she tried to look for him again.

The attic was a better challenge than the bedroom. She forgot their angry words for moments at a time as she tackled the trunk that contained Nancy's school papers. After a layer or two of test papers and surprisingly well-organized essays, she found the high-school yearbook for her mother's junior year and sat back on her heels to page through it.

Even though Nancy had warned her, Tessa was surprised by how few activities her mother had been involved in. She wasn't in the photographs of the chorus or drama club. She hadn't been a cheerleader or a member of any athletic team. She was absent on the pages devoted to service organizations, honor society and special interest clubs. Tessa wouldn't have known this was her mother's album except for the thumb-sized face in a line of five others, a cherub-cheeked Nancy smiling tentatively amidst a sea of more confident faces.

Nancy had said she worked too hard at home to participate in much at school, but Tessa had filed that away as just another complaint about Helen. Tessa wondered if the yearbook from her mother's senior year was here, too, with the usual notes about what had been accomplished during her sojourn at the school. What would it show? The simpering well wishes of favorite girlfriends, sentimental poetry from acne-cheeked admirers, a school life rich in academics if not activities?

She knew her parents had met and married during the spring her mother turned twenty-two. Theirs had been a whirlwind courtship, an unlikely but passionate alliance, and the unexpected appearance of one Tessa Whitlock had crushed Nancy's plans to continue her education. But what had her mother dreamed? What had she hoped for before she fell in love and married a man as different from herself as an eagle from a butterfly?

Tessa set aside the yearbook and dug deeper. As she'd hoped, she found the one for the following year. She opened it and turned to the senior class photographs, smiling at this larger photo of her mother draped in black with the requisite 1960s strand of pearls.

Nancy wasn't smiling here, but somehow she still looked uncomfortable, as if this touch of fake elegance was more than she was used to. Her blond hair was short and carefully curled around her face. Her eyes were huge, open wide enough to glimpse all the frightening possibilities of her future. Her repertoire of activities had increased. This time she was listed as belonging to the pep club, although nothing else. Her favorite book was *Gone With The Wind*—no surprise there—and her fondest ambition was to become somebody.

Tessa closed the book and held it against her chest. Even then, Nancy had known exactly what she wanted. And look where it had gotten her. Just a few years later she had married into the Richmond version of the aristocratic Wilkes family and gone to live at her very own Twelve Oaks, or close enough. And in Richmond, she *was* somebody, a steel magnolia with enough power and prestige to suit her at last.

Or maybe not. For the past month Tessa had picked up hints that Nancy was not satisfied with her life. She made the trip back to Richmond once a week but never stayed the night. She never had news of Billy, and Tessa thought it was unlikely they saw each other. Also, Tessa had noted the way her mother avoided her father on his infrequent visits.

She had never given much thought to her parents' marriage, other than how odd it was that they had found each other, but now she wondered if there was trouble brewing in the Whitlock mansion. Or had she simply not recognized the obvious, that there had *always* been trouble, and Nancy and Billy had only stayed together for their daughter or for the sake of appearances?

That thought gave her pause and a sinking feeling in her stomach. Nancy could be exasperating, but Tessa loved her. She couldn't imagine Nancy without Billy. Everything Nancy had become was wrapped up in him and in their life together. Without him, what would she do and where would she go? And even though Tessa was well beyond the age when she needed her parents to stay to-gether to keep her own world intact, the thought of a divorce, of the shattering of family as she had known it, made her un-easy and sad.

Sadder. Her own marriage was hanging by mere threads. And now, perhaps, her parents' marriage was, too.

She hoped she was imagining this. Maybe last night's scene with Mack was coloring everything else. She stood to slide the album back in the trunk, and something that had been stuck between pages fluttered to the floor.

She picked up the piece of paper to return it to the yearbook, but stopped instead. It was her parents' marriage certificate. She wondered if Nancy knew it was here, or if the certificate had been missing for years.

She started to tuck it under her arm to take to Nancy when something clicked in her mind. She lifted it into view again and stared at it for a moment. Then, with the certificate in hand, she left the attic and descended the stairs.

Nancy was pleased with her day. She and Helen had gone through a dozen quilts, and by the end they'd been laughing and talking like friends. There were few subjects where the two women could have a meeting of the minds, but quilting was definitely one of them. As Nancy had drawn out stories about each one, Helen had asked Nancy for her opinion, listening carefully as she told her what she liked, or even what she didn't. They had discussed pat-terns, colors, scale. By the time Helen tired, Nancy felt closer to her mother than she had for years.

Now she stood in the old bank barn and watched as a slim young man, whose hips were just wide enough to hold up a pair of baggy jeans, fiddled with one of the cobwebbed, rusted pieces of machinery lining the barn's rear wall.

He faced her after another moment or two. "I hate to say it, Ms. Whitlock, but I believe I've seen newer tractors at the Smithsonian over in Washington, D.C. And I haven't seen this much rust outside of Detroit."

Nancy had to smile. Zeke Claiborne was not what she had expected. He was no stranger to droll country humor, and he was clearly intelligent, to boot. He wasn't much to look at yet, but put a few more pounds on him and shave off the scraggly, adolescent goatee, and he would be better than passable. Considering he'd gotten Cissy pregnant and hadn't bothered to marry her, she'd assumed he was poor white trash. But since then, she had figured out that Zeke was anything but.

"I had an antique dealer look at all the old farm machinery," she told him, "but he said there's not much chance anybody would want it."

"We could haul this one outside, take off what rust we can get to and let your grandkids play on it."

Nancy's heart squeezed painfully. "No grandkids, I'm afraid."

"Too bad." He put a long, unfarmerlike finger to his cheek. Then he grinned. "You could use it as a planter. Put a pot here, and here..." He demonstrated.

She smiled, too. "I guess you'll have to haul it away, Zeke. You know we'll pay you, don't you? We really don't expect you to do all this work for free."

"No, ma'am, it's my pleasure to help out. You folks have been good to Cissy. She talks about you all the time. I'm glad to give back."

Nancy heard the rustle of straw on the barn floor behind her and turned to see Tessa approaching. She wore green shorts and a knit shirt with thin straps that bared her tanned arms and shoulders. She had braided her hair, and the braid swung behind her as she walked.

"Tessa, have you had a chance to meet Zeke? He comes and goes so fast most of the time, he's hard to nail down."

"No." Tessa came up beside her and stopped, eyeing the boy as if he were a face on the post office wall. "Hello, Zeke. I'm Tessa MacRae."

"Afternoon, Ms. MacRae. Cissy's told me a lot about you."

"There's not so much to tell."

"She's been talking about the book you gave her. I didn't know she liked to read that much. We went to the library a couple nights ago, and she came home with an armload." He sounded proud. "I'm going to make sure she gets there every week."

"She's a smart girl." Tessa paused. When she spoke again, her voice was even cooler. "I hate to see her drop out of school the way she did."

"Me too." He shook his head. "But she wouldn't go while she's carrying the baby. Said she just couldn't. I figure after the baby's born, maybe I can convince her to work on a GED, and when she sees how well she does and gets some confidence, maybe take some courses at Triplett Tech or do some long-distance courses over the computer. I looked into it already, and it sounds promising. I know she won't want to leave the baby at first."

Nancy was impressed, and beside her, Tessa had nothing to say.

"You decide what you want to do," Zeke said, "about this equipment. I got a friend over in Edinburg who likes to tinker with stuff. He might get a piece or two up and running to sell."

"Tell him it's his if he wants it. I'd rather recycle it than junk it," Nancy said. "And you'll haul the rest of it away?"

"I'll check it all first. Anything too far gone, I'll just take over to the landfill."

Nancy started to protest his refusal to be paid, but he held up his hand. "Now you don't want to go making trouble for me with Cissy and my dad, do you? They just wouldn't stand for it, and neither would I."

Nancy closed her mouth and nodded.

"Nice talking to you both. You have a nice evening." He walked away, and only when his back was to them and he was nearly out the barn door did he pull his cap out of his back pocket and set it on his head.

"He's not what I expected." Nancy turned to her daughter. "Am I right?"

"I don't know what you expected."

"About the same thing you did, I'd guess."

"He seems nice. And concerned about Cissy."

That morning Nancy had noticed a new, grimmer set to her daughter's lips. It was still there. She hated seeing Tessa this way. She was beginning to forget what a more relaxed Tessa looked like. A happy Tessa was an imaginary figure from another lifetime.

"Why don't we take a day off tomorrow?" she offered impulsively. "There's a wonderful little restaurant in Woodstock right in the middle of this indoor mall of sorts, and the chef is as good as anybody in the city. Maybe we can even convince your grandmother to come with us. We could browse some of the antique stores, check out—"

"Mom, I'm okay."

Nancy knew she wasn't. But how did you tell a beloved daughter you knew she was lying? That you knew as much about her mental state just by looking at her as a therapist might after a dozen sessions?

"Mack didn't stay last night," Nancy said. "And I heard raised voices."

"Let's talk about *your* marriage for a change." Tessa pulled a rolled up paper from her pocket and handed it to her mother.

Nancy glanced down at the marriage certificate she hadn't looked at for decades—more than three decades, in fact. Every joint in her body seemed to seize and lock. "Where'd you find this?"

"In your high-school yearbook."

Nancy tried to remember putting it there and couldn't. But her wedding had been such a long time ago. And maybe it made sense, after all, to have put the certificate in her beloved annual. She had been so young, a baby, really, who even at twenty-two still had dreams common to high-school girls and no place to go after graduation. Until Billy came along.

"William Lee Whitlock and Nancy Ann Henry." She gazed down at the document and shook her head nonchalantly, but her heart was beating rapidly. "I remember thinking that William Lee Whitlock was a wonderful name when the minister pronounced it, and Nancy Ann Henry was so common. The first time somebody called me Nancy Whitlock, I didn't know who they were talking about."

"The minister pronounced both your names three months later than the day you've always claimed you were married."

She took a deep breath. "I know when I was married, Tessa."

"You were pregnant with me, weren't you? That's why you claimed you were married in the spring."

"It's not exactly something you blurt out, is it? When would have been the right moment to tell you? I just let sleeping dogs lie."

Tessa was silent.

Nancy was embarrassed but resolute, and denial was futile. "I met your daddy when I was still too young to know anything. I was a diversion, I guess, while he waited to start his final year at UVA. When he left here that summer, I thought I'd never see him again. You might think I'm an unbelievably foolish woman nowadays, but the truth is that even then, I knew facts when I saw them. I never really expected Billy to marry me, not even when I found out I was carrying you. But Billy, being Billy, did the gentlemanly thing."

Tessa's face softened. "Mom, he stayed married to you. That's more than the gentlemanly thing."

Nancy didn't know what to say about that. She had turned herself into the kind of woman Billy needed, and she supposed he had seen the value of keeping her. Her social and political savvy had earned him points with clients and business connections. She kept everything in his life well oiled and trim. Even after menopause, when her friends claimed they would rather shoot a man than sleep with him, she was still there for Billy when he wanted sex. Heck, she wanted it, too. She loved the ungrateful bastard.

"How did it all happen?" Tessa said. "I guess everything I've ever been told was a lie. You didn't meet at a party and fall madly in love, did you?"

"It was such a long time ago."

Tessa put her arm around Nancy's shoulders, more like a friend than a daughter. Her tone was cajoling. "Let's go for a walk. It's cooled down a little. We might be getting another storm if we're lucky. But it's nice enough now for a little stroll."

"There's nothing very exciting to tell."

"It doesn't have to be exciting. The truth would be nice, though. Or whatever part of it you feel like telling me."

Nancy thought maybe the timing wasn't so bad. She'd always known Tessa might find out she'd been conceived out of wedlock. Now that particular cat was out of the bag. And clearly this new turn in the soap opera of their lives was taking Tessa's mind off Mack and her own marriage. And Kayley.

She started to twist her hands, then shoved them in her pockets, instead. "Let's walk toward the river. I always like that hill that looks down on it. I used to think I'd build a cottage there some-day, and your daddy and I would use it as a getaway."

"Didn't he want to?"

"I guess not." Nancy wondered if she had ever asked Billy his opinion or just assumed his answer. After all, what would William Lee Whitlock want with a rustic country cottage, when he owned vacation homes in Hilton Head and Vail?

"Where did you meet?" Tessa said. "Were you at a party, the way you always told me?" She started to walk, and, reluctantly, Nancy followed.

"No, I was selling tomatoes, and when he said something fresh to me, I threw one at him."

Tessa stopped. "You're kidding, right?"

Nancy thought about Billy's lack of interest in her this summer, and her mouth hardened into a thin line. "You think I'm kidding? Someday soon I'll demonstrate. Then you'll see what a pitching arm I have."

CHAPTER
19

June 1964

High-school graduation had come and gone, and there'd been no money for college, although Nancy hadn't really wanted to go, anyway. She didn't want to be a teacher or a nurse, and the high-school guidance counselor had tried to steer all the smart girls toward one or the other. She thought she might like to be an interior decorator, although she wasn't sure how to go about that. The one thing she had been absolutely certain of was that she wanted to leave Toms Brook and everything it represented behind her.

Unfortunately, four years later, she was still standing smack-dab in the middle of town.

Nancy watched as her mother paused on her way to the red mud parking area just in front of the shabby little farm stand where she marketed her vegetables and preserves. Scratching a shoulder, Helen faced her daughter one last time.

"Nanny, you sure you got everything you need? I filled the Thermos with tea and put your sandwiches in the cooler. Make sure you hide the cash box all the time."

Nancy rolled her eyes. "I know, Mama. You think a masked man with a six gun is going to raid some old hick vegetable stand?"

Helen looked tired, and older than her forty-four years. She wore a shapeless seersucker wraparound skirt and a white blouse with old-lady lace-up shoes. Her dark hair was already more than half gray. Nancy didn't know why her mother couldn't try a little harder. She was younger than the mothers of many of Nancy's friends, and she might be almost attractive if she would dye and set her hair or use a little makeup. But nobody could tell Helen Henry anything.

The twin lines between Helen's eyes deepened. "What I do know is that I worked hard to get this produce, and I don't want somebody else making off with my rewards."

"You'll be back after lunch?" Nancy said.

"I said I would be, didn't I? That's when it'll get busy. All you have to do is tidy up 'til then. And put aside all those soft tomatoes."

Nancy watched her mother make her way to the old Ford pickup. Helen would be back by two o'clock with new bushels of tomatoes, cucumbers, green peppers and sweet corn. Last night's thunderstorm had left such deep puddles in the garden that she'd decided to wait until the worst of the water drained off before she picked more produce for the afternoon rush.

Once the pickup was gone, Nancy relaxed a little. If she was lucky, nobody she knew would stop by or see her here. Most of her high-school classmates had left town for good or found jobs farther afield in Woodstock or Strasburg. The class president had gotten a job in a real estate office down in Mt. Jackson, where his uncle lived. Most likely someday he would own the office and half the countryside, too. He was such a smooth talker that at least two female members of the senior class had become personally acquainted with the back seat of his daddy's Pontiac.

After high school, Nancy had gotten a job helping at the elementary school library and office. She was taking some classes at night to learn to type and do shorthand, but she didn't seem to be talented at either. She was afraid she was going to spend the rest of her life helping out at the school for minimum wage, struggling to get her shorthand curlicues just right and selling tomatoes when school was out of session.

She glanced at her wrist. The Elgin watch Helen had given her for graduation claimed it was only 8:00 a.m. That meant she had eleven hours to go before Helen rolled in the outdoor display stands, and secured and locked the folding doors. Eleven excruciating, boring hours until she was free, at least more or less.

She had wanted a better summer job. She could have found one, too, if her mother hadn't insisted she mind the stand for the summer. But how could she refuse? She hated farm work, but she knew their market garden paid a sizeable portion of her mother's bills. No matter how much she fought with her mother—and she certainly did fight with her—she also felt bad about how hard Helen worked. She couldn't leave her to work harder. So this summer she would serve as free labor, but hopefully it would be the last time.

She had brought two magazines to read, one with poor Jackie Kennedy staring right at her from the cover, but first she had to prepare for the day. The display stands were framed wooden platforms that tilted at a slight angle. She picked out the trash, corn husks, leaves and overripe produce, then took cloths and a bucket of water from the spigot by the front door to dust and scrub, moving vegetables back and forth as she did.

She liked to make attractive displays. It was the only part of working here that she found tolerable. In the fall she polished apples and piled them in geometric stacks, yellow nestled with red so they showed to their best advantage. Now that the tomato season was underway, she saved the largest, reddest tomatoes for the top of the quart and half-bushel baskets, and stacked the smaller, greener tomatoes in the bottoms. Eggplant, with its gleaming purple-black skin, looked most attractive if paired with peppers. Later in the season she would have red peppers to sell, as well, and she would place the eggplant in between the green and the red to show them off to advantage.

She graduated to the jars of preserves. They gleamed, jewel-like, in neat rows on a shelf near the front. She dusted and turned them so each label was in full view.

Helen complained about the time Nancy took arranging the stands, but what else did she have to do all day? The gravel floor didn't need sweeping or mopping. There were no records to keep, no windows to wash. There were vegetables and jars, and there was time to fill.

This morning she took her time over the tomatoes. The best specimens had been snatched up yesterday almost as soon as they'd been put out. Only the overripe and the underripe were left, until Helen returned with a fresh crop. She had promised her mother she would take those that were too soft to sell and put them in a bucket to take home. Helen planned to can them that evening after supper. Nancy knew she would feel obliged to help.

There were more soft tomatoes than she had expected, due to a heat wave that made the valley feel like a swamp. She filled two buckets before she quit and set them under the table where she took money and made change. The metal cash box was hidden between the table legs under a board that swung out to reveal it. Her mother was proud of her hiding place, but Nancy figured Helen's invention wouldn't fool anybody who really needed the money.

She was lining the corn up end to end outside under the awning when a car swung in and pulled up to the stand. They were close enough to Skyline Drive that tourists sometimes came through and stopped, although they didn't get as many as the nearby towns with stores and banks and things to see. Toms Brook was a place to receive mail and maybe go to church, but there wasn't much more to it. Just that and some old houses with wide front porches where you could sit and stare at the people across the road, who were staring at you.

The car was unfamiliar, a shiny red convertible with toothy grillwork on the front and a white V-shaped panel on the side. Nobody she knew had anything half as cool.

The door opened, and a young man about her own age unfolded gradually until he was standing beside the car, looking down at his tire. To her eyes, he was as exotic as the car, broad-shouldered, clean-cut and utterly confident. As he turned to look at her, she saw that his short dark hair set off dark-lashed brown eyes and a straight sloping nose. And when he grinned, his teeth were absolutely straight.

"I was bouncing around so much I thought I might have a flat. I guess it's that road. It needs some work."

"Always will," she said, trying not to stare. As she was busily not staring, though, she noted his crisply ironed shirt and the knife-edged pleat in his tan pants. She thought he looked a lot like Ricky Nelson without the pout, but with every bit of the glamour.

"I'm supposed to buy a bushel of tomatoes, anyway. I'm working over at the Dan-D restaurant for the summer. They want some for salads."

She knew the Dan-D. She tried to picture him there and couldn't. It was an ordinary place, not too far from the river, flanked by half a dozen tourist cabins set back toward the woods. It was the kind of place people not much better off than her mother went to spend a few days of vacation.

"I've got tomatoes cheap." She tried to sound nonchalant. "We'll have better ones by afternoon, though."

"I'll take whatever you've got right now. They'll be good enough. Old Wallace—that's the cook—can't make a salad to save his life, anyway."

"I'll pick out the best ones." Nancy thought her heart was going to leap out of her chest, it was beating so hard. She felt as if she was talking to a celebrity. The car, the clothes, the way he stood. All were signs of a life she had never lived herself.

"Thanks, that would be great."

She made good on the offer, retrieving a bushel basket and choosing the best tomatoes from the tops of the baskets she'd readied for display. She wanted to ask him about himself, what he was doing at the Dan-D with a car like that one, how long he would be staying, and if he might be stopping by for more vegetables as summer wore on. But she knew better. She sold tomatoes, and he drove a car that probably cost as much as her mother made in a very good year. Or two.

"I'm glad we got some rain," he said, wandering between displays, looking them over as if he was really paying attention. "But now I'm going to have to scrape the mud out of the coves."

"Coves?"

"Those white indentations on the side of my car. All Corvettes have them."

"That's a Corvette?"

"Heck, I thought every girl in the world knew what a Corvette looked like. What's the point of having one?"

"So you can scrape mud out of the coves when you don't have anything better to do."

He laughed as if she'd said something really funny. "You must live around here. They don't import you for jobs like this one, do they?"

"They imported you, didn't they?"

He leaned against the table as she carefully transferred his tomatoes into brown paper bags. "My dad went to school with Dan." When she didn't respond, he said, "Dan, the guy who owns Dan-D? Dad called Dan and asked him if he had a job for me this summer. Unfortunately, he did."

"You don't want to be here?" It was just barely a question. Of course he didn't. Who did?

"God, no. But Dad's furious at me. I was supposed to graduate from UVA this summer, but I didn't take all the courses I needed. I wasn't even this close." He held his thumb and forefinger an inch apart. "He says it's time I learned about real work and what's waiting for me if I don't finish up next spring."

He was so friendly, so candid, that she almost forgot to be shy or flustered. "So, have you learned anything new?"

"Really? Well, no. Not so much except that I like it here. Dan's got me doing KP, you know, peeling potatoes and shucking corn and scouring pots and pans. I don't like that part. But I like exploring when I'm not working. I like hiking and things like that."

"Why'd you goof off?"

"Oh, drinking. Parties. Women. Taking classes I liked better than accounting and economics." He grinned and shrugged.

She tried to imagine having that kind of time and freedom. Working and night school were just an extension of high school, where there had never been time to fit in or have fun. The few dates she'd accepted had been anything but exciting, and typing classes were not the place to meet eligible young men.

"You're looking wistful."

She found he was staring at her. "Nothing of the kind."

"Sure you were. Are you in college somewhere? This is a summer job?"

For a moment she considered lying, but Helen had drummed into her the importance of honesty, and besides, she wasn't sure she was thinking straight enough right now to keep up with her own lies. "I work over at the elementary school. In the library. I haven't decided what I really want to do yet."

"I haven't met many people our age."

That didn't surprise her. The Dan-D was a family place, not one of the spots anyone their age went for excitement. She wasn't even sure where those spots were. Young men from Fitch Crossing liked to go off in the woods, drink beer and shoot anything that moved in the dark. It amazed her any of them had made it to graduation.

"You drive that car slow enough and smile that smile of yours, and you'll meet every girl in Shenandoah County," she said.

"You like the car and the smile?"

She might be a country girl, but she knew better than to say yes. "Just the car."

He laughed. "You're a cool customer, aren't you?"

She was anything but cool. She was afraid that when she took his money, her hands were going to drip a gallon of perspiration on the counter. "That'll be two fifty."

He reached in his pocket and pulled out a wallet. From one quick glance she thought it might be real alligator. All it needed was a head and teeth. "My name's Billy Whitlock," he said. "What's yours?"

"Nancy. Nancy Henry."

"How do you do, Nancy?" He held out three dollar bills.

When she reached for them, his hand closed around hers, and he shook solemnly.

She was afraid the bills were going to wilt or dissolve, and she snatched back her hand. "I'll see if I have enough change. We just opened."

She lifted the lid of the cigar box where she kept petty cash and was relieved to see there were several quarters. She gave him two, dropping them quickly in his palm before they tarnished.

"Well, enjoy your stay at Dan-D's," she said. "It's probably the last time in your life you'll have the chance to peel potatoes."

"Unless I join the service."

She could imagine him in a uniform. He would wear it well. Of course he would be an officer.

He turned to go, but halfway to the door, he turned back. "You have a boyfriend, Nancy?"

For a moment she didn't know what to say. But something was required, because she saw he wasn't going to leave until he knew. "There's not a boy in these parts that ever interested me," she said at last. It was close enough to the truth.

"I'll bet more than a few of them have been interested in you."

"Oh? What makes you say that?"

His gaze drifted lower than her face to the V of her blouse. The gaze was not insolent, not exactly. But when it wandered back to her face again, his answer was clear even before he spoke. "They've got two eyes in these parts, don't they?"

Her cheeks heated. He was clearly a college man trying to stay in shape until he could get back to his college girls. She had been assessed and found promising. For some reason that upset her.

"You forgot something," she said. She reached under the table and found one of the soft tomatoes her mother planned to can that evening. She hiked it back over her shoulder and lobbed it directly at him.

He didn't try to catch it. He was quick on his feet and dodged just in time. The tomato splatted against the door frame and dribbled to the dirt below.

"What was that for?" he said.

"Just one more tomato for your money, college man. Wouldn't want to be accused of shortchanging you now, would I?"

"You know, I don't think you *could* shortchange me." He smiled his perfect smile once more; then he gave a mock salute, turned and started back out to his car. But he moved quickly, like he wasn't quite sure she was done pitching tomatoes.

She watched the Corvette streak out of the parking area and back out to Route 11. She was afraid the most exciting moment of her summer had just come and gone.

Billy came to the stand every day after that. For a week Nancy told herself he was just bored, that he didn't know anybody, and she was a pretty enough face he could chat with. Sometimes he arrived when Helen was there, and he made respectful, easy conversation with her—although Helen resisted his charm with every bit of her considerable natural immunity.

He bought cucumbers and tomatoes, bushels of sweet corn and baskets of green peppers. He claimed that everyone at that Dan-D told him that theirs was the only produce in the area worth having. But Nancy suspected there was more to his visits than silver queen corn vs. golden bantam.

On Friday evening, one week after Billy first stopped by, she was sitting on the front porch of the Fitch Crossing house with her feet propped on the railing. Helen, who'd been up since before dawn, was already in bed. Nancy was too exhausted to sleep after an impossibly drawn-out day in which everyone who had stopped by the market had been long-winded and short on anything interesting to say. If she'd heard one more word about Mrs. Maidie's bunions, she would have dropped a bucket of tomatoes on the old woman's foot just to give her something new to talk about.

And for the first day since their initial meeting, Billy had not stopped by the market.

She heard the purr of an engine before she saw the beams of the headlights illuminating the road. And she saw the headlights for several seconds before she recognized the car. As she watched, Billy Whitlock's Corvette slowed, then stopped, just a little past their driveway. The car rolled backwards, and he turned in.

"I'll be darned." Before the words were out, she realized how she looked. She had showered and washed her hair when she got home, and it was still wet. She had dragged on cheap flowered shorts and a blue tummy tickler like the ones she'd worn as a little girl, and her shoes were up in her bedroom. She had nothing on her face except a frown and some errant annoying freckles. She looked, in short, about twelve.

He was parked and out of the car before she could flee.

"Nice evening," he said, stopping beside the drooping maples in the front yard.

He was waiting to be invited up. Her mind darted in every possible direction, but there was no way around it. She beckoned, and he started up the stairs.

"Don't tell me you were just out driving around," she said.

"May I sit?"

She motioned to the chair across from her, but he chose the swing beside her, nudging her to the edge with his hip.

Sparks shot through her at the feel of his body so close to hers. She'd lain awake at night for a week trying to imagine a moment like this one, but her experience was so limited, her imagination hadn't had much to work with.

"Dan told me where you lived," he said.

"Everybody knows where I live. Everybody knows everything about everybody here."

"This really is the country, isn't it?"

By now she knew he was from Richmond. She knew from the car, from the clothes and the educated accent that he was from *rich* Richmond, no stutter intended.

"You'll have to watch yourself at UVA next year," she said, "or next time you might end up out here in real purgatory, pulling weeds and mucking out the barn."

"I didn't mean to make the country sound like a bad thing. It's pretty out here. The whole area's pretty."

She couldn't see that, of course. Pretty to her would be sidewalks and shops, big houses with landscaped yards, women in pillbox hats and soft white gloves at parties on sweeping green lawns.

"Why're you here?" she asked. "Why aren't you scrubbing pots?"

"It's my night off."

"On Friday?"

"Dan's got family who come in to help on weekend nights. He doesn't need me. I worked hard and got my part done by five."

"That's why you didn't come to the stand?"

"You noticed, huh? Did you miss me?"

She had missed him the way a gray sky misses sunshine. Her job was intolerable. Her *life* was intolerable, and she wasn't sure what to do about it. Then Billy Whitlock had appeared, and suddenly there was a reason to get up in the morning, to plan and dream a little.

"You're not answering," he pointed out.

Her hands were trembling. She was such a novice, such a beginner, such a hick. She closed her eyes. "Billy, what is it you want?"

"What do you mean?"

Whatever veneer of sophistication she had managed until then melted away. "I'm nobody, and you're somebody. I'm poor, and you're rich. I'm a country girl, you're a city boy."

"You're blond, I'm brunette," he said, a grin in his voice.

She stamped her foot, and the gentle rocking of the swing quieted. "I'm serious and you're not!"

"Nancy, I don't want anything except a little company. I'm going to be here another couple of months. Can't we just spend some time together? Get to know each other? Have a little fun? I like you. Don't you like me?"

She opened her eyes and turned so she could see him. It was a mistake. He was leaning toward her. Their lips were only inches apart, and it was too late to withdraw without making a fuss.

She didn't want to make a fuss. She wanted to kiss him. She supposed she wanted more, but that was a start.

The kiss, when it was finalized, was the best thing that had ever happened to her. He was practiced, and she was not, but he didn't seem to care that she wasn't quite sure where to put her nose or how wide to part her lips. He smiled against them.

"You like that?" he asked softly.

"Uh-huh."

And she liked the next one, and the next, and everything else that came after it in the following weeks, even better.

CHAPTER
20

Before Kayley died, Saturday was a special day, and Mack had religiously cleared his schedule to spend it with Tessa and their daughter. After Kayley's death, Saturday became the longest day of the week, and the only way he could get through it was to stay busy.

This particular Saturday threatened to stretch into eternity. There were no household chores to do. The cleaning lady had come the day before, and the house was not only spotless and more austere than usual, the refrigerator was stocked with items he'd asked her to buy.

His computer had yielded no e-mail of note; the answering machine was still turned off; even his Palm Pilot showed nothing on the day's schedule, since a golf game—never his favorite sport anyway—had been canceled. There was no dog to walk in the park, no wife to take out to breakfast, no daughter....

He made himself cereal, showered and shaved, and confronted the fact that he had the perfect day to drive to Toms Brook and no desire to do so.

Dressing in the bedroom, he realized his loneliness had

reached crisis proportions. He was desperate to color in the spaces in his life. His wife was emotionally unavailable; their past had been erased.

Their past had been erased.

He looked around at the empty dresser top and night tables, at the wall where Kayley's framed artwork had hung. Suddenly his day no longer stretched in front of him like an empty vessel with nothing to fill it.

An hour later he stood back and gazed at his handiwork, recovered from boxes in the basement. The living room had been transformed. On the fireplace mantel the lumpy uneven vase Kayley had crafted at summer day camp held a handful of silk daisies. Framed photographs of Kayley alone, Kayley with friends, Kayley with her parents and Biscuit, adorned shelves and end tables. The dragon kite she had given him on her last Christmas hung from a wall.

They had flown kites from the highest hill at Helen's house. He had so many memories of Kayley and her kites....

He felt triumphant that he had brought this small part of his daughter back into his life. He also felt enormously saddened that this was all he could do.

The sound of the doorbell finally penetrated, and he realized it might not be the first summons. He went to the door and found Erin in khaki cargo shorts and a neon orange shirt that was unzipped to the top of her breasts. She had a royal-blue bike helmet tucked under her arm and was just turning away.

"Erin." He grinned at her. "Nice day for a ride?"

"Only until noon. I thought I'd get some exercise before it really turns hot."

"It's what, eighty-seven, eighty-eight out there now? Cool as a mountain stream."

She smiled her Midwestern beauty-queen smile. "Anyway, I saw your car and wondered if you'd like to take a spin. You have a bike, don't you?"

She had seen his car, but not his wife's. He was sure she must have checked carefully.

He had a bike. He hadn't ridden it since his daughter's death. He wasn't sure, but he thought it might still have a child's seat on it from the days when Kayley hadn't been able to ride a bike on her own. She had ridden solo by the time she was four. He had been so proud. . . .

"You don't look like a man who wants exercise," she said after a moment of reading his expression. "I'll be on my way."

"No, it's just that my bike is probably a mess. I haven't ridden it. . .in a while. But you look like you could use a drink. I've got iced tea. Fruit juice. . ."

"You're not busy?"

"No." He realized he should have been, that even if he wasn't busy, he should have said he was. He was lonely, vulnerable and very attracted to her. It was a lethal combination.

"Well, I'll take a short break, then I'll be off." She unclipped her hair and shook it out. He was reminded of sunbeams.

She followed him inside. They stopped in the living room, and she gazed around. "It's a lovely house, Mack." She went to the photographs immediately, lifting one of Kayley posing on a birthday party pony. "They don't make them cuter, do they?"

He admired her careful phrasing. No past tense to be found. "She was already after us for real riding lessons. Tessa was shopping around for a good program."

"I'm glad you have reminders in view. When Jeff died, my parents packed up everything in the house. They're unhappy with me for having his photos on the wall in my apartment."

"Let's see what I've got in the fridge." He led the way into the kitchen. He had been here earlier, as well. Pot holders Kayley had woven hung from hooks. Ceramic canisters of a cat, a mouse and one big wedge of Swiss cheese lined a counter. A Cookie Monster cookie jar straight from Sesame Street perched on another, as if asking to be filled with Kayley's favorites. She had chosen it on a family shopping spree.

With the refrigerator door open, he catalogued the contents out loud. "Bottled tea, ice water, apple juice——"

"Ice water will be great."

He took a glass from the cupboard and filled it with ice, then added filtered water from a pitcher. She took it gratefully. "My bottled water was as hot as I was." She leaned against the counter and sipped. "How are things, Mack?"

He hadn't seen her since their aborted dinner at the Siam Palace. He was surprised she had sought him out again.

"I'm busy at work." He couldn't think of anything else to say.

"I thought we ought to talk about the other night."

"I'm sorry, Erin. I should have called to apologize sooner. I just wasn't sure whether it would make you feel worse. We weren't doing anything wrong, but I know it was awkward."

"For you, too."

That was like her. She was a generous woman, and more than half in love with him. He had accepted both the generosity and the affection like a drowning man grabbing for a life buoy.

"I just wanted to say that…" She paused. "That I don't want anybody to get hurt here. I think we should back off until your life is in order."

That was code, he knew, for "until you've filed for divorce."

"I'm not cut out to be the other woman," she added ruefully. "Not even when your marriage is hanging by a thread."

She tried to smile, but her eyes were glazed with tears. Maybe he wouldn't have reached out to her if they hadn't been. He didn't really know. He was close enough to touch her cheek, and he did.

Maybe if she hadn't nestled against his palm, even for a moment, he would have dropped his hand and the intimacy would have ended. But instead his fingers crept to her hair, and he brought her face to his.

And maybe if she hadn't kissed him back, if she had withdrawn or protested or not parted her lips... But they were so soft against his, so available, so ardent.

He moved closer and pinned her to the counter with his body. She was soft against him, her breasts full and lushly female, her scent an earthy mixture of cinnamon and sweat. Her arms came around him, enfolding him so that he was half of something again, part of a couple united by desire. He felt himself growing hard against her softness, and he knew that if she didn't stop him, if he didn't stop himself, they would be united by more than a wish very soon. And he didn't want to stop. He wanted to be part of something again, part of *someone*.

He circled her with his arms, and his hand brushed something cool and smooth on the counter. Before he could react, the cookie jar, Kayley's cookie jar, fell to its side and rolled to the floor with a crash.

Erin pulled away and looked down where the shattered jar lay in brown and bright blue pieces. "Oh, Mack, I'm so sorry."

He wasn't touching her now. He wasn't sure how he had moved away so quickly, or how he had moved toward her in the first place. Reality washed over him. And still, staring at the woman who was not his wife, the woman who might replace Tessa if he ended his marriage, he wanted to go back in time, not to the moments before he had taken Erin in his arms, but to the moment when she had been there, when he had been part of something again, when he had felt almost whole.

Shock hadn't reduced his erection, but now he knew that he could no more make love to her than he could explain himself in words.

He wanted this woman, but he knew she was not the woman he really wanted. He liked Erin; perhaps he was even a little bit in love with her. But it wasn't Erin he needed. He wanted and needed what he could never have again. He wanted the life he and Tessa had built together. He wanted the little family that had gone to the store and chosen the cookie jar that now lay shattered at his feet.

A sob rose in his throat. He put his hands to his cheeks and took a deep breath to choke it down.

"I'm the one who's sorry," he said. "And now I'm going to ask you to leave."

She backed away, sliding along the counter. "I'm going to stay away, Mack. For good. I've been coming to the meetings to see *you*. I realized it this morning. I've moved beyond needing to attend so often, but I've come to meetings anyway because you're always there. And that's wrong. I'm going to stay away."

"This isn't your fault."

"No, it's both our faults," she said. "And I've become exactly the kind of woman I despise the most, the kind who goes after another woman's husband. Maybe I was even trying to force the issue by coming here."

"Maybe I was trying to force it by asking you inside."

She continued to slide along the counter until she was nearly at the kitchen door. "Go back to her, Mack. You're not ready to pull the plug. Do whatever you have to."

It was a noble speech, and he was pretty sure it was honestly meant. But he couldn't tell her he appreciated it, because he couldn't speak.

A minute later he heard the front door close.

And he was alone again.

Tessa had finally admitted to her mother and grandmother that she was staking out Robert Owens's house. She had come to Manassas twice already, returning home late both nights, and after the second time the questions about her whereabouts had worn her down. Neither woman had been happy, but they had been more understanding than Mack.

Tonight was officially Diana's shift, but she had a family birthday party she needed to attend. Diana was taking Tessa's shift tomorrow to make up for tonight, and Tessa was watching for the second night in a row.

This time she had dared to park directly across the street from the house, since a much-needed thunderstorm was supposed to move in, and she knew she probably wouldn't be detected. Not many of the tiny ranch houses in the Owenses' development had carports or garages, and because the front yards were narrow, most driveways had room for only one car. This street was lined with vehicles, and with the added bonus of tinted windows, she doubted anyone would ever notice she was sitting here.

So far Owens hadn't been spotted leaving his house at night, although he had been seen at home either picking up the mail in the roadside mailbox, doing yard work, or sitting on the stoop smoking a cigarette. If he was drinking, he was doing it in the privacy of his own home, and he wasn't driving. At least, no one had caught him.

They had only watched his house for four nights, though, counting this one. But this was Saturday, the hardest night to stay away from the bars or parties. He was a young man fresh out of prison. Young men with a record like his were prone to showing off and acting out. Tessa was sure that if she was patient, if she bided her time, he would make a mistake.

She shifted in her seat and tried to make herself more comfortable. She had considered bringing headphones, but she was afraid music might put her to sleep or a book on tape would become so interesting she might not watch as carefully. She had packed pen and paper to write a letter to a college friend, but she was afraid to concentrate on anything except the Owenses' front door.

Two hours passed, and the storm moved in, splashing the first raindrops on her windshield at about eight o'clock. She hadn't seen any sign of Owens tonight, although she knew he was home, because she had heard his mother calling to him from the front yard when she went out for the mail.

To Tessa, the mother looked beaten down, like a dog who'd been kicked once too often and never quite recovered its trust or vitality. She was probably only in her forties, but she looked considerably older, stooped and pasty-faced. Tessa had noticed a flicker of something younger, though, something brighter, when she turned toward the house to call to her son. Tessa was sorry to see that hopeful expression, that momentary thrusting back of shoulders. She obviously cared about Robert, and she was bound to be hurt again.

The sky was now a mass of angry clouds. Lightning slashed the horizon, and ozone scented each gust of wind. It reminded Tessa of the night she, Nancy and Helen had danced in the rain. There was no reason for late-night treasure hunts anymore. Last week, tired of digging fruitlessly for the third tin, Nancy had rented a metal detector. The women had found the third one in fifteen minutes' time. Now Helen's money was safely in the bank, and generous sprigs of periwinkle thrived in the freshly dug areas.

The front door opened, and Mrs. Owens peeked out, as if hoping the rain would halt momentarily. Then, with no umbrella, she scurried to the car parked in her driveway, opened the door and dropped into the driver's seat. Lights and windshield wipers on, she backed out of the drive and drove away.

Her son had not been with her. Robert was still at home, and now there was no car for him to drive.

The rain began in earnest, and Tessa considered abandoning her post. Robert was marooned. The storm would make the drive back to Shenandoah County longer tonight, and she was already exhausted. What were the chances Owens would leave his house on foot in this downpour?

What were the chances a drunk separated from his alcohol would care about a little rain?

She settled down into her seat and arched her neck. Her eyes closed. She was definitely more tired than usual. The nightmare had visited twice last night after she finally got to bed, spurred on, she supposed, by her hours of surveillance. She had slept very little, forgoing her morning jog to sleep later than usual. But she needed more.

She needed so much more than sleep and had no idea how to reach for any of it.

She opened her eyes just as an old silver conversion van pulled into an empty space across the street, directly parallel to her own parking spot. As she watched, a stream of young men poured out into the rain, laughing and cursing. They ran toward the front door, shoving each other as they went. With the help of a streetlight, then the sudden illumination of a porch light, she counted five, two carrying brown paper bags. They disappeared into the house; the porch light flicked off, and the street grew quiet again.

Tessa was wide awake now, adrenaline shooting through her body. She knew a party when she saw one. All the ingredients were right there. The raucous young men. The shopping bags filled with six-packs or hard liquor. A rainy night just meant for getting drunk in the privacy of somebody else's home.

And Mrs. Owens, the good influence that the court depended on to keep Robert in line, gone.

She sat forward, hands on the wheel, and wished she could be a rose on the wallpaper. Although she didn't know every fine detail of the probation agreement, she guessed that spending time with friends was probably allowed, as long as Robert didn't break any other rules. Maybe they had gathered to watch a baseball game or a wrestling match. She didn't know and didn't care. But if they were drinking and Robert joined them, then he was in violation of his probation, and he could go back to jail. *Would* go back, if Judge Lutz was telling the truth.

Robert was supposed to attend AA meetings every morning before work. She doubted he had missed a one, since that was part of the agreement. But what he did in the privacy of his house, when no one else was there to monitor him? That was the question mark.

The rain was coming down in sheets now, but even though it was drumming hard against the roof and windows, Tessa heard music, and she knew where it was coming from. Loud rock music, with a beat as steady as the rain.

She could call the probation officer, but what would she say? *I'm parked outside Robert Owens's house, hoping to send him back to jail? He might be drinking? Send somebody to check his blood alcohol level, but wait a little while until it's higher?*

She had one chance to get this right. Less than one, if the probation officer ignored her, even when the evidence was incontrovertible. She had to use her opportunity wisely. Once she admitted she had been watching Robert, she would not be able to continue.

She needed to see what was happening. She couldn't go to the door and ask to be let in. Even if she manufactured an excuse like a flat tire, Robert would recognize her. The only viable option was to peer through the windows like a peeping Tom. She was fairly sure the darkness and the rain would protect her. Light spilled out of windows in the back, and she knew the curtains were open. If she was careful and didn't take too many chances, she could look in without being seen. If he was drinking, she would go back to the car and make the call. She had the probation officer's name and home phone number. Diana had gotten it for her, although Tessa didn't know quite how that had been accomplished.

She debated silently. Sitting in the car on the Owenses' street was one thing, but padding silently through the backyard, peering through their windows, was something else. Yet the inclination to do it was so strong, so sure, that she abandoned reason at last and turned to get her raincoat from the back seat.

She was glad the worst of the lightning seemed to have moved away. She wasn't worried about getting struck so much as getting caught in a bright burst of light. No one was on the street or front stoops. The houses flanking his didn't have their lights on, which made it easier for her to shoot in between the house on the right and the Owens house, and head toward the back.

Her progress was impeded by overgrown bushes, but they also helped hide her. She passed two darkened windows on her left and noticed with relief that the neighbors' bushes were even higher and thicker, blocking much of the view from the side windows. They'd probably been allowed to grow to provide privacy because the houses were so close together.

Even with a raincoat, she was drenched by the time she got close to the back of the house. Rain found its way under the slight V at her throat, and the hat she'd tied under her chin was no help at all, channeling the water down her back. The coat stopped at her hips, and her jeans were already sodden and stiff.

She heard the party before she could see it. Loud voices, louder music, the laughter of young men egging each other on. She wondered if these were old friends of Robert's, perhaps even some of the ones who'd poured him into his car and sent him off drunk on the morning Kayley died. That party had gone on until well after dawn. She wondered if this one would, as well.

She edged between the bushes and the brick. The passage was narrow, and evergreen branches slapped at her shoulders and neck. She confronted holly and felt the sharp leaves tearing at her raincoat, and then at her hands when she tried to brush it away from her face.

She inched closer, and the noise got louder. She knew better than to stick her face against the windowpane, although the temptation was there. She bent down low and peered in through the corner of the window. Her view was blocked by the edge of a curtain, and she moved closer. A portion of the room was visible now. She saw a television set, although it was unlikely anyone could hear it with the music turned so loud. Her breath caught when a young man walked over and changed the channel. He was dressed in jeans riding low over his hips and an oversized T-shirt. When he turned, she saw an owl and the word *Hooters* in bright orange print. No subtlety there, but none expected, either.

Another man joined him. Both of them were carrying cans, but she couldn't tell of what. The second wore shorts to his knees and a plaid sports shirt unbuttoned to show his entire chest. Both had straggly hair and somber, bored faces. She wondered if they could tell themselves apart.

Neither of them was Robert.

She turned to look past the bushes and decided the only way to get a better view was to get away from the house and beyond the bushes again, then use them to shield her as she positioned herself to see inside. She would be taking a risk by moving away from the house, but as it was, this risk wasn't worth the effort.

The infinitesimal portion of her that had remained dry no longer was by the time she pushed through the bushes and crept closer to the center of the window. She could see better now, although out from under the minor protection of the eaves, the rain was even worse. Two men were laughing in the opposite corner from the television. One shoved the other, palm against shoulder, and the second shoved back. They were obviously playing. She was reminded of young stags butting horns, testing their mettle, finding their place on the testosterone curve.

Then Robert walked into the room. He was the essence of her nightmares, this broad-shouldered, heavy-chested youth whose short legs didn't live up to the promise of his upper body, and whose posture was almost ape-like. He had short hair the color of dried leaves, and a high, wide forehead that made closely set eyes even less appealing.

Had he simply been her student, and had she been the woman she was before Kayley's death, she would have reached out to him, the way she always reached out to kids who seemed to have little going for them. She had seen his presentencing report. His

IQ was high enough that he should have made Bs without trying hard. As a younger boy, he had been a leader in Cub Scouts, and later, as a Boy Scout, he had earned a dozen merit badges before his life fell apart.

But from that point on, his record had changed. Vandalism. Petty theft. Drunk driving. Good grades turned to bad. Problems with anger management. One fistfight that had left a fellow student unconscious and bleeding on the gymnasium floor. Suspension. Reinstatement. Suspension.

As she watched, he joined the two who now seemed to be arguing over what to watch on television. He moved between them, and in a moment the channel had been changed again. There was no drink in his hand, but she knew that didn't mean anything. In the time his friends had been there, he could have chugged a beer, maybe even two, if he was desperate enough. And wouldn't he be desperate after the long dry spell called prison?

If she watched long enough... If she waited patiently... If she...

Robert turned and headed straight for the window. He was arguing. She could hear the rough singsong of his voice, and his fists were flying in punctuation. She realized he was only seconds away from discovering her. It might be dark, it might be raining, but if he got all the way to the window... She sank lower and turned to move away, and there, right in front of her, was a man, stooping in the rain and reaching for her.

He clapped his hand over her mouth just as she opened it to scream. "Tessa," he hissed, "for God's sake, shut up."

She was limp with fear, stunned and shaking, and it took long moments to realize the man was Mack.

He removed his hand and put his finger to his lips. Then he motioned toward the street, taking her arm to pull her along. There was no possibility of argument. They could not afford to make a fuss. But she knew that if she didn't go with him, a fuss would be made anyway.

They ended up in his car, which was parked farther away than hers. She dripped water everywhere as he shoved her into the passenger seat. Inside, he turned and rummaged in the back before he came up with a towel, which he tossed on her lap.

"I just use it for the windshield. It should be clean enough."

She mopped her face. She was still trembling, and the simple act drained all her energy. "How the hell did you find me?"

"Your mother asked me to talk some sense into you. She said this was the second night in a row you'd come out here. She's afraid you're going to set up a tent."

"And you went along with her? That's a first."

"What in the world did you think you'd accomplish back there? Do you know how many laws you broke? Trespassing. Invasion of privacy. Just for starters. Stalking's a real possibility, too. Have you lost your mind?"

"My mind? No. My inhibitions? Apparently." Tessa didn't look at him. The towel was already sopping, but she continued to rub it over her face and hair as a shield.

"Tess, honey, look at me."

She hadn't expected his tone to change so suddenly. She dropped the towel in her lap and faced him. "Mack, I don't want a lecture. And I don't want to be cajoled. I knew what I was doing."

"And what you were risking?"

"Of course! Do you think I've suddenly grown stupid?"

"Robert Owens has rights."

"Unfortunately our daughter no longer does."

He winced, and she wasn't happy to see it. She looked away. "As far as I'm concerned, he lost all his rights forever when he ran Kayley down. If I could plant evidence against him and get away with it, I would do it."

"No, you wouldn't."

She didn't argue, because she wasn't sure which of them was right. Where would she stop? It was a question she'd pondered for days.

"What did you see in there?" he asked. "Was it worth it?"

"It might have been if you'd left me alone."

"In other words, there was nothing going on that doesn't go on in a million homes."

She wished she had seen Robert with a beer can in his hand. She wanted to throw that in Mack's face. "His mother left, and not more than five minutes later his friends arrived. Do you think that was an accident? They were waiting for her to go, waiting to have a party. Party to this set means drinking."

"You can prove it?"

She couldn't.

He put his hand on her thigh, and there was nowhere she could go to get away from it except back out in the rain. "Please, don't do this," he said. "I'm worried about you. More than you even know. This isn't like you. You're fair. You're wise."

"I'm a mother."

"I've been running through our last meeting in my head, Tess. I can't tell you how many times I've replayed it."

As many times as *she* had, she was sure. "Nothing's changed," she said. "I'm still going to watch his house."

"I'm afraid something has changed. You told me the other night that you weren't doing anything illegal. You stepped over that line tonight."

She took his hand and moved it off her leg so that they were no longer touching. Then she sat there and considered what he'd said. And in the end, after minutes had passed, she closed her eyes.

"All right. I blew it."

His sigh filled the car. "I'm glad you see it."

"Are we done, then?"

"I'm afraid you're going to make more mistakes along the way. I'm afraid you're going to end up in jail."

She felt the icy fingers of reality begin to tear aside her defenses, and what she saw when she looked inside her own heart frightened her. "I won't peer into windows again," she said at last. "But that's the most I'll do for you."

"For me?"

"Yes, for *you*." She looked at him again. "I don't care if I go to jail. I'd go in a minute if I thought he'd have to go, too."

"But that's not the way it works."

"I know, Mack. I said I blew it, okay?"

He leaned his head back and closed his eyes. "Sometimes I think you'd be better off without me, do you know that? I'm a reminder of better times. Sometimes I think that's *all* I am to you anymore, that maybe I ought to just step aside. If I did, would you be able to move forward with your life? Would that be enough to kick you out of Reverse gear?"

"It's not Reverse gear. I want justice."

"But you know what?" he went on as if she hadn't spoken. "Every time I think I can let you go, I realize I'm not quite there yet."

She stared at him. In the dim light of a rain fogged street lamp, she stared at her husband, and her heart felt like it was twisting in her chest. "No?"

"I've been looking for you in other women. That's what my thing with Erin was about."

"Your thing? Oh, please."

"And you've been pushing me at her."

"I don't even know the woman."

"Anybody would do." His voice became steely. "It's the only way you can make that final retreat and be alone with your anger and sadness."

"You're blaming your affair on me?"

"There *is* no affair. There won't be, either, although we damned well came close. And no, I'm not blaming it on you. I've been lonely. I've let this happen. I let you push me farther and farther away with every action and inaction, every important conversation we didn't have, every night we didn't make love. But I'm not playing the game anymore, Tess. If you want me out of your life, you have to tell me. Directly. I'm not going to be the one to do your dirty work. I'm not going to let you blame this on me, claim I fell in love with somebody else and just moved on."

She didn't know what to say. She was too honest to insist he was wrong. But was he right? Did she want Mack out of her life so that she would have no reminders of Kayley? Did she want to pack him up with the drawings and the photos and the stuffed unicorn?

Tears filled her eyes. "I see her everywhere. I even see her when I look at Robert Owens, do you know that? I have nightmares about him. There's a car coming closer and closer—"

"Tess, don't. I can't take it."

"No, you don't understand. *He's* not driving the car. I am! I have the same awful dream night after night. I'm in the car, and he's the one on the sidewalk. And I aim for him, Mack. I put my foot on the accelerator and I aim for him, and I don't stop until he's lying dead under my car. I don't stop...." She put her face in her hands.

He didn't touch her, he didn't speak, and she was so glad he didn't. "I want him to suffer the way we have," she said at last through her tears.

"You need help."

"No, I need Robert Owens in jail. That's the only way my life is going to be any better."

"It wasn't any better when he *was* in jail. Don't you see it? You suffered just as much. You've got to get a handle on this, and you can't do it alone."

"I'm coping. I'm doing something about him. That's why I'm here."

"No, you're pushing everybody away. Haven't you learned anything from spending the summer with your grandmother? Don't you see the similarities? Don't you get it? You're going to turn into a bitter, lonely old woman, Tess, just like Helen, unless you do something about this now. You've been pushing me away to make sure the same thing happens to you. But you're going to have to take the final steps alone. I won't help you. I'm here, and I'm going to stay here until you tell me to go away."

She wiped her eyes on the drenched sleeve of her raincoat. Then she turned to him. "I don't want you. I don't want your help."

He stared at her; then he shook his head. "I don't believe you." He leaned over and reached across, opening her door. "Go home."

She stood on the sidewalk as he pulled away. The music was still audible from the Owens house as she walked in the rain to her car. But she got in and drove away.

CHAPTER
21

No matter how tired Helen was during Nancy's childhood, she'd always made sure they went to church as a family. The Shenandoah Community Church was nothing fancy, white clapboard, gracefully wrought steeple, musty-smelling rooms in the back and in the basement for the youth program. There was always coffee and conversation after the services, and Nancy was free to run and play outside with the other children before she went back home to finish her chores.

This morning Nancy drove her mother to the little country church, only to find that since her last visit, a large social hall had been added where the classrooms had once stood, and now a new, light-flooded wing housed the children and their programs. The parking lot had been paved; the fine old trees had been pruned and cared for; a rose garden perfect for outdoor weddings graced a side yard that already had a stunning view of distant mountains. The updates were wonderful, and the congregation had grown.

"It's such an improvement," she told Helen later over midmorning coffee in the farmhouse kitchen. Helen had refused to stay for the social hour, and Nancy hadn't wanted to push the issue.

"Don't go much anymore." Helen stirred three teaspoons of sugar into her cup. "Seems like a wasted effort at my age. Either I'm going to heaven or not. By now, there's not much more I can do about it."

Nancy retrieved pastries she'd bought in Woodstock to go with the coffee. "Maybe you ought to just go so you'll have people to talk to, Mama. You spend too much time alone."

"Not these days. Can't draw a breath around here anymore without somebody else breathing the same air."

Nancy let that ride. "I like the new pastor. He asked a lot of questions about you. And he said he's been trying to visit, but you won't let him inside."

"So that's what the two of you were chewing over?"

"I told him he'd be very welcome now."

Helen grumbled, and Nancy turned away so her mother wouldn't see her smile.

"You think Tessa's all right?" Helen asked when the grumbling had faded.

Nancy brought the pastries to the table. "Why do you ask?"

"I haven't seen her this morning."

"She's up in the attic. While it's still cool enough to be there." Nancy hesitated. "I think she needed some time to herself, and there's not much chance you and I are going to make it up there any time soon."

"She got home late last night."

Nancy wondered if Helen had stayed awake listening, as she had. "I don't like this surveillance she's doing, and I told Mack as much. It's like rubbing salt in a wound. But she's not going to listen to us. She's going to do what she thinks she has to."

"Like her mama."

"No, Tessa's more like Billy than me. She watches that boy's house because she thinks she has to, even if it's ruining her life. And Billy married me because he thought he had to, no matter what the consequences."

"I haven't heard you talk about that for more years than I can count."

Nancy settled herself at the table and took a cheese danish. "Tessa found our marriage certificate in the attic a couple of days ago. She found out I was pregnant before we got married."

Helen didn't look surprised. "It was bound to happen. Better now than after you're gone and there's no way of explaining it to her."

"What's to explain? I met a man, we had sex, I got pregnant. It's such a common little story."

"There was always more to it than that."

Nancy was amazed that the conversation was still in play, but her mother's understanding tone made her pause and tilt her head in question. "More?"

"Don't you think I know you were never cut out for your life here? That you saw Billy as somebody who could take you away?"

"I didn't get pregnant on purpose, if that's what you're saying. I'd admit it at this late date, if it were true, but it's not."

"No, but you were living in a dream when you were with him. I saw the dreaming part of you practically from the time you learned to walk. You were like a little fairy child, sensitive to sound and color and tone of voice. Everything either delighted you or plain-out scared you to death. There was no in-between. You lived in your imagination."

"That's how children are."

"Not me. Nobody in my family was like that, except maybe Tom. Maybe Fate was like that, and he had it bled out of him one bad piece of luck after another, I don't know. I know he didn't like farm life, either, not really. He wanted to travel, see new places and things, drink in life in a way that was outright foreign to me."

Nancy was surprised. She had never realized that Helen understood, much less accepted, who she was. "You tried so hard to make me into somebody else. Why? Did you just want me to be different?"

"No, I just wanted you to survive. And what else could I offer you? I had the farm, and just barely that. I didn't have a way to make things easier or better for you."

"It would have been better just to know you understood."

Helen didn't look angry at the criticism. "I can see that now. Back then, though, there wasn't time to think twice about anything. The way you were, well, it was going to be trouble if you had to stay around here. I thought I was just preparing you. Now I know I was holding you back. So many of the things we try to do for the right reasons are wrong. That's about the saddest thing in life."

Nancy didn't even know what to say. Her entire world needed readjusting. Somewhere inside her was the little girl who had believed her mother thought she was worthless. To find out that had not been the case at all took more than a moment to accept.

Helen seemed to know. She reached out and put her hand on Nancy's. "And maybe I was just trying to weight you down, Nanny, so you wouldn't fly off and leave me. Maybe that's the saddest thing of all. If that's what I was doing, then I'm just real sorry about it."

Tessa wasn't sure where Nancy was taking her. All she knew was that she had come downstairs before noon to find her mother, car keys in hand and "command performance" in her eyes.

"I don't want to talk about watching the Owens house," she told her mother once they were in the car.

"That's fine." Nancy backed out of the driveway and started down Fitch Crossing. She didn't chatter, and she didn't nag. She just drove silently and slowly, as if she were enjoying the view.

Tessa couldn't let it go as easily. "Mack found me. He said you told him where I was."

Nancy turned off Fitch and headed north. "I thought you didn't want to talk about this."

"I wish you hadn't told him where I was."

"You'd prefer I lie?"

Tessa fell silent. She had awakened with a headache and a lump in her throat that might be unshed tears. Aspirin was not the cure.

"He misses you, sweetheart," Nancy said. "And you miss him."

"I don't want analysis." The words weren't out of her mouth before she regretted them, and the tone, as well. "I'm sorry. I don't feel well."

"Then just lie back, close your eyes and relax. This is going to be fun. You'll like what I've got planned."

No recriminations. No guilt. Just motherly concern. Tessa did as she was told, and by the time they stopped and she opened her eyes again, she felt better.

"Gram's church?" She sat forward and gazed at the picturesque building. Well-wishers from the late service were still shaking the pastor's hand. But as they sat there, the last stragglers had their word with him and left.

"His name's Sam Kinkade. He's a nice young man and a good preacher," Nancy said. "Today he spoke about loving yourself. He said we have to love ourselves before we love God or our neighbors. It was something to think about."

Mack had attended church regularly after Kayley's death. Before, they had gone intermittently as a family, but it had been more for their daughter than for themselves. Now Mack went because he wanted to be there, and Tessa hadn't set foot across the threshold.

"We have an appointment," Nancy said.

For a moment Tessa was afraid her mother had dragged her here to talk to the pastor, to spill her feelings in his clerical lap and receive some sort of mini-salvation. But Nancy put her hand on her daughter's arm.

"He's going to give us a tour. I have an idea, and I think this might be the place to pull it off. I want to put on a show of your grandmother's quilts. And I think this is the place to display them." Nancy got out and started toward the church, and in a moment Tessa caught up with her.

"Does Gram know?"

Nancy laughed. "Are you kidding?"

"It would be a surprise?"

"Just until somebody spills the beans. Then we'll have to hogtie her and throw her in that old truck of hers to get her here."

"But it's a wonderful idea!"

Nancy stopped and turned, even though the pastor had seen them and was waiting. "Really? I'm glad you think so. That means a lot."

"What made you think of it?"

"Your grandmother has gotten very little validation in her life. She kept the family farm against terrible odds, she raised a daughter with no help from anybody else, she made those incredible, out-of-this-world quilts. And who knows about them? Who knows about this woman's life? She deserves a little applause before she dies, don't you think?"

Tessa started toward the church again when her mother did. "You'll do a terrific job of it, too."

"You think so?" Nancy looked pleased.

"Of course. Nobody can organize the way you can. And you're wonderful at displays. You could take broken eggshells and make something special out of them."

"Most likely I'm blushing about now. But thanks."

Tessa saw Nancy *was* blushing, and she realized how little praise she gave her mother. Apparently it was a family failing.

Reverend Kinkade came forward to meet them. He was dark-haired and handsome enough to make the young women in the congregation attend more regularly. He was about Tessa's age, perhaps a year or two younger. He seemed like the kind of man who would be more comfortable in blue jeans than his simple black robe.

Nancy introduced them, and they shook hands. His grip was firm, his blue eyes unwavering. "I have visits I have to make in a little while," he said, "but you're welcome to linger as long as you like after I've showed you around."

They wandered through the rooms, and Nancy pointed out where quilts could be hung. Sam—as he preferred to be called—was enthusiastic about the idea.

"I've been told Helen's given away dozens of quilts to church members," he said. "And I hear she's quite a character, to boot. I'd have to agree from the little I've seen."

No pussyfooting there. Tessa thought this might be a minister she could relate to. "Yes, to both. But she's an artist."

"If I had my way, this building would be in use every minute of every day. I'll have to get permission from our lay leaders, but there shouldn't be any problem. Particularly if we can leave some of the quilts up for the following Sunday?"

"That would be wonderful," Nancy said. "More recognition."

"I wonder if any of the people she's given quilts to would bring them back for the show, maybe with stories about what they've meant to their families," Tessa said.

"What a great idea." Nancy put her arm around her daughter's waist. "What do you think about hanging some of them outdoors if it's a good day? As dry as the summer's been, we're probably safe. We could hang them from the lowest branches of the big trees."

"Or display some of them between stepladders in the rose garden?" Sam suggested.

By the time he left, there was little question the quilt show was almost a fait accompli. "It's too bad I don't have more time to pull it together," Nancy said, "but it's going to be big enough to please her."

"Maybe too big."

Tessa gazed around the sanctuary. Sam wasn't sure they would be allowed to use it for the show, but Nancy had asked him to try to get permission. It was a quiet room, and it probably held a hundred people if they squeezed together on the pews. There was only one stained glass window above the altar, but the side windows looked out on mountains and trees, holy enough to suit even the fussiest parishioner. Fresh roses and linen adorned the altar, and the cherrywood pulpit had been polished to a high gleam.

"I'm just going to sit here a moment." Tessa expected Nancy to fuss, to ask if she was feeling well and did she need a drink of water? But Nancy just squeezed her shoulder before disappearing into the hallway.

Tessa wondered if there was any place on earth as quiet as the chapel of a country church. The silence seemed to thrum against her eardrums. The air-conditioning was off now, but the cool stillness seemed to embrace and surround her, a tangible presence. She thought of Mack and understood for the first time what he had found in church and what she hadn't even looked for. She was uncomfortable here, not willing or ready to yield to the comfort within these walls, much less give any consideration to the more academic question of God. But by the time she got up to find her mother, she understood her husband better.

Nancy was outside, gazing up at the branches of an oak tree. "Ready?" she asked when Tessa joined her. "I'm starving. Let's go home and make some lunch."

Tessa put her hand on Nancy's arm. "No, let me take you out. Let's go to that place you mentioned in Woodstock. We can bring back something for Gram."

Nancy looked touched. "Well, that would be lovely. You'll like it."

They drove in silence and parked on a side street. The little town, with its historic limestone courthouse and attractive log and brick buildings, was quiet, and they ordered sandwiches without fuss at Honeycutt and Sugarbaker, the little café within a larger collection of shops and booths of collectibles.

They took a seat by the window, gazing out over the street, and Tessa dove into the best chicken sandwich she had ever eaten.

"I used to take you out to lunch a lot when you were a little girl," Nancy said.

"And instruct me on the proper way to eat, sit and cross my legs."

"You learned well. You do me proud."

Tessa laughed. She was surprised to find she was really enjoying herself. This new, more relaxed mother was someone she didn't know. "You always bought me Rocky Road ice cream, remember? If a restaurant didn't have it, we went looking for it afterwards."

"You were unbelievably set in your ways."

Tessa wondered if she still was. Despite herself, she thought of the conversation with Mack last night, as she had at regular intervals all day. Had she coped with her daughter's death by becoming so rigid, so afraid she might encounter more pain, that she wasn't coping at all, merely atrophying?

"How do you see me now, Mom?" She lifted her head. "Do you think I'm coping?"

She didn't need to elaborate. It was clear from Nancy's expression that she understood. "Do you want the truth?"

"Yes."

"No, I don't think you are."

Tessa waited for her to go on, but Nancy chose this one time in her life to be silent.

"Mack doesn't think so, either," Tessa said at last. "We're this close to a divorce." She didn't even illustrate. She was sure Nancy knew.

"Is that what you want?"

Tessa really didn't know. But she did know that Mack had been right last night when he said she'd been pushing him toward one.

She'd thought about it through the long night, and she knew that part was true.

"Mack says that maybe I can't come to terms with Kayley's death until all reminders of her are gone, and that includes him."

"I suspect he said that hoping you would deny it."

Tessa looked up from her plate. "I didn't."

"They don't come better than Andrew MacRae. The alternative is a life without anyone, because no one else will measure up."

"I've been thinking about your story the other day, about the way you met Daddy. You must have gotten pregnant soon after?"

"I was a farm girl. I should have known better. Unfortunately, animals don't demonstrate the use of condoms, and neither did your dad."

Tessa laughed, despite herself. "He should have known better."

"Let's just say we got carried away."

"What was it like? Not getting carried away, but being pregnant so young and without being married. And I don't want the sanitized version. Maybe I need to hear about difficult times and the way they're overcome." She said it lightly, but she knew it might be more than half true.

"Do you really want to know? It doesn't show the best side of either of us."

"I think I really would like to know." Tessa toyed with what was left of her sandwich. "You got through it."

"More or less. And you were our reward. No matter how it came about, neither of us was ever sorry we had you."

Tessa considered. "I was never sorry you did, either."

"Until Kayley died. Then you were sorry you'd ever been born."

Tessa wondered if that was true. Was she that bitter? And why hadn't she allowed herself to think of any of this until now, to look at her own reactions and question them?

She stood, resting her hands against the small of her back for a moment. "I'm ready for cappuccino. Shall I get you some?"

Nancy smiled a little. "No, I'll just sit here and figure out how to explain what idiots your father and I were thirty-eight years ago, right before we brought you into the world."

CHAPTER
22

August 1964

Nancy hadn't really made plans for her life. Sure, she'd dreamed a lot, imagining modeling agents or talent scouts who found her amidst the tomatoes and the sweet corn and signed her to lucrative contracts. But she was too smart to think those were anything but dreams. If she had any particular strengths, she wasn't aware of them. If she had any resources outside her own quick wits and passably pretty face, she wasn't aware of those, either.

Then Billy Whitlock entered her life, and suddenly plans, strengths and resources seemed inconsequential. She had Billy for the summer, and that was plan enough.

She was still stunned that someone like Billy, even with a limited field to choose from, had settled on her for a summer romance. He was handsome and smart. He was a considerate, passionate lover, and once she got over the fact that she was no longer a "good girl," she reciprocated with all the love she'd never found a home for.

And she *was* in love, despite knowing how foolish that was. Where would she find a more perfect man? His manners were impeccable, and his ability to talk to anyone about anything—even Helen—was remarkable, although Helen still couldn't be swayed. Nancy's mother was suspicious and wary, and from the moment she realized Billy was in the picture, Helen began to find more for Nancy to do, so that the little free time she had was used up.

Nancy still found ways to see him.

This night, though, seeing Billy was not a pleasure but a necessity. He was leaving for home in three days, and eager to go. He was not crass enough to tell her he could hardly wait to get back to a more rarified existence, but she had seen the signs. She had expected this, and she had never fallen prey to false hope. In her mind, the divide between them was so wide that of course Billy would forget her as soon as he returned to Richmond.

Tonight, though, she was going to have to tell him that she wasn't as forgettable as she had expected to be.

Helen had never understood Nancy's desire for a little privacy and fumed nonstop about closed doors and girls who put on airs. As Nancy dressed to go out, Helen barged into her room without knocking, which had always been her way.

"You spend too much time with that boy," Helen said bluntly. "You'd be better off staying at home tonight."

Nancy finished powdering her nose. Her hands were trembling, and the face in her mirror was pale, and not from Cover Girl bisque. "He's leaving in a few days, Mama. Just let it go."

"Should have left before he even got here. A boy like that don't need anything we got to offer around here."

Nancy knew that was Helen's way of saying that Billy didn't need *her*. For once in her life, her mother was right.

The air was turning cooler, and she pulled a Bobbie Brooks blouse with a Peter Pan collar over a Madras wraparound skirt. Billy had offered to take her out for dinner, and though she doubted they would get that far, she wanted to dress nicely enough to match whatever he showed up in.

"Nanny..."

Nancy closed her eyes and waited.

"You be careful," Helen said at last. "That's all. Just be careful."

The warning was already too late.

Billy picked her up fifteen minutes later, attempting polite conversation with Helen for a few moments until it was clear there was no hope of detente. Once they were out on the road, he put the top down on the Corvette and cranked up the engine.

"Pull over," she said, when the combination of the rushing air and the speed made her stomach lurch.

"Why?"

"Now!"

He braked to a halt, and she stumbled out just in time to lose the little she'd eaten since breakfast in the roadside weeds.

To Billy's credit, he gave her his handkerchief and opened a Coke from a stash on his backseat to rinse her mouth with. Then he waited until she was able to speak.

"You should have told me you weren't feeling well tonight," he chided. "You ought to be home in bed."

She began to sob, and he put his arms around her and rubbed her back. "Hey, it's okay. Don't be embarrassed. It happens to everybody."

"Not to men it doesn't!"

It took him a moment to understand. She knew the instant he did. His hand stopped, and his body stiffened. "Are you saying...?"

"That I'm pregnant? Yes."

"Are you sure?"

Now she really was embarrassed. "Yes! I've missed two periods. I'm sick in the morning. My breasts hurt. I looked it up in a book at the library yesterday. I'm going to have a baby."

He didn't ask whose. He knew better.

"God damn," he said.

"Don't curse at me."

"Why didn't you say something before?"

"Because I kept hoping and hoping it wasn't true. And you can't always tell, you know, and for a long time I just felt normal. And sometimes periods can be late or even skip. I've heard that happens. And I thought maybe everything we've been doing just upset things a little. And you were careful most of the time, Billy. I just couldn't believe it."

"God damn!" He turned and slammed his fist against the hood of his car.

Her heart was breaking. She was too realistic to think he would be over the moon with joy, that he would grab her and promise to marry and protect her for the rest of their long lives together. But she had hoped for better than this.

The summer had done funny things to her, even before the pregnancy. She had begun to think about herself in a new way. Before Billy, she had only yearned for something different, for love and a place where she really belonged. Now, after a taste of something better, she had begun to believe she deserved a different life, that she might really find her way out of Toms Brook, that even if Billy wasn't a permanent route, he'd been a helpful signpost.

"We should have been more careful." He was leaning against the car now, his arms crossed over his chest.

"That's pretty clear." She didn't know where to look, so she looked just over his shoulder.

"You need to go to a doctor to make sure it's true."

She *knew* it was true, but she supposed it made sense from his viewpoint to get the news signed, sealed and delivered. "I can't go to our family doctor. He'll tell Mama."

"Don't you think she's going to figure it out soon enough?"

"Later would be better."

"What's she going to do?"

Nancy wasn't sure, but she didn't think Helen would throw her out, although there would surely be hell to pay. Could she bear to stay in the house with her mother, listen to her criticism, be chastised every time she tried to do something for the baby that Helen disapproved of? Did she have the right to bring a child into the world the two women inhabited, a somber, poor existence where even the sweetest baby would be a burden?

"She's going to be hard to live with," Nancy said, and knew it was an almost comic understatement.

"She's already hard to live with."

"I thought about not telling you. I just wanted to be a good memory. I didn't want to be the mother of your baby. I didn't want to trap you."

"Trap me?"

She stared at him and realized that the possibility of marrying her might not even have occurred to him. The idea of marrying her might *never* occur to him. She was like the job he had finished at the Dan-D, a taste of what awaited him if he screwed up his life. And he'd learned what he needed to know.

"I wasn't trying to get you to marry me." She turned her back on him. "I didn't do this on purpose. I never set out to get pregnant."

"I haven't even graduated from college yet."

"Don't you think I know that?"

"I'd just about decided to go on with…" The sentence trailed off. "It doesn't matter now."

"Go on with what?"

He didn't answer.

"Go on with what?" she demanded.

"I changed majors in my junior year. My father wanted me to get an accounting or economics degree so I could join his business. He's a financial consultant, the best in Richmond. But I changed without telling him. I thought I might want to be a forest ranger. He only found out when I told him I wasn't going to graduate on time. That's why I'm here for the summer. He told me the only courses he'll pay for are the ones I need to complete the accounting degree. I'm supposed to decide if I want an education his way or not at all."

Billy had hinted at this previously, although she hadn't understood how the pieces fit together. "And what had you decided?"

"To screw up my life, apparently. To screw up yours. To screw up a baby's."

"Are you going to tell your parents?"

His eyes widened, as if he couldn't believe she'd asked. "What do you think?"

She didn't know. She didn't really know him. They'd laughed together, had wonderful sex, talked about inconsequential things. But she didn't really know Billy Whitlock. In the ways that most mattered, he was a stranger.

"I'll get you a doctor's appointment. Somewhere they don't know you," he added when she started to interrupt. "Okay? That's what we'll do first. Then we'll figure out where to go from there."

"I won't get rid of it."

He pushed away from the car. "I didn't ask you to."

"I don't care if you find a place that's safe and private. I'm not that kind of person."

"What kind of person are you?"

She was afraid she might never find out now. She felt like any growth she'd made this summer had been stunted, and now everything she was and was going to be had to revolve around the life inside her.

"I'd like to go back home now," she said.

"What will you tell your mother?"

"That you're getting a cold and I don't want to catch it."

"Wouldn't it be great if things were that simple?"

* * *

Somehow he found her an appointment in Winchester the following day. The doctor agreed she was pregnant, due sometime in March. She was healthy, young and strong. He foresaw no complications. She thought the last part was the only funny thing he said during the brief appointment.

Billy was waiting outside when she emerged. She told him the news, showed him the prescription for prenatal vitamins and the card for her next appointment. He gave a curt nod, helped her into the Corvette, then took her right home and dropped her off.

"I'll be in touch," he said, when he came around the side of the car to open her door.

"Billy, don't we need to talk?"

"I have to think about things first. Give me a little time, okay?" He was abrupt, but not quite rude.

"Is there a way to get hold of you?" She watched him hesitate, as if the last thing he wanted was to share his family's phone number. With a grimace, he relented, taking a scrap of paper from his pocket and scribbling on it.

He handed it to her. "Don't call unless it's an emergency."

"I think this just about qualifies, don't you?"

"I said I'll be in touch, and I will."

She wondered if she would hear from Billy or his lawyer next.

The following week her nausea grew worse, but she hid it from Helen, who was too busy keeping food on the table to notice anything. Helen seemed relieved that Billy was out of the picture and eased up on the work she required of Nancy now that summer was ending. Nancy spent her free time fretting and pacing. She was due back at the school once the first semester was in gear, but that seemed light years away.

Billy called a week later, when Helen was gone. Halfway into the first minute, she realized he was checking, among other things, to see if somehow a miracle had occurred and she'd lost the baby.

"Wouldn't that make life simple?" she said. "I'm sorry I can't just make it go away by wishing. I know that would suit you."

"Come on, Nancy, don't tell me it wouldn't suit you, too."

"If that's all you've been doing, Billy, waiting and hoping that I'll have a miscarriage, then maybe you'd best put your mind to better use. I'll be showing before long. My skirts are already tight. I had to move the button on two of them. I don't see how I can go back to work."

"I'll call in a couple of days."

But he didn't. By the end of the next week, she was frantic. She even called and left a message at his home, with a woman who called him Young Mr. Whitlock and spoke with a liquid drawl. Just as she was about to hang up, the woman said, "He won't be home again for a while. You might want to try him at school."

Nancy hung up, stunned. Billy had already gone back to school. Without telling her. Without caring if she knew. He had gone back to UVA hoping that Nancy wouldn't find him and the baby would simply disappear.

She cried herself to sleep that night, but when she woke up, she knew she couldn't go on like this. Before she told her mother, before she changed the entire course of her life, she had to see Billy face-to-face one more time and demand that he help her. The baby was his, too. Was it fair that only she suffered the consequences?

Their stand was closed on Sunday. Nancy found an excuse not to accompany her mother to church, and as soon as Helen left, she drove the old farm pickup down the road to the house of a girl she'd known in high school. Patricia wasn't eager to loan Nancy her car, particularly when she heard how far she intended to drive it, but she softened and agreed when Nancy pressed her graduation watch into Patricia's palm with a promise she could keep it if Nancy didn't come up with twenty dollars to buy it back.

The trip took hours, and Charlottesville was unfamiliar territory. She paid little attention to the historic buildings or the UVA campus once she found it. She asked for directions to the Zeta Psi house, which Billy had mentioned several times, and parked just down the street. Then she made her way on foot to the front door.

The girl who had given her directions had told her the house looked like a smaller Monticello, but that meant little to Nancy, since she'd never been to Charlottesville and knew little about Jefferson's home. She straightened her skirt and made sure her blouse was tucked in before she knocked.

She was an immediate hit. Young men flirted with her, offered to duel Billy for her hand, even pretended they'd never heard of him, but in the end, someone went to get him and Billy appeared at the top of the stairs in shorts and a basketball jersey.

He was polite, taking her by the arm and moving her away from his admiring frat brothers and back outdoors before she could even say goodbye. He didn't say anything until they were well away from the house, in a parklike cove that was probably somebody's private property.

"How did you know where to find me?" he asked.

"Someone at your house said you'd gone back to school."

"Did you talk to my parents?"

"You mean did I tell them I'm carrying their grandchild?" She shook her head.

When he didn't say anything, she filled the silence. "You said you would call. I trusted you."

"You trusted me not to get you pregnant, too."

And look where that had gotten her. She wondered if he was trying to tell her she couldn't trust him, that he had no plans to help her and wouldn't be swayed. His parents were rich. They could hire lawyers. For the first time she wondered if she was wrong to push him, if he might decide to take the baby, or insist she give it up for adoption because she was unfit to raise it. Her mind flicked through terrible possibilities.

"I'm sorry," he said, before the possibilities bloomed three-fold.

"I've been trying to figure this out. I should have called just to say that. But with coming back here, trying to settle in, explaining myself to—" He stopped abruptly.

"To who? Who did you have to explain yourself to?"

He looked away. "A girl from back home. We were pinned."

"Pinned?"

"I gave her my fraternity pin."

"Like being engaged?"

"Not quite. Don't look like that."

"You mean you had a steady girlfriend while you were sleeping with me?"

"We broke up, or just about did, before the summer. I just made it final, that's all."

"Why? Why did you?"

He looked back at her. "Because I'm going to be a father. Do you think she would want me right now?"

The *right* answer would have been "Because I'm going to marry you." A wave of nausea swept over her. She was exhausted, terrified, at her wits' end.

She sagged against a tree, resting her head and closing her eyes. Her head was swimming. She'd had nothing to eat all day except a slice of dry toast, and she'd been in Patricia's clunker of a car for hours. She was one step from total exhaustion.

"Do you know what this will do to my life? I'm an unwed mother. No one will ever look at me the same way again. I'll be 'that Henry girl.'" She gave a bitter laugh. "And the baby? The baby will be 'that Henry bastard'!"

"Who do you think I am? I'm not going to let any kid of mine grow up like that."

"No?" She opened her eyes and stared at him. "What do you plan to do about it?" All the terrible possibilities she'd fantasized loomed in front of her. "Because don't you dare—don't you *dare*—think you can take this baby away from me, Billy Whitlock. You may be rich, and your family may be powerful, but I'll go so far away you'll never see me. And if you try, if you try to stop me, I'll…I'll kill myself before I let you!"

She was as close to hysteria as she had ever come. When he stepped closer, she shoved him away. "This is *my* baby, you son of a bitch!"

"Get hold of yourself!" He grabbed her hands.

"What's wrong, frat boy? Too much real life going on here to suit you?"

He stared at her, his eyes angry. Then he dropped her hands. "We'll get married right away. I was trying to clear things up, Nancy, make this work somehow. And that's the only way it's going to work. But get one idea out of your head. *I'm* not rich. My folks are rich, and they're going to be furious. They aren't going to put us up in a cute little apartment while I finish school. They're going to cut me off—like that." He snapped his fingers. "And they're going to make our lives a living hell."

"Marry me?"

"It's the best way, the only way. Believe it or not, I've been trying to figure out a way to make everything come together."

"Why didn't you call me, then? Why didn't you tell me?"

"Because I still hadn't come up with a good answer. I'm still at a loss. But I know this much. We're not telling anybody what's going on. We'll get a license tomorrow and go ahead with the ceremony. We'll find somebody who'll do it. I already checked. There's no waiting period. A couple of weeks into the marriage, we'll make the announcement. It will be too late for anybody to do anything at that point. Then we'll see where we go from there."

He took her hands, not tenderly, but as if he hoped it would stave off another attack. "We can't think of ourselves anymore. We have to think about what's good for the baby. And to begin with, we're going to tell everybody that we got married a couple of months ago, right after we met, and that we knew our parents wouldn't approve, so we got married secretly."

She was crying. This calculating man holding her hands was not the Billy she'd fallen in love with, but he was all she had. And he was saving her from raising this baby alone and in poverty.

"Thank you," she said, as tears slid down her cheeks. "I can get a job here. I'll work. Maybe we can get you through school on our own."

"Let's find a place for you to stay tonight. Tomorrow we'll take care of business."

"I have to call my mother and tell her where I am."

"Don't tell her much."

"I have to return the car. I borrowed it." Nancy had promised to have the car back by evening. She knew her watch was a goner now.

"We'll figure out something."

She searched his face. He didn't look happy. She supposed the tears were proof that *she* didn't look happy, either. This was not the way she had hoped to marry. And while Billy was more than she had ever hoped for, forcing him this way was the wrong way to start a marriage. She was young. She was immature. But even so, she knew this was the worst sort of way to begin.

"We liked each other," she said huskily. "We had fun together."

He dropped her hands. "I think the fun is over."

The next morning they drove to nearby Nelson County, where nobody knew them. That evening the boyish Pentecostal minister who performed the ceremony stumbled through the words as if they were brand-new to him. But it didn't matter, because they were legally married once he was finished.

"I'll get you a ring," Billy promised as they left the old church, which looked more like a run-down convenience store than a house of God. "As soon as I can."

She nodded. Mrs. William Lee Whitlock. She was numb.

"I saw a motel on the main road. Nothing fancy, but just about all we can afford."

She nodded again. She and Billy. Married. In a motel.

At the front desk, the clerk raised a brow at the absence of a ring and the shopping bag with a few things they'd bought for the night. Billy pulled out the marriage certificate and held it up for the man to read.

He smirked and gave them his best room, which simply meant the roaches were smaller and there was only one mousetrap in the corner.

Nancy wanted the wedding night to mean something. It seemed to her that if she could just show Billy one more time how well they fit together, how easy it was to be in each other's company, he would feel better and their marriage might flourish someday.

But stress and exhaustion took what had been simple morning sickness and blew it into something so fierce, so frightening, that she spent most of the night in the tiny bathroom with the cracked linoleum and the rust-stained sink.

Billy slept alone.

CHAPTER
23

Monday morning's jog was longer than usual. Tessa could almost feel the ounces dropping off her already thin torso. She didn't stop to rehydrate along the way. Instead she splashed herself with her bottle of water until halfway through her route, when she gave in and poured the remainder over her head. She kept running and thought about her mother's confessions over yesterday's lunch.

Nancy had been matter-of-fact, but the wound had bled through every word. Tessa was not as surprised to find she'd been conceived out of wedlock as she was to find how much pain Nancy felt about her own shotgun wedding. Clearly Nancy still believed that Billy had married her out of duty, and nothing that had come afterwards had remedied that. She felt closer to her mother because of this revelation, and understood so many things that much better.

Marriage had always seemed simple enough to Tessa. A woman met a man who attracted her. She tried on the relationship, like an off-the-rack dress at a specialty boutique. Then, if it didn't fit or look promising, she discarded it and went on to another. If it almost fit, she made tucks here and there, raised or lowered the hem, and surveyed the final product. If the dress met her approval, she kept it and wore it everywhere.

In hindsight, Tessa was surprised she had ever been that cavalier. Until Kayley's death, she hadn't been a particularly complicated woman. She'd had a host of advantages. Parents who loved her, money, education, status. She had a highly developed social conscience but no paroxysms of guilt over her own good fortune. She had loved deeply, forgiven easily, and always given everyone in her sphere the benefit of the doubt. Truth was that her charmed life had not prepared her for Kayley's death. Evil, sorrow, hatred, were abstract concepts, and she'd had no deep, personal knowledge of any of them.

Nancy's life before marriage hadn't taught her what *she* needed to face a crisis, either. Helen had kept her daughter busy so she wouldn't have time to dream, but, of course, with few friends and even fewer dates, she'd done nothing but. Nancy had never experienced love, security or desire. She hadn't even experienced much laughter. In a way, she had been like the princess in the tower, waiting for the handsome prince to rescue her. Only Tessa's father had been anything but glad to have her once she escaped.

Marriage wasn't simple at all. Like so many others things Tessa had learned in the past years, that was a lesson she would rather have skipped.

By the time she was only half a mile from her grandmother's farmhouse she was thinking about Mack. She had slowed her pace, and now she walked the rest of the way to cool down.

She hadn't spoken to him since Saturday night, when he had found her peering through Robert Owens's window, but she had been thinking of him ever since. How clear a demarcation existed between the conscious and unconscious mind? How long had she been pushing Mack away, and when had it turned from instinctive to deliberate? At what point had she told herself she would be better off alone?

She realized now that since Kayley's death, she had been trying not to love Mack, because he reminded her of better times. And wasn't she also afraid that someday he might leave her, too? That if she pushed *him* away, the moment of departure was under her control?

Would a therapist have helped her see this more clearly? Helped her find ways to cope that were healthier?

Something inside her was broken. With help, could she have mended it? Could it be mended still?

She was so lost in thought that she nearly stumbled over Cissy, who was walking toward her from the direction of Helen's house.

Tessa stopped and smiled a vague apology. "I was thinking. I didn't even see you. Have you been to see Gram?"

"Not yet. I'm coming over later for a quilting lesson." Cissy was dressed in a blue plaid sundress, her freckled arms bare, her hair a soft sunrise-colored cloud floating over her shoulders. "I feel better if I walk a little before the day gets too hot. I just go back and forth on the road a piece. My back aches if I sit too long."

"Mine did, too." Tessa surprised herself. She had stored that memory in her mental attic, along with all the others.

"I know you lost a little girl," Cissy said. "It must have been so hard."

This was the moment when Tessa always changed the subject. She started to now, then caught herself and wondered momentarily what might happen if she uttered just a few sentences about Kayley's death. She tried, but nothing would come.

Cissy filled the space. "When my grandma died, I thought I was going to die, too. Losing a child, well, that would be worse."

"It was." Words, not sentences, but Tessa felt lighter.

A beat-up Plymouth passed, slowly enough, since the road was too narrow and rough for speed, but the two women waved and waited until it was gone.

"I wrote a few pages." Cissy looked down at the ground and re-arranged dirt clods with the toe of a dusty tennis shoe.

"Good for you." Tessa considered her next words. "I'd like to see them. Do you feel like showing me?"

"You'd really be interested? Because I don't want to make you sorry you offered or anything."

"I'd like to see them." Tessa was being honest. Working with Cissy reminded her how much teaching had once meant to her, even as it also reminded her that she was no longer performing well in a classroom setting. That last part had been on her mind a lot.

"I'll bring them when I come for my quilt lesson."

They parted ways, and Tessa finished her walk back to the house for a quick breakfast before she began her newest project, the root cellar and hundreds of jars of home-canned fruit and tomatoes.

When Cissy arrived after lunch, Tessa was relaxing on the front porch. Cissy was a wilted flower, hot and bedraggled and heat-flushed when she climbed up to take the chair beside Tessa's.

"It can't get much hotter, can it?" Cissy complained.

"Don't tell me the mobile home doesn't have air-conditioning?"

"Just up and stopped for no reason last night. Zeke'll fix it. He can fix anything. But he's been gone all day. I spent part of the morning in the house, but I don't want them thinking I'm a burden or nothing...anything."

Tessa wondered if Nancy had felt like a burden when she was pregnant and living with Billy's parents in Richmond. She decided to ask her mother when she had the chance. Obviously there was more to her mother and father's story.

Cissy frowned, as if she'd just realized how her comment had sounded. "Nobody *says* I'm a burden. I don't want you to think bad about Mr. and Mrs. Claiborne. They been good to me. Real good. They treat me like I was a real member of the family."

Tessa wanted to ask the girl why she wasn't. What was keeping the two young people from marriage? Good sense? Selfish disregard for their child? An age in which marriage simply wasn't important, and illegitimate was a word losing its hold on an entire culture?

"How'd you meet Zeke?" she asked instead, hoping that Cissy would feel comfortable with a more casual topic.

"He was playing fiddle in a string band over in Mt. Jackson, and I stopped to listen. Next thing you know, here we are."

Tessa thought there was probably a bit more to it, since Cissy was hugely pregnant. "I've been thinking today about the reasons men and women find each other. What was it about Zeke that made you fall in love?"

Cissy squirmed in her seat. "He was good to me. In a way nobody else ever was."

"I don't know Zeke, but I like what I do know."

Cissy looked up. "Do you?"

"I wasn't sure I would."

"Why?"

"I wasn't sure he was treating you the way a woman deserves to be treated."

"Nobody ever treated me this good. I feel right, like everything's working the way it's supposed to, when he walks into a room."

It wasn't the most romantic definition of love that Tessa had ever heard, but at its core it was as good as any. She'd once felt that way about Mack.

"I wrote about Zeke," Cissy said. With her coloring and the heat, it was hard to tell if she was blushing, but Tessa thought it was a safe bet.

"I'd like to see it," Tessa offered.

"It's not lovey-dovey. Nothing like that." Cissy fished through her purse, a beat-up canvas and straw bag that was big enough to hold lunch, dinner and a midnight snack. "Here it is."

Tessa held out her hand, afraid that if she actually reached for the paper, the girl would snatch it back.

Cissy relinquished it slowly and with great ceremony.

Her handwriting was painfully neat. Fifth grade cursive, Tessa thought, as if she'd been practicing with triple-lined paper, measuring the tails of her letters with perfect precision. Tessa read the paper slowly to herself, then she smiled.

"Cissy, what good ideas you have."

Cissy slumped in her chair. "You're not just saying that, are you? Nobody ever told me I had good ideas when I was in school."

"Well, someone should have. I'm not sure what they were thinking. Maybe they were just more concerned with grammar and spelling. Some teachers are that way." Tessa was afraid that maybe she was becoming one of them.

Cissy had taken the two major male characters in *Tess of the D'Urbervilles* and compared their actions and personalities to Zeke's. It wasn't expertly done, and everything needed work. But she clearly saw the flaws and strengths of each of the three men, and compared them while organizing her opinions in a sensible yet creative way.

Cissy would benefit from a class discussion of the book, which would help her broaden her viewpoint, but there was no getting around the fact that the girl had understood the most important points of Hardy's characters and drawn interesting conclusions about them. She was Tessa's favorite kind of writing student, an astute and quirky observer, able to express her observations in a meaningful way.

"I'll tell you what," Tessa said. "Let's break up our time into two parts. We'll go over some of the simple stuff like punctuation and grammar and get it out of the way. Then we can talk about the way you expressed your thoughts. That's the dessert. Because you did it so well."

Cissy's smile turned a dampened, disheartened pregnant teenager into a Madonna. "You're not just saying so?"

Tessa smiled, too. "I am not just saying so. I never have the energy to lie. It's just not in me, even when the weather's cooler."

Cissy's laugh was low, husky and more adult than Tessa had expected.

* * *

Helen had gone up to her bedroom early that night. After Cissy's quilting lesson, she had gone down to the root cellar to help Tessa identify the jars of food that were probably still safe to eat, and the experience had worn her out. She was a strong woman, but throwing out what seemed like perfectly good food—even if it was ten years old—took the starch right out of her backbone. She went upstairs right after an early supper and never returned.

About seven, Tessa took the wedding ring quilt out to the porch, where the light was still good, and settled herself in the swing, spreading the old quilt on her lap and over the wooden arms. She had successfully replaced three patches with fabric that was not too different from the original. The patches had been sewn into place and pinned with big safety pins to the batting and lining, waiting until the rest were added and she could re-stitch the carefully snipped lines of quilting.

She was lucky in a way that the quilt had been Nancy's first and only project. She could mimic her mother's stitches, but never her grandmother's, which were tiny and straight. Nancy's were more like the woman herself. Erratic, exuberant, although certainly falling short of a desire to please.

A car slowed on the road, and Tessa glanced up to note it was her mother's.

"Like some company?" Nancy asked a few minutes later.

Tessa was struck by how different her mother looked. Nancy had missed supper and called to tell them to go on without her. Now she could see where her mother had been and what she'd been doing. "Wow!"

Nancy's hand went to her hair. "I got my hair cut in town. I told her to whack it all off, and she certainly did. Then I went to Wal-Mart."

This was a new Nancy. The haircut was very becoming, not masculine, but wispy and curly. Curly! "You have curly hair?" Tessa said.

"Well, I guess I must. There it is. I've blown it and pulled it and wound it around so many brushes in my time that I didn't remember what it was really like. Now I can just ruffle it with my fingers and I'm all done for the day."

"Wal-Mart?"

"Shorts, T-shirts, flip-flops." Nancy wiggled her rubber-sandaled feet. The sandals were adorned by large plastic daisies. "Two-ninety-nine. I liked them so much, I bought three pairs in different colors and put these on in the car."

She rummaged through a shopping bag and held up some of her purchases. The shorts were bright lemon-yellow. The shirt was horizontal stripes of yellow, red and black. Horizontal stripes, one of Nancy's biggest no-no's.

Tessa tried not to smile. "I hesitate to say this in case it precipitates a heart attack, but you look cute."

"Cute? At my age? That's something."

"Is this mid-life crisis?"

"I'm past mid-life, aren't I? I don't plan to live to be one hundred and twenty."

"It's such a change."

Nancy settled herself across from her daughter. "I just got tired of trying so hard. Does that make sense to you?"

The last wasn't a plea for understanding. Nancy seemed genuinely interested in Tessa's response, whatever it was.

"It makes sense to me that you'd buy some cooler clothes and cut your hair, Mom. It's hot as the dickens in this house. Makes me want to go chop all mine off."

"Don't you dare!"

Tessa grinned. "The old Nancy speaks."

"No. I love your hair. It suits you perfectly. And you can put it up off your head and never fuss with it. I just got tired of fussing. Used to be, when your grandma was a girl, women of a certain age got to let themselves go. Well, I never got to, and I'm tired of the pretense."

"You're hardly sagging and bagging. You cut your hair and got some comfortable clothes. You look great. Dad's going to think so, too. He called a little while ago to say he's coming for the night so we can go birding early in the morning. He had to see a client in Harrisonburg for dinner, so he's coming up afterward."

Tessa expected the announcement to create a flurry of activity on her mother's part, but Nancy didn't even seem to register it.

"I feel great." Nancy leaned back in the chair and stuck her legs out in front of her. "I used to get in trouble for doing this. Your grandmother had a fit if I lounged this way."

"Gram had the time to notice something that trivial?"

"Not *my* mother. Billy's. Grandmother Caroline."

That made more sense to Tessa. Her father's mother had been a tiny woman, bird-boned, long-necked and slender-legged, a swan with a similar temperament. She looked serene, even stately, but she could strike out with a vicious snap if anyone got too close. Tessa had learned early not to cross her grandmother and not to tell her anything important. With those rules in mind, they had gotten along just fine until Caroline died at an untimely fifty-five of breast cancer.

"You went to live with them before I was born," Tessa said. This part of her mother's life was vaguely familiar. The family had referred to that year politely, if rarely.

"It was the worst year of my life." Nancy kicked off her flip-flops and tucked her feet under her bottom, exactly the way she had so often instructed her daughter not to.

"She was hard to live with?" Tessa asked.

"Your grandfather, too. Harry drank. Steadily, from the moment he got up. As the day got longer, he got quieter and more controlled. He moved like a nineteenth-century Chinese courtesan with bound feet, mincing little steps...." She walked her fingers along the chair arm to demonstrate. "And by dinnertime he had nothing to say to anyone. Caroline would berate him, and he wouldn't even raise an eyebrow. She berated me, and he didn't even notice."

Nancy hesitated. "But I shouldn't be telling you this, Tessa. They were your grandparents."

Nobody knew better the damage that alcohol could do. Tessa felt her own breathing quicken in protest. "Dad used to drink quite a bit."

"Yes, he did. But he hasn't had a drink in years."

"Three years, to be exact," Tessa said. Her father hadn't had a drink since Kayley's death.

"Yes. But Billy never drove when he drank. And neither did Harry. They had a driver in the old days, a man named Randall, who drove Harry anywhere, saw that he was put to bed, mixed his first drink of the morning. A paid enabler."

Tessa carefully snipped a thread, then another. "What was it like living with them? And why did you? Didn't you say you wanted to help Dad through college? Didn't you want to live with him in Charlottesville?"

"I haven't upset the apple cart enough by telling you what I told you yesterday? You understand there are always two sides to every story?"

Tessa hadn't sensed any desire for payback in her mother's version of events. She didn't think Nancy was trying to get even for the way she'd been treated by enlisting Tessa's sympathy and support. She'd simply told the story.

Tessa looked up from the quilt. "I think I need to understand myself better. Maybe this will help."

"Give me a mission, any mission, and I'll perform?"

"No, just tell me the truth the way you saw it."

"I can do that," Nancy said at last. "Because there weren't any villains and definitely no saints. Just people caught up in a situation."

"*I'm* the situation," Tessa reminded her. "Your love child."

"No, sweetie, *marriage* was the situation. I was quilting mine together, the way I quilted that top you're working on. And you know what? Marriage can really be a bitch." She laughed when Tessa's eyes widened at the unexpected and uncharacteristic profanity. "Well, can't it?" she demanded.

Tessa smiled, and her gaze drifted back to the quilt as Nancy began.

CHAPTER
24

December 1965

Billy's parents had been thrilled when he gave Mary Lou Stalcourt his fraternity pin during his junior year at UVA. "Lou's" Atlanta family had Old South heritage and New South money, and Lou understood every nuance of gracious living.

Billy's parents were *not* thrilled when he gave Nancy a wedding ring. The resulting conversation had contained so many words like *annulment*, *misjudgment* and *entrapment* that Nancy wondered if she had stumbled into a quiz show with "words ending in 'ment'" as the only category.

Now she had new words to add to that list: *disappointment*, *discouragement*, *disillusionment*.

Two weeks before her second Christmas as a married woman, Nancy woke up in the room she shared with her baby daughter and peeked out of half-opened lids, hoping, as she had every morning for a year, that she would see the narrow confines of her farm-house bedroom.

As always, she was out of luck.

Her room in the Whitlock house was high-ceilinged and spacious, with multi-paned windows draped in sheer curtains that danced as heat from the floor register wafted through the room. The furniture was French Provincial, even Tessa's crib and changing table. Nancy's ornate white-and-gold canopy bed was hung with yards and yards of floral polished cotton that matched the bedspread and the overstuffed chairs by the fireplace. Thick white area rugs covered the polished wood floors.

Two dressers and a walk-in closet hid all their clothes and anything else that was remotely useful. If Nancy dropped one of Tessa's blankets on the floor, Hattie, the Whitlocks' housekeeper, picked it up, folded it and stuffed it in a drawer before Nancy could even apologize.

A discreet knock sounded on her bedroom door, and Hattie came in without waiting for permission. She was a middle-aged woman whose dark skin was not suited to the dove gray uniform she was required to wear. Nancy couldn't guess Hattie's age, although she suspected she was younger than she looked. Mrs. Whitlock demanded long hours, and Nancy knew that when Hattie went home, she cooked and cleaned all over again. By herself, Mrs. Whitlock was enough to age anyone.

Hattie set a breakfast tray on Nancy's nightstand. A baby's bottle sat at one edge, a glass of orange juice at the other. "Brought you one of those biscuits you like so much. Just don't tell Mrs. Whitlock."

Nancy smiled her thanks. Eating habits were among the many changes Caroline Whitlock had demanded of her new daughter-in-law. A cottage cheese and canned pear dieter, Caroline saw nothing positive in Nancy's love affair with Virginia country cooking. Nancy was not overweight, but in Caroline's mind, she was only one biscuit away from becoming the side-show fat lady.

"Is she gone for the day?" Nancy asked.

Hattie gave a brief shake of her head. "She'll want to see that baby before she goes."

Nancy was sorry. Caroline's desire to see Tessa would mean waking her daughter, who had been up for hours through the night because she was cutting a new tooth. Caroline would expect Tessa to be bathed and dressed in one of many frilly dresses she had bought for her granddaughter. And Caroline had little patience with a fussy baby.

"She won't understand if I tell her Tessa needs to sleep, will she?"

Hattie had perfected the ability to keep her thoughts out of her voice and eyes. The skill automatically went with serving rich white people, but her guard was down with Nancy. Over the months, the two women had developed a mutual interest in keeping Caroline Whitlock off their backs. Now she just gave Nancy the look that silently said "Are you kidding?"

"Maybe I can give Tessa a bottle while I eat, and she'll be awake enough afterwards to put on a good show," Nancy said.

Hattie looked doubtful. "You go take a shower, and I'll give it to her."

"Would you?" Feeding Tessa was not among Hattie's myriad duties. The Whitlocks had made it clear that caring for Tessa without help was Nancy's punishment for the sin of marrying their son. That and living with them in the cheerless Georgian mansion that backed up to the James River, while Billy finished his education in Charlottesville.

"You go on. And take that biscuit with you, case she comes in," Hattie said.

Nancy returned ten minutes later, awake, full and dressed in one of the insipid flowered shirtwaist dresses that her mother-in-law had chosen for her. A protesting Tessa was snuggled deep into Hattie's arms, but she wasn't happy about it.

"There's my little girl." Nancy reached for her daughter, and a grateful Hattie relinquished her burden.

"She ain't happy to be up," Hattie said. "Not one little bit."

Nancy made a face. "She'd be happier if she didn't have to wake up to a command performance."

"Mrs. Whitlock says a baby has to be on schedule, and it's up to you to make sure she is."

Nancy's gaze flicked to Hattie's tired face, and the two women gave each other a brief conspiratorial smile. "I don't know how poor Billy turned out as good as he did," Nancy whispered.

"Young Mr. Whitlock got himself raised up by *my* mama, that's how. His own mama was too busy."

Nancy was surprised at the revelation. "Your mother?"

"The family business."

Nancy giggled. "She did a good job, don't you think?"

"Mama raised eight of her own. She could have raised him up with one little finger after that."

Hattie departed, and Nancy was sad to see her go. Hattie was her only friend in Richmond.

"Good morning, Teresa Michelle," Nancy crooned. "Dood, dood morning…" She rubbed her nose against her baby daughter's soft cheek.

Tessa babbled a greeting as she batted at her mother's face. As always, Nancy's heart filled with such love that she was afraid it was going to spill out for everyone to see.

The next fifteen minutes did not go as well. Tessa was still tired, and she was not in the mood to be bathed and dressed in one of the stiff, lace-edged dresses that Caroline had bought her. But given the choice between a scene with her daughter and one with her mother-in-law, Nancy chose wisely and continued to dress the baby, adding matching lace-trimmed ankle socks and tiny patent leather shoes. Tessa's fine hair wouldn't hold a barrette, but she combed it with water and stood back to see the final result.

Her daughter was breathtakingly gorgeous.

Nancy scooped Tessa out of the crib, where she was frantically gnawing her favorite teething ring. "We have to leave this," she said softly. "Grandmother Whitlock doesn't like to watch you chew."

She swung the baby out of the crib and held her in the air, jiggling her a little until Tessa laughed with delight. And when she swung her down to her hip to take her downstairs, she found that her mother-in-law was standing in the doorway watching.

"Oh," Nancy said, startled. She couldn't think of another thing to say.

"I'm on my way out. I thought I'd stop and see my granddaughter."

Nancy didn't need an explanation. Clearly Billy's mother was not there to see her. "I was just bringing her downstairs to say goodbye."

"Yes, well, I didn't have all day."

"I'm sorry. I just——"

Caroline waved off the explanation. "I don't think you should be jostling the child the way you do, Nancy. It's not healthy, and it overstimulates her."

"I was trying to distract her. She wants the teething ring."

"She doesn't need it."

Nancy approached Caroline. When she was only a few feet away, she held Tessa out for her mother-in-law to claim, but Caroline shook her head.

"I don't want her drooling on this dress."

Privately, Nancy thought the unadorned sweater dress could do with a little drool. "I hope you're going somewhere enjoyable."

"My garden club meeting. I would bring you with me, but Tessa needs you."

Nancy knew that was only an excuse. Her mother-in-law had made certain to introduce Nancy to only a select few of her friends. Nancy was not yet up to Caroline's high standards and probably wouldn't be for some time, if ever. Nancy wasn't sure what excuses Caroline used not to bring her along to social gatherings, but they seemed to be working, since Nancy never received invitations on her own.

"Is there anything you'd like me to do for you today?" Nancy switched Tessa to her other hip, hoping it would delay more fretting.

"I'll be bringing some women home with me to see our holiday decorations. Please put Tessa down for a nap by one o'clock so she won't disturb us."

Nancy waited to see if she would be invited downstairs to meet her mother-in-law's friends, but Caroline only smiled thinly. "You'll need to stay upstairs with her, of course, so you can hear her if she wakes."

"Of course." Nancy's tone was not as accommodating as her words. Caroline's eyes narrowed.

"I'm sorry you find your duties with the baby so onerous, Nancy, but perhaps you should have considered how much work a child would be before you got pregnant."

Nancy usually backed down from any confrontation with her mother-in-law, but this morning she was exhausted and more than a bit annoyed that she'd had to wake her daughter for what amounted to nothing more than a military inspection. She answered without taking the time to think.

"I don't find Tessa onerous in any way. I do find isolation tedious."

"Then perhaps you should have thought about the effect your presence would have on the lives of others."

"Perhaps your son should have thought about it, too. Or maybe his Southern Gentleman lessons weren't as complete as they should have been."

Caroline took a step backwards, but not from dismay. She put distance between them so she could regard Nancy more fully. "You are a guest in this house. And if you're trying to prove that you're ready to be introduced to my friends, then you're doing a dismal job of it."

"There is no proof under the stars that would be good enough for you. Don't pretend there is." Nancy felt tears of exhaustion, loneliness, frustration, rising inside her.

"William is coming home in a few days. I'm going to discuss this behavior with him."

"What behavior? And why would I care what you say to Billy? What can you do that you haven't done already? Get a lock for the door? Put bars on the windows?" Nancy turned before Caroline could see her cry. She heard the door close behind her mother-in-law, and for a moment she wondered if Caroline might actually take her suggestions seriously. But there was no dead bolt to shove into place. Caroline depended on the force of her personality to keep her daughter-in-law in line.

Tessa cried, frantically shoving her tiny fist into her mouth, and Nancy cried right along with her.

After a few minutes Nancy took Tessa back to the changing table and stripped off the shoes and socks and dress through her tears. Despite everything she'd said, she believed the problem was hers more than it was Caroline's. Faced with the prospect of their son quitting school to live a hand-to-mouth existence with a new wife and child, the senior Whitlocks had made the choice they deemed best for everyone. They had invited Tessa and Nancy to live with them while Billy finished school

The third choice, lending Billy enough money to finish school and rent an apartment large enough to accommodate the three of them, had not been an option for a number of reasons that the Whitlocks had carefully listed. Billy could not be expected to study with a baby and a wife in close quarters. Nancy was too young to be left without supervision in proper mothering skills. Richmond and Charlottesville were close enough that the young couple would see each other whenever Billy wasn't occupied with school or the part-time job he'd taken to pay his new wife's expenses.

A circumstance that fell somewhere between rarely and never.

Once she was dressed in corduroy overalls and a soft shirt, Tessa's sobbing and fidgeting subsided. Nancy washed her own face and combed her hair, then, with Tessa on her hip, she went downstairs, past artificial wreaths and swags that adorned the circular stair railing, past the parlor where a silver Christmas tree decorated with royal blue balls glistened under rotating, multi-colored spotlights.

They settled in the kitchen, where Tessa's high chair resided. The baby ate a big breakfast of rice cereal and mashed banana, and chewed enthusiastically on pieces of a day-old sweet potato biscuit that Hattie had brought from home and hidden away for her.

"You don't be crying over anything that woman says to you," Hattie told her, after taking one look at Nancy's red-rimmed eyes. "She knows she can get to you, she be doing it more often."

Nancy was too miserable to protest. "Why do you stay here?"

"I got a family I got to feed. Better question's why do you?"

Nancy had thought many times of leaving. She could wait until Caroline left for the day, get Randall to drive her downtown, then get on a bus. She could go to Charlottesville, or a town where Helen could pick her up and take her back to Toms Brook.

The problem was that she knew she wasn't really welcome in either place. Helen had been furious to find her daughter was pregnant and married, and their conversations ever since had been brief and filled with criticism. She had only seen Tessa twice, and she hadn't seemed impressed.

Billy was even less likely to want her. He was living in a tiny apartment with three other men, and there was no room for a wife and baby, particularly a wife and baby he had never asked for in the first place.

"I want to give this marriage every chance," Nancy said. "This is the only way I can figure to make it work."

"Mrs. Whitlock don't want it to work." Hattie kept her voice low, even though Caroline was gone. "That's why she be pushing at you the way she do."

In her heart, Nancy had known this was true, but to have it confirmed so openly frightened her. "If I leave, will they try to take Tessa?"

Hattie shrugged. "Can't say."

"What do you think?"

"She be a boy, I'd say yes for sure. But a girl?" Hattie shrugged again.

"In a divorce, the mother almost always gets custody, doesn't she?"

"Mr. Whitlock knows a lot of judges. Plays tennis and golf with 'em."

Nancy could feel what little security she had slipping away from her. "What would *you* do?"

"Sugar, this ain't a colored woman's problem. No judge in Virginia gonna care who gets my kids."

Nancy was sorry that was true, but for the moment, civil rights had to take a back seat to her own personal crisis.

Tessa happily shredded what was left of her biscuit and tossed the crumbs on the floor. Nancy cleaned it up; then, coats donned and buttoned, she took the baby outside for a stroller ride around the spacious grounds.

They stopped in front of a life-sized Santa's sleigh drawn by eight stuffed deer that had probably put groceries on some lucky taxidermist's table for a year. Santa himself looked lifelike enough to give Nancy pause, but Tessa loved the display and tried to wiggle out of the stroller.

The Whitlock ancestors had once lived downriver on a flourishing tobacco plantation, and although the house in Windsor Farms might be modest in comparison, it was still an imposing structure. Nancy had killed many a lonely hour imagining all the changes she would make if the house were hers, beginning with the Christmas decorations.

Continuing with the prissy white-and-gold bedroom in which she was being held prisoner.

She came from poor people, yes, but she was no dummy. She might need a little tutoring—and she was even grateful for some of the things she had learned from Caroline—but she was sure that someday she could take her place here with the Richmond elite as Billy's wife. Her yearning to fit in and find a place for herself was so strong she knew nothing could stand in the way if she was only given the chance. But that chance seemed to slip further and further away every day.

Back inside and upstairs, Tessa grew fussy again, and Nancy knew her daughter needed a nap. But if Tessa napped now, she might not nap again when Caroline wanted her to.

Nancy could feel her palms grow damp as she debated what should have been an easy decision. She did not want to further incur Caroline's wrath, but weren't Tessa's needs more important? The baby had slept very little last night, and clearly she was ready to catch up. Now, not later.

Tessa settled the matter by falling asleep mid-fuss in Nancy's arms. Nancy looked down at her sleeping daughter and didn't have the heart to wake her again. She laid the baby carefully on her back in the crib and covered her with a blanket. Tessa's rose-petal cheeks and curling black lashes were the most perfect creations on God's green earth.

There was no other place in the house where she could relax and still hear Tessa if she awoke. Nancy resigned herself to several hours of isolation and went to the closet. She removed a large cardboard box from the top shelf and took it to the window, where she unpacked it. She set a round wooden quilting hoop on the floor beside her, a small cigar box with needle and thread beside that, then, finally, she removed the half-finished wedding ring quilt and draped it over her lap. She positioned the hoop over and under the quilt, took her favorite needle and threaded it, and began to follow the curving designs, quilting just beside the seams. As she did, she thought about Billy.

She had been married to William Lee Whitlock for more than a year now, but for the most part he was still a stranger. In reality, their marriage existed in name only. They lived in different towns. They slept in separate beds except when he made duty visits to Richmond. They shared no activities, no interests—besides Tessa—or hopes for the future. Billy was polite, even kind, when he was with her. They made love on the rare occasions when they had the opportunity. But Billy was an actor repeating his lines. Nancy might not have known much love in her life, but she could recognize it when she saw it.

She recognized love in herself. She loved Billy. The feeling was not mutual.

Billy was coming home in a few days, and although she should have been overjoyed to see him, she was worried, instead. He adored Tessa, a fact that still amazed her. The way in which Tessa had come into Billy's life seemed irrelevant. He loved to play with his daughter, rock her to sleep, take her for walks in her stroller. As life in Richmond deteriorated, Billy's interest in the baby worried Nancy more. Billy's attachment to his daughter could well mean that he would fight for custody when the inevitable split came about. And what could Nancy do about it?

What would she do, anyway? She was hopelessly in love with Billy. She asked herself why and found no good answers. She was afraid her love was part of a new quiz show category: words beginning with "un."

Unreasonable, unpredictable and unmanageable.

Tessa woke up just a little before one, exactly as Nancy had been afraid she would. Nancy put the quilt away and considered her options. She knew she could ask Randall to take her Christmas shopping so that she and the baby would be gone when Caroline and her friends arrived, but Tessa still seemed fussy and might even be running a slight fever. Nancy didn't want to take chances that the baby's symptoms might be caused by something more than an erupting tooth. Exposure to crowds seemed like a bad idea.

Hattie came up with a lunch tray, and while she gave Tessa her bottle, Nancy asked for suggestions about what to do.

Hattie was silent for a long time, as if mulling over the question. "Me, I'd take her down and show her off," Hattie said at last. "But don't you dare tell Mrs. Whitlow I said so."

"Hattie, you know she doesn't want me there. She as much as told me to stay out of sight and keep Tessa out of sight, too."

"These ladies don't know you're here, they don't know when you're gone. She can tell them anything she likes about you. She be telling them you a bad girl and worse mother, and what they got to go on but what she say?"

Hattie's logic made sense. Right now Nancy was an unknown to Caroline's friends. She could have three heads or a rotten disposition. There was no way to tell what Caroline was saying about her. Perhaps Caroline's friends had been led to believe that Nancy was too spoiled or ill-mannered to come down and chat with them.

"I'll need an excuse," Nancy said.

"Christmas cookies."

"Cookies?"

"That's what I be doing when I go downstairs in a minute. You just say you wanted to help, only put on something pretty and fix your face. Then come down and decorate them. And when those ladies get here, you can take a platter in and tell them you made those cookies just for them."

Nancy was intrigued. "Hattie, you've been thinking about this?"

"Sure have." Hattie winked.

Nancy giggled. She knew that Hattie liked her, but she also knew the other woman's plan wasn't sheer altruism. Hattie wanted to thwart Caroline Whitlow as badly as Nancy did.

Nancy put on her prettiest mohair sweater and pleated wool

skirt, and carefully applied makeup. She dressed Tessa in red velvet and apologized as she did. Downstairs, Tessa forgot to be unhappy about the dress as she batted at Cheerios and miniature marshmallows on the high chair tray, while Nancy decorated cutout sugar cookies with colored icing and sprinkles.

At ten minutes after one, she heard the front door open and the sound of women's voices.

"You wait a few minutes," Hattie cautioned. She went to the cupboard and took down a polished silver tray and lined it with a snowflake doily. Then she handed it to Nancy to adorn with cookies.

Nancy chose the prettiest. The tray was just small enough that she could balance Tessa on one hip and carry the tray in the other hand. Once she had everything set to go, she took the baby from the chair and dusted off the crumbs.

"I think I'm all ready," she said.

"I'll be in soon with coffee and wine punch. You be surprised what those ladies can drink."

Nancy grinned. "Wish me luck."

"You don't need it. You'll do fine."

Nancy took a deep breath, then walked through the kitchen door with Tessa and the tray.

She followed the sound of women's voices toward the parlor. Hattie had told her to expect about ten women, but there were only half a dozen besides Caroline, and Nancy wondered if the others were coming later. Heads bobbed as she and the baby walked across the threshold, although Caroline's back remained turned. Then one of the women, with silvering hair and wide, square shoulders, got to her feet with a smile.

"Oh, will you look at this darling little girl. And we'd so hoped to see her."

Nancy beamed. "And I so hoped to show her off."

The woman held out her arms to take Tessa, and her face glowed with pleasure. There was nothing wrong with Nancy's instincts.

She knew that if she handed over her daughter to this woman, she had made a friend for life. And since Tessa had no qualms about going to strangers, the little girl would probably be pleased to have new buttons and jewelry to explore.

Nancy leaned toward the woman, and Tessa chose that exact moment to switch her focus to the cookie tray in Nancy's other hand. Momentarily off balance, Nancy couldn't do anything but gasp when Tessa grabbed the edge of the tray in her tiny hand and tilted it.

Cookies slid to the carpeted floor and broke into a hundred icing-adorned crumbs. There was an immediate flurry of activity and kind words. The women jumped to their feet and started to pick up cookies. The silver-haired woman took Tessa. A pink-cheeked Nancy murmured apologies, as she stooped to help.

"I'm so sorry. But we made plenty. I'll clean up and get a fresh platter."

In the midst of the groundswell of goodwill, Nancy heard the front door close, and she realized her clumsiness was about to be witnessed by even more of her mother-in-law's friends. She swallowed the lump in her throat.

"Don't worry, dear," a woman with straight black hair and silver-rimmed glasses assured her. "I was simply amazed you made it in here at all with the baby and the cookies, too. You are a wonder of coordination. Do you play tennis?"

"I'd love to learn."

"Then you must come to the club and I'll teach you. It's my passion."

Someone else took Nancy gently by the elbow and lifted her to her feet. All the women were laughing and trying to comfort her. For the first time in a long time, Nancy didn't feel like a stranger.

Then a familiar voice sounded. "I thought I told you to put the baby to bed for a nap this afternoon, Nancy."

Nancy's cheeks deepened with color. She faced her mother-in-law. "I'm sorry, but she napped earlier today. I'm afraid she was up most of the night."

"Oh, is she teething?" one of the women asked. She'd been making silly faces at Tessa, and Tessa was smiling and clapping her hands in response. "I just don't see why a baby can't come into the world with all her teeth intact. It would be so much more civilized."

The other women laughed, but the laughter died when Caroline moved closer.

"A baby needs a routine," Caroline said. "I've told you that before."

Nancy could feel herself wilting, yet some part of her refused to give in. She smiled grimly. "I'm afraid somebody forgot to tell Tessa, Mrs. Whitlock. She seems to have a mind of her own."

"Yes, well, babies do pick up things from the people who care for them, don't they?"

The room had grown silent now. Nancy weighed her options and knew she had no good ones.

She sighed. "Well, I just hope Tessa learns to stand up for what she needs, no matter who she learns it from. And this morning I'm afraid her biggest need was more sleep. But I'll certainly take her back upstairs if we're in the way."

"Take her upstairs?" the black-haired woman asked. "Don't you dare, dear. We're just getting to know her. I sense another tennis player in our midst. Look at the way she bats her hand—"

"I would like you to take her up and put her to bed right now," Caroline told Nancy. "Hattie will bring us more cookies. You can visit with us another time. When it's appropriate."

Nancy's eyelids fluttered closed. She had never been this humiliated, not even when she'd stood at the side of a country road and told Billy she was pregnant with his child.

"I'm afraid Nancy won't be visiting with *any*one in Richmond for a while," a male voice said.

Nancy opened her eyes and turned to see her husband standing in the doorway.

"Nancy is moving to Charlottesville with me," he said.

Nancy had never seen Billy so angry. Even when he first learned she was pregnant, he had not been this upset. Now the skin around his lips was deathly white, and a muscle jumped in his jaw. He strolled toward her and kissed her cheek, then he reached for Tessa. The silver-haired woman relinquished their daughter quickly.

"Ladies, if you will excuse us? Nancy and I have plans to finish." Balancing Tessa on his hip as Nancy had, Billy put his free arm around his wife and pulled her to stand beside him, taking time to kiss her hair in a show of husbandly affection. Then, with Nancy in tow, he started out of the room.

Caroline followed, but she waited until they were in the upstairs hallway and the other women were out of earshot before she spoke.

"How dare you make a scene in front of my friends, William?" she said. Like Billy, she was clearly furious.

"How dare *you*?" He whirled and faced her, eyes blazing. "This is my wife! You were treating her like the exterminator or the garbageman. I knew things weren't good here, but I had no idea they were *this* bad."

Caroline exploded. "Bad? I've put up with this…this hillbilly for more than a year now. She has no manners, no education, no abilities worth discussion. And why? Because you couldn't keep your trousers zipped!"

Billy stepped toward his mother, and for a moment Nancy was afraid he was going to lift his hand against her. Then he stepped back slowly. "You will apologize," he told his mother. "Immediately. Or you will never see any of us again. Is that clear?"

"Apologize?"

"Now! And then we will forget this ever happened. The whole family will return to pretending we care about something more than the way we look. Nancy, Tessa and I will visit on holidays. You will pretend you're glad to see us and glad you have a beautiful little granddaughter. You can tell your friends what a perfect family we have and even show them photographs. But if you don't..."

There was no need to repeat the threat. Caroline's anger had changed to fear. Nancy wasn't certain at what point in Billy's tirade that had happened, but clearly her mother-in-law was no longer in charge of the situation, and she knew it.

Caroline looked at Nancy; then she looked away. She lifted her chin. "I'm sorry I lost my temper."

Nancy tried to find the words to forgive her and failed. "So am I," she said at last.

Caroline looked at her son as if to say "See?" Billy shook his head. "You're lucky she didn't just take Tessa and disappear," he told his mother. "You're damned lucky she's still standing here. Because I never would have forgiven you if you'd run her off."

He turned to Nancy. "Can you forgive *me* for leaving you here so long?"

She would have forgiven him anything. She smiled tremulously. "You didn't know."

"Oh, but I suspected. It was just easier not to act on it." He turned back to his mother. "We'll be celebrating this Christmas alone. Now we're going to pack, then we'll be out of here for good."

Caroline's eyes filled with tears, which surprised Nancy. "Don't let her turn you against us, William. We're your family."

Billy nodded toward Nancy and Tessa. "No, *this* is my family."

CHAPTER
25

"That afternoon was the real start of our marriage," Nancy told Tessa.

The sky had darkened as Nancy told her story, and Tessa had finally folded the quilt to work on another day. Besides, her mother's reminiscences were all the entertainment she'd needed. Only now that Nancy's story had ended she didn't feel entertained, she felt angry.

"I can't understand why you put up with so much from Grandmother."

"Can't you?" Nancy slapped a mosquito on her thigh.

"The way you've told it, she was making a calculated effort to drive you away."

Nancy considered. "That's exactly what she was doing. I don't think your grandmother was a bad person, and I don't really want to leave you with that impression. But she wasn't a warm woman, and she was very protective of her image. I didn't fit. I'm afraid it's that simple and that complicated."

"You put up with it for more than a year?"

"Tessa, you can't possibly understand how insecure I felt, because you've never experienced anything like it. I was young. For all practical purposes I was alone. I had a baby I adored and no other place to go with her except home, where I thought I wasn't welcome. Now I know Mama would have been more understanding than I gave her credit for. But you have to remember, I'd had a lifetime of her pushing me away, and that's all I knew about her. And we were so poor. I knew another mouth to feed would be her undoing."

Tessa tried to put herself in Nancy's place. Young. Alone. Pregnant. The words rang a bell. Did Cissy feel what Nancy had? Was she at the Claiborne house simply because she had no other alternative?

Nancy focused on a spot just beyond Tessa. "Your daddy and I moved back to Charlottesville that night. He found us a room in the house of an old woman who lived right in the center of town. She was lonely, and having a baby in the house delighted her. He sold his Corvette and bought an old Chevy that broke down every week or so. I got a part-time job to help with expenses, and our landlady took care of you. It was a nearly perfect situation. Harry relented and continued sending checks so your daddy could finish school. And when he graduated, we went back to Richmond so he could join the firm. We bought a little house on the other side of town and settled in. By then your grandmother was resigned to the inevitable, and she was always polite to me. She even made sure I was welcome in her social circle. In her own way she was good to you, as well, particularly as you got older. She wasn't a baby person."

"Happily ever after?"

Nancy shrugged.

"It doesn't sound happy to me, Mom." When Nancy didn't respond, Tessa went on. "You settled for so little. You married a man who didn't love you, lived in a situation where you were treated like Cinderella before the ball. And you've stayed with Daddy all these years, even though the two of you don't have a thing in common—"

"We have you. We had Kayley."

The mention of her daughter's name didn't even slow Tessa down. "You settled for so little," she repeated. She was appalled. She had always believed that her parents stayed together because there was some strong emotion that bound them, emotion that was invisible to the naked eye, perhaps, but there for the two of them to draw on. Now she knew that only circumstance had kept their marriage intact.

"There's a lot you don't understand about marriage." Nancy sat forward, and her eyes sparkled with anger. "Marriage is about working toward common goals. Love isn't all it's cracked up to be. It plays a part, sure, but common goals and ideals are what hold a marriage together."

"Come on! I share a million goals and ideals with a million different people. And I wouldn't want to be married to any of them. You gave up on love and settled for security. Isn't that incredibly shallow?"

"And isn't that what you've always thought about me anyway? That I'm shallow and silly and useless? That I always settle for less than your own lofty goals? That I wouldn't know love and loyalty from a Kate Spade handbag?"

Tessa knew her anger was out of control. She even knew she was aiming it at her mother because she was a safe target. But she couldn't stop herself.

"No, I think you're comfortable with your life. You got what you wanted, and you didn't want to give it up. I think you've tried to make the best of it, but in the end it's a house of cards. What exactly do you have besides an address in Windsor Farms and membership in a prestigious country club?"

Nancy sat back and stared at her. Tessa was instantly contrite when she saw the wounded expression on her mother's face. "I'm sorry. What's wrong with me? This really isn't my call, is it?"

"Maybe you're sorry and maybe you aren't," Nancy said quietly. "But here's the truth, Tessa. I've struggled my whole life, and struggle is the right word. I've tried to do what was right for you and your dad. I've tried to be a good wife and a good mother, to make up for getting pregnant by doing everything I could to make your daddy's life a happy one."

"But Daddy was there when it happened, too. Nobody asked you to struggle by yourself."

Nancy held up her hand. "And now we're going to talk about *you*. Because how can *you* talk, how can you dare criticize me, when you've taken the coward's way out and stopped fighting for your own marriage? Is your way better? Is it better to abandon somebody you love when the going gets rough? Maybe I have a membership in a prestigious country club, but your personal club is even more exclusive. You're the one and only member, and you won't let anyone else in the front door."

Now it was Tessa's turn to fall silent.

Nancy got to her newly sandaled feet. "It's getting late, and I'm tired. I'm going to bed. I'll make up the bed in the room at the end of the hall for your father. The bed in my room is narrow, and he'll sleep better by himself. It will be cooler."

It *wasn't* late, but Tessa didn't argue. Their entire conversation, particularly the last minute of it, was still whirling in her head. She watched her mother walk gracefully into the house. The screen door flapped behind her. She wondered if now, on top of everything else, she was going to be responsible for a rift in her parents' marriage.

She was still on the porch an hour later when her father pulled into the driveway. He looked tired as he came up the steps, his shirt wrinkled, his tie no longer in evidence. "Hi, sweetheart. I hope you're not sitting out here waiting for me. I'm later than I thought

I'd be. I just couldn't get away as soon as I wanted." He paused and looked around. "Where's your mother?"

"She's gone to bed."

"Oh."

Tessa tried to read his expression and couldn't. That was usually the case. Her father had been well-trained as a child not to inflict his feelings on anyone else.

"Mom made up a bed for you in the room at the end of the hall." She waited again to see if he reacted. He looked slightly puzzled, she thought, but even that disappeared quickly.

Tessa started to her feet. "Would you like a drink? I made lemonade."

"That would be nice. It feels like pea soup out here, but it's even hotter in Richmond. At least here you can catch a breeze."

Tessa let him make himself comfortable and took her time in the kitchen. Back out on the porch with two cold glasses of lemonade, she found him reclining with his eyes closed and his head back. He looked older than usual, and even more tired than she'd noted earlier.

"Daddy?"

He opened his eyes and smiled. "Just catching up on my sleep."

"Aren't you sleeping well at home?"

"I don't seem to be sleeping as well as usual. Maybe it's the heat."

She doubted that, since the house in Windsor Farms had four zones of air-conditioning and was as climate-controlled as the National Gallery of Art.

"Did your meeting go well?" she asked.

"As well as these things ever do."

The remark was unlike him. Billy rarely complained or even hinted he was unhappy. She supposed that and a monumental blind spot were the major reasons she had not realized her parents' marriage was so bloodless and contrived.

"You don't enjoy your job?" she asked.

"It's nothing for you to worry about. I'm good at it. That's the main thing."

"Well, no, it really isn't the main thing. I mean, do you make a habit of doing what you don't like to simply because it's expected?"

He seemed to wake up then, to really focus on what she was saying and her tone. "I didn't say that."

"No, but it fits with the other things I've heard tonight."

"What things?"

"The story of your marriage. How you married Mom because she was pregnant, how you made the final commitment to her when you realized that your mother was mistreating her."

"Nancy told you that?"

"I found your marriage certificate. It explained a lot. Mom explained the rest when she realized I wasn't going to take no for an answer. She's a lot like you in that regard. Putting on appearances is important to both of you."

"Your mother and I have been married for almost forty years."

"That's proof of inertia, Dad, nothing more."

"I'm sorry, Tessa, but when did we give you permission to question our marriage or our lives?"

"When you decided not to use a condom one hot summer night."

"Stop it!"

"I don't think so. The truth is, I need to understand what's kept you together. If it's me, then I'm bearing a huge burden here, and I don't want to anymore."

"This really isn't like you."

"Maybe this is who I need to be."

"This is not your business."

"Oh, come on. Whose business is it, then?"

"Mine and your mother's."

"How could you marry her and live with her all these years when you didn't love her? Didn't she deserve better? Didn't you? Didn't *I*?"

"I'm not sure how you got into that equation."

"Because I spent my whole childhood trying to please her, that's how. And she was trying to please you, and maybe even your mother. Because, damn it, she wanted you to love her. That's all she wanted." Tessa realized she was about to cry. She swallowed hard and looked away.

"A lifetime of people trying to please each other and never quite succeeding," he said.

She looked up to find her father staring at the stars.

"We failed you," he said. "Even though we tried so desperately not to."

"I never said you failed me."

He turned his gaze to her. "No, but we did. Nancy and I, trying so hard to please everybody, pleasing nobody, not even ourselves. You never saw the kind of marriage you needed to, the kind where people talk about their feelings, about what really matters to them—"

She knew where this was leading and tried to head him off. "Dad, it's not about me."

"You just told me it was, remember? You can't have it both ways. You didn't learn how to deal with sadness by watching us. You've tried to deal with it by yourself, just the way your mother and I would have—and did. You didn't learn how to share, and now you're paying the price."

"Don't turn this into therapy. This is about you and Mom."

"There are a million things between your mother and me that you will never be able to understand. We've been married a long time. There's a lot I can't and won't explain. You'll have to be satisfied with that." He stood. "You said the end of the hall?"

"I'm not trying to make things worse. I'm just trying to..." She stopped, no longer sure what she was trying to do.

"If we're going bird-watching tomorrow, I need some sleep. You do, too." He left her on the porch.

She asked herself why she had chosen this moment, this place, this situation, to finally begin exploring her feelings and the feelings of the people she loved.

CHAPTER
26

Cissy arrived for a quilting lesson Thursday morning, and before she left, she went to show Tessa the progress she'd made on piecing her top.

Tessa was lounging under the maple trees on a blanket she had spread to take advantage of the shade. Until Cissy's arrival, her only company had been one of Helen's barn cats, a black tom with white markings who was perched like a sentinel on the porch railing. The day was cooler than usual, with a light breeze blowing from the north and fluffy cumulus clouds protecting them from the worst of the sun. When Cissy approached and flopped down beside her, Tessa had the wedding ring quilt spread over her lap and was removing another of the patches that had disintegrated.

Clearly Cissy was taking a great deal of pride in the baby quilt, and the six pinwheel blocks she'd made so far had been sewed into a perfect rectangle. "The colors are lovely, and so is the workmanship," Tessa told her.

Cissy shyly smiled her thanks. "Now that I'm down here, no

telling if I'll be able to get myself up again without getting on all fours like an old hound dog."

"Stay a moment. Did Gram give you something to drink? I'll be happy to get you something."

"She made me spearmint tea. She makes it like my granny did. I like to have cried when she handed me that glass."

Tessa wondered if Helen realized that she was coming to represent family to this homeless, pregnant waif. She hoped her grandmother would continue to soften and provide Cissy with some of the love she so obviously needed. It would be good for both of them.

"What are you working on?" Cissy asked.

Tessa gave her an abbreviated version of the wedding ring quilt history. "It's too nice to work inside today, so I gave up and came out here. Who knows if we'll have another day like this one this month."

"I think it's about the prettiest quilt I ever saw," Cissy said. "All those little pieces, all different. And knowing it was made from all that love."

Tessa smiled at the adolescent sentiment, but the truth was that she loved the quilt for the same reason.

"I just wondered..." Cissy stopped, as if she was searching for words. "Well, I just thought maybe you might come over to our place tonight. We're having an old-fashioned music night, the way they always used to around here. Zeke's friends are all coming over to play outside on the Claibornes' lawn, and there'll be supper, too. Everyone's bringing something to share."

Tessa looked up and saw that Cissy's eyes were sparkling. She'd been about to say "no thank you," but now she realized she couldn't. Cissy wanted to give something back to the women who had taken an interest in her, and this was her way.

"Did you ask Gram?" Tessa said.

"She said she don't—doesn't—go out of an evening. But I think she might come if you did."

Tessa thought her grandmother might, too. Then an image of Mack passed through her mind. Mack, who loved country music best, not the kind that was only a step from rock music, but roots music, the old-fashioned kind. He had played the soundtrack from the film *O Brother, Where Art Thou* so many times she had committed every cut to memory.

She spoke her thoughts out loud. "It's too bad my husband isn't here. He'd love to come."

Cissy managed to get back to her feet without resorting to sinking to all fours, but only just. "Maybe you can call him and ask him to come up."

Tessa had no intention of asking Mack. She wasn't even sure why she'd mentioned him to Cissy. "I'll be there, at the very least, and I'll see if I can convince Gram. We'll bring a strawberry cream cake. She made one yesterday and put it in the fridge. If we eat it by ourselves, we'll gain twenty pounds apiece."

"Yum. I'll save some room." Cissy looked pleased with herself. "We'll get started around six, when all the men come home from work."

"I'll look forward to it."

Cissy started toward her pickup; then she turned. "Your mother's invited, too. I forgot to say that. I'm sorry."

Tessa tried to imagine Nancy at a down-home music night. "I'll be sure to mention it to her."

Cissy departed, the old truck coughing and sputtering, and Tessa rested against the maple trunk and stared at the newly unleashed cloud of dust that went with her.

"I like that girl."

Tessa looked up to find her mother standing over. Nancy was wearing a lime-green jumper and more of her frivolous Wal-Mart flip-flops.

"Do you? You weren't so sure at first." Tessa made room, and Nancy joined her on the blanket.

"She reminded me too much of myself. That's why."

"And now?"

"I'm getting in touch with my inner Nancy." Nancy smiled to let Tessa know she was, at least partially, joking.

Tessa wondered if it was the inner Nancy who was so staunchly ignoring Billy these days. Nancy hadn't spent even a few minutes alone with her husband on his visit at the beginning of the week. She had risen late, and by the time Tessa and Billy returned from bird-watching, Nancy had already left for the church to make more decisions about Helen's quilt show. From what Tessa could tell, her mother had every woman in the congregation helping her.

Tessa realized she couldn't ignore this any longer. "Mom, I think Dad is hurt that you're never available when he comes to visit."

"You're officially off the case, Tessa. Your dad and I will work out our relationship the way we need to without your help."

"I feel like I caused new problems by talking to you both." Although she and her father hadn't discussed anything important on their bird-watching trip, there had been a new restraint in their interactions that had sobered Tessa.

"You're absolved of all guilt."

"I love you both."

"Tessa, sometimes the hardest thing you can do when you love somebody is stand by and watch them make mistakes. I've been watching you make your share these past years, and now maybe it's your turn."

Tessa knew what mistakes her mother was referring to. Once more she thought about how Mack would enjoy the gathering at the Claibornes'. "Cissy invited all of us over for a potluck supper and music tonight. Zeke's friends are bringing their instruments."

"What fun."

"You'll come?"

"Of course. Maybe your grandmother will give up her strawberry cake for the cause."

"It's just country music, Mom. Mountain music. Bluegrass, most likely."

"And you think I won't enjoy it? I grew up with string bands, remember?" Nancy rose and dusted herself off. "Here's some advice you didn't ask for. Call Mack. He'll be in his element, even if he is a California boy. If you have any interest in trying to save your marriage, this would be a good start."

After Nancy left, Tessa stared at the horizon, the quilt clutched to her chest. Why did something that had once been so easy seem so impossible now?

When was the last time she'd had the courage to ask Mack for anything?

Late that afternoon, Mack was still mulling over Tessa's phone call as he neared the turnoff to Fitch Crossing Road. He had expected something quite different when he picked up the receiver. Exultation that she'd caught Owens drinking or driving. A request for a meeting to discuss a divorce.

The possibility that she might be issuing an invitation to do something fun together hadn't even entered his mind.

He'd been planning to call her himself, only he was a coward and had put off the call. Now he could talk to her in person and see her reaction. But which Tessa would he find? The one he had married? The one who had turned to stone at their daughter's death? Or some new hybrid who was learning, at last, to breathe again?

He slowed once he was on Fitch. The drought was still in effect, and the trees had subtly closed in on themselves, as if sheltering their trunks under drooping branches might conserve what little moisture they could draw from the earth. He understood only too well how they felt and knew Tessa did, too.

He arrived at Helen's to the hustle and bustle of three generations getting ready for the party. Nancy greeted him, kissing him on the cheek as if their last encounter hadn't been filled with tension. He admired her new haircut and told her so, reaping a broad smile as harvest. Next Helen came out to the porch and kissed his cheek, too, but her expression was dour.

"Don't know why I have to go. Never been over to see Ron Claiborne and hoped to keep it that way 'til I died."

"We're driving," Nancy told him, ignoring her mother. "Tessa said you might walk. We'll see you there." Nancy took firm hold of her mother's arm and guided the grumbling Helen down the porch steps. "Go on in," she called behind her when she glanced around and saw that Mack was still standing at the door. "Tessa's in the kitchen."

He admired the changes in the house as he strolled through. He imagined Helen had groused about every one of them and still enjoyed them, the way she would probably enjoy tonight's party.

He found Tessa in the kitchen, setting a cake on a cake plate. She hadn't heard him approach, so he watched undetected for a moment from the doorway. Her hair was loose, flowing straight to the middle of her back. She wore a turquoise sundress he didn't remember and shoes that reminded him of Kayley's ballet slippers. Around her neck was the squash blossom necklace he had bought her on their Arizona honeymoon. She hadn't worn it in years. He wondered why she had even packed it.

"You look lovely."

She turned, startled, and for just a moment she looked vulnerable, as if she wasn't sure what to say or do. Then she smiled a little. "If you'd gotten here sooner, you would have caught me sneaking crumbs off the old plate. This is my grandmother's specialty."

"Is it? I don't remember it."

"I don't think she ever bothered to make it for *us*."

They laughed at the same time, then sobered together, too. "You do look lovely," he said. "I'd forgotten how much I love you in that necklace."

She held it away from her breasts. "Do you remember the Navajo silversmith who sold it to us?"

"He said the crescent was to remind us that even a good marriage waxes and wanes like the moon."

"He was some salesman. He spotted us as newlyweds right off the bat." She released the necklace.

"Because I couldn't keep my hands off you."

"I thought it was the way I looked at you." She turned back to the cake, reaching for the domed cover. "Gram and Mom are gone?"

"Grouching all the way."

"Which one?"

"Your grandmother."

"Mom seems determined to have a good time." Tessa glanced at him and frowned. "If it weren't so incongruous, I'd say I'm worried about her."

"I don't remember ever seeing her so…" He searched for a word. "Contented?"

"It's odd, isn't it, because I think she and my father are heading for a separation."

"Your parents?"

She stopped fiddling with the cover. "You thought we'd beat them, didn't you? So did I."

"Is that an announcement, Tessa?"

"I don't know what it is. I feel like every day I'm walking on shifting sands. I don't seem to be able to figure out who anybody is anymore."

"Including you?"

"Most of all me." She looked up again. "Or you, Mack. You're so far away from me that I'm not even sure I can see you anymore, much less figure you out."

"What about your parents?"

"They got married because Mom got pregnant. They stayed together because it was easier to raise me that way. And for some reason they stayed together once I was gone. I'm just not sure they understand why. I certainly don't."

"Do you want them going their separate ways?"

She shook her head. "That's the crazy part. We're all grown-ups, but I want them together. I feel like a little girl again."

"It doesn't sound crazy." He joined her in the kitchen, but he didn't touch her. He didn't think he could bear another physical rejection.

"It's out of my hands, isn't it? There are just so many things I have no control over." Clearly that bothered her.

"And some you do." Mack edged past her and lifted the cake from the counter. "Like tonight, for instance. We could just have fun. No strings, no expectations. No thinking about things we can't change. We can control that much, can't we?"

"I'd like that."

He was surprised but didn't say so. "Then it's a done deal."

"Mack, there is a little business…"

He nodded toward the door. "Shall we walk? We can talk on the way."

"You're willing to carry that?"

"I'm willing to share the burden."

"Deal."

Neither of them spoke until they were out on the road. "I did surveillance yesterday," Tessa said, as they left the farmhouse behind. "And there's something you ought to know."

Mack was sorry the "business" was about Robert Owens, but he had his own business concerning the young man, and it looked as if this was going to be the time to conduct it.

"If you'd caught him doing anything illegal he'd already be in jail," he said.

"It probably was illegal. I'm assuming he's not supposed to go to bars."

Mack switched the cake to the other arm. "You saw him?"

Tessa was silent for a while, as if gauging her own answer. "I saw him leave the house with some of his friends. I followed them, but with no intention of getting out of the car and peering in windows. I promised you I wouldn't do anything illegal."

"And?"

"They ended up at a sports bar, one of those chicken wings and billiards places down the road from his mother's house. When they left, I went inside and talked to the server who had waited on him."

"And?" he repeated.

"All of them were drinking. Except Robert. She said he made a point of ordering a Coke even when his friends kidded him."

He felt something very much like relief. Not only because Owens had behaved himself, but because Tessa had not been faced with an opportunity to wreak the revenge she so desperately sought.

"How do you feel about that?" he asked after a moment of digesting the news.

"Disappointed." She hesitated. "Sorry I am."

More relief filled him. "Tessa, I've come up with a way to make sure Owens stays on the straight and narrow *and* get you out of the action at the same time. Are you willing to listen?"

The sun was sinking behind the mountains to their west. The air was beginning to cool, and a light breeze fanned their faces. As Tessa contemplated his question, Mack wished that on this lovely evening they could get past this quickly, that they could pretend for just this one night that their lives weren't ruled by the man who had killed their daughter.

"I need to be out of it," she said at last, surprising him. "But I can't let go knowing he could kill again."

"I've got a private investigator who's willing to do the surveillance for us. He has assistants who do this kind of work."

"It would cost a fortune."

"It's not as expensive as your well-being. And the assistants come at a reduced rate. Besides, he owes me, and he knows it. He does most of our investigative work. He owns a summer house on the Chesapeake, courtesy of the firm."

She stopped walking and turned to him. "You would do this for me?"

He gazed down at her, noted the pinched grooves between her eyes, the tight skin around them. Even without those signs, he knew what this meant to her. "I don't agree with following Owens. I don't think we should take the law into our own hands, but I know how important this is to you."

"The last time you and I were together we as much as said goodbye."

"Is that what you heard?" He remembered his exact words. He had told her she would have to be the one to push him away. She hadn't pushed hard enough.

He hoped she hadn't wanted to.

She took the cake out of his hands. "Every time I go to Manassas, it's like stepping back in time to the day Kayley died."

"That's why you can't keep it up."

"I would like it if someone else watched the house. I can't ask my friends to give up any more time. This would be a blessing." She lifted her eyes to his. "Thank you."

He leaned down and kissed her lightly, quickly on the lips.

The food was delicious. They feasted on fried chicken, potato salad, deviled eggs and sweet corn that was smaller than usual, but delicious anyway. There were platters of fresh tomatoes and icy-cold pickled watermelon rind, casseroles of green beans and baked beans and crowder peas with ham hocks. Helen's cake was a huge success, and even she seemed pleased by all the compliments and the empty platter at the meal's end.

From the moment they arrived, Mack fit right in. Tessa watched him talk to everyone, old and young. He played patty-cake and eensy, weensy spider with the babies, swapped stories with a local attorney, listened intently to the opinions of two old farmers who were still—at least theoretically—fighting the Civil War.

He made friends with Cissy immediately, and Tessa could see that her protégé was entranced with him. When the music started in earnest, he stood close to the band and swayed to the sawing of fiddles and picking of banjo strings. There were a total of eight musicians who seemed to move in and out of the action. Tessa counted three guitars, a string bass, two fiddles, a mandolin and a banjo.

She felt physically lighter, despite all the food. Even the thought that Kayley, who had inherited her father's love of music, would have loved being here tonight didn't sadden her. She felt a bond with her daughter that had survived the little girl's death, and for the first time the feeling that went with it was more pleasure than pain.

After she had helped Cissy and her mother-in-law refrigerate leftovers and carry out more pitchers of iced tea and Thermoses of coffee, Tessa joined Mack, who was tapping his foot to a rousing chorus of "Will the Circle Be Unbroken."

He took her arm as naturally as if the past three years had never happened. She nestled her hip against his and swayed side to side with him.

Zeke, wearing an unbuttoned Hawaiian shirt and cutoff shorts, was playing the banjo, and while Tessa watched, he picked a complicated solo that drew applause from the gathered crowd. Flushed with pleasure, he grinned and stepped back so the bass player could plunk out a few solo lines.

"I always wanted to do that," Mack said.

"Why don't you take lessons?"

"When? In that pregnant pause between 'we find the defendant' and 'not guilty'?"

"Maybe you ought to give yourself a little free time."

"I will if you will. Why don't you take up the fiddle? We could form a band."

She laughed, because they both knew that despite eight painful years of piano lessons with one of Richmond's finest teachers, she was still only a "Chopsticks" virtuoso.

The band started another selection. "'Black Mountain Rag,'" Mack said, right before he started to hum along.

"How do you know this stuff?"

"It's all I listen to when you're not around."

"And even when I am."

"Honey, you married a mountain man."

Before she could respond, he grabbed her and began to dance her in circles. She threw back her head and laughed as she stumbled and tried to keep up. He was clutching her so close she could feel his denim jeans scrape against her bare leg, feel the hard curve of his hip brush against hers. Her breasts sank against his chest, and her arms circled his neck.

Her breath hovered uncertainly in her lungs, as if she no longer remembered how to expel it. And this wasn't exertion. No, never that. She recognized desire, the harsh thrust of it that had blindsided her the first time she was ever close to Mack, and she knew it was working its magic again.

She hadn't felt desire, not like this, for years. She'd only felt anger and sorrow, and a cold, gray wind extinguishing everything she'd felt for him. Tears sprang to her eyes, and she held him closer, clutched him harder against her to bask in his warmth.

They stopped dancing, but he didn't stop holding her. The sky had grown dark, and he stepped back out of the makeshift circle of light that illuminated the band. Mack wrapped his arms tighter around her, and they swayed together, listening to the fiddle screech and moan, the mandolin trill, Zeke's banjo weave improvisational counterpoint against the guitar's melody.

"I feel young again," he whispered against her hair.

She did, too, as if someone had lifted her from quicksand and deposited her on firm earth. She knew it wouldn't last, that she would sink again. But just feeling the firm earth for a moment, just knowing it was still there and she might find it again for longer and longer moments, lightened her spirit even more.

"Mom and Gram are enjoying themselves." She nodded toward them, sitting at the edge of the lights on plastic chairs. Nancy was conversing with Mrs. Claiborne, and Helen had made friends with the ersatz Confederate soldiers. At one point in the evening Tessa had heard the three of them extolling the virtues of Stonewall Jackson.

"How much, do you think?" he asked.

"What do you mean?"

"Enough that they'll be here a while?"

"I think you'd have to take a bulldozer to Gram to get her away right now."

"Good. And we can make it back to the house in say, ten minutes?"

She understood where this was going, and her heart beat faster. "Quicker, if we need to."

"Good. Now watch how I do this." He pulled her farther from the light. They waited a moment; then he pulled her even farther. In no more than a minute they'd edged far enough away that they were lost in the shadows. Then, taking her hand, Mack started toward the road at a fast clip.

They laughed, taking turns pulling each other along the road, at times playfully chasing each other but enjoying getting caught even more. He pulled her to him each time for long, luxurious kisses, which she returned with fervor. They were home sooner than she'd expected, winded, still laughing, their eyes shining brightly in the light of a crescent moon.

They kissed their way upstairs, taking their time on the old steps. Her dress was unzipped by the time they arrived in her room, and his shirt was unbuttoned. She removed the squash blossom necklace and placed it on the dresser. His arms went around her, and he held her against him. Even through his jeans she could feel the fullness of his erection, and she leaned harder against him and began to sway.

"I have missed you more than you'll ever know," he said softly.

She couldn't talk about the past. For tonight she wanted no past. Just this moment and the moments to come. Not days, and certainly not years. Just moments to help her back into a life that was still too far in the distance.

She turned in his arms. "I want you, Mack."

He slipped the dress off her shoulders, and it pooled at her feet. The bra was easily dispensed with. She removed his shirt the same way and unsnapped his jeans.

The bed was narrow, but it hardly mattered. They nestled together as only longtime lovers did, so aware of the curves and planes of each other's body that there was no need to adjust or accommodate. His hands found the familiar places that gave her pleasure, and she responded, kissing the hollow of his neck, the sensitive places of his chest, then lower, as he sighed and moved in response.

Moments later he was inside her, making slow, torturously slow strokes. She was suffused with feeling, a nearly forgotten rush of passion and yearning for completion. She wondered how they had lost this, how she could have pushed him away when she needed to hold him closer.

And then she remembered, like a communication from some faraway land, that she had forgotten to put in her diaphragm.

He mistook her attempted retreat as a shift in response. He moved faster and she was lost in the mindless surge of a body that had too long denied its need. Even as she felt herself falling over the edge of desire, she was gripped by terror.

He came when she did, a powerful, mindless merging of flesh to flesh, seed into womb, hearts beating in matching rhythm.

They lay panting, chest to chest, until she moved away and sat up.

He knew immediately that something was wrong. He gripped her arm so she couldn't stand. "Tess?"

"We didn't use birth control."

He didn't respond. She turned to look at him. "Did you remember?"

He shook his head. "No, honestly. You were on the pill for so long after…"

She'd gone on the pill after Kayley's death, terrified to take the chance she might get pregnant again. She'd stopped taking it six months ago, not pleased with the problems she'd encountered. And what had been the point, after all, when their lovemaking had dwindled to almost nothing?

She looked away. "How could we have made a mistake like this?"

"Mistake?"

She got to her feet, shaking off his hand. "What would you call it?"

"I'd call it hopeful."

"Hopeful?"

He swung his legs over the side of the bed. "Aren't there worse things in life than having another child together?"

"How can you even talk about another child after everything that happened?"

"We can't replace Kayley. I don't want to try. But can't we affirm that what we had with her was so wonderful, so miraculous, that we want another little girl or boy to bring that joy back into our lives?"

Panic had filled her, and now it overflowed. She couldn't stop her next words. "I never want another child."

"Never is a long time. Never is as final as it gets."

With trembling hands, she slipped back into her dress and turned. A flurry of calculations assured her that the chance she might get pregnant tonight was slim, but she was still overwrought. "When I went off the pill I talked to my gynecologist about getting my tubes tied. That's how final it is."

"You didn't do it?"

"Not yet. We talked about the fall."

"When were you going to get around to telling me? Afterward?"

She looked away. The conversation with her physician had been casual, the decision unmade, but now, with Mack's seed inside her, with even the slightest potential for new life blossoming, she couldn't see any other way. If she wasn't pregnant because of this mistake, how could she ever take that chance again?

How could she stand the possibility she might lose another child? How could she survive?

Mack got to his feet. "You know I want a family. But I seem to be out of this equation forever."

She watched him pick up his clothes and slip them on. She couldn't speak. She couldn't reassure him. She was gripped with such apprehension that she could only think of what they'd just done.

He straightened, his shirt unbuttoned. "*Am* I out of the equation? Have you made this decision for both of us?"

"My body. My decision." She turned up her hands in supplication. "It has to be."

"So you've made your decision, and now I make mine? You, Tess, or someone who isn't so afraid of what might happen in the future that she's willing to take a chance on life?"

She was tempted to say yes, to push him so hard he left forever, taking with him the demand for normalcy, for the things other couples took for granted. Perhaps she would have done so at the beginning of the summer, before warmth began to seep back into her soul. But now she couldn't.

"I love you," she said softly. "I wish that could be enough."

He closed his eyes for a moment. Then he moved past her, carrying his shoes in one hand and buttoning his shirt with the other. She heard the front door close a few moments later, then the sound of a car engine.

And the quicksand sucked at her feet once more.

CHAPTER
27

On Saturday morning the sun rose with such attitude that by nine the temperature inside the old farmhouse was almost unbearable. Tessa had barely made it through her morning run, and Nancy was already on the telephone over Helen's objections, calling for estimates on central air.

"You think I'll let them come here, tear up everything in sight just so you can cool off a little?" Helen demanded when Nancy came out to the porch to join her panting mother and daughter.

"Darned right you'll let me. I'm the one they'll call one of these days to scrape you off the floor when you melt like the Wicked Witch of the West, or wherever the hell that woman was from."

"Don't you curse at me."

Nancy kissed her mother's weathered cheek. "It's cursing-hot, Mama. Damned hot. Frigging hot. You don't ever even have to turn the air-conditioning on. Nobody'll know if you do or you don't."

"I lived this long without it."

"Mama, you want to keep this house in the family, don't you?"

Helen made a wicked witch face. "What's that got to do with anything?"

"Do you really think we'll come back here in the summers if there's no air-conditioning?"

"I don't expect either of you to come back. You'll sell it just like that." Helen snapped her perspiration-damp fingers.

"No." Nancy lifted what little hair adorned the back of her neck and fanned herself. "If you leave it to me, I'm going to keep the old place. My mind's made up. I need somewhere to go outside the city that's all mine. Who knows, I might even live here some-day. And Tessa will want to have it as a retreat, too. She's a teacher. She needs a place to relax in the summer. It ought to stay in the family."

Tessa was as surprised as her grandmother. "I thought you couldn't wait to get rid of the farm."

"Wrong again, and that's beginning to be a habit."

"I won't turn on the durned thing," Helen warned. "But I guess they can put one in if it'll make you happy."

"Just for the hottest days," Nancy said, struggling unsuccessfully not to smile.

The three women sat in silence for a moment. Tessa watched with interest as a black minivan drove along the road in the di-rection of the house. In the city she never would have noticed it, but here it was of primary interest.

"Haven't seen that van before," Nancy said, clearly in the coun-try mode, too.

"It's slowing." Tessa shaded her eyes. "Maybe they're lost."

The van pulled into the driveway, slowly and carefully, and the driver's door opened. A woman got out and came around to the side to pull open the sliding panel door.

A familiar Old English Sheepdog bounded out and streaked to-ward the front porch.

Tessa got to her feet and watched as Biscuit, long shaggy fur ruffling in her own breeze, leapt up to the porch and jumped up, paws to Tessa's shoulders, nearly knocking her to the ground.

"Biscuit!" Tessa burrowed her face against the dog's fur for seconds before she pushed her down. Biscuit took off to sniff the other two women, but came right back to Tessa and jumped up again, tongue ecstatically searching for available flesh.

Tessa managed to quiet the dog a little, as she watched the woman who was walking toward her carrying a sack of dog chow. "Bonnie? How on earth did you find me?"

"Mack gave me directions." Bonnie Hitchcock was a short woman with pixie-cut dark hair and an athletic body. She set the bag on the ground before she searched Tessa's face for clues. "He didn't tell you we were coming, did he?"

Nancy got to her feet. "He didn't tell her, but he told *me*."

Tessa glanced at her mother. "Did you forget to mention it?"

"No, I was afraid to."

Tessa had known Bonnie for years. Her son Danny had been Kayley's best friend in preschool. "So what's going on?"

Bonnie looked increasingly uncomfortable. "I thought you knew. We can't keep Biscuit anymore, Tessa. Danny's developed asthma, and in addition to everything else, he's allergic to dog fur." She hesitated. "And it's never really worked out the way it should have, I'll be honest. Biscuit misses you. We had to keep an eye on her every minute or she tried to run away. She likes my kids, and when they're home with her she's okay. But she's never been ours. Not really."

Tessa felt her throat tighten. "Why didn't you tell me?"

"You had enough to handle. Mack said you could take her for the rest of the summer. I can try to find her another home, but this will give us some breathing room." She tried to smile. "No pun intended."

Tessa once again quieted Biscuit, who was clearly overjoyed to be there. The dog plopped down on Tessa's foot and rubbed her muzzle against Tessa's knees.

"Don't worry," Tessa said. "We'll take care of it."

"I'm really sorry. She's a great dog, she really is." Bonnie straightened a little. "But, Tessa, she's a one-family dog. She *knows* who she belongs to."

"She belonged to Kayley," Tessa said.

Bonnie didn't back down, and she didn't flinch. "No, she belonged to all of you. Just look at her right now if you have any real question about it." She looked as if she wanted to say more, but she didn't. She smiled ruefully; then she raised a hand in farewell, peering around Tessa to wave goodbye to the other women before she started back to her van.

"I'll be durned," Helen said. "That mangy rotten dog is back." Then she rose, stooped and rubbed the mangy rotten dog's floppy gray ears.

By afternoon Biscuit owned the farm and the house, and she'd chosen a shady corner of the porch as her own after scaring away two of the barn cats who'd come looking for a handout. She snoozed there now, unaware that she was the topic of conversation between Tessa and her grandmother. Nancy was at the Claibornes', picking up Cissy for a trip to Wal-Mart. The two had arranged it during a particularly rousing chorus of "Waiting for the Boatman" on music night, and now Nancy also had a mission to buy dog supplies.

"That dog. She's like that thing those Australians throw," Helen said.

"A boomerang." Tessa sniffed. "Exactly what am I going to do with her?"

"Seems easy enough. You keep her. She's not a pup. She'll be all right at home during the day alone. And she can run with you in the mornings and keep you company in the evenings when Mack works late. You needed company."

Tessa's heart melted a little every time she looked at the dog. "I gave her to Bonnie because I thought she needed to be with children. She was Kayley's companion."

"I think you gave her to those folks 'cause it pained you too much to see her without your little girl."

"Just like you to go right to the heart of it."

"Just like me."

"Some of both." Tessa decided to be honest. "But mostly because it hurt so much." She was surprised she could admit it so easily.

"The dog seems perfectly happy to be with you now. I don't like dogs, you understand, but if somebody had to have one, that'd be a good one to have."

Tessa thought of Mack and the things she'd said to him. "It seems like everything I've done for years has revolved around Kayley's death." She looked up and saw understanding in her grandmother's eyes. "You appreciate that better than anybody I know."

"Some time ago you asked me what I'd learned after Fate was killed, from losing all my family so sudden like. And I told you maybe you weren't ready to hear it."

"I remember."

"Here's what I learned, Tessa. There's only one thing worse than dying or being left behind, and that's wasting the life God gives you."

Tessa still wasn't sure she was ready to hear it. "Is that what I'm doing?"

"You're the only one who can answer that, but I can answer for myself. I wasted a whole lot of mine, and I wish I could call it back. Your own mama paid the biggest price for that. Now I've got months and days left to me, not years and years. And I'm answering for all the mistakes I made."

Tessa put her hand on her grandmother's. She, of all people, knew how hard this was for Helen to admit.

Nancy arrived home after her shopping trip with Cissy. They had ogled baby clothes and supplies, and Nancy had made a mental list. She planned to have a baby shower for the girl, and now she knew what Cissy needed most. She had already talked to Mrs. Claiborne, who was thrilled to let Nancy make the arrangements.

Then they had visited Helen's church to meet with the women's auxiliary, who had agreed to help set up the quilt show. Now Cissy was in on the plans, and she had been welcomed by the other women as one of them.

Nancy carried a brand-new giant-sized dog bed up to the porch, along with a bright red collar and matching retractable leash, but Biscuit was nowhere in sight. Nancy went in search of everyone. She found her mother in her room, but no sign of Tessa or the dog.

"They're down at the creek trying to find some blackberries for a pie, but don't go yelling for them. They need some time alone to get reacquainted," Helen said.

Nancy sank to the bed. "Maybe I should have told her the dog was coming. I didn't know what to do. I was afraid she'd say no."

"She doesn't know what to say or what to do, just like you. Family curse."

"What are *you* doing? Or don't you know?"

"Sorting through some old things of mine." Helen held what looked like a batch of quilt blocks up to her chest.

"What are those?"

"Just some old blocks I made a while ago."

Nancy knew something was wrong. Helen looked vulnerable, or as vulnerable as she would ever look. Nancy wondered if these were more of the spectacular Shenandoah Album blocks, like the ones in the quilt she'd amazed her daughter with a few weeks ago, the quilt that would be the centerpiece of the quilt show.

"May I see them?" Nancy put out her hand.

Helen looked torn. "I wasn't going to show these to anybody."

"Mama, porno quilt blocks? Naked ladies and gentlemen?"

"Nanny, who do you think you're talking to?" Helen flushed.

Nancy wiggled her fingers. "Mama..."

Helen thrust out her hand.

Nancy's smile disappeared when she saw what the blocks were. "Oh, Mama..." She spread them out on the bed beside her. They were Sunbonnet Sue blocks, a traditional block of a little girl in an old-fashioned dress, a wide bonnet covering her face. But these had been updated. There was Sunbonnet Sue flying a kite. Sunbonnet Sue in a frilly white tutu and ballet slippers. Sunbonnet Sue reading a book, feeding brightly colored chickens, fishing in a pond.

Sunbonnet Sue playing with an Old English Sheepdog.

Kayley's life in quilt blocks.

Nancy didn't know she was crying until a tear splashed from her chin to her wrist. "Oh, Mama..."

"I was making it as a Christmas present. For her room. I was finishing up that last block, the one with the dog, when I got your phone call saying she'd been..."

Nancy wiped her eyes with the back of her hand. "So you put them away."

"I couldn't finish the quilt. How could I? I knew it would make Tessa that much sadder to see it."

"Just like the wedding ring quilt."

Helen's voice broke. "She was just a little thing. She never did a mean thing to anybody."

Nancy got up and went to her. She put her arms around her mother and felt Helen's shoulders heave. "I miss her, too." She tried to blink back tears and found she couldn't.

Helen's arms came around her, and they held each other for long moments.

"You ought to finish it," Nancy said at last.

"No, I put it away, and that's that."

But Nancy thought differently. "Let me have the blocks, then."

"Why?"

"I don't know. But I'd like to keep them. Somebody should be able to look at them and remember her."

Helen was clearly debating with herself, but she nodded at last. "You take them."

Nancy moved away so she could see Helen's face. She traced the path of a tear with her fingertip. "Let's go see what we can make for supper tonight."

"If Tessa comes back with blackberries, we'll make a pie."

"And finish it in one sitting. That sounds like supper to me."

CHAPTER
28

Early Monday morning, a light rain fell, just enough to mist the air and raise the humidity, but Tessa thought it was progress. The clouds hadn't forgotten what to do. They were just a little rusty, a little out of practice. But the rain, as paltry as it was, seemed a good sign.

There were footsteps behind her, but she didn't turn. She recognized the squeak of her mother's new flip-flops.

Nancy joined her at the edge of the steps, where the rain could spatter her cheeks. "You're up even earlier than usual, sweetie. Too wet to jog?"

Tessa gave her mother a smile. "Do you know where I'm supposed to be this morning?"

"I wondered what was up with school. Aren't you usually back at work by now?"

"I'm taking the semester off." Tessa hugged herself, although it certainly wasn't cold. "I called my principal two weeks ago, and he went to bat for me and found a replacement. She's somebody

I know, and she's good. The kids won't be cheated. But I would have started back full-time today."

"You know, I could have finished up here. No one expected—"

"It's not that."

"What, then?"

Tessa stared into the rain. Mist rose from the parched ground to meet the raindrops halfway. The maples were shrouded in a soft gray haze. Without a certain amount of faith, the presence of a sunrise would have been a question mark.

"I'm not good at what I do anymore," she said at last. "I haven't been good at it since Kayley died."

"You needed to take off more time after the accident."

Tessa couldn't refute that. She had gone back to work after only three weeks, accepting condolences with a frozen nod, sweeping unopened sympathy notes into an empty drawer in her desk, shutting her students out of her heart, because worrying and caring about them hurt too much.

She tried to explain her decision. "I told him I'll either figure out how to be the kind of teacher the kids need again, or I'll quit permanently. But I have to have more time."

"What are you going to do? We won't be needed here after another week or so."

"Gram still needs us."

"That goes without saying. But she doesn't need us right here living with her anymore. We'll both be visiting a lot more often, and so will the neighbors and people from church."

"Then she'll be staying in the house?" As well as her grandmother was doing now, Tessa still wasn't sure she should be living alone. But the alternatives seemed few and unsuitable.

"That's what she wants. I have to believe she knows best."

"We can work out a schedule to visit her so she's never here for too long without one of us. We can hire somebody to come in to cook and clean."

"You didn't answer my question," Nancy said. "What will *you* do?"

"I don't know." Tessa locked her hands in front of her and lifted them to the sky. "I don't know what I'm going to do. I don't know what Mack is going to do, either. I haven't even told him I'm taking the semester off. I just know I don't want to go back to teaching until I'm good at it again."

"I know one young lady who thinks you're the best teacher in the world."

Tessa did, too, even though the sentiment was undeserved. "Yes. Cissy's coming over this morning. I asked her to write her life story. She's going to let me read it."

"Get the Kleenex ready."

Tessa glanced at her mother. "She needs to tell somebody."

Nancy rested her arm around her daughter's shoulders. "Maybe you need a semester off and maybe you don't. But I predict you'll be back behind your desk before your grandmother's had time to collect even one stack of old magazines from her doctor's office."

Cissy's petite body was now distinctly Buddhalike, although there was no placid smile to go with it. From the moment she arrived under the dubious shelter of an ancient green umbrella until she was settled on the living-room sofa with a glass of iced tea and a plate of Helen's old-fashioned sugar cookies, she looked worried.

"Fitch is as slick as all get-out," she told Tessa. "Water's not soaking in, just skimming along the surface. I should have brought the truck. I thought it would be fun to walk in the rain, but it wasn't."

"I'll take you home once we're finished. We don't want you slipping and falling."

"I'm nearly done with my quilt top. Soon as I finish, your grandmother's going to show me how to quilt it up all proper."

Tessa hoped there was still time. Cissy looked as if she could go into labor at nearly any moment, even though she wasn't due until late October.

"I'm glad you made it, despite the rain." Tessa sent a smile, but the words weren't simply for reassurance. Maybe she'd been reluctant to get involved in Cissy's life at first, but now she looked forward to her time with the girl.

"I did what you asked me to. I wrote it all down. My whole life." For just a moment, humor sparkled in Cissy's eyes. "Didn't need a lot of paper, you understand."

"It's always better not to overwrite."

Cissy sobered. "It's not entertaining. I couldn't figure out how to make it, you know, something you'd like to read."

"I didn't expect it to be easy." Tessa leaned forward. "I don't think you've had an easy time of it."

Cissy shrugged, as if words were, at that moment, impossible.

"Shall I read it?" Tessa hesitated. "Or is it too personal? Would you rather just keep this for yourself?"

Cissy seemed to be weighing her alternatives. Then she reached inside the plastic grocery bag she'd brought along and handed the damp-around-the-edges pages to Tessa. She cleared her throat. "It won't take that long."

Tessa settled back in her chair, but Cissy got up and wandered the room, as if sitting still was too hard. From time to time she rubbed her swollen belly, as if to comfort her unborn child.

The story wasn't easy to read. Cissy had laid out the basics with little fanfare. A young mother who hadn't wanted Cissy or her younger brother. A father who only showed up now and then, and never with money in his pockets. A beloved grandmother who had taken Cissy in but couldn't manage the brother, too, and had wept bitterly as he was placed in foster care. The day Cissy learned her brother would be adopted by strangers and disappear from her life forever. The death of her grandmother. Moving into a crowded apartment with her emotionally unstable mother and a new stepfather who drank uncontrollably.

Then Zeke, who had turned her lonely world upside down, who

had reached out a hand to her, told her she was beautiful, bought her flowers and stuffed animals, and finally taken her into his heart and his bed.

Tessa stopped at the next to last page and took a breath. Cissy was sure she had found her knight in shining armor. For the girl's sake, Tessa hoped she was right. Tessa liked Zeke, but they were both so young. So very, very young. And there was a baby on the way and no wedding ring.

She turned the page and read the last few paragraphs, and for a moment she couldn't make sense of them. The rest of the story had been in carefully wrought prose. The handwriting had been neat and easy to read. This page was scribbled, as if Cissy had written it as an afterthought. Several words were misspelled. There was virtually no punctuation. But it was the content that was a knife in Tessa's heart.

"Oh, Cissy." She put down the paper and looked up at the girl. "I don't know what to say."

"Neither do I." Cissy stood with her back to Tessa, her shoulders hunched. "And that's why I never did tell anybody."

"Who is this Lucas?"

"He's a friend of Zeke's, or Zeke thought he was, anyway. They went to high school together."

"How…did it happen? Or do you want to tell me?"

"Zeke and I'd been together a while. Six months, I think. We were happy. It was the first time since my grandma died I'd been happy. I wanted to be with him. He made me feel so good, so special, and we were careful most of the time when we…you know. We knew better than to make a baby while we were so young."

Cissy faced her. "There was a party this one night, and Lucas was there. Zeke got called away. His mama had to go to the emergency room. She got bit by a spider and swelled up something fierce, and his dad called to tell him where they'd gone. Zeke wanted me to come with him to the hospital, but I wasn't sure how they'd feel about me being there. They didn't know me very well, and I felt I'd be in the way."

Tessa imagined that Cissy had felt "in the way" most of her life. "So you stayed at the party?"

"Lucas said he'd take me home when the party was over, and Zeke was so worried he said that would be okay. Only when it came time to go, Lucas, he'd had a lot to drink, so I said I'd drive. I was going to drop him at his house, then take his car back to the place where I was staying. Only, when we got to Lucas's house, he said he'd need help getting inside."

For a moment Tessa wished she had never started this by asking Cissy to write her life story. Then she looked in the girl's eyes and saw how much she needed to talk about it. "And he raped you," Tessa said, trying to make it easier by using the word first.

"I tried to get away from him. But he's big. Over six foot. And strong. And he'd had so much to drink, I'm not sure he knew what he was doing."

"Oh, I suspect he did."

Cissy averted her gaze. "I scratched him good. That was about all I could do. After, he said he was sorry, and he asked me not to tell Zeke."

"Did you?"

Cissy shook her head. She looked miserable. "I didn't think he'd want me. You know."

"Did you think about going to the police?"

This time she shook her head in horror. "How could I prove I didn't want him to do it? He told me if I tried, he'd swear I did. And why would they believe me? I'm nothing to anybody here. I'm nobody."

Tessa was sorry the girl hadn't reported the rape, but she understood why Cissy had kept the truth locked in her heart all these months. She also understood how much damage the secret had done. "The baby?"

"I figured it all out. If the baby comes when the doctor says it's supposed to, then it's Zeke's baby. But if it comes later..."

"Did you tell the doctor?"

"No, I just asked him, you know, when it was conceived."

The word seemed incongruous, an adult word from a little girl who was still trying to put her world into perspective after an ordeal no one should ever undergo.

"And he said?"

"Before I was ra—before Lucas. Two weeks before. Maybe even three."

Tessa reached out and took her hand. "Is this why you won't marry Zeke?"

"He's been asking me since the beginning. He *wants* to marry me."

"And you?"

Her next words were so soft, Tessa had to strain to hear them. "What if it's not his baby? What if the doctor's wrong?"

"You've had an ultrasound recently?"

Cissy nodded.

"They can pinpoint age, Cissy. Particularly later in the pregnancy. If the doctor says—"

"What if he's *wrong*?"

Tessa pulled the girl over to sit beside her. "What will happen if you tell Zeke the truth, honey?"

Cissy didn't protest. She gave one miserable shake of her head. "I don't know."

"But you've thought about it?"

"Not at first. I thought I could never tell him. What if he thinks I wanted Lucas to...you know."

"Have you ever given him a reason to think that?"

"No!"

"What are you thinking now?"

Cissy threaded her fingers into a knot on her belly. "I got three choices. I can tell him and see what he says. I can marry him and lie to him the rest of my life. Or I can just up and leave him right now, before the baby comes."

Clearly she had a handle on the possibilities. Tessa probed a little more. "I can't see you living very well with choice number two."

"I been trying to live without telling him the truth, and it's not working."

"I know. And choice number three means you don't trust him to hear the truth and make his own choices about it."

"I got to tell him." Cissy examined her fingers. "I just don't think I can do it alone."

Tessa had known from the first that this girl would suck her in, that knowing Cissy would complicate her life and demand responses she wasn't ready to give. All her barriers had slammed into place at their first meeting, yet here she sat with Cissy, her own choice as clear as any she'd ever made.

"Of course I'll go with you," Tessa said. "Will that help?"

Cissy gave a quick nod. "What if he throws me out?"

Tessa took and squeezed her hand. "Then you'll come back here with us and we'll figure out what to do together. We aren't going to let anything happen to you, Cissy. There's not a woman in this house who would. We'll make sure you and the baby are taken care of."

"I never did anything, you know, to deserve that kind of help."

"You don't have to do a thing. It's not about deserving anything. It never is. We care about you. It's that simple."

Tears sparkled in the girl's colorless lashes. "I guess I'm just real lucky, then."

Zeke had a small studio in a corner of the Claiborne barn where he repaired stringed instruments. He was so pleased to see Tessa with Cissy that he immediately offered her a tour, but she declined, not willing to put off the moment of truth any longer. Cissy was ready to tell him about Lucas, and Tessa didn't want her courage to wane.

"Is there a quiet place where we can talk?" she asked him.

Zeke looked puzzled, but he led both women to a rough-sawn wooden bench under a willow near the farm pond. The rain had stopped, and he dried the bench with a bandana, even though they chose to stand.

"Cissy, are you feeling bad?" he asked. His exuberance had disappeared, replaced by concern. If he hadn't noticed Cissy's red eyes before, he'd noticed them now.

She was looking down at her hands, clenched over her belly. "Zeke, I got something to say, and I need to say it fast. So let me, please."

He didn't respond. He just touched her hand, as if he knew she needed the courage. Tessa was impressed. In this, as in everything she'd seen of him, she noted the young man's sensitivity and maturity.

"That night last winter when you went to the emergency room to check on your mama and left me at the party? Well, that night I drove Lucas to his house because he'd been drinking. I got out to help him inside and he...he..." Her hands twisted, and she began to sob.

Zeke grew visibly paler. "He did what? What did he do?"

But Cissy was crying too hard now to answer.

"He raped her," Tessa said. "And she's been terrified to tell you."

"I...I fought him. I scratched him up good, but he wouldn't—"

Zeke grabbed her and hauled her against his chest. "Cissy... Why didn't you tell me?"

"I just...couldn't."

He was crying now, too, crying and holding her tighter. "I knew...I knew something had happened. But you wouldn't tell me. I tried to get you—"

"I was afraid."

"He's the one who'd better be afraid!"

"He's gone. Left right after. Figured I'd be telling you, I guess, and he knew he'd better...not stay around."

"I wondered why he just disappeared." He swallowed twice. "Nobody knows where...I'm going to find him!"

"No!" She pulled away. "No. Lucas, well, he's done enough to us, don't you think, Zeke? If you hurt him, kill him, the law will go after you. I been scared to death to tell you, even more scared to marry you."

The truth seemed to hit him full force now. "The baby?"

She shook her head. She looked miserable. "The doctor says you and me, we made this baby before Lucas, before he attacked me. But what if the doctor's wrong, Zeke? What if this baby isn't yours? Now can you see why I didn't want to marry you? Can you understand?"

He looked stunned. His hand brushed her belly, once, then again. Cissy sobbed, low in her throat.

He looked up at her. "That's my baby."

"What if it's not?"

"I said that is *my* baby. No other man can lay claim to it. I'm the one who loves you, who looks out for you, who holds you at night when you have bad dreams. I'm the one who brought you crackers and Coke when you couldn't lift your head off the pillow. That makes this my baby."

Cissy looked as if she wanted to argue again. Tessa knew it was time to step in. "Zeke, Cissy's had an ultrasound. These days they can pinpoint conception very accurately. And the doctor says this baby was conceived several weeks before...the party."

"Doesn't matter. You're not hearing me right. Neither of you is hearing me. So listen. This is *my* baby. I take Cissy to the doctor, and I'm the one that hears that little heart beating. And I'm the one who feels that tiny little body squirming against her belly."

"You haven't had time to think about it," Cissy said.

"Haven't I? Don't you think I asked myself over and over why you didn't want to marry me?" He shook his head. "About a month ago I finally got around to asking myself if maybe I wasn't the baby's daddy. I didn't think that maybe you'd been...I just thought maybe there'd been someone else before me, someone you were afraid to tell me about. I knew it had to be something big like that, because I know you love me, Cissy."

Her eyes filled again. "I do, Zeke."

"So I asked myself if it would matter. Took some time to think it over. So I *have* had time. Don't make the mistake of thinking I haven't. And I figured then, just like I figure now, that it's not one night that makes a father. It takes a lot more than that."

Tessa watched Cissy fall back into his arms, watched Zeke rest his damp cheek against her hair. She knew she should turn away and give them a moment of privacy. But before she did, she drank in the sight of them together.

Children, really. Too young to be parents. Too poor to manage easily. Yet both of them possessed of everything they would need to get them through difficult times. The desire to be fair, to tell the truth, to love each other despite terrible, almost insurmountable, obstacles. Two young people willing to take a leap of faith together.

From the beginning she had been sure Cissy and Zeke were not ready to be parents, that someone older and more stable, more experienced, should adopt their child and raise it. Someone, perhaps, like herself and Mack. Now she looked at them and saw the truth. That nothing was as important to a marriage, to becoming parents, as that final leap, that final hope-filled leap into the unknown.

"I'll leave you two," she said, her throat tight, her eyes misting. "That's going to be one lucky baby." She turned and found her way across the grass and down the driveway to her car.

CHAPTER
29

Tessa watched her mother slip real leather sandals with heels on her feet. It was Saturday morning, and the sun was just barely creeping over the horizon, but Nancy looked fresh and ready for the day. As Tessa continued her inspection Nancy stood and straightened her knit skirt.

"The least I can do is take the quilt show committee out to breakfast after all the work they've done for Mama. I wish you could come with us."

"You know why I can't."

"Uh-huh."

Tessa repeated the facts anyway. "Daddy's on his way. We're going bird-watching. He's going to notice you're not here. Again."

"I have a life." Nancy gave a flippant shrug. "What can I say?"

"Isn't this a little manipulative, Mom?"

Nancy paused to consider. "It's Saturday, Tessa. Some of these women work. They're giving up their free time to help make your grandmother's show a success. Saturday is the only morning I can show my appreciation."

"And it doesn't have a thing to do with avoiding Daddy?"

"Something, I guess. But to be fair, does it matter? I see him for five minutes before you two go off into the hills. That's hardly worth hanging around for."

"He offers to take you out to lunch when we get back, but you always manage to be gone by then."

"Well, today my excuse is impeccable. It's one week till the show. And once your grandmother gets wind of it, we'll be so busy soothing her, there won't be time to take care of details."

Tessa was surprised that Helen hadn't yet learned she was going to be a star. Her relative isolation had made that possible, but it wouldn't last forever. Soon enough she would find out, and Tessa and Nancy were girding their loins for a senior citizen tantrum.

"What'll I tell Daddy?" she asked.

"Tell him the truth, that I've made friends here and I'm out with some of them."

"You haven't told him about the show?"

"I haven't been keeping it from him. I just haven't seen him in private. Besides, he won't be interested. I'll leave him a message at home in case he wants to come and show some support for your grandmother, but I bet he'll think of an excuse."

"I don't think that's fair."

"Has he ever shown the least amount of interest in old quilts?"

"No, but he's shown a great deal in Gram."

Nancy thought it over. "Feel free to tell him yourself. Of course he's invited if he feels like making the trip next weekend. But I bet he'll just send her flowers."

"You're the one who sends flowers. Does he even know how to dial the florist?"

"It'll be a new trick for the old dog. Let's see if he manages." With a wave, she headed out the door.

Tessa had no doubt her mother was telling the truth and that she was entertaining the ladies who were helping her with the quilt show. But she wondered what restaurant would be open this early. It was more likely that Nancy was leaving now to avoid her husband. She would prefer to sit in a hot parking lot, waiting for the restaurant to open its doors, rather than face Billy.

Tessa went to shower, and by the time she came out, her father was waiting in the living room. He'd found the coffeepot and poured himself a cup, and now he was sipping it over that morning's *Richmond Times-Dispatch*, obviously brought from home, since Helen got her newspapers from trash piles.

He rose and kissed her cheek. "All ready?"

"Sure am. There's a new spot down by the river where I thought we might do a little scouting."

"I guess your mother's not up yet."

"Up, dressed and gone."

He narrowed his eyes. "Gone?"

"Uh-huh."

"This early?"

"She's meeting some women for breakfast."

He glanced at his watch. "Or a late dinner."

"Breakfast."

"Maybe I'll have to start coming in the night before to catch her."

"Maybe you will."

He was quiet as they crossed hills, walking softly and stopping from time to time at the sound of bird calls or the sudden flapping of wings. They checked Helen's bluebird boxes, strung out on metal poles along a three-rail fence. They had hoped to remove old nests now that it was late enough that the birds would have fledged, but there was no sign of activity along the trail.

"Most of these boxes are rotting," Tessa said. "We should buy Gram new ones. No telling how old these are."

"I helped your grandmother put them in place one summer

when we came to visit. I think you were still living at home, it's been that long. She said her brother always put boxes out for the bluebirds. She monitored them weekly in those days, just the way they tell you to."

"Where was I?"

"Trying to avoid her."

Tessa was sorry about that now. "It's a nice memorial, isn't it? I wonder which brother." She considered what she knew about the two men. "Tom, I bet."

They fell back into step. On a hill looking over the river Tessa pointed out a clump of trees that were set back a bit. "That seems like a good place to watch for activity down on the bank."

But Billy didn't move. "Tessa, I don't want to put you on the spot, but what's going on with your mother?"

"Going on?"

"Who's she really meeting this morning?"

For a moment she didn't understand. Then a smile tugged at her lips. "You mean, is she meeting a man?"

"She's never here."

"She's here all the time, Dad. Just not when you are." She let that sink in. "This morning she's having breakfast with some women from Gram's church. Next weekend they're putting on a show of Gram's quilts. They've been planning it for weeks. Gram doesn't know, and that's why nobody's said anything when you were visiting, because we didn't want her to overhear."

"You're planning a quilt show to honor your grandmother, and nobody bothered to tell me?" For once his feelings were obvious.

"Look, until this morning, I didn't realize you didn't know. I just assumed Mom had told you at some point. But when I asked her today, she said she doubted you'd be interested. She said she'd call and leave you a message this week just in case."

"Well, that's darned decent of her. My very own phone message."

Tessa lifted a brow. "You haven't exactly been around for her.

You come to see me. That's obvious. Mom's certainly not stupid. She can read a lack of interest as well as anybody else."

"I've been busy. I'm a financial consultant. The economy—"

"Oh, the heck with the economy. Look, Mom's made some pretty significant changes this summer. She's a lot less interested in pleasing people than she used to be. Coming back here has made some very real differences in the way she's looking at things now. And I guess she feels she doesn't have to hang around and wait for you to pay attention to her anymore. She just doesn't need it."

"Doesn't need *me*, you mean."

Tessa held up her hands. She had already said too much. "Look, what am I, all of a sudden? The person most likely to be put in the middle of every emotional crisis? I'm out of this one. I'm not saying another word to you or to her about it. Your marriage is your marriage. I'm having enough trouble hanging on to my own. It's up to you two to straighten this out or tie it into tighter knots. It's not my choice. If you want to find her, try the church. I think they were heading over there after breakfast to finalize plans."

Billy just looked at her, the eruption of feelings carefully tamped down again, at least outwardly.

"Dad," she prompted. "This is not the time to close up shop."

"You're right, Tessa. I shouldn't have involved you."

She put her hands on her hips. "Do you want me to draw you a map? The church isn't that far away."

He considered, looking as torn as a well-bred Southern gentleman ever allowed himself.

"Just what am I going to find there?" he asked at last.

"I don't know. But you're going to have to look and see for yourself."

He gave a short nod before they started down toward the stand of trees.

* * *

Nancy was delighted with the progress she and the women's auxiliary had made. On Friday they would come together one last time to put the show in motion. They were going to hang thirty quilts, eight of which Helen had given away to church families over the years. Each family had promised to write the quilt's story, what it had meant to them when it was given, who had it now and how it was being used. Three of the stories had already come in. Nancy had been moved to tears by each one.

Helen was so sure she'd done nothing of consequence in her lifetime, but her generosity had affected so many people. It was time she felt pride in what she had accomplished.

Cathy, one of the volunteers and a retired insurance agent, came to stand beside Nancy under the shade of a large oak at the side of the church. "It's a week away, but there's not a bit of rain forecast. That could change, but considering the rest of the summer, I think we can plan for the outdoor display."

Nancy liked Cathy. She was unaffected and comfortable with herself, as well as gray-haired and stout enough to showcase her obsessive love of chocolate. She was also a quilter, although a rank beginner, and particularly excited about Helen's show.

Nancy measured the distance between the trees by sight, mentally calculating how much clothesline they would need, then doubling that amount for good measure. "When I was a little girl, Mama would wash her quilts twice a year. She'd wait for a shady day, then she'd wash them in an old tub outside before she hung them on the line. I loved them that way. Waving in the breeze, like dancing rainbows."

"That's how they'll look Saturday. I've got some of those old-fashioned pins, too, without the springs. They'll be perfect."

"Do you think we've done everything we need to today?" Nancy asked.

"We've each got our lists. I think we'll be ready. She still doesn't know?"

"You'll hear her yelling all the way to your house when she finds out."

"Every guild in the valley knows about it, and some beyond. People will turn out, and not just church people."

Cathy had done a particularly lovely flyer and sent it everywhere she could think of. She'd reported dozens of phone calls asking for more information. Helen's quilt show had developed a life of its own, and Nancy was delighted.

"All of us learned a lot watching you work," Cathy said.

Nancy was surprised. "Me?"

"I never saw anybody so organized or persuasive. You should have sold insurance. You'd probably be the CEO of Allstate *and* State Farm by now."

Nancy felt a warm glow. She supposed Helen wasn't the only one in the family who hadn't appreciated her own talents. "Nothing pleases me more than making displays." She thought of the highly polished apples of her youth, the eggplants, peppers and tomatoes. She hadn't changed that much, not in all these years. Most of the changes had simply been window dressing. And not always for the better.

"I hate to lose you when the summer's over," Cathy said. "I've enjoyed getting to know you. We all have."

"You won't lose me. I'll be here whenever I can, and you'll come down to Richmond and visit."

"Sounds like a plan." Cathy lifted a hand in a goodbye wave and started off toward the church.

Nancy glanced at her watch and grimaced. It was still early. If she went home now, Billy might be there. She was avoiding him, of course, just the way Tessa had said she was. Her new vision of herself was too tender to share. She'd given up her identity once— heck, she'd thrown it away with such force, she was surprised she'd been able to find even the remnants. But she knew she wasn't strong, that her need for love and acceptance was still so over-

whelming that she might yet squander any newfound enlighten-
ment on the altar of her husband's approval.

As if just thinking about Billy had conjured him, he came around
the corner of the church, clearly searching for someone. She actually considered stepping behind the tree so he wouldn't spot her,
until she realized—all in a split second—how immature that was.
She was married to Billy Lee Whitlock, and maybe their marriage
had failed and failed badly in the ways that most mattered, but she
couldn't simply pretend it had never happened.

She stepped farther into the sunshine and waited for him to join
her. The moments it took him to reach her were some of the
longest in her life.

"Tessa told me I'd find you here." He leaned over and kissed her
cheek in greeting.

She wondered if any couple their age still shared more than a
quick peck on the cheek at moments like this. Had she and Billy
ever shared more? She could hardly remember. Passion in the
bedroom, that was memorable. But in the other common moments of their life together?

"Is something going on at home?" she asked. "Did you need to
see me about anything?"

"No, everything's fine." He stepped back and looked at her, as
if noticing the differences for the first time. "Your hair's different."

"I got tired of fussing with it."

"It's nice that way."

She waited for the hard slam of gratitude that always followed
his compliments and was pleased when it didn't surface. "I'm glad
everything's okay at home. Work's going okay?"

"As well as it can when pension plans keep shrinking no matter
what I do."

She felt no huge surge of sympathy, only enough to make her
feel pleasantly human. "It probably feels like you have a finger in
the dike. What more can you do, though?"

He smiled a little. "Exactly."

She waited for him to say more, perhaps to tell her why he had come. She wondered how many times she had feared that any new conversation with Billy would begin, "Nancy, you know this marriage isn't working, don't you?" Now she was almost anxious to hear him say it, to put an end, once and for all, to the fear that he would leave her.

Instead he said, "Tessa told me about the quilt show. It's a nice idea."

Nice was not the word she would have chosen. She told herself he hadn't meant to sound patronizing, but she wasn't sure she believed it.

"Yes, well, she deserves the recognition. But she's going to raise holy hell when she finds out about it."

He gave the first genuine smile she'd noted so far. "You'll find a way to bring her in line. You always do."

"I don't want to bring her or anyone else in line."

He looked surprised.

"I just want her to be happy," she continued. "I hope she will be. If she's not, I'll probably spend the rest of my life apologizing. But I don't think I'll have to."

"Why don't you show me what you have planned?"

She considered. She was about to tell him that wasn't necessary when she realized that would be the old Nancy talking. The old Nancy let Billy off the emotional hook. She spoke for him, figured out what would please him most, decided how to provide it no matter what it cost her—and only rarely was the cost financial.

"I'll be glad to," she said instead. "We can start right here." She gestured toward the trees. "We're going to do part of the show out here. It's such a lovely area, we want to use it to best advantage. We'll string the quilts on lines between the trees. Over there," she pointed, "we'll have wooden stepladders with poles between them and some of the quilts hanging from the poles. We'll add some other touches for decoration. An old cider press with a bushel of early apples, a wooden wheelbarrow filled with folded quilts, some potted flowers."

"Very down-home and country," he said.

She bristled. It took her a moment to soothe her own ruffled feathers. "I'll show you what we're planning indoors."

They walked back up to the church in silence. The other women were in the foyer preparing to leave, and Nancy performed a quick introduction to Billy before they said goodbye. Once they were gone, the church seemed deathly quiet. All too suitable for the funeral of a long marriage.

"The church has a new social hall, very simple, clean lines, with white walls and wide windows. We'll display eight quilts in here." She led him into the hall and pointed out the places where the quilts would hang.

"We're lucky," she continued. "They sometimes use the hall as an art gallery. See what looks like a chair rail up high? We'll pin hooks to the quilts—carefully, of course—and hang them from the rail. We don't have to make more than an adjustment or two. Some of the women are working on that now."

"Helen's quilts will certainly brighten up the place."

She was annoyed again. Pink flamingos and neon hotel signs would brighten up the place, too. Did Billy realize how condescending he sounded? Or was she just trying to find fault with him to make whatever was coming easier?

She took him into the hallway where the "giveaway" quilts would hang with their framed testimonials beside them.

"The quilts have meant a lot to people through the years," she said.

"Sometimes even the smallest thing can have such a large impact."

She bristled again. "Small? Mama's quilts are no small thing. It takes her hours to make each one, even the simplest."

"I just meant that at times of crisis, an act of simple kindness, like the giving of a quilt, can start someone on the road to a happier life."

His answer was a good save. He'd been raised to practice tact and good manners, to say the things people wanted to hear. He had turned a put-down into a psalm. She didn't believe a word of it.

"I'll show you the rest of it. The lay leaders decided that using the sanctuary would be appropriate, so we're choosing quilt patterns that fit there. Crown of Thorns. Tree of Life. Job's Troubles."

They peeked into the sanctuary, and he nodded approvingly. "There's nothing that can take you back in time as quickly as a country chapel."

"There's nothing very sweet or simple about this place," she said acidly. "They have an aggressive social outreach program and discussion groups on everything from Liberation Theology to the Jesus Seminar. The minister has turned them on their ears. Some people left in a huff, but more started coming. Mama's not sure whether Sam's an angel or the devil."

He looked surprised, as if she was rarely so perceptive. "How do you know all that?"

She exploded. "I pay attention! That's how I moved up from being the hillbilly you accidentally knocked up to the president of the James River Historical Association."

He took her arm. "What's going on here?"

She shook off his hand. "I'm just tired of your condescension, Billy. This isn't some quaint little country-girl pastime. This is about my mother's heart and soul, about all the things she is inside, about the way life can rob you of everything that matters, and you can still go on and create beauty."

He was staring at her. "I don't think your anger is about Helen's life at all. I think it's about yours. Do you think I'm condescending to *you*?"

She gave a short, humorless laugh. "I think you've done it so long, and I've encouraged it so long, that neither of us recognizes it for what it is. But yes, through the fog of too many years of marriage, I smell the stench of condescension."

"Too many years?"

She turned away from him, staring out a long window that framed a distant mountain. "Too many years of groveling, Billy, of being ashamed of who I am, of wishing you really cared about me instead of merely felt a duty to stay married and remain a gentleman to your deathbed. I am so ashamed I bought into all that. I understand now why I did, what I was looking for that I'd never found at home. But I'm way past the age when I can blame who I am on anybody else. Not Mama, and not you. I just kept going on old feelings, old needs. So in the long run, the only person I can blame is myself."

"Blame?" He took her arm and pulled her around to face him. "For what?"

"For staying in a marriage where I wasn't appreciated. Being home these weeks, doing something constructive, something important right to the bone, it's made me look at a lot of issues. Things are clearer here. People are easier to read, and I realized I'd stopped being genuine the day I said 'I do' in that storefront church in Nelson County. I've been trying to be someone or something I don't even respect. Trying to imitate a woman I didn't even like."

"My mother?"

"Who else?"

He dropped her arm. "Nobody asked you to be like Mother."

"Oh, I see that, and I take responsibility for my own shortcomings. But for the first time I can also see that I'm better than the people in your family, every one of them but you. And I have talents and feelings that matter, and a lot of love to give somebody who really wants it."

His eyes were veiled, as they so often were. She had no idea what he was thinking.

"Was it a contest?" he asked at last. "Your background measured against mine, your family tree standing in the shade of mine? No one told me."

"No one had to."

"How long have you been unhappy?"

She wished it was that clear, that she could say "since the summer of 1976 or 1984," and mean it. But of course things were never that simple.

"I wish I could tell you," she said, staring out another window. "But I've been so out of touch with what I feel, I can't. There were so many things about our life together that made me happy. Tessa, then Kayley. A lot of the committee work I did wasn't important, but some of it was. I had a chance to make a difference. That meant a lot to me."

"And what about me?"

She turned her gaze to him, drinking in all the things she had always loved about Billy Whitlock. "You married me because you had to, Billy. I tried to bury it, but I never forgot. I wanted desperately to measure up, to make you love me, but the harder I tried, the further apart we grew. I didn't want to face up to it, but I should have a long time ago."

"You didn't want to face any problems we had because you didn't want to lose the life you'd made for yourself in Richmond."

His words hurt, but she deserved them. At least partly. Still, there was another part, the most important, he hadn't touched on. "I didn't want to lose *you*," she said. "The life was secondary. I was willing to accept your crumbs because I didn't think I was worth more. Now I know better."

"That sounds like an announcement."

"Better than a plea. That's a significant step for me."

"Why didn't you want to lose me? Because of what I represent? Because I'm Tessa's father? Because in Richmond, when you say you're married to a Whitlock, all kinds of doors open that you thought were closed to you?"

She had danced around the truth. She was as bad as Billy when it came to expressing her deepest feelings. That thought made her sadder. Two people, married for so many decades, yet still unable to be emotionally honest.

The time had come. She knew it, but still, it was the most difficult thing she'd ever said to anyone.

"I had this fantasy that one day you'd look at me, and I would see that you felt a tenth of what I feel for you, and that would have been plenty. I love you, but I can't live with that kind of fantasy anymore. I'm ashamed of myself for groveling. I'm worth more."

His shoulders slumped. Billy, whose posture was so erect it seemed to add inches to his height. "I thought you were going to ask me for a divorce."

"It could come to that." She paused, because he was shaking his head. "Couldn't it?"

He smiled his warmest smile; then he reached out and touched her cheek. "Nancy, I'm not giving you a divorce. You don't want one. I don't want one. We've had a good stretch of time here to think about it, and way down deep, we both know I'm right. That's why we can finally have this conversation. At last."

She had summoned every bit of resolve to tell him this much. Now, to be undone by kindness, seemed particularly cruel. Yet she couldn't move away.

"I love you, too," he said. "Maybe I didn't at first, although I'm not even sure that's true anymore. You were so different from the women I'd known. Insecure, yes. Vain, silly at times, always trying to be more than you needed to—"

She opened suspiciously damp eyes and glared at him. "This doesn't sound like love."

"But also warmhearted, unflinchingly loyal, so very bright and perceptive, except when it came to yourself."

"And how perceptive were *you*? Didn't you think that maybe once in a while I'd like to hear that you loved me? If you really did?"

"I did. Do. Will. But to be honest, I wasn't absolutely sure how *you* felt. You're right, you married me because you had to. I knew

I stood for security, and later there was Tessa. We never seemed able to talk about anything important, like our feelings. I didn't know how to ask. How *do* you ask?"

His hand crept through her hair and cupped the back of her neck. "But it was more than that. I just took the way I felt for granted. I took you for granted. It's taken a lonely summer for me to get it in perspective. That's why I've stayed so far away. I needed time to figure out exactly how to spend the rest of our life together. And now I'm going to need more time to figure out what this new Nancy means."

"It's not new. This is who I am. I'm just getting through the layers again."

"I love the layers, too. But maybe I don't love them as much as I love the woman who threw the tomato at me all those years ago."

She realized with some surprise that she was not stunned by his words. She was not even vastly relieved. She felt very little except joy that this was finally all out in the open.

Because deep down, under all those layers, for all these years, she had been smarter and more perceptive than she had given herself credit for. Yes, now, nearly at the end of midlife, her faith in this man and in herself had faltered, and the sad habits of a lifetime had left her confused and hurting.

But hadn't she known all along that Billy cared about her? Despite all her fears and inadequacies, despite his inability to tell her so, despite her own inability to be honest about her feelings. Hadn't she known that love had grown and eventually come to stay? Wasn't that why she had remained married to him?

Because despite all the mistakes, the inadequacies, despite everything, she had *known*?

"You know, you sure took your sweet time telling me," she said. "You have a lot to make up for."

He pulled her closer. "I'm only getting older, Nancy. If I have anything to make up for, I ought to get right to it."

"There's a lovely little inn on the outskirts of Woodstock. I wonder if they're all booked up."

"I have a cell phone."

"And I, of course, have the number," she said, right before he kissed her.

CHAPTER
30

Tessa watched as Nancy pulled into the driveway, too fast, as always, but with a certain hard-earned expertise. She did not run over the fading day lilies, and she avoided the worst of the ruts. She cut the engine and bounced out of the car wearing yesterday's clothes, like a child heading for the presents under an extravagant Christmas tree.

"You're up early," she called, before she was even halfway to the porch.

The sun was barely up, and Tessa was surprised to see her mother. She didn't know what had transpired between her parents yesterday, but she had hoped it was the start of more time spent together. "Where's Daddy?"

"On his way back to Richmond. He's flying to Boston this afternoon, and he had to get an early start back home to pack. He sends his apologies."

Tessa wasn't sure what to say. Her mother looked so happy, Tessa was nearly blinded by it. "I was just on my way out to Gram's fence line. I bought some new bluebird boxes yesterday, and I'm going to put them out while it's still cool." She held up a plastic bag. Another one sat on the porch floor beside her.

"Want some help?"

For a moment, Tessa didn't know what to say. "You don't like to hike, and it's a ways out there."

"Tessa, I grew up here, remember? I know where the boxes go."

"I'm sorry. Of course you do."

"I feel like a walk. I can carry some of them. Just let me run up and change into better shoes."

Tessa handed Nancy the second bag when she returned a few minutes later wearing shorts and sneakers.

They were nearing the pond before Tessa finally asked the question she'd been forming. "Okay, what happened?"

Nancy laughed. "That's the best you can do? I expected a little finesse."

"One minute you're not talking to Daddy, the next you're shacked up at a hotel with him."

"Hardly a hotel. An inn. A lovely one, too. I heartily recommend it. I'll give you their business card."

"I don't want the card. I want an explanation."

"You're my daughter, not my mother. Besides, I wouldn't tell *her* everything, either."

"I don't want everything. Just relieve my fears."

"Honey, do I look like I'm going to call my lawyer?"

"Then you two have made up?"

Nancy shifted the bag to her other hand. "We understand each other better. We love each other, but there's a lot we were afraid to say all these years. Neither of us was raised to talk about our feelings, and we did our mothers proud."

Tessa felt pure, unadulterated relief. "You're talking now?"

"About time, don't you think?"

Tessa didn't say the obvious, but Nancy seemed to hear it anyway. "You're amazed we could be married so long and not communicate. Right now you're wondering how we could have missed out on so much pleasure and intimacy purely because neither of us could talk about what we were feeling."

"It crossed my mind."

"It should cross your mind. I suspect it sounds familiar, Tessa."

Helen couldn't believe her own eyes. For a moment she stared at the insert in the church newsletter, hoping that she just needed new glasses worse than she'd feared. The newsletter had come yesterday, but she hadn't bothered to open it until now, when she wanted to see what that radical young preacher had chosen to talk about this morning, just in case she decided to go to the late service. But even when she squinted, the words still read the same.

Quilt exhibit? They were doing an exhibit of her quilts and nobody had bothered to tell her?

Nancy and Tessa were living right here, breathing her air, drinking her water, eating her best preserves, not to mention her strawberry cake and blueberry pie, and they hadn't even mentioned it to her in passing?

But, of course, they hadn't mentioned it because they were the ones behind it! She sensed Nancy's hand in this. Nancy, who had never left well enough alone in her entire life. Nancy, who wanted her mother to be more than she was, had always wanted that. Nancy who was pretending Helen was some airy-fairy artist instead of a simple country woman who sewed because she was too old to do much of anything else.

Nancy!

"Mrs. Henry?"

For a moment Helen wasn't sure if she'd really heard her name being called. She was so angry, the words sounded like they were being shouted underwater. Then someone called her again, and she realized it was Cissy, who was standing at the screen door.

"Well, don't just stand there!" Helen bellowed.

Cissy slipped inside. "I can come back."

"Why are you here in the first place?"

Cissy held up a cloth bag. Helen recognized the one she'd given the girl to keep her quilting supplies in.

"You told me to come early this morning, remember?" Cissy said. "I've got all the blocks sewed together. You were going to show me how to quilt them."

"You don't want to learn how to quilt, girl. You know what they'll do to you if you learn?" She thrust out the circular. "Here's what they'll do."

Cissy glanced at it. "Oh."

"You knew, didn't you?"

"I got a bad feeling if I say yes, you're going to ask me to leave."

Helen had been about to shout something new and even meaner at her. But Cissy's response silenced her.

"I did know," Cissy said. "I think it's about the nicest thing I ever heard. They done—did—a lot of work on this show. Mrs. Whitlock's been over at the church every chance she gets, and there are a whole bunch of people helping. Zeke's mom's going to make ten dozen of her best shortbread cookies for the luncheon, and I'm making lemon bars. And they're going to ask for a freewill donation and give whatever they collect to a group of women in India who make quilts to support their families. You know, not those ones where the women just get paid a little for all their work but—"

Helen waved her to silence.

"I guess you're mad," Cissy said after a while.

"They just don't understand."

"Who?"

"My daughter! And that granddaughter of mine. Tessa had something to do with this, too, didn't she?"

"I'd sure hate to get anybody in trouble."

"They're already in trouble."

"It's just that those quilts of yours, well, they're real special. Everybody sees it but you. They want you to see it, too."

"Everybody's just going to laugh." Helen looked up and saw that Cissy was paler than she ought to be. "Just sit down, girl. I don't want you falling over."

"You don't want me to go?"

"I told you I'd show you how to quilt, and I will. Now sit down!"

"Yes, ma'am." Cissy took the closest chair, picked up a magazine and started to fan herself. "Only if I'm gonna stay, I have to say something."

"What do you have to say?"

"That there ain't gonna be nobody laughing. I don't really mean ain't. I mean isn't. Isn't anybody gonna laugh. Your quilts make my heart hurt, they're so beautiful."

Helen wanted to rage, but the girl kept cutting her off. She didn't know what to say to that. Heart hurt?

Cissy leaned forward earnestly. "I think, if you do something that makes the world a beautiful place, well, you're supposed to show it to people. It's a talent. God gave you that talent. And now you have to give it back in the form of pleasure to the eyes."

"Pleasure to the eyes?"

Cissy flushed. "I don't know how else to say it. But it's your job now to show off what you got."

"My job?"

"Yes, ma'am."

"And what if I don't want to?"

"Well, I kind of think that's out of your hands now. They've already got the quilts—"

"They already got my quilts!"

"Yes, ma'am, 'cause they knew you'd be just this way once you found out."

That set Helen back. She dropped into a chair herself and stared at the girl. "They knew I'd be upset, but they took the quilts anyway?"

"They have a lot of people coming, and they couldn't disappoint them even if you, you know, threw a fit."

"I don't throw fits!"

"Yes, ma'am."

"Took my quilts, like thieves in the night?"

"Well, no, ma'am. They just borrowed them till after the show. You can see the difference, can't you? And you probably didn't notice 'cause you got so many."

Helen couldn't speak. Finally she managed a bitter laugh. "I don't know why I'm worried. Nobody's going to be there."

"Well, you'd be wrong about that. The way I hear it, they're bringing in busloads. A couple of the nursing homes are bringing their folks, even the ones in wheelchairs, because they're fussing over handicap access, and all the quilt guilds in the area know about it. They even got it on the radio. I heard it myself. Of course, there were a lot of those public service announcements that day, but yours was sure there, too."

"Radio?"

"And the newspaper."

Helen hung her head and stared at her shoeless feet.

"Everybody you ever gave a quilt to will be there," Cissy said. "And that was a lot of people, wasn't it? And people from church who know you, and people on Fitch Crossing and—"

Helen waved her to silence again.

But this time Cissy refused. "The way I see it, there are a whole lot of people who want to honor you, and you just got to let them."

"I don't have to do a thing, girl. Not one blessed thing. I'm not going to be there. They'll look for me, and I'll be right here, sitting in this chair, my arms crossed just like this." Helen demonstrated.

"Well now, Ms. Henry, you sure could do that."

Helen was glad she had made her point. "Don't you think I'm not considering it," she said.

"I don't. I sure don't. I know you're mad now. But you got to ask yourself why they did it this way."

"Because they knew I'd say no."

"That's exactly right. And they want to do something for you even when you're being bullheaded. Because they love you."

Helen didn't know what to say to that. She supposed it was true, that Nancy and Tessa did love her. It wasn't something she sat around and worried about, but things had changed this summer. Maybe before they weren't so sure whether they did or they didn't. But now, well, even she knew things were different.

"I could just sit right here in my old housedress," Helen said. "Just like this. All those people wondering where I'd got to..."

Wisely, Cissy didn't respond.

The front door opened, and Nancy and Tessa walked in. Helen looked up and saw her daughter's face, saw a smile in Nancy's eyes that hadn't been there before, saw Tessa's gaze flick to the circular Helen had left on the coffee table in full view.

Helen sighed. "Well, it's about time you two got home."

"We walked a lot farther than we intended," Nancy said. "Cissy, how are you?"

Cissy looked from one woman to the other, her eyes wary. "Just fine, but I think I'd better—"

"You stay!" Helen cleared her throat. "You stay, and I'll show you a thing or two about how to make a real quilt out of that top. Just the way I said."

Cissy's eyes widened as Helen stood and pointed her finger at her daughter. "And you, Nanny?"

"Mama?"

"You figure out where I can go to get a new dress. Something that fits me for once. And make me an appointment at that place where they cut your hair." She lifted her chin. "And that's all I'm going to say about this. Cissy!"

Cissy jumped to her feet. "Ma'am?"

"We're going upstairs."

Helen could feel two sets of eyes on her back as she climbed.

"You showed 'em," Cissy said in a stage whisper.

Helen smiled for the first time that morning.

CHAPTER
31

Helen shook one more hand among the many she had shaken that day. It seemed to her that everyone in six counties had come to see her quilts. She couldn't imagine their lives were that boring. Didn't people know how to entertain themselves these days?

The red-haired woman, someone Helen had never seen in her whole life, couldn't seem to stop pumping her hand or talking about the Job's Troubles quilt hanging in the sanctuary.

"My grandma had one on her bed until the day she died," the woman said. "She stitched it herself in red and green. My cousin got it after Grandma passed away, and I still wish I'd spoken up and asked for it. But yours is just breathtaking."

Helen wished the woman, who had talked nonstop, would *take* a breath.

She didn't. "Those earth tones are scrumptious, like a South-western desert at sunset. My husband and I retired to Arizona. We're just visiting for Labor Day. And that quilt would look so perfect on our bed. It would feel right at home there."

Helen nearly tuned out. After three hours of standing there chatting with strangers, she was exhausted, but the woman's final sentences made it through her fatigue. "Unless you just got burned out or flooded, I don't give away my quilts."

The woman laughed. "Of course you don't, although I read every one of those tributes to you from the people you did give quilts to. No, I'm leading up to asking if you'd sell that quilt to me. I promise I would take only the best care of it. And my daughter will take care of it when I'm gone. She'll love it as much as I do."

Helen knew she was tired, but had this woman just offered to buy one of her quilts?

Nancy joined them, as if she'd seen that her mother was fading quickly. "Mama, are you ready for some lunch and some time off your feet?"

"This woman wants to buy my Job's Troubles quilt," Helen said, nodding to the Arizona retiree who was still holding her hand.

"Does she?" Nancy smiled. "I'm Mrs. Henry's daughter." She held out her hand, and the woman reluctantly dropped Helen's to take it.

"Say eight hundred dollars?" the woman asked. When Nancy didn't respond right away, she added, "Or nine hundred dollars?"

"Holy smokes," Helen said. "I don't even know why they hung that quilt in the first place, only because the name comes from the Bible. I—"

"Why don't you give me your name and address," Nancy said, cutting off her mother's explanation. "I'll talk to Mama in private, and we'll let you know what she decides. Will next week be okay?"

The woman looked excited. "You just put a price on it and let me know. If I can afford it, I'll buy it like that." She snapped chubby fingers.

After a flurry of goodbyes, Helen and Nancy were alone for a moment.

"It's not even one of my best quilts," Helen said. "No fancy quilting to speak of."

Nancy made a note on the woman's card before she put it in the pocket of her blazer. "It's a gorgeous quilt. And you were going to give it away, remember? It was in your giveaway pile."

"Think she'd go higher?"

Nancy laughed. "I think we ought to have a good heart-to-heart talk about what you want to do with your quilts when this is over. Then we can talk about selling the ones you don't care about."

"I want you and Tessa to have whatever quilts you want."

Nancy put her arm around her mother's shoulders. "Maybe you didn't notice, but that giant dahlia's been on my bed at the farm since the day you showed it to us."

"You think I didn't know?"

"Let's make you comfortable outside with some lemonade and chicken sandwiches. The women's auxiliary is going to buy a quilt frame for their meeting room in the basement with whatever they make from lunch today, and start a weekly quilting bee. I told them you'd be a regular if they did."

"You sure take a lot on yourself."

"I learned from a master. Look what you took on years ago. A collection of some of the finest quilts in Virginia."

Helen knew better, of course. She could point out flaws in every single quilt. A red that was a shade too orange in this one, applique stitches that were visible in that one. The eagle beaks on her memorial to 9/11 weren't curved or prominent enough, and the quilting pattern she'd chosen for a star quilt that Nancy had named "Celestial Galaxy" would have been peppier in a variegated thread.

But all in all, even she had to admit that her quilts dressed up the church and made it glow. If there was a heaven, and she wasn't taking any bets on it just in case, then she would like to think that her mother and aunts were looking down on her handiwork today and nodding their heads proudly.

Nancy guided her mother toward the door. "Billy set up chairs in the shade near the outdoor display. Tessa's been handing out programs and talking to people all morning, but maybe I can get her to join us, too."

"I haven't seen Mack." Even with all the flurry, Helen had noticed that her grandson-in-law hadn't yet come to see the quilts. She was afraid that was a bad sign.

"Oh, he's coming," Nancy said. "He called this morning to tell me he'd be late. Something about an eviction and a court order. And I think some politician was in jail or ought to be, but he said he'd be here in time for lunch."

"That boy leads an interesting life."

"The question is whether he'll be leading it with Tessa in a couple of weeks when we go home again."

"Weeks? You're going to stay weeks? I thought I'd have my house to myself."

"Soon enough."

They were stopped before they got to the front door by another group of well wishers. Helen figured she'd already heard more compliments today than she'd gotten in her whole life.

She made it outside at last, and Nancy waved to Billy, who came to escort her to the chairs he'd set up. Helen wasn't sure what had transpired between her daughter and her husband, but she wasn't about to ask and jinx it. There was a lot more smiling than she remembered in the past, and a fair amount of touching. Nancy hadn't looked so moon-eyed since their courting days.

"I'll get lunch. Do you want brownies or pecan pie?" Nancy asked.

"I'll take both, and don't think about arguing."

"I'll get the food," Billy said. "You two relax a little. You deserve it."

"Did you see Tessa?" Helen asked Nancy.

"She was talking to somebody and showing her the quilts in the sanctuary. I pointed outside. She'll probably join us here."

Helen slipped her feet out of her new red shoes. They were stiff even though she'd tried to break them in all week. She figured she would be long dead before they were actually comfortable. But she couldn't help noticing how pretty they were. They had a shine to them, like nothing she'd bought for herself in years and years. And they looked good with the dress Nancy had insisted on. The dress was navy blue with a flowered skirt, and there was a cotton sweater with short sleeves and embroidered flowers to wear over it. She felt young just looking at it.

It hadn't cost that much. She thought it was just possible she might buy another before this one even wore out. And she might get her hair cut at that salon now and then, too. It didn't look the same when somebody else cut it. It looked better. Much better.

Not that there'd be anybody much to see it after Nancy and Tessa left.

"Did you get downstairs to see the quilts hanging in the nursery and kindergarten room?" Nancy asked.

"I barely got to peek in the chapel. People just won't leave me be."

"I know," Nancy said in mock consolation. "They seem to think you're a celebrity or something."

"You put some of my baby quilts down there?"

"You ought to see for yourself."

Helen made a mental note to do just that.

Billy returned with stacked paper platters of chicken and potato salad. Tessa was right beside him, carrying drinks.

"I don't see my desserts," Helen noted.

"I'm going back," Billy promised. "Did you want to start *and* end with chocolate?"

"Smart-aleck. Not that different from a college boy I used to know."

He smiled warmly. "I hope not."

Tessa handed her grandmother lemonade. "Gram, there's a woman who wants to meet you. I told her you'd talk to her after lunch and a little rest."

"If she wants my Job's Troubles quilt, well, it looks like she's too late."

"No, she wants the Shenandoah Album quilt."

Helen had been about to raise the lemonade to her lips. She stopped midway. "No chance of that. That belongs to your mother, unless she doesn't want it?"

Nancy stopped just short of her first bite. "It's the most beautiful quilt in the world. Of course I want it when you're ready to give it away."

Tessa spoke before Helen could answer. "That's okay. I told her I doubted you'd sell it. That's not a problem for her. She wants to hang it as much as she wants to buy it."

"Hang it? Where?"

"In the Virginia Quilt Museum. She wants to build an exhibit around it. And she said that you need to have it insured right away, that it's worth more money than you can possibly imagine."

Tessa stood in the doorway of the sanctuary and watched her grandmother and a curator from the Virginia Quilt Museum in Harrisonburg discussing each quilt. Helen still looked shell-shocked. After today she would never be able to think of herself as a simple country quilter again. The woman from the museum was using terms like *luminosity*, *emotional resonance* and *dramatic focus*. Helen was simply nodding.

"Quite a success, huh?"

Tessa turned to find that her husband was standing beside her. Her heart sped faster. She had yearned for Mack to be here to share her grandmother's day. And, too, she had simply yearned for *him*. Ever since their last encounter.

"It is a success," she agreed. She looked him over carefully. She wondered what it would be like never to see him again, never to feel this surge of excitement, this desire to investigate even the minutiae of his days, to catalog each and every change he underwent.

"Do you want to show me around?" he said.

She realized she wanted nothing more, but she had promised her mother she would make sure Helen and the curator weren't disturbed while they were in the sanctuary. "I have to stay here a few more minutes. Why don't you start downstairs? I haven't been there myself yet, but I know there are some quilts in the nursery and the kindergarten room next door. I'll meet you there, then we can come upstairs and I'll give you the three-dollar tour."

"You look good."

"I'm not working. I guess you figured that out."

"I talked to Joe. He called about some technicality with your health insurance."

Joe was Tessa's principal. She was ashamed she hadn't discussed her decision not to teach this semester with Mack.

"It's temporary," she promised. "Spur of the moment. I guess I was afraid to tell you."

"Why? Because I'm such a tyrant? Because I don't make enough money to support us and then some?"

She looked away, as if checking on her grandmother. "No, because it's an admission that I haven't been handling things very well."

"Handling things has never been a competition. We put one foot in front of the other the best way we could. We're both still here. We're talking. That's something."

She could feel stress seeping from her body. In this, as in all things, he had understood. "It's important to me that at least I look like I'm in control."

"I know."

She didn't add what she needed to, that she was not in control and hadn't been for a long time. That she had nearly drowned and might not yet be finding her way to shore.

But Mack knew it. No one knew the facts better than he did.

"You scoot downstairs," she said. "It looks like they're on their final quilt. Then I'll join you."

She missed him when he was no longer visible. She'd gotten used to him being out of her life. But one glimpse, and she missed him already.

She needed to remember. She needed to take that into consideration before she pushed him away again. There were a million things to take into consideration, but none was more important than that.

The baby quilts were bright and whimsical. The committee had draped them over crib rails and the backs of rocking chairs. Some hung on the wall. Mack was particularly enamored of a lime-green frog sitting on a lily pad, watching for the next course of that night's supper. Butterflies, dragonflies and ladybugs adorned the borders. If he had another child, if he ever was blessed that way again, he wanted that quilt. And he was going to tell Helen so.

He heard a noise behind him and expected to find Tessa in the doorway, but Nancy stood there instead.

"I heard you were down here." She walked over and stood on tiptoe to kiss his cheek. "Aren't these adorable?"

"Kayley had a quilt with kittens on it that Helen made for her. She loved it to death. I don't think there was a thread left by the time she moved to a real bed."

"I don't know if we'll be able to live with Mama after today."

"You did a wonderful thing here."

She smiled. "I'm glad you approve."

"I've never been fair to you, have I?"

She thought about that a moment. "You were probably fair. You saw what I wanted people to see. I'd like to think there's more to me than that, though."

He slung an arm over her shoulder and gave her a quick hug. "Truce?"

"Let's just be friends and call it a day."

She hugged him back; then she started for the hallway. "Oh, Mack, have you been next door?"

"I came straight down here."

"There's another quilt to see there. Don't leave without a look."

He enjoyed the baby quilts some more and waited for Tessa, but when she didn't appear, he left the nursery and went next door to the kindergarten room.

He was sitting there, gazing at the lone quilt on the wall, when Tessa found him.

"Hi. Sorry I was late," she said. "They just finished. Gram looks like she's about done in for the day. She's so happy, Mack."

"Did you know about this?" Mack gestured to the quilt just in front of him.

Only then did Tessa turn and examine it. She stared at it for a long time. When she turned back to him, her eyes glistened. "No." The word was spoken softly. Clearly she hadn't known.

The quilt showed a little girl in a silly hat doing all the things their daughter had done. The sign simply said "Kayley's Quilt," and beneath it, "Pieced by Helen Henry and Quilted by Nancy Whitlock."

"Mom quilted it," Tessa said. "And Gram made the blocks. I wonder how long…"

"We'll ask your mother about it. But she wanted us to see it. She made sure I came over here."

"Kayley would have loved it. It would have meant so much to her. Even Biscuit looks real."

"I hear Biscuit's come home to stay."

"You keep hearing things from other people and nothing from me."

"That's not the way I prefer it."

"I'm keeping Biscuit, Mack. I can't give her away again. She's so glad to be with me. I'm glad you sent Bonnie to find me."

She had used "me" twice. The word made him sad.

She faced him. "Biscuit would be even happier to be with both of us."

He took her hands. "Are *you* coming home?"

"I don't know. Not yet."

He squeezed her hands before he dropped them. "I want you there."

"Maybe you don't."

He knew the time wasn't right to talk about this, and once again, as he had so many times before for so many years now, he changed the subject.

"If your mother and grandmother give their permission, would you like to donate this quilt to the library for their new addition?"

"Perfect." She swallowed, and he watched her struggle not to cry as she had struggled so many times before.

He pulled her against him and wrapped his arms around her. When the tears began to fall, he held her closer.

CHAPTER
32

All in all, nearly two hundred people had come through the church that day to see Helen's quilts. When the cleanup crew arrived to tidy the building for the next day's services, Nancy asked Tessa to take the exhausted Helen home, leaving the rest of the family behind to help. Mack was charged with overseeing the removal and packing of the outdoor and nursery quilts. The other quilts would remain in place to be admired by churchgoers and removed the next evening.

Nancy thanked all the volunteers and gave each one a little bag of potpourri bundled in a quilt square from Helen's "reject" pile. Even Helen's rejects were special enough to be lovely gifts.

Billy joined her as she put the finishing touches on two huge bouquets of wildflowers sitting on the simple altar.

"I'm just fussing a little. They'll still be pretty for the services tomorrow," she told him. "A thank-you to the church. I wanted to make sure they look their best. I didn't have time to arrange them as well as I wanted this morning."

He came up and put his arms around her, pulling her to rest against him. "I've got something for you."

She leaned against him, luxuriating in this simple act of affection. "What would that be?"

He held her with one arm and fidgeted in his pocket. Then he pulled out a box and held it in front of her.

The box was small and beautifully wrapped. She sighed with pleasure. "Billy, it's too pretty to open."

"I'll wrap it back up for you when you're done. Open it."

He had given her the requisite gifts on holidays, always generous and somehow impersonal. But spur-of-the-moment gifts had been as rare as words of affection.

She knew the box contained jewelry. The size indicated that. A bracelet, perhaps. She took her time savoring the moment. When the paper was neatly folded in her pocket, she opened the narrow box to reveal two smaller boxes. Ring boxes.

She opened the first and found a beautiful gold band in Japanese *mokume gane* style. She knew enough about jewelry to realize it had been carefully handcrafted. The metal was meticulously forged and layered of contrasting golds to appear finely grained, like wood.

"It's beautiful." The workmanship was exquisite. The ring was plain but extraordinarily unique.

"It's mine," Billy said. "Look in the other box."

She turned to look at him. "Yours?"

"I've never had a wedding ring. I'm married, too."

She didn't know what to say. A week after their wedding day, he had put a narrow gold band on her finger, replaced years later with an ostentatious display of diamonds that she had never really warmed to. But Billy had never had a ring.

He reached around her and opened the other box. A matching ring was nestled there, but a shade narrower and sprinkled with tiny diamonds that were sunk deeply into the surface, like twinkling stars.

It was completely different from anything she'd seen before, and as she took the box from his hands, she fell in love with it immediately. "I don't know what to say."

"Marry me again." He turned her to face him. "Right here and now. No minister, no guests. Our marriage should never have been about anybody else. Just put my ring on my finger, and I'll do the same for you."

"Billy, I'd marry you again anywhere. I'd marry you in a mud puddle in the middle of a rain forest."

He smiled and reached for her ring as she slipped off her old ones. "We'll talk about rain forests in a few minutes."

Tessa heard the slam of a car door, then the toot of a horn. In a moment her mother walked in, minus her father.

"Where's Dad?"

"I knew we'd all be too tired to make anything for supper, so I ordered dinner. He's gone into town to pick it up. We'll have another celebration. Where's Mama? Napping?"

Helen came in from the kitchen. "I won't sleep for a week. I'm all stirred up. I can barely remember my own name." She headed straight for her favorite chair.

"You look tired," Tessa told her mother. "You and Gram sit, and I'll bring you some tea."

Nancy flopped down on the sofa as Tessa left the room, and Tessa heard the thunk of shoes hitting the floor. She smiled, since that was exactly what Helen had done the moment she returned. The two women were more alike than they let on.

When she came back with the tea, Nancy was curled up with her feet under her. She did look tired, but as happy as Tessa had ever seen her.

Each woman took a glass and sighed after the first swallow. The new air conditioner was on. Helen herself—grumbling, of course—had turned it on when she arrived back home. The contrast to the temperature at church had been too much to bear.

"So what do you think, Mama?" Nancy asked. "Was it a good day?"

Tessa figured her mother might as well have drawn a bull's-eye over her own heart, but Helen surprised her.

"I don't know what's wrong with all those people, spending their Labor Day weekend that way. But if somebody had to entertain them, I guess I'm just as glad it was me."

As thank-yous went, it was a roaring success. Nancy beamed. "I'm glad you enjoyed it."

"I still can't figure out why that museum wants my quilts. They gave me an invitation to go down there and visit. Now how am I going to do that?"

"I'll come up and we'll go together. I'd love to see it myself."

"Then you're leaving? Soon?"

"Not right away," Nancy said. "But I'm going to have to go back pretty soon. Billy and I are about to make some big changes."

Since her mother was smiling, Tessa knew they couldn't be too bad. "Like?"

Nancy set her tea on the end table. "We're selling the house."

For a moment Tessa couldn't believe what she'd just heard. "No." She paused. "It's the market, isn't it? Dad's in trouble."

"Dad's as good at what he does as anybody in the world. No, it's not the stock market. It's just that neither of us wants the responsibility for keeping up with the house anymore. There are only two of us, and one of these days we might lose each other in all those rooms. I want something a lot smaller and easier to take care of. Maybe something north of the city, so we can bypass the worst traffic when we come to visit you, Mama." She aimed the last at Helen.

Tessa was still trying to imagine life for her parents without the house that had been Nancy's pride and joy. "I can't visualize you living anywhere else."

Nancy's smile faltered. "Is this going to upset you, sweetheart? Did you expect to inherit the house and live there someday?"

"Lord no!" Tessa was horrified at the thought. "I mean, you've done wonderful things with it, and it's a beautiful house. But it's a museum."

Nancy looked relieved. "Someone will be thrilled to have it. Someone with more pretensions than I have anymore. I want something that's just big enough for the furniture we really love and my paintings. Something Sarah can clean all by herself whenever she feels like coming over. She's been hinting she might want to retire pretty soon."

"And Dad doesn't care? It is his family home, and you entertained all the time for business."

"He's only too glad to sell it. But that brings up something else." Nancy's eyes danced. "Dad's taking early retirement. He's passing the reins to his associates."

Selling the house. Taking retirement. Tessa felt like she was standing on shifting sands. "What in the world is he going to do?"

"Well, for once he's going to do what he loves most. Travel. Hike. Canoe. Add birds to his life list. We're going to Costa Rica for a long-delayed honeymoon. We're going to work with a project that helps sea turtles for two weeks, then we're going to explore on our own for another month. If you think we can be away from you that long, Mama?"

"I don't want you hovering all over me, Nanny. Never asked for that. Something comes up, Tessa can handle it."

"Your dad's going to teach me to be a birder, Tessa," Nancy finished. "Then, next trip, I'm taking *him* to Paris to spend two weeks at the Louvre, and Mama's invited, too, if we can pry her away. And while I'm on a roll, I'll just finish up and then be quiet. Your dad's retiring, but I'm going to work. I've been offered a job at that gallery in Carytown I was telling you about. Among other things, I'll be in charge of developing new displays every month or so. It's been in the works for a while. I just got the real offer on Wednesday. I've been waiting to talk to your dad and see how he felt. It's just part-time, and I'll be able to take time off when I need to."

"Dad was thrilled," Tessa guessed out loud.

"He was delighted. He wants me to support him." Nancy laughed, clearly pleased with herself.

"That's a lot of changes," Helen said. "A whole lot all at once."

"Mama, we're going to buy a house with a guest suite just for you." She held up her hand to stop the protests. "Not for anything but visiting. I know you don't want to live with me, but I want you to come and see me and stay whenever you feel like it. We can fix it up any way you want."

Helen chewed her lip. "Nothing fancy?"

"Something plain and simple, with a room big enough for a quilt frame. I'll even disconnect the air conditioner."

"Don't you dare."

"I'm happy," Nancy said. "It feels so good just to be happy."

"I know how you feel," Helen said. "Although I don't want to put too fine a point on it, you understand."

Mack wondered if everyone else at the table realized how unusual this gathering was. Unless they had gone to California to visit *his* mother, he and Tessa had gotten together with her parents and occasionally her grandmother for holidays and special occasions. But he couldn't remember ever feeling this relaxed in their presence, or hearing so much laughter.

Tessa had taken him aside to tell him about all the changes coming up in her mother and father's lives, and he had duly and genuinely admired their lovely new wedding rings. The food had been excellent, nobody had fussed over it, and once the meal had ended, the family had sat together on the front porch watching the final fireflies of a hot summer. As they sat there, a cooling breeze signaled the promise of autumn. Biscuit, who had been wildly excited to see him, was settled on the porch at his feet.

The stars came out in full measure, and eventually they simply sat quietly and admired them. When Helen finally announced she was calling it a day, Nancy and Billy went upstairs with her. Everyone was tired. Mack could see it in Tessa's eyes. He felt it, too, and although he planned to stay the night, he had to leave for home early in the morning to make sure a client hadn't been thrown out on the street despite the firm's intervention.

"It's been a remarkable day," he said.

On the swing beside him, Tessa shifted to see him better. "In every way."

"Who would have thought the summer would turn out like this?"

"Not me."

He hated to spoil the mood, had even considered ignoring his best impulses. But he knew he would regret it if he didn't tell Tessa the truth. He shifted, too, so he was looking right at her. "I don't want to inject tension into a beautiful evening, but I have to talk to you about something."

She was silent a moment, as if debating whether to object. "It's about Robert, isn't it?"

"Barry, the investigator, recommends we go to twice-a-week surveillance. Partly because he thinks that's all we need. Partly because he's going away for a month and his staff will be stretched thin without him. Partly because in the nearly three weeks they've been on the job, no one has seen a thing that would send Owens back to jail."

"Twice a week?"

Biscuit sensed the change in Tessa's tone and sat up, head cocked. Mack patted her head until she flopped at his feet again. Then he forced himself to keep his voice low and calm.

"As a matter of fact, he suggested once a week, but I knew you'd never buy it."

"Maybe we're not paying him enough."

"It's not the money. He says if Owens falls off the wagon, they'll find out, even if they only monitor him occasionally. He'll start drinking in earnest, and he'll get careless. It'll be simple then. Or he won't drink, he'll continue living up to the probation agreement, and he won't need monitoring anyway."

"You don't get it, do you?" Her voice was low, but the anger was clear. "It's not just about sending him back to jail. I want to catch him before he hurts somebody else. This way, months could pass before we're sure he's breaking the law, and on one of those nights when we're not watching, he could kill again."

"Are you planning to monitor the boy for the rest of his life? At what point do you just accept that he's doing his best to stay sober and live up to the agreement he made?"

"Never. And certainly not now." She was struggling to stay calm, but the lines of tension were back. She was pale. "Is this what you planned all along, Mack? To wean me away from following him? Convince me to let someone else do it, then gradually decrease the nights?"

What had he hoped? He wasn't sure now. He tried to be honest. "I thought either we'd catch him in the act right away or your need to follow him would wane. But I never planned to wean you from anything. I just hoped you'd see the light."

"I have seen the light—the flashing red light on the ambulance that took our daughter's body away!"

He let long moments pass before he spoke again. "Do you want me to hire somebody else, then, until Barry's staff can go back to doing surveillance nightly? Are you willing to compromise and try for three times a week?"

He expected her to lash out again. But after giving it some thought, she folded her hands, as if forcing them to be still.

"What nights will they cover?" she asked.

"Barry suggested Fridays and Saturdays, since those are typically party nights. That's where we left it, starting this week, but I could try for Tuesday, too."

She was silent again. Just as he thought she wouldn't agree, she gave a brief nod. "Will you let me know if they can't do Tuesday?"

"Is it a deal breaker?"

"No, I'd just like to know what's going on."

She still sounded angry, but he thought she was struggling to be reasonable. He told himself it was a good sign, that if she could be reasonable about this, it meant she might be loosening her grip on the past. He had never officially set the end of the summer as the deadline for their personal moment of truth, but he could feel that moment coming the way he could feel the cool breeze changing one season into another.

They could not go on as they had, but he didn't know if Tessa was willing or able to go on any other way.

She got to her feet. "Are you coming upstairs?"

"Do you want me there?"

"More than I want you out on these roads on the Saturday night of a holiday weekend."

She had neatly turned a question about their relationship into another indictment of drunk drivers. He couldn't let it go.

"Will there ever be a point in our life again, Tessa, when everything won't be about Owens? When who we are and what we feel about each other comes first?"

For a moment she looked ashamed. Then she shook her head. "If I had the ability to see the future, Mack, I never would have let Kayley walk to school that morning."

"By now you should have figured out that there are things we can't control. And things we can."

"Which is why I started watching the Owens house in the first place."

He stood, too, tired of verbal swordplay. "I'll be leaving early in the morning. I hate to wake you. I'll just sleep on the couch."

She held out her hand. "Sleep with me."

He took her hand and let her lead him upstairs. But in the double bed where they had made love after the Claiborne party, they slept with their backs to each other. And just after dawn, he left without waking her.

CHAPTER
33

Tessa jumped when a car door slammed across the street from Robert Owens's house. She had debated whether to come here tonight. Last night she'd tossed and turned beside Mack, asking herself if she could let go of her quest to trap Robert the way Mack wanted her to. She needed to move on. She could see that as clearly as he did. Life was too precious to waste on revenge.

Yet here she was again. This morning she had taken Biscuit for a marathon hike over the hills instead of their usual roadside jog. This afternoon she had unearthed a hand-cranked ice cream freezer in the root cellar and helped her father churn a gallon of ice cream made with the Claibornes' final peaches of the season.

Labor Day Sunday. A *day* for barbecues, for Frisbee matches and watermelon seed spitting contests.

Labor Day Sunday, a *night* for beer kegs and wild parties with no fears of hangovers or punching time clocks the next morning.

Labor Day Sunday, and she was no closer to moving on than she had been at the beginning of the summer. She was a prisoner of her own need to put Robert back in jail.

The dashboard clock claimed it was only a little past nine, but Tessa was sure it had to be later. She was exhausted. She had slept very little the night before, and the long drive to Manassas had stripped away any lingering energy. The Owenses' street was busy, with people pulling in and out of parking spaces, carrying sleepy children to cars and calling goodbye to family and friends after the day's festivities. She half expected someone to rap on her window and ask why she was sitting there. But no one paid any attention.

The Owens house was quiet. A lamp burned in what was probably the living room. The family car was parked in the driveway, and she was sure she'd seen movement behind the sheer curtains. She wondered if she had come all this way just to keep tabs on Robert's mother. There was certainly no guarantee Robert was here. For all she knew, he might have spent the day with friends. If so, how long could he resist the enticement to drink? The icy cold six-packs, the colorful Jell-O shots? How long would he resist driving himself to and from these parties?

Her eyelids were heavy, and the car was growing warmer. When the air got too hot, she would turn on the engine and run the air conditioner. But for now the temperature simply made her sleepier.

She turned on the radio and found a political talk show. She settled back to listen to dual pundits discuss the presence of air marshals on all flights leaving Reagan National Airport. And before they had decided whether it was a good idea, she fell fast asleep.

She awoke to the sound of a car starting. For a moment she didn't know where she was or why. She forced her eyelids open and struggled to focus. She felt as if she were swimming toward a distant surface, her lungs bursting. The air in the car was stifling, and there was a saxophone wailing on the radio.

Before she could pull all her thoughts together, someone rapped on the passenger side window. She drew a startled breath. A palm slapped the window, making more noise.

"Tessa!"

She recognized Mack's voice. She fumbled for the button that would unlock the side door, but as she found it, she saw a car careen out of the Owenses' driveway. She caught a glimpse of Robert at the wheel.

Mack opened the door and dropped into the passenger's seat. "Follow him."

Tessa was fully awake now. She already had the engine running and the car in gear. She screeched out of the parking space before Mack had his seat belt buckled.

She tried to make sense of her husband's presence. "What...?"

"Just drive."

She turned the corner in pursuit of Robert and saw him just ahead. He was driving at least fifty in a twenty-five mile-per-hour zone, and she struggled to keep up along the narrow development streets. "Get my cell phone. In my purse. I've got a local cop on speed dial. First number. He knows the situation. Tell him where we are and what's happening."

She had to concentrate on driving, but beside her she heard Mack fumbling through her purse; then, as she turned another corner on to a wider road, she heard Mack explaining the situation.

Mack gave directions; then he spoke to her. "He says to keep Owens in sight if you can without taking any unnecessary chances. He's in a patrol car not too far away, and he's calling it in on the radio. I'll give him updates if I can."

"What are you doing here?" she demanded.

"I promised you coverage every night."

"But you said—"

"I know what I said, and I know what I promised. And whether I think this is a good idea doesn't matter. You need coverage. I decided to make sure you got it."

At that moment, everything in her marriage seemed to fall into place. She had been right about Robert, but she could just as easily have been wrong. Despite this, Mack had seen her need, and despite his own misgivings, he had tried to fulfill it.

She saw how much Mack loved her and exactly how much that love meant. And she saw how close she had come to throwing it away.

"You were right about him," Mack said.

She felt no exultation, although she had expected to. "The way he's driving, he's going to kill somebody else."

Mack, who rarely cursed, let forth with a torrent of blistering profanity.

She turned another corner. Robert was farther ahead of her now, weaving from one side of his lane to the other. She wondered if he knew he was being followed. He was clearly drunk. He had to be drunk to be driving so erratically.

"I don't know if I can drive fast enough to stay with him," she said.

Mack finished updating the cop again before he spoke. "Just concentrate on the road. I'll tell you if he turns. But don't drive any faster than you're comfortable with. The police will get him. We just have to keep him—"

She swerved just in time to avoid a dog who stepped into the street from the curb, even as the man who was walking him tried to haul him back.

She struggled to straighten the wheel. She heard Mack's breath catch as she nearly hit the opposite curb. Perspiration glazed her palms and forehead. She was breathing too fast, and her heart was as loud as a jackhammer in her ears.

"Slow down, Tessa."

Some part of her wanted to; a larger part knew that she couldn't. "I'm not going to have another death on my conscience. If somebody else dies because Robert gets away, it will be my fault!"

"Slow down!"

She saw Robert's car on the next block, making a sharp right turn on to a four-lane street. There was no one else between them. She was beginning to accelerate again when she heard a siren coming up behind her. If she was stopped, Robert would get away. Panicked, she pressed harder on the accelerator, but the cop was faster, and not in pursuit of her. He passed her.

She touched the brake gently, pressing slowly and carefully until she was going a safe speed.

"They'll get him," Mack said.

She was gulping for air. She felt as if she were strangling.

Mack touched her arm. "You said *another* death on your conscience."

She was trying to breathe slowly, but she was not successful. She could see the police car just ahead and Robert farther in the distance. "She was my baby," she gasped. "I should have seen what would happen. I should have known. I should have protected her. I owe her this!"

"Tessa…"

She heard tears in his voice. She was nearly crying, too. She wondered if she would be whole now, if she would be absolved of her guilt. Robert Owens would be going back to jail tonight. For the remaining years of his sentence, he could not kill again.

With growing despair, she realized she felt no pleasure and no absolution.

"He's not stopping," Mack said. "He's ignoring the siren."

"He's scared." Drunk or not, she knew the young man must be terrified. He deserved to be, yet some part of her could understand his panic, his desire to flee, his vision of a future behind bars. She wished now that she had been wrong. She wished that he had changed, that the time he had spent in prison and in rehabilitation had really turned his life around. For the first time she realized that on some level she had been wishing for this all during the past weeks, even as another part of her had hoped for the worst.

"There's another cop coming." Mack pointed and she saw another patrol car turning in from a side street, lights blazing and siren splitting the air.

Robert turned again, followed closely by both patrol cars now. She fell back, not willing to be involved in a high-speed chase, but she kept them in sight and made the same turns they did. She needed to know the ending, to see Robert led away again so that she could finalize this chapter in her daughter's death.

Then she saw an attractive brick building and saw the sign for Prince William Hospital.

"He's slowing down," Mack said.

She saw he was right. Robert was turning into the entrance. As she watched, he stopped and almost before the car stopped shuddering, he was out and running around the side.

The first patrol car caught up with him and, with lights still flashing but sirens off, pulled up beside him. The driver got out. She thought she saw Robert waving his arms.

"Is he giving himself up?" She couldn't tell.

"I don't know. Pull into the parking lot." He pointed. "We might as well see this through to the end."

She was already turning. She pulled to a stop in the lot across from the main entrance. She and Mack got out at the same time. She was trembling and her legs felt weak. As if he knew, he came around to help her.

"I feel sick." For a moment she thought she was going to vomit. She lowered her head, and he rubbed her back.

When she straightened at last, Mack's head was bowed, his fingertips against his forehead.

"I'm okay."

He opened his eyes. "They just took someone inside."

"Inside?"

"The E.R. The cop got somebody out of the passenger seat."

She didn't understand.

"I think he was bringing somebody here to the hospital, Tessa. When I got to his house, I saw your car. I pulled into a spot down the street and started toward you. That's when I saw Owens backing out. I didn't see anything up to that point. I didn't see anyone else get into the car. Did you?"

For a moment she couldn't speak. "His mother?" she asked at last.

"I don't know." He held out his hand. "Let's go."

She couldn't move. If what Mack said was true, she had been terribly wrong. This had *not* been a drunken escapade. "I can't believe it," she said.

"Let's go find out."

"But if that's what this is, then I reported him for—"

"Don't second-guess yourself. We're going to go in and find out and face up to whatever we've done here."

She couldn't take his hand. She had involved him enough. He might say "we," but both knew which of them had been determined to spy on Robert and catch him in the act.

She followed him around the car, through the lot and, at last, into the emergency room. Two police officers in dark pants and familiar blue shirts were at the reception desk. The young man Tessa had never wanted to see again was sitting not far away, his head in his hands.

She could hear Mack take a deep breath, a man preparing for battle. Tears scratched her throat. She wished she had given in to the impulse to be sick in the parking lot. She felt dizzy and ill, and knew it was too late to indulge either.

Mack approached the policemen. "I'm Andrew MacRae. I called this in."

The policeman, an African-American with wide shoulders and the physique to go with them, turned and sized him up. "The boy's mother collapsed. Might be a heart attack. They've got a team with her."

The second cop, white, portly and at least fifteen years older, turned to Tessa. "I'm Diana's friend. She warned me you might be calling."

Robert looked up then. He didn't seem surprised they were standing there. Tessa supposed the second cop had already told him why they'd caught him driving and followed him here.

"You've been watching my house, haven't you?" he demanded. "Waiting for me to make a mistake."

She wasn't about to lie. She gave a short nod.

"Somebody had to drive her here," he said. "She was dying. She looked to me like she was dying. I'd do it again."

Tessa closed her eyes for a moment, but his face was still there. Not a handsome face, or even a particularly appealing one. Just the face of a boy who was terrified he was going to lose the one person who had always believed in him.

"She's the only reason I'm still here," Robert said, his voice catching. "I wanted to die once I realized what I'd done that morning. I see your little girl's face in my dreams. Every damned night I see it. Don't you know that? I would die right now if I thought it would do somebody some good."

His sorrow wasn't an act. It wasn't a well-rehearsed scene being played before a judge. Tessa saw that it was the simple truth.

She looked away. Something died inside her, and she knew it was the need for revenge. Because what could she do to this young man that he hadn't done to himself? What punishment was worse than the one he would undergo for the rest of his life? In this, they were companions. Neither of them would ever forget that terrible morning. In some vitally important way, they would never move beyond it.

But both of them could pick up the pieces of their lives, even as they dragged the burden of Kayley's death behind them.

If they chose to.

She was not flooded with remorse. She was not flooded with forgiveness. She was not sure she could or would *ever* forgive

Robert Owens for what he had done. But for the first time she could see that he was not the monster she had believed him to be. He was struggling to be something more than he had been, to begin to reach whatever potential he had, to be a good and loyal son, to move beyond the accident to a better life.

She felt a shiver of sympathy. In this last, too, they were companions.

"Tessa, there's nothing we can do here." Mack put his arm around her.

She knew that wasn't true. There was something she *could* do, something she couldn't leave the hospital without trying to do. "Just a moment," she told him.

The cops were still talking, and she moved closer. She waited until they stopped to acknowledge her again.

"He had a good reason for driving this one time," she said softly. "Both of you can see that, can't you?"

"He should have called 911," the younger cop said.

She was clasping her hands to keep them still, but it wasn't working. They twisted with every word she spoke. "Maybe he did and he was afraid they'd take too long. Or maybe he just panicked. We called you because we thought Robert was drunk, but he wasn't. He deserves another chance. He was trying to save his mother's life. He shouldn't go back to prison for that."

Diana's friend shook his head. "That's not our call, ma'am. We have to report the incident. His probation officer and the judge will take it from there."

"What if my husband and I make a statement in his favor?"

The cop shrugged. "Can't say for sure, but it's likely to make a difference. You being…"

"Kayley's mother," she said. "The way that woman lying in that bed inside is his mother and deserves to have her son in her life if she can."

Mack took her hand, and she knew it was time to leave. "You'll put what I said in the report?" she asked them. "That his victim's parents don't want him sent back to prison?"

"I'll make sure the word gets out."

She nodded to both of them. She avoided looking at Robert as she and Mack left the building. She hoped she never had to see him again.

At the car Mack turned to her. "Want me to drive?"

"Please."

She handed him her keys, and he got behind the wheel. She leaned back and closed her eyes as he wound his way through the streets and back to Robert's house, where his own car was parked.

Once he had pulled into a space at the curb, he turned off the engine, but neither of them got out. She spoke at last. "You'll find somebody to represent Robert if he needs it?"

"I'll talk to the judge again. I'll tell him what happened and what we want. I think it'll be okay. The prisons are too crowded to add somebody who really doesn't need to be there. For now, at least, Robert should be free to see what he can accomplish. But there's no way to know if he'll make it to a better life, Tessa. He has a hard road ahead of him."

She hoped Robert made it. The world already had too many people who hadn't been able to. In a different way, she had nearly been one of them, and if Mack hadn't remained beside her, she probably would never have started the journey back.

But it was a hard road *and* a long one, and she had covered only part of the distance this summer. There was farther to go.

"I'm going to see a therapist," she said. "I've needed to for a long time."

He covered her hand with his.

"There are a lot of reasons why I haven't been able to move on," she said. "But most of all I've been afraid if I let go of the pain and fury, I'd lose Kayley for good. That was all I had to give her. The only thing I could still do for her was seek revenge."

"Understanding that's a big step, Tessa."

She still didn't, couldn't, look at him. "I was wrong. Revenge didn't bring her closer. Maybe there will be room for the good feelings some day now."

"Do you want me to come with you to the sessions?"

"Eventually." She finally turned so she could see his face. "We have a lot of things to work out, Mack. And I know we can. But first, let me work on myself a little. Can you be patient a little longer? Can you wait?"

"I'll wait as long as I need to."

Love had been moving through her life all summer, nudging and prompting, forgiving her shortcomings. But she knew the love she still shared with the father of her beloved daughter was the key to her recovery.

"I want a long and happy life with you," she said. "I'm...I'm just so sorry."

He reached for her then. She knew he had been giving her time to say everything she needed to. But what more could she say? In the end, love had brought her to this terrible time in her life.

And love had saved her.

CHAPTER
34

Fall came reluctantly, and with it, just as reluctantly, enough rain to ensure more years of life for the twin maples at the farm. The pond rose by inches; bluebirds checked out the new boxes along the fence line; Helen's chickens preened their rain-beaded feathers and stretched their glorious necks in anticipation of more.

Kayley's Room was dedicated in late September, and the Sunbonnet Sue quilt was installed in the story corner. Mack spoke, and Tessa shook hands and thanked everyone for coming. Her supporters from MADD were there, and his from Compassionate Friends. Erin had called the week before to say goodbye, because she was moving back to her home state to take a job at the University of Minnesota.

Now it was late October, and they were in the midst of another transition.

"Nobody ought to get married looking like this." Cissy gazed at herself in the wavery glass of a mirror that had been in the bride's room of the Shenandoah Community Church since Delilah and Cuddy's day.

"Nobody ought *not* to get married looking like that," Helen said dryly. "You nearly didn't make it to the altar in time."

"The day's not over yet." Cissy rested her hands on the huge mound that would exist in a different environment very soon.

Tessa put the final touches on a circlet of fresh flowers that Cissy would wear instead of a veil. She had opted for a long white dress, but the style was, from necessity, more Hawaiian muumuu than traditional wedding gown. Still, there was no mistaking the advanced state of her pregnancy.

"Sit," Tessa told her. "Let me pin this in place."

Cissy's hair curled softly over her shoulders. The gardenias, orange blossoms and baby's breath looked lovely, but with the loose, long dress, Cissy looked more akin to the Woodstock generation than a bride of the new century.

"When I was a little girl, I dreamed of a wedding like this." Cissy rubbed her belly. "Maybe not quite like this, but close enough."

Tessa fussed with the circlet, fixing it so the pins didn't show in Cissy's fair hair. In the past weeks she had taken on the role of mother of the bride. Nancy had tracked down Cissy's real mother, but the woman hadn't shown any interest in coming today. When Nancy gently broke that news, Cissy had not been surprised or even visibly disappointed, which was even sadder.

The Claiborne side of the match was well represented today, however, and it seemed that everyone else who knew the young couple was there, as well. Tessa had met a dozen of Zeke and Cissy's friends yesterday as she supervised the moving of the couple's worldly goods from the mobile home into Helen's house.

Cissy and Zeke were going to live with Helen after a weekend at the inn in Woodstock that Nancy loved so well. No one was sure who was taking care of whom. No one cared. The arrangement, engineered by Nancy, suited everyone. Cissy and Zeke would be independent of his parents. Helen would have companionship and help if she needed it, while she could keep a close eye on the baby and make sure the young parents were providing the care an infant needed.

Although no one was unduly worried.

A knock sounded on the bride's room door, and Helen, who had installed herself as security guard, went to answer it. "It's Mack," she said, opening the door just a crack.

Tessa handed the hairpins to her mother, who was teasing the ribbons on Cissy's bouquet into perfect form. "Will you finish up?"

Nancy, in an aqua silk suit, took the pins with enthusiasm. There was no chance now that the circlet would slip even a sixteenth of an inch. "Whatever it is, hurry him along. It's nearly time."

Tessa slipped out of the room and closed the door behind her. The bride's room was located near the pastor's study. That door was ajar, and she glimpsed Sam Kinkade in a dark robe, along with Zeke and his two brothers in dark suits. Zeke looked refreshingly pale. She was glad he was taking this step seriously.

Mack pulled Tessa to him for a quick kiss. She relaxed against him, glad to be in his arms. He was an oasis in the wedding storm.

In the months that had passed, she had moved back home and begun therapy to cope with her grief and anger. Most of the time, when she thought about Robert Owens, it was with hope that he would continue his recovery and never harm another living soul. The last she had heard, his mother was recuperating and he had not been returned to prison. If she couldn't wish him well, at least she no longer wished him harm.

She wasn't finished dealing with her anger, and she knew the grief would never disappear. But she was making steps, not the least of which was a return of the trust and pleasure in her relationship with Mack. She was learning that she had no right to hold on to her own pain to insulate herself against more. She and Mack had a future to look forward to. She thought they were going to make it.

"Did you bring the box?" she asked.

"You asked me to, didn't you?"

She touched his cheek. "I did."

"You look lovely."

She was glad he thought so. Her mother had discovered the spruce-green dress on a shopping trip with Helen, and it was perfect for the occasion.

"You're sure you want to give this away?" he asked, stooping to lift the gift box at his feet.

"Sure," she said. The gift was from her grandmother and mother, too. They had planned to give it to Cissy at the reception, but when Tessa had arrived and seen how many guests had actually come, she'd changed her mind. They wouldn't have any personal time with Cissy again today. Now was better, since it was a very personal present.

"I'll wait with your father on the bride's side," he said.

"We'll have a good time at the reception," she promised. Zeke's band was the entertainment. There was no question Mack would enjoy himself.

He kissed her again, and she watched him wend his way past the pastor's study, stopping for a moment to offer his congratulations to a nervous Zeke. Then she took the gift box inside the bride's room and waited for a moment until she could get Cissy's attention.

The girl stood, took one more look at herself in the mirror, and turned. Helen, in the sage-colored suit she and Nancy had chosen, caught sight of the box and nodded. Nancy stopped fussing with the bouquet and laid it carefully on a table.

"We have something for you. The three of us." Tessa held it out.

Cissy smiled brightly. Tessa knew there had been too few gifts in the young woman's life, and that she would appreciate this one immeasurably.

"Should I open it now?"

"We'd be disappointed if you didn't. But you don't have much time."

That was all the permission Cissy needed. She tore into the wrapping paper like a child at her birthday party. Tessa felt a lump forming in her throat at the joy Cissy radiated. Tessa would never have this moment with Kayley, but that no longer spoiled every good moment she *was* able to experience. This moment was special in a different way. Very special.

Cissy took the top off the box and stared at the restored wedding ring quilt. For a moment she froze; then she looked up, tears filling her eyes. "Oh, I couldn't!"

"You most certainly can and will," Helen said, taking charge. "It's our quilt. We made it. We get to say where it goes next."

"You want me to have it?" Cissy might be young, but she fully appreciated the meaning of this.

"We know you'll take care of it, maybe even add your own touches," Tessa said. "We think you're next in line."

Cissy threw herself into Tessa's arms, and Tessa stroked her hair. Her own eyes filled, and when she looked up, she saw she was not alone.